The Waters of Babylon

A Novel About Lawrence After Arabia

DAVID STEVENS

SIMON & SCHUSTER

New York   London   Toronto   Sydney   Singapore

SIMON & SCHUSTER
Rockefeller Center
1230 Avenue of the Americas
New York, NY 10020

Book design by Ellen R. Sasahara

Manufactured in the United States of America

1   3   5   7   9   10   8   6   4   2

Library of Congress Cataloging-in-Publication Data
Stevens, David, date.
The waters of Babylon : a novel about Lawrence after Arabia
/ David Stevens
p.   cm.
1. Lawrence, T. E. (Thomas Edward),
1888–1935—Fiction. 2. Soldiers—Great
Britain—Fiction. 3. Arabists—England—Fiction.
4. Gay men—England—Fiction. I. Title.
PR6069.T445 W38 2000
823'.914—dc21   99-088093
ISBN 0-684-86210-7

For Loren

The Waters of Babylon

From William Lawrence, an observer with the Royal Flying Corps, somewhere in France. The letter, with corrections by William and censored by the army, is dated 10 September 1915. William was killed in action within the week.

My dearest brother Ned,

You'll probably be a bit surprised to get this letter. I haven't written to you very much over the past couple of years and I'm sorry about that. There's a lot of things I want to say, ~~but I have to be a bit careful, because of the censor.~~

I can't tell you where we are but you can probably guess. ~~I'm where almost every young man from England is these days. Thousands upon thousands of us, stuck in muddy battlefields, or near them, and grieving for the thousands upon thousands who will never see home again. I'd like to think that~~ they're all sleeping safely with Jesus, ~~but I can't imagine there's enough space in heaven for all of them. I pray that God found room for~~ our sweet brother Frank, ~~and that maybe there's a tiny corner for me, although, to be honest, I'm not sure that I believe in God, or Jesus, anymore. (Don't tell this to mother when you write, it'll only give her more to worry~~ about, ~~and~~ she's got enough on her plate with Frank dead and me ~~in France~~ out here.)

~~I'm with the Royal Flying Corps, as you know.~~ It's a fine life, ~~if any part of this sodding war can be called fine. I "observe" all the battlefields, and I see the smoke and hear the guns, and it makes me sick that a lot of brave lads are copping it down there. What's it all for, anyway? Who cares about France, what's it got to do with us? What are our lads doing here so far from home, being gassed and wounded and slaughtered for a country that none of us gives a shit about? Our average life expectancy is one week. I've been here seven days.~~

I love you, Ned. I always have. Like I say, I'm sorry I've been a bit funny the last little while, I'll try and explain why.

It all started when I came out to see you at Carchemish on my way to the teaching job in India. It was the best adventure I've ever had. My eyes were popping out of my head at all the funny things I saw (I don't mean funny ha-ha, I mean funny peculiar, you know, different). The boat trip and landing at Beirut, and meeting you at Aleppo. I hardly recognized you. Crumbs, Ned, you looked like a real pirate. Your hair was down to your shoulders, and that embroidered jacket and red slippers looked funny with your white cricket ducks.

I loved Carchemish. Everyone treated you like a king, and I was so proud of you, gosh, I thought you were a real hero, Ned, all the stories you told. Is it true that the Turks wouldn't let you build the house until you threatened them with a gun? And did you really walk across the desert to the Persian Gulf? Or that other business when those Kurds were dynamiting fish in the river, and you arrested the lot of them single-handed? I used to wonder even then how much was true and how much was ~~bullshit. (Sorry about the coarse language, but I've learned quite a few new words recently, and dirty words don't seem to matter anymore.)~~

Carchemish was living and I'm embarrassed, and even ashamed, about what happened afterwards.

This isn't easy for me to say. It's about you and ~~Dalhoun~~ S. A. I knew that you two were really good pals, you were always together and sometimes I felt excluded. The last day I was there you went off down to the river with S. A. I followed you there, because I wanted to have a swim. ~~I got to the river and saw you, the two of you, together, doing something. I didn't like it, Ned. I was disgusted. I'm sure you can guess what it was, and~~ anyway, it doesn't matter now.

But it mattered then, it mattered like stink. I never wanted to speak to you again, ~~I couldn't bring myself to accept that my big brother was—I don't know what to call it~~, Ned. I wanted to punch the living daylights out of you.

~~I hated you for a while and I think you know I did. Mother kept asking questions about Carchemish in her letters, about you and S. A. and I think she knows. I didn't tell her anything, I didn't tell anyone, I didn't even tell Janet, but I think she guessed.~~

I've changed since then, Ned, this last week, anyway. ~~We're so close to death here, it is our constant shadow, and I don't care where a chap finds love as long as he finds it. I've been a fool~~ myself. I should have married Janet years ago. ~~(I was terrified I was going to die without ever having had a woman, so I went with some of the chaps to a place in town. I felt a bit dirty about it, but it was the best, Ned. I hope you're not shocked, and please don't ever tell Janet. I know you'd never tell mother!)~~

I want you to be happy, Ned. I couldn't bear the idea of you getting old alone. ~~Mind you, most of us here would appreciate the chance just to~~

~~get old at all, alone or~~ even ~~shoving it up some darkie's bum!~~ or otherwise. ~~(I crossed that bit out because it's very crude. All our jokes are a bit off color these days. Can you blame us? You've seen the casualty lists.)~~

Please be careful, Ned. ~~I mean, it might be all right out there, but it wouldn't go down too well in England. They court martialled two chaps the other day because they caught them shagging each other doing something. It'll be a wonder if they don't shoot them, they execute chaps for anything here. It's a bunch of farts in charge of us, Ned, white-haired arm-chair generals dreaming up lousy battles~~ they're too old to fight.

That's about it. It's nearly dawn already, and the others are getting up. ~~If by some remote chance I come through all this, and you do,~~ we'll have a drink at some pub in London, and have a good laugh about it.

~~If I don't ever see you again,~~ pray for me, ~~just in case I'm wrong about God.~~ And don't let the buggers get you down. Especially not mother. ~~She's not everything she claims to be anyway, she and father have been going at it like knives ever since they've been together, in spite of all her ranting about sin and wickedness (you probably know that better than I do). I reckon she's probably been more wicked than all of us brothers would ever know how to be, all rolled into one.~~

I'm sorry I wasn't a better brother to you when we were young. I want you to know that I have always loved you, and that you have always been in my thoughts, and that I'm thinking of you now. Please give my best regards to ~~Dahoum~~ S. A. if you ever see ~~him~~ that person again.

Your loving brother

William.

PS: Wouldn't it be funny if ~~I did come through all this, and~~ we all met up again, in Carchemish, and we all became friends? You and S. A. living there, and me and Janet on our honeymoon? It is a dream I had last night.

Silly, isn't it, the things we dream.

. . . but the dreamers of the day are dangerous men, for they may act their dream with open eyes, and make it possible. This I did.

—T. E. LAWRENCE

The Bitter Lake

1926

1

Who am I?

I have many names, given, taken, chosen, adopted. Take your pick. I was christened Thomas Edward. But Thomas was my father's name, and he was a faithless man—to his heritage, to his true wife and daughters, and to his bastard sons and their heritage.

I was never known as Thomas, or even Tom, not even as a boy or in the days of my other self's achievement. There has never been a great Tom, except the genius Hardy, whom I once longed to emulate, and the warrior Thumb, with whom all I share is physical size, and perhaps, ambition.

Nor can I be Edward, gentle, wise and grand. A royal name, Edward. The first king of that name was also called the Confessor, and that is not inappropriate, for these pages from my journal are an admission of my many sins and failures, a squaring of my account.

Mother called me Ted, to distinguish me from my father, but I don't want to be distinguished from anyone, I want to be forgotten and ignored.

Once I was known as Lawrence, but I am not that man anymore. I killed him long ago. That name was taken in sin, to disguise a beastly lust that disinherited me from what should have been mine. Mother was the cause of it. She forced my poor, saintly father to change his name from Chapman to Lawrence, to disinherit himself, to abandon his birthright for her. She, who would do nothing to offend God or the social graces, but who did mightily offend the heavens, would rebel at being so described, and beat me for it, as she has beaten me so many times, to exorcise her sin from me.

I giggle now at the thought of her wrath, but when I was young there was only the pain, the wrenching, wondrous pain, which I bore with all the fortitude I could muster and never let her know the ecstasy that I discovered, the flawless jewel deep inside my soul. I would not cry out, which is what she wanted. I would not let her find her redemption in my pain, her penitence, her salvation.

I am Sparta, rock hard, because of her.

Sometimes I am known as T. E., but because I giggle rather too often (they say my balls never dropped), I am usually called Tee-Hee, not when I was a leg-

15

*end, but now, when Tee–Hee reduces me to the level of those with whom I live
and work. I have been John and Hume and Ross, and recently I became Shaw,
which changed me from TEL to TES. Or Tess, as some will have it.*

*(Winston Churchill tried to dub me Tessa, but I was sharp with him and
told him that if he did I would call him Winifred. He turned on me angrily, port
drunk, and thundered his detestation of the name. My name is Winnie! he cried.
We both laughed and agreed on Winnie and Tess.)*

*Years ago, at Carchemish, they called me, simply, English, and later, when I
was the man I thought I wanted to be, the Arabs called me many things—
Lurens Pasha, El Aurens, Laurens and El Aurance—but these were only different spellings of the name I hate. Some Australians in that same war tried to dub
me Lofty because of my tiny height, while in the mundane Tank Corps I was
mundanely known as Shortarse. (In the more imaginative Royal Air Force, my
nickname is Coughdrop, because I can be difficult to swallow.)*

*And I have been designated Hero, Legend and Genius, King of the Desert,
and, by the hyperbolic American, Prince of Mecca. Less generously: Fraud,
Charlatan and Mountebank (with which I do not necessarily disagree). And
Bastard (with which I cannot argue), Pervert (which I refuse to admit) and
Liar (well, who knows what "the truth" is, anyway? Who cares? The truth is
only what we want it to be).*

*Now I have this new name, Shaw, which I took from the army list (or, when
the mood takes me, say I adopted as a tribute to GBS). Perhaps it will stay with
me, but if not it doesn't matter, because then I will become someone else, and
nothing matters, not anymore, not anything, least of all, a name. Even a number designates me as someone, and I am a nobody and nothing matters. I give
myself a name simply to avoid confusion.*

*Who am I? At this dark moment, some small time before dawn, I am Shaw,
T. E., 338171, Aircraftsman 2nd Class, on board SS Derbyshire, adrift in the
Great Bitter Lake, somewhere south of the Mediterranean, near Egypt, bordering Sinai, closer than I have been for many years, closer than I ever will be
again, to Zin, the wilderness that was once my sublime happiness. Leaving
Europe, bordering Africa, edging Arabia, not yet in Asia, a tiny speck of nothing
who is nowhere, who really doesn't matter in this vast universe, because what
can possibly matter? Who can believe (except my mother) that there is any
scheme of things, any grand design? The only thing that ever did matter is gone
from me, existing only in my soul and in my memory, and now, not anywhere
will I ever find rest or peace.*

Call me Ned.

2

ALL NED COULD SEE was darkness, the shielding, ebony night. The few lights of the ship were dim and shaded, the stars had disappeared and the shy moon was flirting with some other hemisphere, but soon, Ned knew, the magic must begin. Black would become, imperceptibly, indigo, then cobalt and aquamarine, revealing the shadow of the dark, surrounding land. The water would form before his eyes, and the horizon, and the deck of the ship on which he stood, Odysseus looking for home.

Temporarily deprived of sight, he was keenly aware of how his other senses sparkled. The wood of the rail seemed living timber; the unpainted deck, holystoned to flawless white, and the strips of tar between the planks, cushioned his naked feet. Smells bewitched him, undefined, sensual, not of spice, but scents that communicate heat and dust even when it is neither hot nor dusty, and which confirmed to him that he was, again, in the East.

It was not hot by summer desert standards, but warm enough (Brighton on a June day), and some few of his fellows, men who had not previously left their native land, had crept up to the deck to sleep, snuggled beneath blankets, to escape their dank, overcrowded cabins.

Nor was it dusty. It could not be, they were, technically, at sea, actually at anchor in the Great Bitter Lake, halfway point of the Suez Canal, waiting for dawn and the pilot to guide them farther south. Surrounded by sand, the water was salt, undrinkable, canal fed from the sea at either end, a bitter mirage to desert travelers. To Ned's right, to starboard, the desert tracks led to Cairo, the starting point of his famous adventure. To port, across Sinai, was Aqaba, the place of his most celebrated triumph, and the wasteland where he longed with all his heart to be, the wilderness that was known as Zin.

He imagined that he was the only man in all the world awake, but reason told him there were others. The watch must watch, the bridge keep vigil, the stokers tend the coals and the cooks make ready for breakfast, but since they could not be seen, they did not at that moment exist.

At rainy Southampton he had volunteered for night watch, partly to be by himself, partly for time to write—his book and journal, and letters home—and partly because of the perspective night would give him on those alien creatures, his companions and shipmates, who were the people with whom he had chosen to share the rest of his life.

At first, it had been easy. Hardly out of sight of England, the troopship had become a pleasure boat of drunkenness and some debauchery. Wives were traveling with their husbands or to join them, and freed from constraining land, illicit passions flared. The foggy Channel and the stormy Spanish bay had hardly claimed Ned's attention, for he was intent on recording the nocturnal frolics of his fellow travelers. As they passed through the Gates of Herales, he had tried to ignore Gibraltar and had seen only its lights and the ruined, drunken wrecks of young, untraveled men coming back to the ship after their first foreign shore leave.

Sailing across the Mediterranean, he spent what time he could chatting with the Duty Watch or insomniac sailors or those who loved to hear him talk. But for hours he would be alone, and then the other man that he had been—himself when young—came back to haunt him.

Past the land of the Lotus-eaters. Past Sicily and divine Calypso. Craggy, mysterious Crete loomed through a misty dawn, and beyond that, Cythera and Ithaca, Pylos and Illyria, and all the cascading legends of Hellas and ruined Ilium. If they kept on their present course, they must run aground on that disturbing shore where his youth, his life, had once seemed limitless, and which now left such emptiness in his heart.

But the ship had avoided these hazards of his past and swung south, to Suez. Not even the night could save him from Port Said, where the raucous merchants were no respecters of time, not when money was to be made. From their fragile, crowded boats they besieged the ship in a cacophony of vending screams, hawking cheap souvenirs and tin antiques; gaudy carpets and tours of ancient glories; dirty, faded postcards of corpulent, scantily clad temptresses, and offering the bodies of sisters unrelated to them.

Knowing he had no defenses against the relentless Egyptian attack, Ned had surrendered to the insistent energy and joined in the fun. He played the fool and the veteran for his green companions, even allowing himself to remember Arabic, bargaining for them for cheap trinkets they would give to their wives and mothers as treasures of their voyages. He allowed the locals to spring all the traps that the age-old port town lays for the unwary traveler.

He echoed most solemnly (and, because he was known to be wise to this world, was more believed) the imprecations of the sergeants against the pitted whores whose pimps beset them. Young, wide-eyed, callow Wilson, whose parents were Salvation, had turned pale at Ned's lurid description of what would happen to his private parts from the merest contact with one of these raddled harlots and refused to leave the ship.

Wanting a friend, needing to test himself, daring the past to hurt him even more, Ned had visited, only half unwillingly, an old companion—Stewart Newcombe. Newk, who was stationed here, had known him through all the golden years, almost from the very beginning. Newk had visited Carchemish and surveyed Zin, had ridden beside him in the Hejaz and blown up railways in Palestine. Newk had followed him as his commander and cared for him still, despite his newfound, lowly rank.

And Newk had known Dahoum.

They spent pleasant, dangerous hours together, half remembering the glory days, tiptoeing over acres of their youth as carefully as they would any minefield, venturing into volatile, forbidden zones, unable to resist the call of their untrammeled morning.

Perhaps it was that day of too sharp remembrance that made Ned here, on this bitter lake, so vulnerable. Only a silent stretch of water, not a mile wide, lay between him and the place where he yearned with all his heart to be, where he could remember happiness again.

Soon, he knew, it must begin. Soon, for a thousand miles to the east and to the west, north and south, panting muezzins would climb the stairs of graceful minarets, and, finding breath, would sing the song that was the harbinger of morning, fanfare to his return, rain to his parched soul. He could not allow himself to go back, but he could permit himself, just for this moment, to remember. So he stood alone in the limpid night and dreamed.

He needed to be naked. Sometimes, in the other times, the yesteryears, waking at this moment he would go to the river, alone or with Dahoum, strip and let the pure desert air caress his body, then wade into the icy stream and bathe in the waters that flowed on down to Babylon.

He could not be naked here; some must be awake, he would be seen. Prepared for this, he unwrapped the little bundle of cloth he had with him, took off his shirt and vest, shook out the cloth and slipped it over his head. It billowed about him, voluminous, diaphanous, the gentle weight of the cotton falling, soft as any breeze, about him. When he was covered by it, he unbuck-led his belt, slipped off his shorts and underpants and let them fall aside, while the sheer white garment embraced him in soft folds of gossamer.

A match flickered. A cigarette was lit. Of the sleeping men sprawled around the deck, one, at least, was awake, and watching.

Ned didn't care. He was hardly even aware of it, for this was the moment. It happened exactly as he knew it would.

All sound seemed to cease. The lake was millpond still. The breathing of the slumbering men was suspended in silence. He was not even aware of the little crimson firefly that was the unknown smoker's cigarette, which flared from time to time as the smoker inhaled, a tiny, intermittent beacon. There was only himself and the approaching dawn. On what would become the horizon, where had been only black, there appeared a narrow wash of indigo, silhouetting the land on the edge of the desert he adored.

A distant, impossible sound called to him across the sea. There was not a minaret within twenty miles in any direction, but he could hear it all the same, the beckoning, austere song, the reminder of mortality, the summons to thoughts of God: a muezzin calling the faithful to prayer, the immaculate sound of Islam. And Islam is the desert, and the desert was his home.

Tears smarted in his eyes.

If he seemed a fool to the smoker, or to anyone who saw him, it did not matter; he did not care, for his torments were temporarily forgotten or assuaged, and he was in another place, a golden, fragile sanctuary. To the north were the dreams of his youth. To the west was a teeming city where he had made preparations for his adventure. To the south was a desert where his ambition had flowed. To the east was a wilderness, and beyond it an ancient city where once he was a prince and might have been a king.

The smoker took another drag on his cigarette, then flicked the butt away. The pinpoint of crimson fire arced through the night and died to nothing, while the silent smoker stared at the tiny, white-robed figure standing, in some evident, private rapture, at the ship's rail.

Queer bastard, Slaney thought.

Karachi

―――◦◦◦――

1927–1928

3

A new year and a new beginning. And this will do. Karachi is as good a place as any to while away the days that are the rest of my life.

I'd rather be in England, but that's too dangerous. There are letters, scores of them, so many that the postage for reply almost beggars me (Charlotte is the most assiduous; she writes at least once a week, regular as clockwork), all congratulating me with the worst news of all, which they think good. I am become famous again. So I cannot be in England.

The book is published again, and fabulously well received. A shorter, public version of the lengthy, private lie, that record of the man I was, that stranger I once knew. Money tumbles in. I cannot, will not, take it. I have to give it all away, get rid of it, or burn, like Judas.

Another writer, Robert Graves, is commissioned to do a life of me. Aren't two enough? Wasn't one too many? Well, he will do it well enough, but he won't find me. I have covered my tracks. I have left enough confusion to confound those who would rattle my biographic bones. I have been honest enough for them to draw their own conclusions, and vague enough to hide the truth. (I even gave them sweet S. A. and told them of Deraa.) I cannot give them more. I wrote my history for the ages, the public record of my private war. And Graves is a poet too much in love with posterity to imagine my self-disgust or to comprehend that if I profited from this enterprise I would hate myself for being like a Port Said whore, who sells for ready money the virtue that no money should be able to buy.

I knew it would be like this, that there would be a tremendous fuss about the book. I am safer here, in this scrawny desert by a windswept sea, but without enough of my beloved wilderness to make me remember things I would rather forget.

No, not forget. Simply not remember.

The base, the Drigh Road depot, is competently run by an incompetent CO, who has the good fortune to have an excellent staff. We do too much drill and not enough work, only five half-days a week, with Thursdays and Sundays off.

We still call the barracks of my sanctuary "huts," but they owe nothing to the cramped and crowded wooden sheds of Cranwell. They are newly built, of stone, wide and open, and my monastic cell is one-fourteenth of a spacious room, which thirteen others share. As in England, I have a cot and three little biscuits, padded squares that together form a skimpy mattress, a thin pillow and a thinner blanket, which I hardly use, a sheet being all the cover I need to hide my scars. I have a trunk for my kit, and one little cupboard that I can lock, in which to keep my private self, my letters, which might be provocative, my few photos. Sometimes, alone, when I cannot bear to be so lonely, I gaze at them, staring at the record of that other man's life as if it had meaning to my own. A few books, Homer, Mallory (of course) and Hardy. I have a gramophone, a gift from Charlotte, and she keeps me sufficiently supplied with records. (Bless her cotton socks, but she wants to know too much about me, wants too much from me.)

We have native servants, mostly Moslem, a few Hindu, in uneasy alliance. They sweep, futilely, daily, to keep the dust at bay, and try to be friends with us, but only to earn—or filch—our money. An obsequious lot, they polish our boots, blanco our belts and puttees, shine our brasses and even do our laundry, proving that I am a very long way from England. A cushy number, the others call it, for in England an airman is his own housewife.

Charlotte asks me what I think of India, or this small part of it she assumes I have seen. But I know nothing of the world outside, except those few miles I saw when on the truck from the docks to here. I will not go outside the confines of this camp.

Outside is dangerous. Outside there are temptations that I must, I will, resist. I have no interest in these thin, excitable Indians. I do not want to know of their deprivations under British rule. It is not my fault! They must take their own chances, fashion their own future. I will not involve myself in their political fate, or provoke them to throw off their Imperial yoke. I did that once with another, grander, bolder people and almost destroyed myself. I will not be that other man again.

The other fellows are congenial enough, but they are wary of me (one particularly, Slaney, a surly, Cumbrian beauty), suspicious of my education, accent and age (I could give the oldest of the fellows in my hut ten years). Slaney watches me constantly, distrustfully, so with him I keep my guard.

Wilson is funny, innocently gullible, and Jones, in the bed next to mine, listens attentively when I talk and asks sensible questions and has already borrowed two books that will open new worlds to him that his foolish teachers never thought him bright enough to discover. There is no John Bruce in him—he is not dour enough, not tough enough, not monumental enough, for that.

Only Slaney has the potential for punishment. I will watch him, as cautiously as he watches me. A cobra and a mongoose—but which is the mammal and which the snake?

Here I can exist, then, cushily, secretly. I have no need to go outside.

But I wonder—I wonder—what on earth am I going to do with myself, except exist?

4

NED SAT SLUMPED at his desk, pen in hand, paper before him, going through the necessary motions of his work, but emptily, without a spark of vigor in him.

His fellow workers, who knew the reason for his mood, avoided him, speaking to him only when necessary, wary of his melancholy.

They had an uneasy relationship with Ned at the best of times. Several of them knew who he had been, what he had done in the war; that man was adored, so what was that man doing here, with them? That man was an officer of legendary achievement, that man was a friend of the most powerful people in Britain. How could that remarkable man be Ned?

Several of them did not even like Ned very much; they imagined dark motives for his presence, some speculating that he was a spy reporting on them to his posh friends. Others, more tolerant by nature, believed Ned to be shell-shocked, recovering from inconceivable war wounds of the mind. A few regarded him simply as a crank, a nutter, a loony. Yet none could deny the man he had been, and, forced to accept him amongst them—of them but not one of them—they became fiercely protective of him, a precious icon of Imperial Britain given, for reasons they could not imagine, into their safekeeping.

But whatever they thought of the man, they loved his words. Words were Ned's palette and their minds his canvas. Sometimes at night, Ned would sit on his cot and tell them of the war, of that other man, or of the famous people that he knew. Or he'd paint word pictures, mostly of England, and when he spoke they listened in rapt attention. They were far from home and often homesick, and sometimes they weren't sure if Ned's stories made the pain greater or less, but Ned's England was a different England from theirs, and although they recognized his country as their own, they felt privileged to be with someone who had been to places they would never go.

It didn't happen every night. Some nights, Ned was not in a mood to talk and would lie on his cot, a stubby pencil in his hand, a notebook on the pillow, and he would write, words flooding from him, and sometimes they were envious of the stories being written, for he never shared those words with them.

Even Ned's engine reports were crafted as carefully as his books and letters. As a clerk in the ERS, the Engine Repair Section, it was his job to record the state and progress of every engine that came to them for overhaul or repair. Most clerks regarded the reports as simple statements of fact, but to Ned they were five-finger exercises of his craft, essays on the health of what he regarded as his dependents, love songs to machines.

These reports had caused consternation at first, seen as some gigantic hoax, because each machine as he described it began to assume a personality of its own. But familiarity bred favor, and now, just as the buses—the aircraft—all had their individual markings and numbers, and, to the airmen who loved them, specific personalities, so the engines that powered those buses came to be regarded with a similar affection.

For Ned it was abundant pleasure. He earned his living being what he wanted to be remembered as, a wordsmith. A very amateur mechanic when he first came to Karachi, Ned's intimate association with every stage of an engine's welfare had given him a formidable theoretical knowledge of their structure, function and capacity. So he found a place and purpose among the crks, the enlisted airmen, who would watch him at his desk and wink among themselves and display him, the chipper writer, to visitors less fortunate than they.

Three days ago, a letter had come, and as Ned read it, those near him could sense it was bad news. Ned had thrown the letter to the ground, punched the stone wall behind him, hurting his hand, then flung himself facedown on his bed. The others exchanged glances of surprise, but none dared talk to him. Children of the Great War, they guessed it was news of bereavement. Perhaps it was his mum. They knew she had been—was?—in riot-torn China and that she was old. Surely, it must be his mum. They arranged that Ned should not be left alone. One man, at least, would always find reasons to remain in the hut until Ned passed through his grief. At teatime, Wilson stayed while the others went to eat. Jones came back early and sent Wilson away. Jones brought with him a mug of sweetened tea and a small plate of food. He set them down near Ned, then sat on his own cot.

"Thought you might like a cuppa," he said after a suitable pause. "Best drink it while it's hot."

He received the silence he expected.

"Had some bad news, eh?" Jones said, after another little pause. "Your mum?" he asked softly.

"An old friend." Ned spoke so softly that Jones strained to hear and thought he had misheard.

"Good mate, was he? Young fella? Friend from the war?"

He was surprised that Ned almost smiled. "No," he said. "My prof at Oxford. He was seventy-five."

"Well," Jones said, at a loss for words. He fell back on a cliché and couldn't keep a gentle smile out of his own eyes. "At least he had a good innings."

Ned nodded, and Jones felt uncomfortable, as if he had intruded into a private world he never would understand.

"Best drink it while it's hot," he repeated, of the tea. He pretended to busy himself, tidying his immaculate bed, and tried to puzzle it out. Ned's reaction to the letter had been extreme, and Jones could understand had the death been of a close relation—a parent or sibling—or a loved one. That the passing of such an old man, a teacher who was not even related, could have such a profound effect was unusual to him.

Still, you never knew with Coughdrop, never knew what he was going to say or do, could never guess how he would react to anything. He was an odd one.

Jones could not know that the dead man, Hogarth, had been the most important influence in Ned's life, mentor to the bulging, extravagant, undirected promise of the boy who was the young Ned. Always encouraging, always demanding, he had it within his power to offer Ned astounding opportunities. It was Hogarth who encouraged Ned's inquiries into the farthest shores of classical antiquity and the most arcane details of past military glory. It was Hogarth who had provoked him into wandering alone, on the threshold of manhood, through the Turkish-held Holy Land.

It was Hogarth who had taken him to Carchemish, jewel of the Oxford archeologists, a rediscovered Hittite city by a river whose waters had once washed Babylon. At Carchemish, Ned had spent the three most exciting years of his life, his only time of genuine happiness and his only exploration of that alien land, his heart.

It was Hogarth who led him to the wilderness of Zin, Hogarth who took him to Cairo and sent him to the Hejaz. Hogarth had laid all the foundations of Ned's greatness as that other man that he had been, and it was because of Hogarth that Ned had found Dahoum.

Now, like Dahoum, Hogarth was gone. Unlike Dahoum, his had been a very good innings, and Ned had been expecting his death for some years, dreading the day when it must come. Still, it was surprisingly painful to Ned, as though some last part of any reason for his own existence had been violently torn from him.

He drifted through the next two days scarcely able to function, except by rote. He sat at his desk, writing his reports, hating himself, unable to think of any good reason to go on living. His wartime exploits, which meant so much to others, were meaningless to him, for ultimately he had failed in his self-appointed quest. The promise to himself was broken.

He had tried to salvage what he could of the promises he had made to others. Feisal sat on a throne, at least, but it was the wrong one. Ned's book, his grab at immortality, at greatness, the child that he had labored so long and so painfully to produce, was gone from him, and he did not believe that it was the masterwork he had intended to write. His second book was effectively finished, but it would never see the light of day, and if it did he would be accused of treachery to those who were dearest to him, those who had been kindest to him. There was nothing else in him to do, nothing else to achieve, nothing else to write about, because all he had ever written about was himself, and now he was nothing.

Is this what Hogarth had trained him for? Is this what the world of words he could command was intended to describe—these mundane engines, the problems of a faulty magneto?

The corporal barked his name.

"Here, Shaw! The CO wants you in his office. Quick sharp!"

Everyone else stopped what they were doing and looked at Ned. Ned looked at the corporal with startled, frightened eyes. Why would the CO want to see him? It could only be bad news. Not more bad news. He could not bear more bad news.

"What for?"

"How the bloody 'ell should I know?" The corporal was a cheerful realist. "The effing CO don't tell the likes of me what's up."

Please, no, thought Ned, don't let it be. Without the Royal Air Force, he would be less than nothing. Don't let them chuck me out.

He couldn't imagine it was anything else. Commanding officers don't send for airmen, not in the first instance; sergeants do that. Then warrant officers.

Then adjutants. Only at the end of a long chain of command is an ordinary airman summoned to the CO's office, and then only for potent reasons.

But Ned was not an ordinary airman and Sir Geoffrey Salmond had been here yesterday. They had not talked, had not even seen each other. Ned had deliberately kept out of his way—safety first in all things. But Sir Geoffrey must have spoken of him to the CO, Wing Commander Aubrey Stapleton.

"It's maybe news from home, or summat," the corporal said in the face of Ned's evident distress.

That was unlikely. Ned's mother and Bob, his brother, were safe home in England from their missionary work in China. Ned glanced down at his slightly grubby overalls, and the corporal shrugged. "Now, they said. On the double."

Ned glanced at the watching men, and in his anxiety found a ridiculous frivolity.

Who cares?

What does anything matter? If it is to be my execution, he thought, I will show them how I go to it.

He jumped to attention.

"On my way, Corp!" he snapped, and set off at the double. He knew he looked silly and didn't care. No one runs on the high, stepping double in overalls—they don't do it often in uniform, except at the whim of some sadistic sergeant—but it had the intended effect. The watching airmen cheered and called out encouragement.

Ned waved back to them merrily, but once away from the workshop, out of their sight, he slowed his pace, dreading to go where he must. He was thrown out of the RAF once before for the sin of being Lawrence, and his life became unbearable. It was only when he threatened suicide that influential friends had interceded for him and had him reinstated. To be kicked out again would be the end of everything.

He had never met this particular commanding officer before, but they had crossed swords, indirectly, in that other man's life. In Cairo, years ago, some other officers and Ned, appalled by Stapleton's incompetence, had successfully petitioned Kitchener to have him removed from the Middle East and stationed elsewhere.

Stapleton had been transferred, but had survived and eventually risen to his present status. Perhaps he had discovered Ned's role in his earlier eclipse and was seeking vengeance. Fear burgeoned in Ned's mind.

Hawkins, the adjutant, was waiting for him in the outer office. Ned came to attention and saluted.

"At ease," Hawkins said. He was puzzled to see Ned so clearly anxious. They had first met when Ned asked to be excused from Sunday church parade, and Hawkins had been intrigued by this reserved and withdrawn man with such a spectacular history. He had determined then to do what few small things he could to make Ned's life easier. He could not think how to do that now.

"I'm afraid he knows who you are," he said.

Ned raised his eyebrows questioningly

"Not the best," Hawkins confided.

It was a considerable understatement. The fuss had begun the previous evening, at dinner. Air Vice-Marshal Sir Geoffrey Salmond had come from Delhi for an inspection and in the mess, over port, had asked how Shaw was getting along.

Wing Commander Aubrey Stapleton was puzzled. "I do not believe we have an officer of that name here," he replied.

"He isn't an officer," Salmond said, but didn't elaborate. His tone suggested that any good CO would know the names of all the men—officers, NCOs and other ranks—in his charge, which was, of course, impossible at a depot as large as Karachi. Hawkins could not hide a small smile. He did not know the names of *all* the men at the base, some several hundred, but most of them.

"A little gift from Providence, sir," Hawkins told Sir Geoffrey. "He seems to be well and happy; the other men like him and appreciate his sense of humor."

Sir Geoffrey nodded and moved on to other matters, but the wing commander scowled at his adjutant in astonishment, and Hawkins knew it was only a matter of time before he must explain himself.

It had happened this morning, soon after Sir Geoffrey had left to return to Delhi.

"Can you give me any good reason why the air vice-marshal should be so concerned as to the welfare of one particular airman under my command?" Stapleton had demanded of Hawkins.

"I take it you mean Shaw, sir," he said.

"Of course, I mean Shaw!" Stapleton could scarcely control his irritation.

"He is curiously well connected," Hawkins said, calm in the face of an impending storm. "Because of his knowledge of Arabian affairs."

Stapleton bristled. He considered himself to be an Orientalist, an expert on the Arab world. Some years ago, during the war, he had served briefly in the Middle East before being sent home, unexpectedly, under circumstances that were still puzzling to him.

"What knowledge?" he snapped. "And how is he known to Sir Geoffrey?"

"You might know him better by another name, sir." Hawkins was a little shocked that Stapleton didn't know already. Almost everyone else on the base did.

"Lawrence," he said, enjoying the moment. "T. E. Lawrence."

Stapleton's reaction was entirely satisfactory to his adjutant. The wing commander blinked and tried to remain impassive, but Hawkins could almost see his mind whirling, an antic propellor.

"T. E. Lawrence, Colonel Lawrence, Lawrence of Arabia, is serving as an ordinary airman here?"

"Sir," Hawkins affirmed.

"How on earth did he get in?" Stapleton demanded.

"Friends in very high places, I would imagine, sir."

That much was obvious to Stapleton. That Shaw should know Sir Geoffrey was a shocking surprise, but not that Lawrence would. Colonel Lawrence was astonishingly famous, extraordinarily well connected. He was a close confidante of the Chief of Air Staff, Sir Hugh Trenchard, and had been Winston Churchill's most trusted adviser in all that Middle Eastern nonsense after the war. Even the prime minister knew him. He was a friend of kings and emperors. It was rumored he had turned down a knighthood. Potentially a very dangerous fellow—especially skulking about in the ranks.

"How long have you known this?"

"Since shortly after he first came here," Hawkins replied.

"And you did not see fit to inform me?"

"I was told privately, confidentially, by a friend in Delhi. I've spoken with Shaw. He is not keen to have it broadcast about."

The wing commander's face flushed. "I hardly think that telling me is broadcasting it about! Who else knows?"

"Not many, I think," Hawkins responded blandly. "The men in his barracks, I suppose. A few others. Those that do know are keen to respect his desire for anonymity."

Hawkins was a thoroughly competent officer, a fair and honest man, liked by his peers, respected by the enlisted men, the erks. He disliked Stapleton intensely, thought him arrogant and overly fussy, trying to impose boarding-school discipline and the Victorian traditions of the army on the bright new force of the air. Ned, on the other hand, was exactly the sort of new thinking man they needed, looking to future possibilities, not clinging to past conventions.

Hawkins knew that Ned's life could not be easy, that a man of his background and education must be suspiciously regarded by his fellow erks, yet Ned behaved with grace and humor, and exercised reticent leadership. A sensible suggestion of Ned's was more readily accepted than many of Stapleton's punctilious orders, and Ned was the only A/C 2 that corporals and sergeants obeyed.

To Hawkins, Ned represented a tantalizing future, a breaking away from the old, class-bound conventions of military service, a lodestar for a brave, exciting world, in which a man was judged by his ability, by his merit, and not some accident of birth. If Ned, once a glittering officer, could successfully serve in the ranks, then the brightest and the best of their ranking men might rise to officer status. Hawkins felt an odd stirring somewhere in the pit of his stomach. He could think of half a dozen of the erks who would make fine officers, and one or two who might be better leaders of men than the intemperate, bumbling Stapleton. What a future that would be, Hawkins thought, what a Britain. Suddenly, and for the first time, he realized that what Ned was doing was revolutionary, and that he, Hawkins, had wholeheartedly signed on to the cause. Thus inspired, he went into battle.

"He is a very good airman, sir. Keen and conscientious. He causes no trouble, keeps to himself and the men like him." He couldn't resist a touch of humor. "The quality of reports from the Engine Repair Section has improved dramatically since Shaw came here."

Stapleton had no interest in elegantly written reports. "Bring him to me," he ordered.

Now Ned was here, patently frightened and curiously downcast, like a man on his way to the gallows. No, Hawkins corrected himself, that was too extravagant: like an errant schoolboy about to get six of the best from the Head.

He could not smile encouragement because he didn't know what Stapleton might do, but he tried to look encouraging and knocked on the commanding officer's door.

There was a barked order to enter. Hawkins opened the door and led the way. Ned marched to the desk, stamped to a halt and saluted.

"Sir, 338171, Shaw, sir, reporting as ordered." Ned's voice went up an octave, as it often did when he was nervous.

Stapleton stared at him, as if taking the measure of him, and did not give the stand-easy. How could this man be the fabled Lawrence of Arabia? How could this noodle be the legendary hero of the Great War? How could this be the man who melded a dozen, disparate tribes into a formidable army and conquered the Turks? With that silly, high-pitched voice, no one would follow this little pipsqueak anywhere. He almost smirked as he wondered if the great Lawrence's balls had ever dropped.

Stapleton stood up. A tall man and impeccably uniformed, he believed himself impressive, a true leader of men.

"I do not approve of your presence here, in your present rank," Stapleton said. "It is untenable. Surely you must see that you are a most provocative influence?"

Ned didn't reply.

"Your proper place, if you have one here, is as an officer, and it is beyond my understanding that you are not commissioned. Obviously, because of some wretched oversight, you have not been given that opportunity. I offer it to you now. I am prepared to recommend that you be accepted for Officer Training immediately."

He waited for an enthusiastic response, but none came.

"It is your duty to your king and country," he urged.

No, this was too easy, Ned thought, a ton weight of worry falling from his shoulders. This he had learned early, at his mother's knee. He wasn't going to be chucked out, this man didn't have the guts to do it. He was being invited to a different rank, to settle a societal embarrassment, that was all. It was a demand, but not an order; it couldn't be. He would have needed authority from Boom—Sir Hugh Trenchard—or Sir Geoffrey at the very least, to kick Ned out and would have hidden behind their names. By revealing the limits of his power, the wing commander had lost any power he might have had, and Ned was immediately himself again and in command. Hawkins, watching carefully, thought the man seemed to grow, almost visibly, in stature.

"Not educationally qualified, sir," Ned said.

In his mind, it was true. Shaw had never been to school, having been born at the age of thirty-six. Lawrence was a different matter. Lawrence had formidable educational qualifications. But Lawrence was dead.

Hawkins turned away to the window, to hide his smile. Stapleton was furious. This nervous, diminutive figure had become someone else. The room was charged with a new presence, a new energy. The voice that had been so weak was now crisp and commanding, and the tone mocking. The soft, blue eyes hardened to sapphire. And of course, the answer was inarguable.

Stapleton understood his own impotence. He could not order the man to be an officer. And although he could demand Shaw's dismissal, he did not want to be remembered as the man who had Lawrence of Arabia chucked out of the RAF. In any case, the demand might not be met. He could write complaining letters, but would all those friends in the highest places pay any attention, or would he only discredit himself? He could put the man on a charge, but for what? Insolence? How had he been insolent? He could make life as unpleasant as possible for Shaw, but always there were those friends, those powerful friends, who held Stapleton's promotion, or otherwise, in their hands. What infuriated him most of all was that he did not know how he had lost, and so abjectly.

"Don't play games with me!" he almost shouted. "I've read your bloody book! I know what your qualifications are!"

Inwardly, he cursed his lack of temperance, but lost control of his tongue. "Not one of those bloody Bolsheviks, are you?" he snapped. It was a stupid question, and Stapleton regretted it even as he spoke.

"Sir?" Ned questioned smartly, as if he didn't understand. The arrogance had faded almost as quickly as it had come, he knew he had made an enemy and wanted to make some small amends. He prayed he would now be dismissed, but Stapleton hadn't finished.

"I know what you did in Arabia," he said. "I trust you're not stirring up trouble with the natives here."

"Haven't left the base since I got here, sir," Ned said, hoping it would help.

His response almost made it worse, because it could be checked, and if found to be true, which Stapleton was sure it was, then the accusation was simply ridiculous.

"Then keep it that way. Nationalist nonsense doesn't wash with me." Stapleton was loath to dismiss the man. He wanted, somehow, to hurt. "I will keep my eye on you," he warned. "And if you put one foot out of line, if I smell one hint of trouble, I will have you posted away from here, up-country, to the worst hellhole I can find! Dismiss!"

Ned saluted, made a sharp about-turn and marched out of the office.

Stapleton hit his desk in fury. "That man is dangerous!" he insisted. Overly ambitious, he was a strong believer in conspiracy theories to explain his own less-than-spectacular career. "I'll lay money he's been planted, put here to snoop on us all. I dread to think what he's telling Delhi about us. Or London."

He turned to Hawkins. "Talk to him. Find out."

"I hardly think—" Hawkins began. He could not think that Ned would answer honestly if it were true, but he was also intrigued. He didn't want Ned to be a spy, didn't think he was one, but he was a copious letter writer: what did he write in those letters to all his highly placed friends about his officers?

"And keep him out of my sight!" Stapleton commanded. Hawkins saluted and left the room.

Alone, Stapleton considered the interview and nursed his grievances. He remembered stories that Lawrence had been discovered, under an assumed name that was not Shaw—Roberts? Ross? Rose, perhaps?—at some other air base in England, sometime before, and after a hoo-ha in the press, was dismissed the service. He had heard rumors that Lawrence had reenlisted, first in the Tank Corps, and then again in the RAF, but under yet another name. What he had not known was that the new name was Shaw. And that he was here.

Stapleton had read Lawrence's book about the Desert Campaign and thought it an outrageous piece of self-aggrandizement, a tissue of lies from beginning to end. A fabrication that made a hero of the writer and ignored the valiant efforts of so many others in the Middle Eastern war—others such as himself.

What offended him most greatly, though, was that a gentleman and an erstwhile officer, no matter how vainglorious, was serving in the ranks. It cocked a cheeky, destructive snook at all his concepts of leaders and men, of the military establishment, of all that he, Stapleton, stood for, fought for and probably would have died for. It made a mockery of all he held most dear. Not overly wellborn, Stapleton had high social aspirations, and Shaw's position suborned his concept of the natural order of blood and birthright, of authority and command. It sabotaged the entire class structure of Britain. It was as if the King of England had abdicated his throne to work in a miner's pit. How dare the man turn down a knighthood?

The foolishness of the decision to place him in India astounded Stapleton. Lawrence had made it very clear, in his book, that he had little time for colonialism or imperialism and thought all subject nations should have the right to self-determination, although preferably under some form of dominion status with Britain. The fellow had already fomented one successful revolution among restless natives. What dreadful harm he could do here! The political situation was already volatile enough, with Moslems and Hindus constantly at each other's throats, united only in strident and increasing calls to be free of the shackles of Imperial Britain.

Putting Lawrence in the middle of this, roaming free to voice his postcolonial views, was madness, and that appalling book could be read as a manifesto for revolution by the wrong minded.

Stapleton liked to think of himself as a fair man, especially where the welfare of his troops was concerned, and, for better or worse, Shaw was one of his men. He would give him the benefit of the doubt. Perhaps, despite all his strong feelings to the contrary, there was some innocent reason for Lawrence's—Shaw's—bizarre behavior. And if none of his superiors in London or Delhi had been clever enough to divine that reason, he, Stapleton, would.

And then get rid of him.

5

June 1927

I do not want you to think I am unhappy. This is the life I have chosen, the life for which I have fought battles as fierce as any in Arabia. I try not to think about the past, the real past, because it can overwhelm me; the legendary lie is better. Nor dare I think about the future. I am terrified that my position in the RAF is insecure, and in any case, it must end while I still have life to live, and then what shall I do? I have no yesterday and no tomorrow. I am only, always, today, and I am not unhappy.

Nor do I want you to think I blame my mother for what has become of me. Although I have already said harsh things about her, and shall say more, I am mine own executioner. My mother did her best for me, what she believed was right, did what befits a Spartan boy.

In her gymnasium of virtue, my mother trained me to my destiny. She gave me chastity and obedience, and taught me that the heart can be a treacherous enemy. She made me understand that strategy can vanquish force, guile can subdue legions, and meekness, real or apparent, can subdue strength. Above everything, she beat into me a resolute determination never to surrender to pain. I am a son of Sparta.

I cannot remember the first time she spanked me for being naughty, but I remember the first time I remember being spanked as if it were yesterday.

It is then I learn the power I have over her authority.

I am five, nearly six. It is 1893, and we are living in Dinard, in France, but my father is talking of moving. Again. We move quite often. Since I was born in Wales we have lived in Scotland (where William was born), the Isle of Man, the island of Jersey and now here. And Mother says that another little brother is on the way.

It is Friday night, bath night. Every Friday night the maid drags a big zinc bathtub to the kitchen fire and fills it with hot water. Then Mother brings us in and the maid is banished. (It is not seemly for her to see male nakedness, even puny, unformed boys, she is not our nanny; we don't have a nanny here. It is France.)

38

Bob bathes first—he is older by three years, my big brother—soaping himself, although Mother scrubs his back. She questions him about his day and God while she sponges his back and bum. Then he relaxes to rinse and I climb in. Bob shouts (but not too loudly, for mother gets cross) that I'm taking up too much room, or getting him wet. I laugh because he is already wet. I love Bob because he's big and strong, compared with me, and nice to me sometimes. He's a bit serious and doesn't laugh a lot, but I don't suppose big brothers can—they've got too much to think about. (I like to laugh a lot, but I don't laugh too much, because Mother gets cross—she says life is a very serious business.) I love bathing with Bob. I want to be like him, to be firm and strong and considerate like him.

I am small for my age.

I wash my face with the flannel cloth and then stand up while Mother soaps my back with the sponge. Sometimes she tells me stories about the baby Jesus, what a good boy he was, and how kind he was to his mother, who suffered so much pain when she gave birth to him, and about when he was crucified for our sins, to be our Savior and our Salvation. Sometimes she sings pretty hymns as her soapy hands caress my soapy back and move over my bottom, kneading it clean until I have the cleanest bum in all the world. (I am never to say that word in front of Mother, but I love saying it to myself. Bum. Bumbumbum. Bumbum-dibumbum, bumbum.)

Sometimes Bob climbs out before me, but I like it best when he stays in, and we sit at opposite ends of the tub, knees pulled up so we both fit. The tub doesn't seem as big as it was. Am I growing up? Am I getting bigger? I hope so. When Mother asks me what I will pray for that night, I tell her that I will pray for her and Father and Bob and baby William, and that Jesus will guard me through the night and keep my soul if I should die before I wake. But mostly—I don't tell her this—I will pray to be big.

She smiles and tells me I am being good, but I must make a sacred, solemn promise to her that I will never grow up to be a naughty boy. She turns away to get the towels, warming on the rack, and Bob stands up, ready to get out of the bath.

I see his willy.

I stand up too, and cover my willy with my hands, because it is so tiny compared to Bob's. It's never seemed all that important before, but tonight it does (am I growing up?), and I am so surprised that his willy is so much bigger than mine, that I reach to touch it, to see if it is real.

Bob lets me touch it, as if he understands my admiration, and then whispers, "That's rude," and gently pushes my hand away.

Too late. Mother has heard him. She turns around and sees Bob pushing my hand away from his willy.

She smacks me, hard, across the bum. It hurts all the more because I'm wet. She grabs me, pulls me sopping from the bath. She orders Bob to cover himself. She sits down and pushes me across her knee and smacks me hard on my bare bottom, and again, hard, and it hurts, and again, calling me a naughty boy who'll never go to heaven, a rude and sinning boy who is condemned to hell, hits me again, hard, oh, sweet baby Jesus how it hurts, and I am crying, and she hits me again, hard, it hurts so much, and I'm screaming because it hurts so much and because suddenly I know it is not the first time it has happened. I am scared of her and her open hand, and she's shouting above my screams, demanding that I beg forgiveness of Jesus for being such a rude boy, a naughty boy, a sinning boy, and never to touch Bob, or anyone, there again.

Bob is cowering by the door, scared of her anger, wrapped in a towel, trying to lose himself inside it, and holding back the tears he wants to shed. Big brothers don't cry. Little boys shouldn't cry. It is unmanly to cry. She tells him to put on his nightshirt, say good night to Father and go to bed.

She towels me dry, roughly, and tells me to stand in the corner and not look at Bob again until he has put on his nightshirt.

I stand in the corner, shivering, crying, my bottom screaming from the awful pain. I hear her kiss Bob good night. I hear him leave the room, and hear her doing things, tidying up, and I shout out my sorrow, admit my naughtiness, confess my sin, beg her to forgive me.

She does not speak to me, does not tell me to turn around. She does not tell me to come to her, and take me in her arms and hold me to her and forgive me. Which she should do, because she is my mother, and she should love me (Jesus loves me), and not hurt me (Jesus would forgive me). Because I am truly sorry for what I have done.

Not sorry because I touched Bob's willy. I'm sorry that I made Mother so angry that she could hurt me so much.

She sits down and calls me to her. I turn around, terrified in case she hits me again.

She demands I come to her, and I, sniveling, creep like a snail, eyes to the floor, until I can see the tips of her sensible black leather shoes sticking out from under her long dress, and I know I am standing in front of her. "Look at me," she says.

I raise my eyes to her, but not my head.

"Are you truly sorry for being such a naughty boy?" she asks me.

"Yes, Mother," I whisper.

She seems to believe me. "Turn around," she says.

"Don't hit me again," I beg.

"Turn around," she insists.

I turn around.

She takes the towel away from me. I start crying again. I know she is going to hit me.

Then I feel something warm and soothing on my bare bottom. She is rubbing embrocation on my injured bum. Caressing my bottom. And in a voice as soft as honey she is telling me that she will forgive me this time, and pray to God to forgive me as well, as long as I promise her that I will strive even harder to be a good boy, and to love her.

I do love her, I do, and I'm so sorry to have been naughty and to have made her so angry. She rubs my bottom, rubs, rubs, rubs my bum until her soothing hands (or is it the ointment?) have taken the worst of the pain away, and I feel another sensation, and, to my shock and horror, my willy does a little jump, as if it has a mind of its own. How can it do that? It's just a silly piece of meat, useless except for doing number ones. Will it ever do it again? It does! It jumps again!

Dear Jesus, will she hit me for that too? It isn't me! I swear I didn't do it. Happily, my willy stops doing those little jumps, and I thank Jesus with all my heart and beg him never to let my willy jump again.

Of course, I promise Mother that I will strive my utmost to be good, and eventually she seems to believe me.

"Turn around," she says again.

I am naked, and I don't want to turn around and let her see my willy. What if he jumps? An hour ago it would not have bothered me to face her, I would have done it without a second thought, but something has happened since I touched Bob. I don't want anyone to see me naked anymore.

"You promised me you would be good and do as you are told," Mother says.

I turn around. I do not look at her.

"Do you want to know why I was so angry with you?" she asks me, and, of course, I nod my head.

She points to my willy. I blush.

"That thing is the curse of all men and an intolerable burden for all women. It is the serpent that caused Adam and Eve to be banished from the Garden of Eden," she says. "It is the cause of all sin. Good Christian boys don't ever touch their own, or anyone else's."

I am amazed. I can't imagine my willy to have so much power. I know he jumped all of his own accord, but who would have thought that tiny piece of flesh to be so dangerous? But I believe her. Mother never tells me lies.

"Now put your nightclothes on."

I put on my nightshirt, dressing gown and slippers.

"Very well," Mother says at last. "I think you have learned your lesson. I hope so. You may kiss me and tell me you love me, then go in and say good night to your father."

I lean forward and kiss her on the cheek. Suddenly, she clutches me to her and holds me tight, much too tight; the hard jet of her necklace is pushing into my chest and hurting me.

"Oh, Ned," she cries. "I am so worried for you. I know you try to be a good boy, but I fear for your immortal soul. Do you really love me?"

"Yes, Mother, of course I do," I say. I would say anything she bade me, I want her to stop, I want to be away from her suffocating embrace. "May I have a biscuit?"

As I expected, she relaxes her painful clasp. "I don't think so," she says. "Not tonight."

I don't want a biscuit. I want her to let go, and I know how to get her to do it. Distract with innocence. Be naïve. Talk about biscuits. Never fight back.

I rub my sore chest. "Good night, Mother," I say, and leave the room.

I go to my father's study and knock on the door. He bids me enter. I go in. He's sitting at his desk, looking at snapshots he has taken. He loves to take photographs. He's taught me how to do it, and those hours with him are some of my favorite times in all the world. I stand beside him.

"I've come to say good night, Father," I say.

Father puts down a snapshot, pushes his reading spectacles onto his forehead and looks at me.

"Are you all right, Ned?" he asks me.

I nod my head. I think I'm going to cry again, because he is so sweet and kind and gentle and he cares about me, I know he does, and I want him to take me in his arms and hold me close to him and stop her from ever hitting me again.

He doesn't hold me. He never holds me. He never touches me, except to shake my hand.

"Your mother loves you very much, you know," my father tells me. He never tells me that he loves me. "Try not to be naughty."

Have I been so very naughty? Has news of my sin traveled so far, so fast? From the kitchen across the hall through the closed door of his study. Who told him? Bob? Or did he hear my screams and know?

"No, Father," I say. "Good night, Father."

"Good night, Son," my father says.

I leave the study and go upstairs. I share a bedroom with Bob. William, who's only three, sleeps on a cot in my parents' bedroom. Bob isn't in his bed, he's lying on it, facedown, reading the Boy's Own Annual. *He looks at me, and I blush. He's accusing me of something, but I'm not sure what. Of touching his willy? He let me do that.*

"It's rude to touch people there," he says. "It's a sin." He is my mother's son.

"Does it still hurt?" he asks me, and I nod and climb into my own small bed.

"Silly little beggar," Bob says, and I can hear the love in his voice. "You shouldn't make Mother cross."

Well, I know that!

"Do you want me to read you a story? Any one you like, special treat."

"King Arthur," I say.

"Which one?" Bob asks, laughing. "I'm not going to read the whole thing."

"'Sir Gawain and the Green Apples,'" I tell him. Bob finds the book and reads me the story. A simple version, I suppose, with easy words and bright pictures, suitable for boys of my age, but thrilling to me.

When the tale is done, he reminds me to say my prayers.

"I can't kneel down," I tell him, and start to cry again. "It hurts too much."

"Hush now, Ned," he says. "Big boys don't cry. Say your prayers in bed. I'm sure Jesus won't mind, not this once."

I scrunch my eyes to try and stop the tears because I want to be a big boy. I whisper my prayers and beg Jesus to understand that I wasn't trying to be a sinner tonight when I touched Bob.

I didn't understand that touching someone there is an enormous sin. I will never touch anyone there again.

Not even myself.

6

HAWKINS, HURRYING TO find Ned, knew that something unusual had happened during the interview with Stapleton. At the moment the balance had swung, he had seen—no, he had felt—the change in Ned. The small, unremarkable man had become something else. Whereas immediately before, Ned seemed to him to be a very ordinary airman who would, without outward argument, obey any order, some internal combustion had ignited his personality, had changed him into a man who was used to giving orders, and used to having them obeyed, someone who was, without question, remarkable.

Yet when he found Ned not far from the wingco's office, obviously waiting for him, there was no evidence of that other man. Instead there seemed even less of him than there had been before—only a little, nervous airman, older than all his fellows, with shaking hands and a harried frown. Nor could Hawkins swear that Ned had not been crying.

"It's all right," he said. "His bark's infinitely worse than his bite."

"I didn't mean to cheek him," Ned said, his voice wavering toward the upper registers. "I just—"

He stopped and took control of himself. "I have to keep a clean sheet," he said.

"He thinks you may be spying on us." Hawkins saw no point in beating about the bush. "It isn't so unreasonable. Your position is quite unusual, and you do know some influential people."

Ned's nervousness disappeared, and something of the other man returned.

"They are my friends," he said. "And that is all." Ned liked Hawkins but was suddenly angry at what he had been put through by the wing commander. He would show them just how powerful his friends were and thus what power he himself had, if he chose to use it.

"I can prove it, if I must." He knew that Hawkins believed him, but he needed to do it anyway.

Hawkins considered this. "You must know that this is very distasteful to me," he said.

Ned nodded. They walked together to Ned's barracks.

"Are you writing anything new?" Hawkins asked.

Ned shrugged. "A thing about the RAF, my experiences. Myself, I suppose. Everything I write seems to be about me. Not here, but at Uxbridge, when I first joined up. It's fairly down to earth. I doubt it will ever be published. The language is pretty salty, and it wouldn't be fair to Boom. Or the fellows."

The use of "Boom" jolted Hawkins. It was the nickname by which Air Chief Marshal Sir Hugh Trenchard, the chief of air staff, the big wallah, was known. But he was called that only by his familiars. It was odd to hear a lowly A/C 2 use it. Then again, he thought, not odd at all when you knew who the A/C 2 is. Was? It was all so silly, and because it was so silly, he did a silly thing. He giggled.

Ned giggled with him, and they walked the rest of the way to the barracks in comfortable silence.

They went up the stairs of the stone building. The airmen lived on the upper level, to take advantage of the breezes. The lower part was reserved for the native servants and for storage.

The big room was empty, apart from Slaney. He had been on night duty at the guardhouse and was lying on his cot, asleep.

Ned went to his cupboard and unlocked it. He took out some letters and flicked through them, then settled on two, which he gave to Hawkins. "Sir Hugh," he said of one. "Winston Churchill," of the other.

There was a hint of arrogance in his voice again, but Hawkins thought it allowable. He scanned the letters, both congratulating Ned on his book, in epic terms. Both were also intensely personal, and Hawkins was almost embarrassed to read them.

"Do I have clearance?" Ned asked, smiling to soften his insolence. Hawkins smiled too, and nodded. He looked about the room. He tried to imagine Ned's life as one of its fourteen occupants.

"Do you need somewhere to write?" He spoke softly, in consideration of the sleeping airman. "I know of an office you could use—there's a typewriter . . ."

"I write in longhand, mostly," Ned said, but appreciated the offer. "An office would be very pleasant. Life gets a little"—he glanced around the barracks—"crowded."

Hawkins gave back the letters.

"What makes you certain that this is the life for you?" Hawkins asked. "It seems so very unlikely."

"It is the only life I have," Ned said wistfully, staring out of the window at the barren, dusty, endless plain beyond, as if looking for something he'd lost, something unbelievably precious to him. Hawkins was determined to help.

"There's a job coming up next year that might suit you, given your experience," he said. "In Afghanistan."

"I don't know anything about Afghanistan," Ned said, but it was not a rejection. It was a lie.

In fact, he knew quite a lot about Afghanistan, a critically important pawn in the complex game of international diplomacy. Afghanistan lay trapped between the increasingly expansionist Soviet Union and the subcontinent of British India, linchpin of the Empire. He and Winnie had discussed it often, while drunk, over one of those many dinners during which they conquered the world together. In Winnie's view, there must eventually be a resolving conflict between the rising force of Communism on the one side and all those that opposed it on the other. Imperial Britain and her Commonwealth, with their capitalist ally, America, against the Russian Soviet Empire, with its avowed goal of world domination. The British had long understood the importance of Afghanistan as a fortress against an invasion of India, but so had the French and the Americans and the Chinese and now the Bolsheviks. The country was a quagmire of shifting alliances.

"It's not actually a military job, but they want a serviceman to do it," Hawkins explained. "Clerk to the British attaché in Kabul. It could be right up your alley. There's trouble brewing, and we have to protect our position."

He thought he saw a glimmer of curiosity in Ned's eye. "You'd have to learn to type," he ended with a smile.

"A spy?" Ned smiled with him.

"In a roundabout kind of way, perhaps," Hawkins agreed. "It's a bit of a political stew up there, the nationalists, the Soviets and ourselves, all vying for control. There's even a few Americans spicing the mix. The king is a crafty fellow, but he has his hands full, playing all sides against the middle."

Obviously, the idea was attractive to Ned, but his next question surprised Hawkins: "Are you so anxious to be rid of me from here? Have I blotted my copybook, after all?"

"No," Hawkins assured him. "I think you are an exemplary airman. It's just that I hate to see your splendid talents wasted. Think it over. You don't have to give me an answer for a couple of months."

When Hawkins had gone, Ned sat on his cot and glanced at the letters again, drinking in their praise of his writing, of his Arabian triumphs, of his contribution to world affairs. Afghanistan frittered across his mind. Well, I have the qualifications, he thought.

Something was stirring inside him, some sense of wanting to be involved again, somehow, somewhere. It scared him too, and he was not sure what he feared most, the possibility of success or the probability of repeating a failure. He didn't know that much about the current political situation in Afghanistan, but it shouldn't be too hard to find it out. At the very least, he would brush up on his rudimentary typing skills.

Then he realized that for the last hour or so, since his petty triumph over Stapleton, for the first time in days, he had not thought once of Hogarth. Or of failure.

He locked the letters away and glanced around. It was all right. They had talked softly enough. Slaney was still asleep, facedown on his bunk.

Ned moved a little closer. Slaney's puttees were half undone, his calves fleshy beneath them. His muscular thighs were shaded dark with hair. His shorts were tight across his chunky buttocks, his shirt showed the shape of a powerful back, and the armpits were wet with sweat. The very smell of him was man. A breeze fluttered his thick, brown hair, his sometimes surly face was buried in a muscular arm, in sleep.

A worthy arm, Ned thought. An arm that could do damage. An arm that could hurt.

Staring at him, Ned was shocked as he felt an old urge come upon him, a feeling he had not known for months, since he last saw John Bruce at Clouds Hill before embarking for India. A need. A quick and sudden hardening. Are you awake again, old serpent? he wondered of that part of himself. Has the life not been beaten out of you yet? Do you need more punishment? Have I been so very bad again?

He hated himself for thinking it, for wanting the pain, hated this momentary loss of control, this desire that urged his surrender. He could subdue it; he had to conquer the wretched worm, he must be master of his body. Knowing that Slaney was the cause and focus of it, he turned away abruptly and left the room.

* * *

But Ned was wrong. They had not talked softly enough. Slaney was not asleep. He had been dozing when Hawkins and Ned came into the room, had only half heard their talk.

Until they mentioned spying. Then he was wide awake, and, feigning sleep, enthralled.

They had talked of spies and clearances, of famous politicians, of kings and Soviets and revolution. And Coughdrop was right in the middle of it.

For a moment, Slaney allowed himself to think that he had been an intimate, if only by association, in world affairs, in things that mattered. It was heady stuff to a young man from a dank English village, whose only real expectation of life was insignificance. The feeling fed some part of him that had never been touched before, and he was filled with a thrilling sense that somehow, if only for a moment, somewhere in the scheme of things, his life might have some meaning.

He let his mind roam free in the limitless landscapes of youthful dreams. For spying is adventure, especially in wild Afghanistan. And what young man's blood does not pump hard at the thought of being important?

7

It is the beginning of the new century, I am nearly twelve, and I have just had a revelation.

I am not ordinary. I am blessed with a glamorous curse. I am different. I am not like the others.

My father tells me I am descended from a noble family, and that if things were different, Bob would have a title and I would be second in line until Bob has a son. Father won't tell me who our family is, except to say that our ancestors were related to Sir Walter Raleigh. When I ask him questions, he says he'll explain it all to me one day. But I think I already know:

She is not my real mother.

She is not my father's wife.

My real mother was a wellborn lady who fell in love with a great knight who wasn't her husband (my father), and when I was born she had to send me away to live with my father, and he employed a nanny (Mother) to look after me.

Of course, they have to pretend to be married, but I think they do more than that. They sleep together in a big double bed, my father and the woman who calls herself my mother, and they make babies (they've just made another). My friend Janet Laurie told me how babies are made, and the boys at school have confirmed it. I can't believe my father and the woman who calls herself my mother would do that thing. They are sinners, and they compound their evil every time they make a baby. Or perhaps Mother is a fallen woman, like the strumpet Guinevere, who could not keep her virtue to save a noble kingdom.

We live in Oxford now. We moved here four years ago so we boys can go to a good school. It's the first time I've been to a proper school; we had a governess when we lived in the New Forest. (We didn't have a governess or a nanny in France, because Mother didn't trust French women.)

I'm good at Latin and Greek and history, and I adore English grammar and literature. The other boys are all right, but some of them think me odd. I don't like to play football or cricket or hockey, I don't like to be part of a team. I like doing things by myself, swimming is my favorite sport.

(I like wrestling too. I'm good at it. Sometimes, especially when I wrestle with Bodger, my serpent gets hard, and I know his does too. We giggle and fight harder. He's bigger than I am, but not as fleet or cunning. Quite often, I win.)

We all envy and admire Bodger. He is a year older and very sure of himself, very worldly. He knows all about girls and says he is not a virgin. We don't believe him.

Once a week we have a swimming class, at the municipal baths. I go to the changing room one day. Bodger is there with Coleberd and Wilson. Bodger's swimming costume is pulled down, and he is showing the others his serpent.

It is fat and thick, much fatter and thicker than mine. It is magnificent. I want it—not to touch it or admire, but to possess, to be the proud owner of a serpent such as his, engorged between my legs. If you are going to sin, why not do it on a gargantuan scale.

Bodger grins and offers to let me touch it, but I won't ever touch anyone there. What if Mother found out? She is a sorceress and has eyes everywhere, eyes that seek out evil. Cassandra could learn from her.

We're not allowed to know girls. Mother doesn't like us knowing girls, except Janet. I like Janet a lot, but I don't know why Mother lets us play with her. I think she hopes that Bob will marry her one day. Or perhaps it's because Janet's more like a boy than a girl; she can climb trees and run nearly as fast as me, and she's a wizard shot with a catapult.

She knows all about boys' willys and asks to see mine because she says she's never actually seen one before. I undo my belt and braces and push down my trousers and underpants and let her see my willy, but I don't let her touch it. She laughs and says it looks silly, so I get dressed again and ask her to show me hers. She tells me girls don't have willys. I ask her what they do have, and she says "Nothing." I don't believe her, but she won't show me because she says nice girls don't show boys that. *I offer her a penny (half my pocket money), and she pulls up her skirt and petticoat and pulls down her knickers and shows me—nothing. What a waste of money.*

Bob sees us, the prig, and, of course, he tells Mother. She beats me really hard that night, and tells me I can't play with Janet anymore.

I don't cry out. I scream inside. I will not give her the pleasure of knowing how much she hurts me. I bear the pain; she must not win. My will is greater than hers, and I know how to make her stop. If I admit my weakness, if I confess my sins, she bursts into tears and holds me to her and tells me she loves me. I tell her I love her too (and sometimes, I do), but then she gives me big lectures about

Jesus and heaven, and about my immortal soul. If Jesus forgives everyone, why can't she?

Even though I have this power, I don't always use it. I don't always make her stop. Sometimes when she beats me I feel wonderful, my bum howling in agony and my little, hard willy all warm and soothing, and I don't know which I like better, the beating or the feeling in my serpent, and suddenly I cry out, but it isn't in pain, and it's the most wonderful feeling I've ever known and something hot and sticky comes out of my willy.

I know what it is, because the other boys brag about it. I know that it is wrong—really, really wrong—and I know that if SHE finds out, she will kill me. But after it happens, I feel wonderful, all drowsy and calm, and the beating has stopped, and she's rubbing my bum with embrocation and whispers how sorry she is for me and tells me to be on constant guard against the devil and warns me all the time about girls.

I feel sorry for the new baby: what will she do to him? I shall protect him from her, to the very best of my ability. It is the duty of the strong to protect the weak, like knights of old, and I am strong, for she has made me so.

In some of the old churches nearby, there are monumental brasses, engravings of knights and their ladies who are buried beneath them. The knights look calm and peaceful, resting in eternal slumber, their eyes closed, their hands on the hilts of their swords, their ladies beside them: perfect, perpetual partners, the ultimate union.

I go there sometimes and take rubbings of the brasses, inspired by them.

I want to be a knight.

I want to do brave and bold things. I want to find someone to love and cherish and protect, someone to fight for and conquer kingdoms for, and finally, when all the battles are done, I want to come home and govern my grateful country justly, to be loved by all the people, my beloved at my side, until we reach the end of our days and die together, and sleep together forever, lulled by angels.

I want to be Galahad, the only knight pure enough to see the Sacred Chalice.

I will be Galahad, Keeper of the Holy Grail, whose bones lie in Jerusalem.

I am Galahad, whose shield bore the bend sinister. And when I am Sir Ned, my shield will show the same.

It would be awful to be ordinary.

8

SOME EVENINGS, AFTER DARK, when Ned's hand was tired from writing, he would wind up his gramophone and play records.

So the men went about their domestic chores to the strains of Brahms, Beethoven or Schubert. Or, bored with their own company, they might gather near Ned's bed, as troops to a leader, to be closer to the lovely sounds.

They would talk to Ned between the records, warily at first, about their lives, their families and their aspirations. The breadth of his experience, his special perspective on the world and his sense of humor made accessible to the men subjects they might otherwise have dismissed. He encouraged argument and debate among them, and never derided their opinions, however simplistic.

It was not all one sided. These men had knowledge of things about which Ned knew little and they shared what they knew gladly, although they laughed at his ignorance of their mundane worlds, and wondered what it must be like to be born, as they thought him, to privilege.

"What shits me," Thompson said one night, "is that my parents are so effing smug about being working class."

"What's to be ashamed of?" Cameron, the Scot whom Ned suspected of communism, asked belligerently, ready for a fight.

"Nothing," Thompson said. "I'm working class, and I'm proud of it. But they've never wanted to be more than what they are, never wanted to be any better than what they were always going to be."

Clearly, he wanted to be more. They all did. It was why they had joined the Royal Air Force—the new force, conquerors of the limitless sky. It satisfied their thirst for adventure while giving them security and a trade. It was more than the army and more than the navy, because airmen, ground or sky, were something the world had not known before, fledgling technocrats. Without them, and their knowledge and their skill, the aircrew could not fly. They were necessary to the system, and feeling their own wings of confidence, they were questioning the system that had reared them.

Cameron made many speeches about the evils of their class-ridden society, and he found receptive ears. Trade unionism had flourished in their lifetimes. Women had the vote. The terrible war, with its senseless slaughter that achieved nothing, had wrought a desire for change in all of them—but what would the changes be and what would they bring? The Scotsman's revolutionary ideas of independence for the British colonies provoked contentious argument.

"Imagine the nignogs ruling 'emselves," said Jones, who couldn't.

Inevitably, the men would ask Ned what he thought, and he offered them his vision of an alternative, a middle way, a commonwealth of the British Dominions together with any other nations that subscribed to the Westminster system of government, suitably refined, as an ideal.

This vision found considerable favor. The men loved their country, believed that Britannia ruled the waves and should rule the air as well, and that British government of the colonies was essentially benevolent, in the best interests of the native peoples.

"All wogs start at Calais," Rogers said, voicing the general opinion.

Ned did not entirely disagree. His greatest bitterness in life was directed toward the untrustworthy French, who had helped to destroy everything he had striven to achieve. Even afterwards, when he had tried to make something of the mess, to keep his promise to Feisal, at least, and to give him the crown of Damascus, the French had brought him undone.

But his prejudices were color blind. He loathed his wartime enemy, the Turks, but he had adored the Arabs, and often his life had depended on their grace. And he would have given his life for, and did give his heart to, the dusky Dahoum. For Dahoum, he would have abandoned everything he was brought up to be, would have dwelt the rest of his life in a remote desert fortress, his beloved at his side.

Of course, he could not tell the men this. He could not tell them that for Dahoum he had dared everything. For Dahoum's sake, he had become legend.

So he told them what they wanted to hear, tales of Arabia and what they believed he had been. He told them how he—or that other man—had inspired a native people to rise up against their Turkish oppressors and seize their freedom, the right to govern themselves, under benign British influence. If the men didn't comprehend all the political ramifications of what he told them, they were enthralled by the telling. For Ned, in their simple company, was unthreatened. Home was them, not his family or a house where he lived, and he allowed himself to relive that other man's life and made it a sweeping adventure.

He spoke of the small flame of revolt near Jeddah that he fanned into the fire of a mighty revolution. Of how he had convinced a minor prince of a small desert tribe that they could march north and defeat the Turks, even to Damascus, and enter that distant city in triumph. Of how he had dreamed of the conquest of Aqaba, by land, not by sea, and how he led a tiny army across a sun-scorched waste to victory.

He communicated the thrill of blowing up railways. He shared with them the heat and dust and cold and sand and thirst and bad food and flies and camel rides and attacks by flimsy aircraft. He conjured up the excitement of riding to battle at the head of a wild, rampaging Bedouin force and vanquishing a formidable, mechanized army. He let them laugh at his stories of the fleeing Turkish foe. He elaborated his own role to the one of glory that they wanted, and offered a small group of airmen in a dusty barracks far from home some feeling of how magnificent it must have been to ride in triumph to Damascus with Lawrence of Arabia, some sense of the immortal.

Of the dark side, he told them nothing, of his true reason for his campaign, and of its awful, abject end. He did not speak of the arguments and bickering and prevarication. Of the betrayal of his many promises. Of slinking into Damascus, with a desolate soul, bereft of the reason that might have made sense of his life. He did not tell them of Dahoum dying in his arms.

This dark side he kept secret from the men until one night when he had an irresistible need to explain some small part of when it had first gone wrong. Not the fulfillment of it—that scalding moment when everything became just wasted time—but the public part, the part that he had already written of in his book. And if it shocked them, or offended them, what did it matter? Who cared? Anyone in England who bought the book could read a version of it. Why shouldn't these, his friends, his transient family, know the truth? Not all of it, of course. Not that. Not his heart.

He explained that he had become a proscribed outlaw with a fabulous Turkish price on his head. The Arab army was bogged down not far from the Turkish railway junction of Deraa, some sixty miles south of Damascus. Deraa was critical to their success, so Ned had gone there in his Arab clothes. To spy.

He looked at Slaney as he said this, and saw a rapt attention.

He had been caught, and the Turks took him to their commander, the Bey, who recognized him. Who tried to "have his way" with Ned.

The airmen were stunned to silence.

"Bloody brown-hatters," Ned heard someone mutter. Dare he go on? This night, he dared do anything.

Ned had resisted the Bey violently and had been attacked, violently. The Bey had even pushed a bayonet through a fold of flesh at Ned's ribs.

Ned casually opened his shirt and pointed to the scars. As one man, the airmen stared at those scars.

Still Ned refused the Bey, and he, viciously, malevolently, told his men to teach Ned a lesson. They dragged him downstairs, tied his hands to a post, stripped him and took turns flogging him. They flayed him till he screamed for mercy, whipped him till his back was a mass of bloody, opened flesh. Beat him till he fainted. Threw cold water over him and flogged him again.

He took off his shirt, and they saw the scars on his back.

"Bloody 'ell," wide-eyed Wilson muttered.

Ned could have told them anything now, and they would have believed him. So he told them what his tormentor, but not the Bey, did next.

The silence that followed this revelation was thunderous. Every airman in the hut was battling to come to terms with what Ned had said.

Rogers was the first to speak. "He fucked you up the arse?"

Ned had used a milder verb, and Rogers wanted to be sure he understood.

Ned nodded. He didn't have to defend himself. Others would do that for him. Besides, he was watching Slaney, who couldn't meet his eyes.

"How could he stop 'em?" Jones asked Rogers and the world. "He was tied up and being flogged."

They considered the implications for a moment.

"Wouldn't let no cunt up my arse," Rogers said, voicing a salty impossibility.

"Why not?" Cameron asked him. "Half of bloody Pompey's been up there already."

The others laughed. Rogers came from Pompey—Portsmouth—a naval town, and sailors were notorious.

Rogers took the joke in good part. He jumped off his cot toward Cameron. "Yeh, and all of fucken Scotland's been up your kilt, sweetheart," he said. To show his good humor, he minced the last few steps, but he was a big man, and the effect was like an elephant dancing on a pinhead. Cameron laughed, threw a biscuit at Rogers and, for a moment, they pillow fought.

"Did it hurt?" Wilson, more wide eyed than ever, asked Ned.

"More than the worst pain you can imagine," Ned told him, and the others nodded agreement. Few of them had any experience of sodomy, but it was one of their worst fears made real.

"Of course it bloody hurt, you worm!" Vine said, with no authority.

They fell silent again, contemplating Ned's awful fate.

"What happened then?" Wilson wanted to know.

"They dragged me back to the Bey," Ned told them, "but he bawled them out. He wasn't interested in a piece of bloody pulp, he said. He told them to take me away, but ordered his corporal to stay."

"What, and shagged him instead?" Rogers leaped ahead. "Serve the little shit-shoveler right."

"They took me to a sort of hospital room and dumped me in there," Ned continued. "A medic mopped me up and put some stuff on my back. He was very kind and whispered that a window in the next room was open. He left me alone, and I got up and went into the next room, a sort of pharmacy. He was right. A window was open. I climbed out and got away, back to my people."

He was aware that the escape was a mild anticlimax for them. Blood up, incensed at the outrage that had been done to him, they wanted more, a revenge or a bolder, more dashing escape.

He was also aware of something else. He was aware that Slaney did not believe the story.

"What I don't understand is this," Slaney said. "If this Bey bloke knew who you were, why did they let you go? Wasn't there a big price on your head?"

"I don't know either," Ned agreed. It had always been the sticking point of the story, and he had never found a version that made sense, because he didn't understand it himself. "The medic wasn't Turkish," he said. "I think he was Druse, an Arab. He didn't say much, but he spoke in Arabic, and he might have been on my side."

This possibility satisfied the others.

"Prob'bly been rogered by the Bey too, and was getting his own back," Thompson said.

There were murmurs of assent. "Did you ever get your own back on him?" Wilson wondered.

Ned nodded, but his mood had changed. He had opened too many old wounds. Deraa still had the power to hurt him. Besides, Slaney wasn't there anymore, he had slipped away while Ned wasn't looking.

"Sort of," Ned answered Wilson, as an evident postscript. "But after that, it all changed. It was different."

They recognized the change in his mood. "Not surprised," he heard someone whisper.

"But you still won, didn't you?" Wilson insisted.

"Oh, yes, we won," Ned agreed. "But it was—different."

"Course he bloody won!" Jones took command, ending the party. "He's Lawrence of Arabia, isn't he?"

"Yeh, that's right. Three cheers for you, Coughdrop." Thompson led the appreciation. But whether the cheers were for his exploits in Arabia or his evening's prowess as a storyteller, Ned wasn't sure. What did it matter? Who cared? Soon it would be lights-out anyway.

They drifted away, chatting about the world and what he had told him. Ned busied himself putting away his things, his mementos, his memories.

"After all that, everything you've done," Jones said quietly, making ready for bed, "why are you here, with us?"

It was an old, familiar question, for which Ned had no simple answer. He tried to be as honest as he could with Jones.

"Lots of reasons," he said with a shrug. "I got tired of authority, sick of command. I wanted to be ordinary. One of you."

"But you're not, are you?" Jones went on. "You're not one of us. You're not ordinary. You're different, you speak different, you've been an officer, a colonel. Why do you want to be in the ranks with a bunch of yobbos?"

Because you are real, Ned wanted to scream at him. I am fleshless, effete, false. You indulge your senses; I deny mine. Your minds see uncomplicated truth; I can only find complex lies. You are innocent; I am guilty.

But he said none of this. He knew he would be wasting his time. They didn't want him to be ordinary, to be one of them. They wanted him to be the man he was. Or had been.

Did the stories of his epic past confound his search for an ordinary future? Did the men cherish his difference, his acts of daring, deeds greater than any of them believed they could ever achieve? Did they want to be burned by the sun of him? Did they have so much need for heroes?

"Perhaps I'm just lying fallow for a while," he told Jones, and saw a grateful understanding in the other man's eye.

"I should think so," Jones said. "You deserve a break, after all you've done. But you couldn't be happy, not for long, just being one of us."

Forever and forever and forever, Ned might have said yesterday. But tonight Afghanistan tickled in his brain. That could be different.

"Maybe something will turn up one day," he said, knowing it tantalized Jones. "Something that I need to do."

"Hope so," Jones said. "It'd be a bloody waste, otherwise."

Slaney came back into the room, freshly showered, just as lights-out sounded around the camp. He did not look at Ned, or at anyone.

The corporal came in to check that they were all in bed. He bid them a gruff, vulgar, futile good night, turned out the lights and left them in the dark.

There was some desultory, whispered, idle chatter as they settled to sleep. Then silence for a while.

"Fucken queers," Rogers whispered to the silent world. "I'd shoot the lot of them."

No one responded because there was nothing to say, and no need. But Ned shivered. Sometimes the price of conformity was extraordinarily high.

The room was still and silent for a while, and then the ritual began. Some were already sleeping, but some others needed something more before they slept. It happened everywhere that men were, in lonely bedrooms or bulging barracks. Here, it was at its most tranquil. A few of the men slipped their hands under their sheets and began caressing their private selves. They did it furtively, although everyone knew what they did. They joked about it in the daylight, made fun of themselves and others, and sometimes at night, if one man was too noisy, the others might, cheerily or angrily, protest the disturbance. But usually, apart from a heavier breathing or a stifled moan at climax, the wankers kept discreetly quiet.

That they could bear the guilt that must attend this activity was constantly astonishing to Ned. The muffled sounds caused him to get hard, but he forced his mind to fight his body and never touched himself. For the most part, he kept his vow of celibacy, and on those few, rare occasions when he did seek satisfaction, or when Nature found its own release, in necessary dreams, no direct human contact was involved.

Still, it excited him to hear the other men, these men, bringing themselves to climax. The challenge was not to submit. That they tried to keep it so secret suggested to Ned that they understood it was a sacred thing, part of their innermost selves; and that they battled not to surrender, just as he struggled now against that release of desire that his body craved, was proof that he was not so different.

I *am* like them, he thought. Or nearly.

It had been different when he was in the Tank Corps, and, long before that, before the war, a boy soldier in the Royal Artillery. In the Tank Corps, those awful, ugly, degrading years, the ceremony had been vile and violent, a public display, as if each man had to prove his manhood by the loudness and the audacity of his masturbation. There it was verbalized and vociferously encouraged. No one could climax silently, it seemed, but yelled of the violence they would do to the imaginary bodies that were destined to receive them.

Ned had hated it, this nightly ritual, and had tried to shut his ears to it, pulling his thin pillow over his head to block out the awful sound of it, for it made the holy act of sex, which was already an alien sacrament to him, degrading, bestial, profane.

Only when they had finished, and the last man had broadcast the excellence of his orgasm and quantity of his come, only then did silence fall. Only then could Ned compose himself for the night.

His one true friend in the Tank Corps, John Bruce, had seemed to understand how much the ritual affected Ned. One night, early on, when it was at its most raucous, sensing Ned's horror, he had held out his hand across the small space that separated them. Ned, who could not bear physical contact, took his offer gratefully, in the need of reassurance that there was not only beast in man.

They did no more than this. Shielded by dark, they lay together, side by side, in separate beds, two feet apart, each man holding the other's hand, until Ned had drifted to a fitful sleep, secure in the strong Scotsman's grasp.

9

I am a fool. A stupid, careless fool. I can't go to Afghanistan. It would be dangerous, too much like the past. Oh, why did I tell them about Deraa? How could I have been so stupid? Why was I so vain? How could I have imagined that the scars have healed? Pick at them and they are suppurating sores again. Talk—even think—about Deraa, and they spring open, newly cut, gushing blood.

I want the men to think me one of them, yet I set myself apart. I want to be ordinary, but I boast of my difference. I want to be forgotten, and I make myself immortal. They look at me in awe now, as a man who has suffered what they can scarcely imagine. They don't understand that it wasn't the pain that hurt, it was the betrayal. They treat me differently, diffidently, tread warily around me, deferentially, as dogs regard the leader of the pack.

But I will betray their trust too, just as I have betrayed everyone who ever put faith in my promises. As I betray Charlotte, who believes me capable of love. As I betray Newcombe and Hogarth and Boom and Winnie and all the others— betray them just by being here. As I betrayed Feisal. I promised him Damascus and I gave him Baghdad. And as I betrayed Dahoum.

It will soon be Christmas again. (Will they never end?) I must abscond myself. The men cannot be themselves when I'm around (the specter at their feast), and Christmas is their festival of loutish celebration.

Some American wants me to translate the Odyssey. *I cannot think of anything better for me to do. It is a mighty work, ringing in my mind. Its people breathe my air, are dear, living friends; their artifacts are my familiars, their landscapes are as known to me as Dorsetshire to Hardy. How does it begin?*

"By now all the others, those who had survived the battles or terrible shipwrecks at sea, were safely home.

"Only Odysseus wandered. . . ."

No. Not wandered—tarried, that's the word. "Only Odysseus tarried . . ."

Is this who I am? Do I tarry? Have I sailed with Odysseus, constantly searching for home, longing for that which I can never find? Have I so missed my place in time?

Should I have lived four thousand years ago, as I did at Carchemish, the place where I was happy?

At Carchemish I cast aside the modern world and lived as they did, Homer's heroes. And that other man was not a stranger to me, I liked him then, that man I was creating. I was the young Achilles then, invincible, with my Patroclus by my side, before they sailed for Ilium, before the grief of Troy.

I know the cruel, careless arrogance of the gods, the games they play. At least they let Achilles die. The arrow only killed my soul; my body lives. Would this have been Achilles's fate if he had lived? To mourn Patroclus all his days, cursing the dreadful war that robbed him of his other self?

Well, to translate the mighty work is a fancy, but at least it will give me something to do, something that touches me. If I cannot write greatness myself, I will be the key to it for others and unlock the door to kingdoms lost. I have read all the other translations and I can do better, because I have been the darling of the gods, in war, so sweetly smiled upon, and I have drunk a fill of bitterness.

I cannot go to Afghanistan. It would not be safe.

Safe? Me? A translator? A librarian?

It isn't what I had in mind for me, but it is better than the nothing I have become.

10

ROGERS SAW HIS CHANCE. He clamped his hand to the horn and his foot to the accelerator. The truck lurched forward. The sergeant, sitting beside Rogers, grabbed the dashboard for support. The men in the back of the truck, bouncing on the benches, grabbed the sides. The crowd, alarmed by the blaring Klaxon, began to part. The possibility of triumph tempered Rogers's simmering frustration.

Yet, as always, India defeated him. Veiled women dashed pell-mell across his path to join their families. The driver of a cart, determined on a right-of-way he didn't have, flicked his camel. The braying animal jerked forward, pulling the cart directly in front of the truck. Rogers, an instinctively good driver, swerved to avoid disaster, and the truck bounced over a bone-shuddering rut, scattering beggars and children.

The men's vertebrae clashed together. "What a godforsaken, bloody dump," Slaney shouted, to no one in particular. No one responded, there was no need; they all agreed with him and none had words more adequately to convey their collective opinion of K.

Rogers, blood up, would not admit defeat. His biceps strained as he pulled the heavy wheel this way and that, swerving to avoid the milling crowd, but he point-blank refused to admit the existence of a brake. The sergeant felt the need both to encourage and to assert his rank.

"Stick to the road, lad," he ordered, approvingly. "Stick to the road."

Rogers glared at the river of people. "What fucken road?" he yelled.

Drigh Road (wet road in the rainy season). The road from the air depot to town. Seven miles of Indian confusion. A bad road for the most part, hardly a road at all, a track through the desert. An unsealed, rutted, potholed road. A road for an unmechanized population. A road of camel carts and donkeys, of wandering water sellers, vegetable vendors and straggling, errant families. Of Moslem imams and Hindu godmen, fortune-tellers, itinerant tinkers and traveling tailors, assertive merchants and aggressive beggars. A road of crowded mosques and occasional temples. A road not designed for the motor.

The men always set off with high hopes; their weekly trip to Karachi was their only adventure. They were going to town, if only a very poor man's London. Despite their repeated disappointment, they cherished the fond hope that each new journey would end differently. They dressed in their best, spit-polished and clean. They climbed into the truck in exuberant spirits, chattering their expectations to bolster their mood. By the time they reached the city, the optimists were cynical and the realists, smug.

"I reckon Alexander the Great got it right," Thompson said, in an effort to break a gloomy, sixth-mile silence. "He come all this effing way, conquering 'alf the effing world, saw this effing mob and went 'ome."

The destination was worse than the journey, for once there they no longer had the protection of the truck. Deposited at the army barracks, they milled about, unwilling to separate, until a few took the plunge and headed off to buy more unwanted souvenirs to send home, to explore the stores they already knew or just to be in town. Others inclined to beer.

Jones and Vine decided on the native market. It was exotic, an adventure, part of what they had come for, and they were determined to take its measure, if only to tell their children.

Slaney and Wilson tagged along with them, Wilson wanting the protection of his friends, Slaney because he had nothing else to do and didn't enjoy getting drunk. They set off through the mass with only their uniforms and their collective sense of superiority to protect them, pigheadedly British, determined to vanquish the local onslaught.

Because his expectations had been high, Slaney's disappointment with Karachi was acute. Of a darker nature than his fellows, he lacked the armor of a cheerful disposition. Everything about the place appalled him, the wayward traffic and dirty streets, the decrepit buildings, the straggling, strident people and the ubiquitous poverty. Any wall was a public lavatory, and the stench disgusted Slaney.

On every side he was assailed, beset, urged to buy this or investigate that, or met with insistent, screeching, demands for money by beggars. Jones and Vine strode ahead, repelling all comers by simply ignoring them. Wilson trotted in their wake, vainly muttering dismissives in his few words of Urdu and, in case and to be equitable, Hindi, but safe because he kept pace with his protectors.

Slaney lagged behind, engulfed by India. A reed-thin woman approached him, a dirty-faced, sleeping child in her arms, other, older children swarming around her, all begging for money. Slaney walked on. The woman and her brood followed him, too close for his comfort, crying their hunger. Slaney tried to quicken his pace. The woman fell behind, but one of her children, a tiny tot, detached herself from the others and ran at Slaney's side, demanding money.

"*Yellah,*" Slaney said, but couldn't remember if that was Arabic or Urdu, and didn't know if the child was Hindu and wouldn't understand anyway. "*Jow,*" he said sharply, in case.

The little girl ignored all his commands, relentlessly demanding money. It was a battle of wills, and Slaney wasn't sure he would win.

"Get out of here, you little brat," Slaney muttered. He could see Jones, Vine and Wilson just ahead, on the verge of being lost in the crowd. He quickened his pace again, but the girl responded by launching herself at Slaney's leg and holding on tight, arms clutched around his thigh, legs clamped around his calf.

"Jesus Christ!" Slaney shouted. He tried to march on, a limpet child attached to his leg, but he knew he looked ridiculous. He dug his hand in his pocket, pulled out some coins and threw them to the ground. The child jumped again, scrambling for the money, along with her family (and half of India, Slaney thought), but he was free.

It was not for long, however. Perceived as an easy touch, he was immediately surrounded by beggars and shoe shine-boys. Slaney couldn't see his friends, and, for just a moment, he was frightened, feeling as if he were drowning. That tiny stab of fear was quickly replaced by anger.

He shouted at them to go away, but they would not. He tried to control his temper. His boots were mirror shiny, freshly cleaned, albeit filmed in dust, and he kept yelling that he didn't need a shoe shine, but it made no difference. One of the boys opened a little tin and threw something over Slaney's boots, a thick, sticky, filthy mixture of egg and dog shit.

It was an old trick, Slaney knew that. They'd seen it in Port Said, had joked about it and admired the mock-angry way that Ned had dealt with the offender. Slaney tried to be that calm now, but his temper snapped. He grabbed the youth, dragged him to the wall and, fist up, almost punched him. The threatened violence shocked the shoe-shiner to wide-eyed fear, the crowd to anger, and Slaney to control of himself.

"Go away, go away, what are you doing in my country?" the shoe-shine boy cried, tears spurting from his eyes. The crowd took up a similar chant, and Slaney worried that he had started a riot, and, if he had, whether he would survive.

He let the sniveling youth go, glared at the crowd, which kept its distance, and walked away, the mob parting enough to let him through, but still yelling its displeasure.

Slaney felt dirty, disgusted with himself. He didn't want to go to the mess—the others would be drunk, and the talk would be foul. He didn't want to be anywhere in India; he wanted to be home, and home, for now, was his barracks, his cot, his small piece of territory, safe behind barbed wire, with the things he understood. But the truck wouldn't be going back for another three hours. He thought about taking a rickshaw or, if he could find one, a taxi. But in either case the driver would be Indian, would want to talk, would want to sell him all manner of things he didn't want and, at the end of it, would gyp him.

So he walked. He knew he had to run the gamut of Drigh Road, but he didn't care. He had a purpose and was determined to achieve it.

At first it was almost pleasant. He walked past the officers' club, all trim and clean, with a spacious, kempt approach, an open space mercifully free of crowds. Near the club was a shop, tidy and well ordered, for the British officers' wives. Wanting closer contact with his real home, he went inside, but immediately felt out of place. The women shopping there were well above his class, all trim cotton, cool and smartly dressed. He bought an English newspaper and left. He walked on, past the homes of the ruling British—grand residences set in lovely, well-tended, well-watered gardens—and wished with all his heart that everywhere was like this. It is, if you're an officer, he thought bitterly.

Soon he was through this privileged district and Drigh Road assailed him once more, but he was ready for it, going home. He marched rather than walked, keeping his eyes straight ahead, and refused to respond to anything, to any question, any demand for money, or to anything he saw, no matter how odd.

The sun was hot, the wind was hot, he was hot. He was sweating, his shirt clinging to his back.

"What a godforsaken, bloody dump," he muttered to himself, but he still had another four miles to go and self-pity wouldn't help. He put his shoulders back, stepped smartly and began whistling a march, "The British Grenadiers." It made him feel better. He knew he was attracting considerable attention, a strutting, whistling figure, but he didn't care.

He had walked another mile when he heard a familiar droning overhead. An aircraft was coming in to land at the base, a Bristol. He stopped and stood looking at it, admiring it, loving it, envying its pilot, wanting with all his heart to be up there in that extraordinary machine. Longing to fly.

It was all he had ever wanted to do. He was a child of flight, his earliest memories were of the bedtime stories his brother, Harold, used to tell him, of the new gravity-defying machines, and it was with Harold he had seen his first aircraft, droning over their dumbstruck village. Everyone had stopped to watch, folk had come running out of their houses to see, and old, mad Mrs. Herriott had flung her pinny over her head and run shrieking inside to hide. The telling of it made young Slaney laugh, but that was the way with Harold, who always saw the funny side of everything.

Slaney loved his big brother, a sunshine man with an embracing personality that made everyone near him feel that the rain had ended. Slaney was more serious, a darkling boy; it was as if God or the gods or fate had given all life's joy to the firstborn and all its gravity to the second. Slaney never attempted to compete with Harold, but was content to live in his big brother's warm shadow. If that meant coming second at everything, or third or fourth, or even being forgotten, it didn't bother Slaney in the slightest. It seemed to him to be his right and proper place.

It was Harold who enlisted Slaney into the Scouts and the church choir, and Harold who taught his young brother how to use his fists, handily, in the defense of others or himself. And, when the time came, not long before he left for the war, it was Harold who instructed him in the rudimentary mysteries of life, good-humoredly, but with an unyielding morality. Women were to be respected at all times, sex outside of marriage was beastly and self-abuse, unmanly. Young Slaney battled to believe the first all his life, nearly managed to obey the second, and when he occasionally failed with the third his guilt was magnified by this betrayal of his hero brother.

If one was Earth and the other Air, their mutual love of flying sealed the brothers together. Scarcely ever seeing an aircraft, they followed with breathless, shared excitement the soaring achievements of these new gods, airmen, and dreamed of the day when they might do what only the bravest, most valiant could do: cast off the shackling ground and fly. When war came and they had to face the realities of the society into which they had been born, the dream, in Harold, was tempered. Only officers could be pilots, and Harold was not of the officer class.

He enlisted late, bleakly, grimly and only because it was his duty. He was dead within three months. It was unbelievable to Slaney. On the first night after learning of his brother's death, he lay in the big double bed that he and Harold had shared for as long as Slaney could remember, unable to sleep because his brother lay in wet French mud. Toward dawn he left the bed, lay on the hard floorboards and slept there, as penance, or communion, and accepted the truth and felt winter settle on his soul.

His mother, when she heard of Harold's death, lost her hold on reason. She wept. She screamed and ranted and cursed God. She would go out, be gone for hours and come back drunk. She disappeared for three days. The police in Carlisle found her, and Slaney's father went to fetch her. When Slaney came home from school one day, his father was sitting alone at the kitchen table, sipping tea.

"She's gone," he said to Slaney, who never knew why, or what his father thought of her going. "Thou'd best look lively around t' house."

Slaney said nothing, because he couldn't think what to say. His father made a meal for them, fried eggs and boiled potatoes, and then never cooked, nor mentioned his vanished wife, again.

Slaney took charge of the housekeeping, as much as he could, less than was necessary. Always a diligent student, he studied harder. Only education would enable him to realize his ambition of flight, which he had made a vow to fulfill, as much for his brother as himself. He went to the cathedral in Carlisle for the memorial service after the Armistice, and felt distanced from God until a boy soprano sang "I Know That My Redeemer Liveth." The tranquil hymn and the innocent voice combined in a purity that deeply affected the lonely young man, and, for the first time since Harold's death, he wept.

His father married again, a sensible, house-proud widow from the village. She was kind to Slaney, but was more concerned with her new marriage than being surrogate mother. She treated him well, but he felt in the way. He found a job in Sunderland, far from home, in a motorcar repair shop, and he moved into comfortable lodgings with a motherly woman who didn't charge him much because she had lost her two sons to the war.

. He joined a choral society. He didn't have an exceptional voice, but he had a competent, natural baritone and loved to sing. Mixing with people of his own age, for the first time without Harold, he enjoyed their company and was quite well liked by everyone, but he formed no lasting friendships. One or two of the young women flirted with him, and he went out with them a few times, but he was socially inadequate with women, and, because of his mother, he never entirely trusted them. He became a man who was liked because he was there, but he was never part of the group, which is what he had always expected.

He had not forgotten his ambition. In 1919, he applied to join the Royal Air Force and won a scholarship to the college at Cranwell. He loved it. Service life gave him the security he needed and the home he had lacked for so many years. He was content in the company of men, and he was recognized as a fine engineer. Thus he would achieve his own and Harold's dream. If he couldn't be a pilot himself, he would make it possible for others, and with the ever larger aircraft and more complex engines, increasingly, engineers were required to fly. After Cranwell he was posted to Farnborough, and he was content.

He was rock solid, steady, with a heart of soundest oak, and he lived his life by the moral precepts he had learned from his brother. He had girlfriends, but owing to a certain reserve, whether a lack of passion or desire, or a refusal to commit to anything lasting on his part, the relationships never endured. He assumed that the right woman for him would come along one day, and he saw no need to pester his fate. He loved his country—his brother's death would be meaningless otherwise—and believed implicitly that Britain had a sacred covenant to bring civilization to the world, that the British Empire was the greatest force for the greatest good ever conceived. He was an ardent royalist and despised anyone who criticized or questioned the monarchy or the established order of government. He was the stuff without which the Empire could not have been made.

After three years at Farnborough he was posted to India. Journeying there on the SS *Derbyshire*, he encountered Ned.

It was not the first time he had seen him.

On his way from Cranwell to Farnborough, Slaney had spent a couple of nights in London and had gone to the Albert Hall, to a famous lecture and picture show, the epic story of Lawrence of Arabia, being given by an American reporter, Lowell Thomas. It was thrilling stuff. The speaker likened Lawrence to the most gallant heroes and his exploits to a crusade. Slaney, and the packed audience, devastated by the horrors of the war in Europe, agreed. The golden adventuring of Lawrence burst upon them, suffusing them with pride and sunlight.

The war had begun in a blaze of Victorian glory and ended mired in stalemated carnage, with no true heroes to make sense of it all. There were brave men aplenty, and astonishing stories from the front of gallantry and courage in the face of death. But there was no Drake or Raleigh, Clive or Gordon, only the decrepit Kitchener, the callous Haig and the tainted Churchill.

In the whole of the Great War, not one romantic hero stood above the carnage, a champion of all that was good and noble, a victor against evil.

Except for Lawrence.

He was adored. He was presented by Lowell Thomas as a visionary and embraced as such by an audience already aware of his name. He had led an unlikely army across a thousand miles of pitiless desert to conquer an unspeakable enemy. He had entered Damascus in triumph and had championed the Arab cause at the Paris Peace Conference at Versailles afterwards. He had laid low tyrants and created kings.

How much of this was true was irrelevant, he filled a void, a visceral, public need. To Slaney, Lawrence's achievements made sense of Harold's death. There were important things to die for after all, and men could still be heroes. When Slaney left the Albert Hall that night, his heart was filled with a mixture of wonder and gratitude, and he thought Lawrence a giant.

Some months later, the newspapers began blaring the news that Lawrence was stationed at Farnborough, as a lowly aircraftsman called Ross. Slaney was shocked. He had seen Ross once or twice and could not imagine him as any kind of a hero, nor could he summon any good reason why a great man would be so belittlingly disguised. Others were as confused. Press speculation as to his motives for being there were frenzied. Reporters besieged the gates of the camp. Questions were asked in Parliament. The consensus among the airmen was that Lawrence was either on a secret mission of national importance, or put there to spy on them. Or, of course, it could all be lies.

Because of the furor, the man called Ross was dismissed from the service, in January 1923. As luck would have it, Slaney was in the guardhouse that day, signing himself out for leave. Ross arrived, in the company of an officer. Slaney stared at Ross as he signed the papers, trying to imagine this small, insignificant, slightly shabby man in a threadbare suit as the glittering hero of Lowell Thomas's lantern slides. Slaney glanced at the sergeant of the day, who winked and gave a slight nod of affirmation. Slaney pretended to be busy with his own papers but stared at Ross again. Certainly it was the same person that he had seen in photographs, but absolutely not the same man.

"Ross" thanked the men present for their company, in his thin, high-pitched voice. He shook hands with the sergeant and walked out of the guardhouse. Slaney watched him through the window. Ross stopped outside and looked around, as if he had nowhere to go. The officer went out and led Ross to his car. They drove away through the crowds of reporters.

That image of Ross standing outside the guardhouse with a look of utter despair on his face stayed with Slaney for several days. The man's behavior was inexplicable, and Slaney was instinctively suspicious of that which could not be immediately explained. A man like Lawrence, in Slaney's mind, would have countless reasons to look forward to the future. He could not make sense of it, or why Lawrence had been in the ranks at all.

His sense of disappointment was so intense that Slaney, on that first night of his leave, found a quiet pub not far from the cheap hotel where he was staying in London and tried to find answers in whisky. If Lawrence was the man that Lowell Thomas had presented, he could not be the man called Ross. If Ross was Lawrence, then everything that Lowell Thomas claimed was meaningless, and Lawrence was a sham. Although he seldom drank to excess, Slaney got drunk that night, and felt, as many in England did, a deep sense of betrayal.

As he walked unsteadily back to his hotel, two louts accosted him, wanting his wallet, and Slaney found a focus for his anger. He did not fight often, but when he did, he fought to win. It was a short, bloody fray from which one thief ran with a broken nose while his partner lay on the ground, nursing cracked ribs from a well-directed boot.

Slaney walked away almost unscathed, feeling both vindicated and disgusted, with both the world and himself. Later, as he drifted to an uneasy sleep on a hard bed in his grubby hotel room, he remembered the fight with satisfaction, but then saw in his mind's eye conflicting images of Lawrence and of Ross.

And wondered why.

11

October 1905

The truth (the real truth) is out at last.

I am a bastard.

My father is a nobleman, will be a baronet one day, but has no true-born sons to inherit the title. If he had married my mother, the title could have gone to Bob, and if Bob died, to me. But he never married my mother. He has a real wife, in Ireland, and he left her and their daughters for the woman who is my mother. He is a lecher and she is a strumpet, they live together in sin, denying their bastard sons their true patrimony.

I find out when Father is planning one of his annual visits to Ireland, and Mother asks about his wife. She looks at me, and I know it is deliberately done to wound me. She says I had to know eventually, so it might as well be now. She demands that Father tell me the whole story.

There is an awful row. She is revealed to me, at last, this woman who claims such godly virtue, for a damned whore.

I cannot live under the same roof as them. I go to my attic and curse God for my affliction. I pack a bag and wait till the house is still and sleeping. I sneak downstairs and steal money from her purse. (I've often stolen money from her purse, but only pennies. This time I take pounds.)

I catch the milk train to London. I wander the city for a day, loving it, vibrant, wondrous, bejeweled London. I sleep in the park (it is summer) and put my mind to what I can do.

I have to find a sanctuary. I have to find a refuge from the carnal world. And from women. I want to live solely in the company of men, for men away from women are honorable and innocent. Women are the downfall of man.

I join the army. There I can hide from the world and work my way through virtuous conduct to be a leader of men, however blighted by the bend sinister. I am too young, seventeen, but they will take me as a boy soldier if my father signs a paper. That's easy. I have been able to forge his signature for years.

I am excited. It is not the future I had planned for myself, but it is a future and it is an escape. I shall make the best of it. I have Plato with me, and I shall live in the brotherhood of like-minded fellows.

But they are not.

They are crass and brutish, the scum of the earth. They are the dregs of the slums of London and Liverpool, and loutish peasant lads. They are foul. They fight, and hurt each other badly, over the tiniest slights, real or imagined. They steal from each other, abuse each other, verbally and physically, and when the lights are out, they abuse themselves. They have no gentleness, no modesty. Their talk is abhorrent to me, and they sneer at my accent and my vocabulary.

They call me a toff, a fairy—and worse: they call me queer.

I am not queer!

Queer is carnal. Queer is lust. Queer is fucking. They call me that name because I have fair hair and am young and slight and well spoken. Pretty, they all say, and they tell me what they will do to me, when desire makes them mad.

There is one fellow who is not so bad, Jackson, a stocky, handsome lad from Manchester. He is uncouth, like all the rest, but I sense some potential virtue in him. He likes me, or says he does. We are almost friends.

Jackson has the bunk next to mine, and we talk for hours, in whispers so the others will not hear us. He laughs at my accent and my manners, but he seems to want to learn about the goodness of which man is capable. Perhaps there is hope in him. Perhaps this is my mission in life: to bring education and an under-standing of a better world to those who have been denied it.

Jackson is not as randy as the others. He plays with himself sometimes, brings himself to pleasure, but not with the potential for violence of the others and not as often.

He asks me why I never do it, and I try to explain to him the precious mean-ing of man's seed. He says I'm queer.

I am angry. I tell him that to live in a world without women is not queer. I tell him of the warrior Achilles and his soul mate Patroclus. He says Patroclus was Achilles's bum boy and asks me if I've ever fucked a woman.

I blush and shake my head.

He says my balls haven't dropped yet.

Why is everyone so obsessed with the dropping of my balls? Scroggs said it, a long time ago, when Bodger was expelled and sent to another school, outside Oxford. We weren't doing anything, we never touched each other. I just wanted to see Bodger's magnificent cock, and he wanted to look at mine. We were seen and Bodger was expelled, and I nearly so. There was an awful beating from

Mother that night. Now Bodger writes to us, telling us what fun he's having. I read it in the company of Scroggs.

"There are tarts aplenty here," Bodger says, "and they all like cream."

Scroggs is lost in a dream of envy and desire, longing to fill countless tarts, or even one, with his adolescent cream. I am so shocked, I giggle.

Scroggs is furious.

"For Chrissake, Tee-Hee," he whispers fiercely, his voice thick with unfulfilled desire and present anger, for my girlish giggle has interrupted his fantasy of well-creamed tarts. "Aren't your balls ever going to drop?"

I giggle now, when Jackson says it, and he looks at me in a funny way.

"I know what you want," Jackson says huskily. "And one day you're going to get it."

Why am I so frightened? Why do I think he is suddenly dangerous?

One Saturday night, Jackson, drunk, asks me to walk with him. I don't want to go but daren't refuse. He leads me to a quiet, dark place, smokes a cigarette and talks about shagging women. He tells me how randy he is. I shrug.

He throws an arm about me and tells me I'm a sweetheart. I try to pull away. We start wrestling. We're on the ground, and he's on top of me, his serpent hard, pressing against me, trying to dry shag me.

Sweet Jesus, why am I hard? Why does my serpent choose this moment to jump to attention? It gives Jackson the wrong idea, and he laughs and forces his mouth to mine, to kiss me on the lips. His tongue tastes of nicotine, whisky and beer. I struggle against him, but the more I resist, the more he is excited. I start yelling for help. This makes him even angrier, and he punches me on the jaw to shut me up.

"You queer bastard," he says, huskily. "I know what you want."

He kneels on my shoulders, pinning me to the ground. He unbuttons his fly and pulls out his hard cock. He uses his hand on himself, whispering violent abuse of me all the time. It doesn't take him long. His body tenses and he groans and the stuff shoots onto me, onto my face, onto my uniform.

He relaxes, still kneeling on me, staring at me, until his gasping has stopped. He buttons up. The look in his eyes is almost affectionate.

"That's what you wanted, isn't it," he says softly. "Next time, I'll shag you good and proper."

He pulls a grubby handkerchief from his pocket and throws it at me.

"Come on," he says. "Clean yourself up, we'd best get back."

I don't get up. I don't move. I don't want to be with him. I am in despair. Because I have come.

Strong as I am, I can't endure this. I send a telegram to Father. He arrives two days later.

Father stares at me as if I were a stranger to him. I am not embarrassed.

"Well, Ned," he says at last. "This is a poor business."

Yes, it is!

Father looks away for a moment, and when he looks back to me, I see pain in his eyes, and deep regret.

"I am so very sorry, Ned," he says, "for the enormous wrongs that we have done to you, your mother and I."

My heart sings! It is what I have wanted to hear for so many years, and it is said with grace and true apology. Surely, my father is a noble man.

"I won't go back to the way it was," I shout, quivering with remembered pain and anger.

"I don't expect you to," he says. "There will be changes, Ned, I promise you."

(I think he knows the truth. I think he knows that sometimes when Mother beats me, I have an orgasm. He came into the room once, the night that Bodger was expelled, and ordered Mother to stop. She was furious. She threw the rod at him and told him to beat some honor into me. He sat down beside me and was very calm. But I think he knew.)

We negotiate my future, and Father arranges to buy me out. The officer tries to make it difficult, but he's no match for Father, who has friends in quite high places. I don't tell the sergeant what happened with Jackson, even when he asks about the scabs on my face and hands. Perhaps he guesses, because he assigns a corporal to me, to take me to the barracks, to keep guard while I pack. Or perhaps he has been told of Father's connections in Whitehall.

Jackson is there, lying on his bunk. Some others too, and they watch in surprise as I come in with the corporal.

I am depressed and filled with an abject sense of failure. They have won. I, who thought myself capable of anything, am not man enough for this. I do not deserve to be Sir Galahad. Or even Sir Ned.

"What's up, Ned?" Jackson asks, as if nothing untoward had happened between us. He's never called me Ned before, only Tee-Hee.

"I'm leaving," I tell him and the others. "My father's buying me out."

They are surprised. To be bought out is expensive, all of twenty pounds. None of them could raise so much money.

They watch me pack and tell me they will miss me, that I would have made a good soldier, but that I am officer class. Then a couple of them come and shake my hand and tell me that it was a real privilege to know me. They say that the help I gave them with letters home, or the stories I told, or just being me, was a great experience for them.

"We gave you some shit, and you took it like a man," one says, and shakes my hand.

I am astonished by this outpouring of respect and affection. Why couldn't it have been like this before?

Jackson, who has stayed silent, gets off his bunk.

"I'd have looked after you," he says, reproachfully I think. "I thought we were muckers."

"Mucker" is their term for very best friends. More than friends, inseparable companions, men devoted to each other's welfare for all their mortal lives. It has great significance. Achilles and Patroclus might have been muckers, or Hadrian and Antinous.

"Take care of yourself," he says, "and good luck, whatever happens."

I can't bear the naked hurt in Jackson's eyes. I turn away, knowing that I have hurt him far worse than he hurt me.

I have betrayed him.

"We had a few laughs, didn't we?" he whispers. "You queer bastard."

And suddenly I understand. It is the only way he can express his love.

He turns to the others.

"What about three cheers for Ned, eh, lads?" he says to them. "Let's hear it for Tee-Hee, the virgin soldier!"

They all laugh and give three rousing cheers. I blush and laugh with them, but I am embarrassed and curiously moved.

I walk away with the corporal, and they start to sing "For He's a Jolly Good Fellow."

I don't look back. I walk out of the hut, into the night, toward a different life.

The lusty singing recedes and is replaced by some filthy jeering of each other, and soon they are at it again, brawling, fighting, yelling.

"They're a bit rough, but they're not a bad lot," the corporal says. "Hearts of gold, most of 'em. They liked you."

I can't speak, because, to my complete surprise, I find that I am crying. The army was a true test of my spirit, a trial of my will. They showed me that I can be a man. A virgin soldier.

It is only now that I realize how very sorry I am to leave.

12

SLANEY FELT MUCKY when he got back to the depot after his long walk from town. The hut was empty, and he guessed the bathhouse would be as well, so he took a long shower to rid himself of sand. He toweled dry, put on freshly laundered shorts and his boots and walked back to the hut.

He knew he would not be alone now. He could hear music coming from the hut, and that meant Ned was there.

Ned was on his cot writing, lost in thought. It was a book he was working on, Slaney knew, about air force life, but Ned would not let any of them read it.

Slaney crossed to his cot without feeling the need for greeting. He stood and brushed his hair. He could see Ned reflected in the mirror and tried to make sense of the man. Ned, suddenly inspired, finished a sentence and then looked directly at Slaney, who was embarrassed. He knew that Ned was hardly seeing him, was actually looking beyond him. Even so, his startling blue eyes seemed to pierce Slaney's soul.

One of the cheap Christmas decorations the men had put up had fallen. Slaney picked it up and started folding it, thinking they should all come down. It was long past Twelfth Night, but no one had bothered.

"How was town?" Ned asked.

Slaney shrugged his shoulders, and suddenly conscious of his seminaked-ness, put on a shirt. "A dump," he muttered.

Ned nodded, unsurprised. The music had finished. Ned got up, wound the gramophone and turned the record over. The silence between them was comforting to Slaney, who was not adept at making conversation. He picked up his newspaper, held it out. "I bought a paper," he said.

"Later, thanks." Ned had gone back to his cot and was scratching at his manuscript. "When you've finished with it."

Slaney shrugged again, made himself comfortable on his own bed and glanced at the paper. The news was recent, the paper had come by air and was expensive, and the gossip columns, the trivia and sports columns held some interest for him. Ned, however, held more. Slaney saw something in the paper that he guessed would be of interest to Ned, an obituary of the writer Thomas Hardy, but he didn't know how to tell Ned. He never knew quite what to say to Ned. Safe behind his newspaper, secure in silence, half a hut from a legend, Slaney could not keep from wondering about this man.

Ned, paper in one hand, pencil in the other, was lying back, staring out of the window at the desert. He's looking at it as if that's where he really wants to be, Slaney thought. How can he bear to be stuck inside with us? Why doesn't he ever go out? What makes him tick?

Ned had absented himself from their company at Christmas. He volunteered for guard duty all through the festive season and took no part in the drunken celebrations of the hut. It occurred to Slaney that Ned had distanced himself deliberately, so that his sometimes melancholy presence did not dampen the men's wild parties. The tactfulness of that decision made Slaney see his fellows differently, and for the first time he felt a small disgust at the lack of restraint shown by the other men.

Ned had come back into the hut at dawn one morning. Rogers, passed out on his cot, had vomited on himself and on the floor. Slaney was cleaning up the mess as Ned came in. The others were asleep, dead drunk. Ned watched Slaney wiping the vomit from Rogers's body.

"It isn't always like this," Slaney said. "I promise it isn't."

Ned had said nothing. He lay down and fell asleep. A small part of his old anger at Ned came back to Slaney. If Ned had such a low opinion of the other airmen, Slaney included, why did he choose to spend his life with them?

He had felt more of that anger when he had embarked on the troopship for Karachi and found that Lawrence, who had been Ross, was also on the ship, now calling himself Shaw. Slaney was convinced that Shaw had ulterior motives for enlisting in the ranks, twice now and under different names, and he still felt that keen sense of disappointment, of betrayal, that the man he had once admired so deeply had proved to be so peculiar.

At Port Said, Slaney had not indulged in the blandishments of the town, but had teamed up with some others—an army corporal and two soldiers—on a day trip to the pyramids. Their Egyptian driver packed them into a rattling, rusty old car, and they traveled to Giza in dusty, jolting discomfort.

At first, Slaney had hated the whole experience and bitterly regretted joining the group. As they drove through Port Said, he saw for the first time the desperate poverty of the East, and because it was so new to him, and so shocking, at first it was all he could see. Slaney knew the slums in English cities, but they were nothing like this. The children affected him most, the poor, begging children, with hideously bent limbs, deformed deliberately at birth by their parents, the corporal said, that they might present a more piteous appearance and thus be given more charity.

The thought of that violence done to a child, and the raucous, narrow streets filled with oddly clad, poorly clothed, dirty-looking people, the constant noise that attended everything they did and the smell of ordure, made Slaney want to get back to the security of the ship, get back to England and never venture beyond her tidier shores again.

Happily, the cheerful corporal was an old Cairo hand who loved the Middle East. He had served in Egypt during the war and was pleased to be back again.

"Life's a bastard for them," he told his companions blithely as they narrowly avoided collision with a fat man on a donkey who was claiming all the narrow road. "The poorest of us is a rich man compared with them. Isn't that right, Ibrahim?"

He nudged the driver, whose name was Mohammed.

"We are very poor in Egypt," Mohammed agreed, grinning toothily.

"Take 'im," the corporal said, "'e can speak three languages. His own, English and a fair wodge of French—'e 'as to, to earn a quid."

He glared at Slaney. "'Ow many languages can you speak?"

Slaney was embarrassed and looked out of the window. They were out of the city and traveling across the desert.

"Bloody 'ell," one of the soldiers said. "I never seen so much sand."

"You ain't seen nothin' yet," the corporal said loftily. He settled comfortably in his seat and, for the next three hours, gave them the benefit of his views on life in Egypt.

As he droned on, Slaney drifted away. He stared out of the window at the awful desert, an endless barren plain with only a few dusty date palms at the side of the road to interrupt the vista.

Slaney wondered if it was all like this. Egypt. Africa. India. The Empire. Was it all just a hostile landscape of empty land and a few mud-brick villages where peasants scraped a frugal living? Was it all just dirty cities clinging to life at the edge of the desert?

Where was the glory? Where was the adventure? Where were the fabulous cities of fabled riches? Where were the caravans of silks and spices? Where were the roaming tribes of magnificent Bedouin warriors, extravagantly costumed, gorgeously bejeweled, or the shiningly oiled Fuzzy Wuzzy tribesmen? Where were the graceful tents and peaceful oases? Where were the exotic women, provocatively veiled? Where were all the processions of magnificence? Where were all the treasures of the East?

And what of Baghdad, Nineveh and Samarkand? Were they just Port Said writ large? Were the legends of them only figments of a storyteller's imagination? How could there be splendor in all this dusty nothing? How could there be anything but worn-out bodies and broken hearts? Was this the white man's burden, a bitter reality after luminous expectation?

Lulled by the heat and the corporal's droning voice, hypnotized by the sand and bored by his own disappointment, Slaney drifted off to sleep.

He awoke to a nudge from one of the soldiers.

"You see?" the corporal said.

Slaney looked, and he saw.

Three graceful pyramids in the middle of nowhere, rising out of the sand. Three ancient pyramids with a breathtaking purity of line. Three simple pyramids that were a bridge to a people's understanding of this world and their belief in the next.

And beside them, a lion-woman who had been standing guard for all of recorded time.

"I thought they'd be bigger," one of the soldiers said, unable to disguise his disappointment. A small argument ensued with the corporal.

Slaney didn't bother to listen, hardly heard them, because what they said was meaningless to him.

To him, the pyramids were the perfect size. To him, the pyramids were more than he had been seeking. To him, they were monumental. As he stared at them, he drank in ancient kingdoms and fell crushingly in love.

On the journey back to Port Said he was silent, contemplating how much he had seen—and how little—and wanting more. As they drove into Port Said, he looked at the Egyptians differently. He was less judgmental of them, but was puzzled that they were content to live like this after what they had been. Then it occurred to him that they had always lived like this. The pyramids were an aberration, not the rule, an expression of their need to understand the infinite.

"Worth it?" the corporal asked, as they paid the driver.

"Bloody wonderful," Slaney replied, and knew that his words were completely inadequate. "How do you say 'thank you'?"

"*Su'chran,*" the corporal told him.

Slaney turned to Mohammed. "*Su'chran,*" he said.

Mohammed grinned toothily again and said, "*Afwan,*" and Slaney felt a thrill of pride. It was the first time he had communicated in a foreign language.

His euphoria didn't last, couldn't last at such an intensity, and shipboard life, service life, was mundane. But the change in his perspective stayed with him, and he began to question things that before had been absolute.

One of those things was Ned.

They had sailed from Port Said and anchored in the Bitter Lake for the night. Slaney, unable to sleep, had sat on deck, smoking and reveling in the tranquil, mystic dark. He had seen Ned come on deck and, at dawn, change into a simple cotton gown, an Arab garment, and stare at the land, lost in rapture.

It made sense to Slaney. If he, a very ordinary man of limited education, had been so mightily moved by a visit to the pyramids, what must it be like for someone such as Ned, a scholar, who had experienced things beyond Slaney's imagination?

What he could not understand was how such a man would abandon the opportunities that must be available to him. Even if Ned didn't want to be in a position of responsibility or high command, if he was determined on an anonymous life, why choose the ranks? Why choose to incarcerate himself with a bunch of uncouth, ill-educated airmen when the limitless acres of antiquity were available? Slaney did not have that choice. Ned did.

The only explanation that made sense to Slaney was that Ned was involved in some secret mission of national importance. If that was the case, then the man should be left alone to do what he had to do. But still it was puzzling. Ned himself was such an oddball.

"Queer bastard," Slaney said to himself. He lit another cigarette, dismissed Ned from his mind and dreamed instead of their destination.

India.

If one day in Egypt had thrilled him to his core, what must an extended period of time in this land of romantic legends do to him? When they first docked at Karachi, he had forgiven the apparent, immediate awfulness of the city. Port Said had been dreadful, and look what treasure he had found beyond. However, as the days passed into weeks, an awful disappointment settled over him. If there was a fabulous, antique India, it wasn't here.

Ned proved another disappointment. The other men listened to his tales of the Desert Campaign with mouths open, but these, Slaney was sure, were only comic-strip stories. Of the true nature of Lawrence of Arabia, his secret heart, Ned revealed nothing.

At least until that day when Slaney had been dozing and had overheard Ned talk of spying with Hawkins. Then that night, Ned told them what had happened to him at Deraa. While Slaney had no interest in the talk of sodomy, he recognized that Ned was revealing some dark moment of his soul, some hint of the price that he had had to pay for his love of Arabia, and Slaney had been enthralled. That the cost was so enormous meant that the reward must have been extraordinary.

Slaney had left when the other men discussed the rape. He went to the shower block to be alone, to plead with the silent stars, to beg the moon with all his heart to be allowed to experience, if only for one tiny moment, some sense of what that extraordinary reward had been.

The sound of a needle scratching on a finished record impinged on Slaney's mind, and he realized he had been daydreaming, exhausted by his long walk back from Karachi. He had no idea how much time had passed.

He looked around. Nothing had changed. The newspaper had fallen onto his chest. Ned, still staring out of the window at the desert beyond the barracks, lost in thought, made no move to turn the record over or change it. The only sound in the still afternoon was that repetitive scratching and the distant tinkling of camel bells. Then Ned roused himself and took the arm off the record.

"What music would you like to hear?" he asked. "Sophie Tucker?"

It was a favorite of the airmen's, the only "popular" record in all of Ned's collection. "I haven't got 'Chu Chin Chow.'"

A spark of anger flared in Slaney. "'Air on a G String'?" he suggested.

Ned looked at him in surprise. "I haven't got that, either," he said. "Do you really like Bach?"

The spark of anger flared to a flame. "Is that what you think of us?" Slaney demanded. "That we're just a bunch of yobbos who don't know nothing about Mendelssohn and Elgar? That all we like is Ivor Novello and *Rose Marie?*"

If he was looking for an argument, he didn't find one. "No, I don't think that at all," Ned murmured. "I said it because I don't know anything about you, and I made a stupid guess."

It was an apology, and Slaney accepted it as such. "That's all right," he said.

There was silence again, until Ned spoke. "I don't even know your name," he said. "Your first name, I mean."

"Slaney'll do," Slaney said.

To his surprise, Ned smiled. "What's up? Don't you like your first name? I don't think I've ever heard anyone use it. You don't even have a nickname. You're always just Slaney."

Slaney shrugged.

"It can't be any worse than what they call me," Ned continued. "Cough-drop. Tee-Hee." He giggled, but there was no humor in the sound. "Some folk think my balls never dropped," he said. He stared at Slaney, and those soft blue eyes seemed to encourage Slaney to reveal some inner aspect of himself.

"Archibald," Slaney said finally, defensively. "I hate it. Don't tell anyone. A few of the blokes found out when I joined up and gave me curry." He looked at his fists. "I took 'em on, gave 'em what for. Everyone's always called me Slaney ever since."

"Archie?" Ned wondered.

"Slaney," Slaney said.

"Slaney," Ned concurred.

A warmth of comradeship flooded through Slaney. He wondered why. He wanted to make some small act of kindness and wondered why. He remembered something he had seen in the newspaper.

"There's something about that friend of yours in here," he said. "An obituary."

News of the death of Thomas Hardy, the famous English writer, had come to them some days before, from Vine, who had heard it in the wireless room and knew that Ned had known the man. Ned had said nothing when Vine told him, but had walked out into the night to be alone.

Now Slaney folded the newspaper open at the obituary and held it out to Ned. "It's very nice, what they say about him."

Ned took the paper and glanced at it. "'Let us now praise famous men,'" he whispered softly. "I used to go to his house in Dorset. He was very old, very frail, calmly waiting for the end. And very wise."

A change seemed to happen to him. The odd, insignificant airman became someone else. Someone remarkable. Slaney thought that time was standing still, felt that he was in the presence of greatness.

"He made the past as real as yesterday," Ned said. "A century ago we were at war with France, but he made it as real as the war I had just fought. Napoleon was a living man to him, as Allenby is to me."

He stopped for a moment, and Slaney prayed he had not finished.

He had not. "He judged all men equally, by what they achieved, and received anyone, no matter how lowly, as generously as he would the great. I wanted to be like him," Ned said. "I never will be, now."

Was this it? Slaney wondered. Was this the secret? Was it just lost ambition? Was it what he had felt when he realized that he would never be a pilot? But Ned was wrong. He had been great. "You've written books—" he began.

"I've written one," Ned said. "And it isn't half bad. It's long, anyway."

That sadness again. "But Hardy wrote dozens, and any one of them could stand with the greatest. Homer would have been proud to know him. Shakespeare would have been happy to call him a friend."

Slaney was moved but didn't quite know how or why, except that it had something to do with pyramids and men who had known Napoleon. He tried to find words of consolation, but felt, again, completely inadequate.

"You're not dead yet," he said, meaning that Ned had time to write many more books, whether they were accounted great or not.

"No," Ned agreed. "Not yet."

Suddenly, the inconceivable occurred to Slaney. He wants to be dead, he thought. He doesn't want to go on living. Then his imagination took an extraordinary leap.

He is already dead.

It was so shocking to Slaney that he rejected the idea almost as soon as he had thought it, but an image of his brother Harold going to war, hopeless of victory, lingered in his mind.

"What other music do you like, apart from Bach?" Ned asked him, as if to change the subject.

"Mendelssohn," Slaney replied, almost in relief. "Sullivan. Purcell."

"The English composers."

"And Handel," Slaney said. "I love Handel. I used to sing in a choir."

"'By the waters of Babylon, there we sat down . . .'" Ned whispered. He winced, as if in pain—a sharp, stinging, astringent pain. A pain of memory. By the waters of Babylon he had sat him down, and he had not wept, he had been happy. But he was banished from happiness now. Exiled from his heart. A stranger to the world and to himself, in a strange land, no matter what country. Only one place could make his heart sing, and he would never see that place again, even if he went there, because what had made him happy was obliterated. Like the Second Temple to a dispossessed Jew, it existed only in his memory. "If I forget thee, O Jerusalem"? How could he forget?

O child of Babylon, you devastator. O Dahoum, you child of Babylon.

Ned looked so abject, so downcast, Slaney could hardly bear to look at him. He felt a compelling need to offer comfort but could not imagine what comfort he could offer to a man who wanted to be dead. He remembered the bleak days of mourning Harold, and how a boy's lovely voice had made him cry and given him solace as well.

He started to sing, softly. "'By the waters of Babylon, there we sat down and wept,'" he sang. Embarrassment tinged with futility made his voice quaver, but because he had started and thought it would be worse to stop than to continue, he went on singing, the baritone part that he had learned in Sunderland.

Ned listened in silence for a while, and then, to Slaney's astonishment, he joined in, but badly, the hymn remembered from his youth, the soprano line he had sung as a boy.

A Hindu servant padded quietly upstairs to deliver freshly shined boots. He stopped and stared in amazement at what he saw. In a stone hut decorated with tawdry tinsel, a pair of men, overgrown boys in shorts and shirts, were singing some odd music, a sound filled with grief, and incomplete, as if other voices were lacking. But still it was not unpleasing.

Although he was used to the odd things that this ruling race did, the servant turned back and went downstairs. He would deliver the boots later. What he had seen was too bizarre to interrupt, too private. It was something only the gods could understand, Shiva and Vishnu and Brahma.

13

My sabots go gaily ringing, clattering along,
Through Lorraine as I go singing, clattering along.
Jolly captains three espy me, shout as they go riding by me,
Ho ho ho, clattering along!

Bicycling through Lorraine, actually, and I'm not wearing wooden clogs, but I am singing at the top of my voice and making a heck of a racket, clattering along!

It is summer, a wondrous, drowsy, French summer, full of fat plums and luscious peaches, dancing butterflies and busy bees, crisp bread, creamy cheeses and simple cider.

I am happy. I am alone.

Last year, Scroggs came with me, and that was fun, but Scroggs can be venal sometimes, constantly in futile search of some tart to fill with cream, to relieve him of his self-absorbing cherry. It is very aggravating to be bathed in the gules of a flawless, ancient, stained-glass window, in some awe-inspiring cathedral, and have Scroggs whisper in my ear, of a pretty, praying mademoiselle: "Gosh, Tee-Hee, do you reckon she goes off?"

This year I am alone. And I am lost in time.

This is French soil, but this is not France. This is the empire of Plantagenet England. This is Lorraine and Aquitaine, Normandy and Burgundy and Tours. These are the battlefields of Crécy, Poitiers and Agincourt. This is the land won for England by the warrior kings, the valiant Edward (another Ned!), the fearsome Black Prince and the magnificent Fifth Henry, and lost by their weak heirs to a conquering Virgin.

(I am a virgin, and the countryside falls to my assault this summer. I am monarch of all I survey.)

Mother hates the French, and I know why. Mother hates anything that smacks of worldliness, and the French are self-indulgent of the world. Their God, they say, is constantly forgiving of their sins because they are constantly contrite, and so, forgiven, are free to sin again and be forgiven again. This makes them weak, but fun, pedantic, arrogant and life loving.

And I love life this summer. I am becoming myself, at last, the man I am destined to be. My mother has abandoned me to the Devil, and I gorge on my freedom. But I am not what she—or anyone—thinks I am. I am not an ephebe lost in the fleshpots of Paris, I am not the bum boy of sailors on the docks at Marseilles. I am not queer. I am a bastard, but I am not queer!

I thought it might be easier if I took a wife. I thought Janet might understand, we've been good friends, and so I asked her to marry me. She declined me, sweetly, but I could see she was laughing at me. She saved me from myself. It would have been a marriage in name only. There is no point in my having sons, I have nothing for them to inherit. I am denied my patrimony by my father's lust. I would not do the same to my own offspring.

Janet's laughter showed me my path. I will never marry. I despise carnality, I live in a chivalrous world, where men are disciplined against lust.

But I like the company of men who like men, for they are dangerous. (And I like their flattery!) Their allegiances are with their sex, not with their nation or their class, their desires cross dangerous frontiers. To test my spirit, I put myself, deliberately, in situations where temptation might make me fail, and every time I am victorious. My friend Vyvyan, at Jesus, is lovesick for me, but we will not be lovers. I will not spill my sacred juice casually, to relieve a momentary want, with him or anyone like him. It is a weakening thing; like self-abuse, it makes mice of men.

When I tell Vyvyan of my monastic life, he tells me he cannot live without my love. I tell him no. But I do not send him away. Am I cruel to Vyvyan? Does my flirting with his affection wound him? Perhaps, but I did not ask him to love me, and I cannot love him. I must make myself pure so that one day I may come to my beloved chaste. And if I never find anyone worthy of my adoration, I will go on alone.

But I shall find someone. I will. When I have proved myself worthy.

I do not know what my Quest is yet, but I know I am close to discovering it, France has pointed the way. I am studying Crusader castles, and struggling with an old question for my thesis. Was the architecture of the castles, the pointed arch and vault, brought back from the Holy Land by the Crusaders, or did they take their knowledge with them to Syria and Palestine and teach it to the Infidels? I have always thought that surely we taught them, but some scholars at Oxford think otherwise, that Saladin's court encompassed advanced academics, deeply concerned with mathematics and its practical application to war. Can it be that I am wrong? Are there, in the Levant, in Syria and in Palestine, civilizations that have, if they do not now, worshipped learning and its pure applications?

Next year I shall go to the East, although Hogarth says I'm mad!

"You've been," I tell him. "You go there all the time."

Hogarth laughs. "At other people's expense," he says, "with guides and servants and comfortable lodgings. Not as a footsore Bedouin."

He wonders if I am ready for it. "Of course," I cry. "I'm ready!"

I am ready, he knows that. Hogarth understands me. He is my professor and the new keeper of the Ashmolean Museum. He is also my inspiration. He is an expert on the Middle East and is leading me to fantastic, vanished empires. His knowledge of the Nabateans and the Medes and the Hittites is astounding. He makes their tiny, long-forgotten histories, buried in the sand, throb with vibrant life.

He goes there all the time, on digs and journeys of discovery. His advice is constantly sought by the most important men in government, and often he presents me to some of these men, and they listen to my lowly, forming opinions and treat them with respect. He knows what makes me tick.

When he talks of there, his eyes grow bright, and he fills me with an urgent longing to see what he has seen. "It will make you or break you," he says. "Either you will fall in love with it, or you will never go there again. But it will bring you face to face with yourself."

How can I resist that challenge? What is there, I wonder, that is so confronting?

"A sense of the wonder of mankind," Hogarth says, "and the futility of our existence."

Shall I find my future there? Oh, please! I am jaded with this old Europe, this sophisticated, decadent continent, obsessed with the pleasures of the flesh. I am bored with the Scroggses of this world, whose groins dictate their lives. I grow testy with Vyvyan, I do not ask him for his love!

I am no longer surprised that we English found it so easy to conquer the French. They are vain and self-indulgent, their minds consumed with the trivia of style. No wonder our stouthearted, disciplined armies and kings were so easily victorious!

Hogarth laughs at me. If the French are what you say, why do we not rule them still? Where did they find an army to throw us off?

I am in Orléans, and I know the answer. There she stands, the sacred Joan, the only one who could triumph against English oak.

Joan of Arc, Joan of Lorraine, Joan the Maid. The Maid of Orléans.

None of these appellations reveal her secret, but it is crystal clear to me. Shakespeare, that old truth-teller, got it right. Joan La Pucelle, Shakespeare called her. La Pucelle. The Virgin. Joan the Virgin. In her virginity was her strength, her purity. Her rigorous chastity among the voluptuous French gave her the strength to conquer the bravest that England could put against her. Of course, we burned her for it, but we could not win back France. No wonder they adore her here. If the French were all like her, France would have the greatest empire the world has ever known. But only Joan could do it. Joan the Virgin, Joan the Alone.

I am a virgin, and I am alone.

I will be like her. I will lead an army against a mighty conqueror, to free a people from another's dominion. But what people will I free and where? Hogarth says these are dangerous times, that one day Europe will explode in war, but I see no place for me in that. No one will conquer England, and without that conquest, how can I set England free?

It will be somewhere else. Ireland, perhaps, but that would be to fight myself, the Irish blood from my father at war with my English blood from my mother.

In any case, I'm not ready yet. My body is rock hard and wiry, despite my size, but I still have flabby edges to my mind. Hogarth can trap me sometimes.

(And I still have serpent dreams. I must cleanse them from my body, waking or sleeping. I can conquer them, I am determined on it. And when I have vanquished them, then, like Joan the Virgin, I shall be ready to take on the world.)

Hogarth, Mentor to Telemachus, tells me to be patient. That I will find what I am seeking, but only when I have been tested by fire.

I am ready for the flames. I will temper my body to steel and my will to iron. But not here. Not in decadent France. I need an Olympian forge.

Next summer, I shall follow Alexander's footsteps. Even to Thebes, even to Babylon. Even to the distant Indus.

14

"RIGHT . . . TURN!"

"One!" three hundred voices shouted, and three hundred right feet pivoted smartly to the right. "Two, three," the three hundred voices chanted the grace notes, and then, to an almighty cry of "One!," three hundred left feet slammed into the ground, each beside its fellow.

"Left . . . Turn!" The drill sergeant was red in the face and hoarse but still could be heard a mile away.

Three hundred men in uniform executed a sharp left turn, yelling out the beats. "One! . . . two, three . . . One!"

"About—" Wilson began a turn in anticipation.

"Wait for it, wait for it," his corporal muttered.

"Turn!" the drill sergeant screamed. Three hundred men turned smartly to face the opposite direction. The fourteen men of Ned's hut were sick of the drill, and one shouted a petty revolt.

"One! . . . balls . . . One!" he yelled.

"'Oo said that?" Their corporal went doolally. "'Oo said balls?"

No one owned up.

"This ain't the effing army, y'know," the corporal screamed. "This is the effing air force; you blokes are supposed to be effing educated! The next effing airman that says balls is on a effing charge!"

"Ah, fuck off," Rogers muttered. The corporal might have heard him if he hadn't been screaming.

Ned giggled, and unfortunately the corporal had paused just then, to draw breath for his next assault. He changed direction in mid gasp.

"That you, Coughdrop?" The corporal advanced on Ned, delighted to have found a victim. "No wonder they call you Tee-Hee, you short-arsed runt, was you the one what said balls?"

"Not fond of the word, Corp!" Ned said smartly, and Slaney and several others giggled.

The corporal had a fine stream of invective ready to rain on Ned, on all of them, but a man in the next platoon fainted, and then, some distance away, another, then a third, and the farce that was the drill parade swooned to a halt. Corporals and a sergeant went to investigate the heat-struck men. The corporal of Ned's platoon, as bored as the erks with this useless exercise, gave his men the stand-easy.

"What is the matter with those men?" Wing Commander Aubrey Stapleton demanded of his adjutant.

"Heat exhaustion, I imagine," Hawkins said.

"There's far too much of this sort of thing," Stapleton insisted. He looked at the muddle of men on the parade ground and knew defeat when he saw it.

"Very well," he conceded. He nodded at the drill sergeant, who called the men to attention and ordered the dismiss. Three hundred men, scarcely able to contain their cheers, fell out and headed for their huts.

Ned, Slaney and several of the others ambled from the parade ground.

"Good on you, Ned," Jones said. "We needed a laugh."

Although he had not actually been the one to say it, Ned had been the instigator of "balls." In the army, especially in the Tank Corps, the men point-blank refused to use the polite "two, three" as the intermediate, but used balls or bollocks instead. Ned had told the men this story, and they thought it funny.

"Yeh, but you fucked it up," Cameron insisted. "It's one, balls, two—it's a joke: one ball, two balls—not one, balls, one."

Trying to explain a joke to Rogers was difficult at the best of times. They moved on, everyone voicing their opinion as to the merits of one or two balls.

Ned, walking more slowly, lagged behind. Slaney stayed with him.

"You all right?" Slaney asked, for Ned looked pale, and his breathing was labored.

"It's because of me, all this extra drill," he said. "The wingco, he's got it in for me. He wants me to fail."

Slaney only half believed him. It was hard to imagine what Ned could have done that warranted such an extravagant revenge. He asked the obvious question. "Why?"

"I'm a threat to him," Ned said. "To his authority. He wants me gone."

It was simple, direct and understandable, but it didn't answer the most basic question. Slaney thought that he knew Ned well enough to ask.

"Why? Why are you here?"

Suddenly, curiously, Ned looked older, tired, worn out. The drill had been tedious on this hot winter day, but not enough to cause this sudden lack of energy. His ice-blue eyes were clouded, but filled with honesty. "I'm all smashed up inside," he said.

Slaney was concerned. "You want to see the doc?"

Ned shook his head. He was smashed up inside, but not physically. Physically, he was in reasonable condition for a man of his years, and to whose body much violence had been done, but the drill was designed for younger men. Most men of his age, if they were still in the service, were corporals or sergeants, or had comfortable desk jobs that kept them away from exertion, very few were simple erks. Yet it was the life Ned had chosen, the life he wanted—the only life possible for him. He could not take the easy way out, he could not report sick with sunstroke, which he didn't have, or give Stapleton, or any officer, any reason to review his situation. His service contract was up for renewal in eighteen months. If he was lucky, they'd let him stay for another five years. If he was not lucky, they'd kick him out. Then what would he do?

He took a breath and changed again, as though drawing strength from the younger man. Slaney, and others like him, made life bearable. With Slaney, and others like him, Ned was young and fit again, bathing at a tranquil oasis, surrounded by vibrant young Bedouin men, unmarried, unsullied, their lives before them, so filled with energy that the conquest of a continent seemed an achievable dream.

It happened now. He looked at Slaney and drew vigor and energy. Years fell away from him, tiredness disappeared, the eyes lost their cloudiness. I am a vampire, he giggled to himself, stealing life from others. "There's a parcel come from Fortnum," he said. "Let's see what Charlotte's sent."

They walked toward the hut, and Ned was chipper. "The trouble with service life is that they kick you out when you get old and sick," he said with a giggle. "I should have joined a monastery, but I'm not religious."

Slaney had become used to these quicksilver changes in Ned. Circling each other warily, they had become tentative friends, cautiously at first, but then, at least on Slaney's part, without reservation.

Sometimes Slaney thought that the best of the friendship was in the silences they often shared. They could be silent for hours, Ned writing, Slaney pondering the world, or Ned, or the things that Ned, when he wasn't being silent, had told him. When the others went to town, to Karachi, Slaney never went with them anymore. He and Ned would lie on their respective cots listening to music, each taking his turn at changing the record and winding up the gramophone. Ned might write or stare out at the desert, and Slaney would read or think or drift or doze, and they were happy.

Yet much as he loved the silence, Slaney loved the words more. When Ned spoke, the words dazzled, not because they were big words, or difficult to understand, but because, in their simplicity and their precision they evoked vast landscapes peopled with living beings, and they provoked, in Slaney's mind, enormous, simple questions.

And if he loved the silence and adored the words, the most precious gift Ned gave him was the answer to his questions.

Slaney had never been shy of asking questions, but those questions were usually of logic: "what?" "how?" and "when?" The question "why?" had not been encouraged in Slaney's life, except by Harold, and was actively discouraged in the service.

Ned was different. Ned was like Harold. Ned told him why.

"Why did they build the pyramids?" was the first of these questions. It came, Ned thought, out of the blue, out of a long silence, but it had been with Slaney since that day in Egypt.

"No one knows," Ned said, and then, inexplicably to Slaney, giggled.

Slaney was disappointed, but then Ned began to speak. In the hour that followed, Ned took Slaney on an extraordinary, if simplistic, journey among the ancient Egyptians. He painted a gorgeous word picture of a people coming to terms with the questions that beset mankind, of the infinite and the cosmos, and of the blessed, life-giving river that sustained them and became a fountainhead of Western civilization.

The answer was so much more than Slaney had expected that it daunted him from asking other such questions for a while. He thought they could not be important enough for such a scholar's time. Ned understood his hesitancy, and, days later when they were alone again, he began to talk of other ancient peoples—of the Medes, the Phoenicians and the Greeks, and of his especial darlings, the Hittites. Slaney realized he could ask Ned anything because the joy for both of them was in the answer. Ned needed to talk about these people, Homer's children, philosophers and valiant warriors and mischievous, capricious, interfering gods. He preferred the ancient kingdoms to any he had found in the modern world. Yet he knew his listener and tempered his knowledge, so as not to patronize.

Troy was besieged and tumbled to Ned's words. Aspiring Athens became a living city, no larger than cautious Carlisle. Alexander swept down from Macedon and conquered the world, from Greece to Persia to Egypt to Babylon, even to Karachi, where they were now.

Like Slaney, Alexander had stood before the pyramids, his friend Hephaestion at his side, and wondered why.

And always there were the Hittites, of whom Slaney had never heard but who were as real to Ned as the other men in the hut. As real as Slaney.

Fifteen hundred years before the birth of Christ, successive, pugnacious Hittite kings had led armies from their mountain strongholds in northern Turkey and conquered all before them, even, some thought, as far east as mighty Nineveh, and south to Damascus. They created an empire that lasted for several hundred years, then drifted into petty squabbling and, lacking a unifying king, had decayed, disintegrated and finally disappeared, to be lost in the shrouding mists of time.

Ned's interest was not so much in their empire as in one Hittite city in northern Syria, a place called "Kargemish," built beside a river whose waters flowed on to Babylon. Ned had spent three years there before the war, rediscovering it, and there, Slaney knew, Ned had been happy.

It was also clear to Slaney that some grievous mischance was connected with the place. Sometimes when Ned spoke of "Kargemish" he conveyed emotions that were similar to those Slaney felt about Harold, of a lost time and a vanished place both centered on one golden person, when all doubts and worries and fears about the world disappeared before the unity and strength of love and comradeship.

Ned didn't reveal who that person was, and Slaney didn't care. That was the past, like Harold. He knew that Ned found comfort in his present company, that Slaney's strength was a balm to him, and that, however minutely, he alleviated Ned's loneliness. He also knew that in Ned he had a friend at last, however odd that friendship might be, and that his friend's complexity and generosity had made him more than he had been before, a better man. He had no desire to compete with Ned, only to encourage and protect.

As their friendship burgeoned, Slaney was able to reconcile the two conflicting images that had once confounded him. The tumultuous hero who had burst upon him in lantern slides at the Albert Hall and the shabby, forlorn Ross he had seen being dismissed from the service at Farnborough were the same man. Now he believed that Ned was a leader lying fallow, and that while he, Slaney, could not aspire to greatness, he had learned from Ned that sometimes great men flourished in the company of a stalwart friend.

He would be that friend.

There were two parcels from Fortnum & Mason, huge hampers of exotic food. They came with infrequent regularity, one every three months or so, and Ned generously shared the contents with all the men in the hut. They came from Charlotte Shaw, and everyone toasted her health as they munched on her tinned ham and pâté and brandied peaches.

"What is it?" Wilson wondered, staring at a water biscuit covered in pâté. Wilson had a cautious stomach and regularly considered and sniffed every forkful of food before he dared put it into his mouth.

"It's like meat paste, only better," Ned said. "It's made of liver."

Wilson nibbled on a tiny sliver. "It's good," he said doubtfully, not wanting to offend Ned, or Mrs. Shaw.

"Is this what toffs eat all the time?" Jones asked, munching on tinned game pie.

"I don't know; I'm not a toff and I don't eat very much meat." Ned grinned.

"You eat sausages," Vine said, his mouth full.

"There's nae meat in an English sausage." Cameron was in a good mood. "Scottish sausages, that's a different matter—"

"Yeh, what would you know?" Rogers said. "You blokes eat 'aggis, and we all know what's in 'aggis."

"What is in haggis?" Wilson asked. They told him, and Wilson paled.

There was a big fruitcake covered in marzipan and icing. Ned cut it into fourteen portions. The cake reeked of brandy.

"She's gotta be worth a few quid," Thompson said, "that Mrs. Shaw." Fortnum & Mason was an expensive shop in Piccadilly that all of them knew but none had dared to enter, except Ned. "What's she like?"

"What's 'e like, you mean," Jones corrected him. "'E's the one with the loot, all them plays and books and stuff."

"He's a brilliant man," Ned said, "one of the finest minds I've ever met. He's been like a father to me."

They loved to hear him talk of famous people. "Told ya," Jones said smugly.

"But Mrs. Shaw is rich in her own right." Ned didn't want them to think of Charlotte as George Bernard Shaw's housewife, she was so much more than that. "She's Irish aristocracy. She gives away fortunes to charity."

"Yeh, well, I know a charity she can chuck some at," Rogers chipped in. "Me!"

The men laughed, stomachs full, intimates, if only by association, of the rich and famous, and grateful to Charlotte Shaw.

"'E's an old codger, in't he, GBS?" Rogers had an unlikely plan. "Reckon she'd like a young ram like me when 'e pops off?"

"There's just one problem," Ned said. He had to be careful. He didn't want them to laugh at Charlotte. Or himself.

"She's celibate, like me," he finished. He glanced at Slaney, who held his look, steadily.

There was a shocked silence, which Wilson broke with a whisper to Jones. "What's celibate?"

"She don't do it," Jones whispered back, although everyone could hear.

"But she's married," Wilson whispered again.

"She don't give GBS none?" Rogers was disbelieving. "I'd chuck 'er out, quick smart."

Ned knew he had made a foolish mistake and tried to end it. "They're very happy," he said.

"Mebbe she's a good cook," Jones said, dismissing Charlotte Shaw's marital problems as her own business. Ned had raised a much more disturbing concept, about his own celibacy; they had all been taught this was admirable in an unmarried man, but none believed it possible. A few remained unrepentant about their visits to brothels or their masturbation, but several felt a pressure of guilt.

"What about you, you must have—y'know—or pulled yer pud sometimes?" Cameron demanded. "All blokes do."

"I don't!" Wilson said, anxious not to be guilty by association.

"Yes you do, you lying little bugger," Thompson said. "I've 'eard you, you wait till you think we're all asleep, then yer 'ands down there faster'n you can say Jack Robinson. Five times a night, sometimes, you randy little shit."

"I never do," Wilson insisted, blushing.

"Who can do it five times a night?" Vine wanted to know.

It created the diversion Ned needed in order to escape. The men fell to a discussion of how many times they could climax on a single night and pretended not to notice when Ned left the hut.

Except Rogers. "P'raps 'is balls 'aven't dropped," he giggled in a stage whisper, to the relief of the others. It explained Tee-Hee's apparent virginity.

Slaney found him, standing alone near the perimeter wire, staring at the moon. He stood beside him and lit a cigarette for both of them. Ned didn't smoke very often, but sometimes he would join Slaney in the ritual.

The silence was comfortable and comforting, although Slaney sensed that Ned was in a different mood from any he had previously known in his friend.

"What did you mean today," Slaney asked eventually. "About the wingco having it in for you?"

Ned took a drag on the cigarette and handed it back.

"Some big brass are coming," he explained. "Scrambled eggs."

"Scrambled eggs" was service slang for the mass of gold braid on the peaks of the most senior officers' caps. "The government wants to start a new airmail service through the Persian Gulf, and there's to be a conference here about it."

"And you've been invited?"

"I know something about the area and the people," Ned said. He looked around uneasily. "The thing is, the wingco hasn't been asked."

Slaney whistled softly.

"So he has it in for me," Ned said. "The drill, the PT, it's all because of me. He's hopping mad." He knew it was true, because Hawkins had told him and had warned him.

"I have to be careful," Ned said. "I don't want to be chucked out."

Slaney could understand the wing commander's anger. If he ran the depot and a lowly erk was asked to a conference instead of him, he'd be hopping mad too. Still, if he ran a base and had a man like Lawrence of Arabia serving under him, he'd want that man's opinions. It seemed a perfect moment to ask Ned a critical question.

"Are you a spy?"

"What's a spy?" Ned said. "A man who gives his country information that his country needs to know?"

Slaney didn't laugh, and Ned understood it was a serious question. He also knew the rumors about him.

"I've done that. Probably any of us would, if we had the information. Wouldn't you?"

Slaney nodded. Perhaps he would. Certainly he would.

"Did I rush around in a long cloak and a mask, wielding daggers? No. It began at Carchemish."

That place again, Slaney thought.

"I was an archeologist, pure and simple," Ned said. "But the Germans were building a bridge a few miles away, as part of the Berlin to Baghdad railway. It had strategic value, and we kept an eye on them. Obviously, we let our friends in London know how they were progressing. It was much the same in the war. We played to win."

It was the absolute truth. Or part of it. Slaney was a little disappointed. It was so very reasonable, but it didn't answer all of the questions. It didn't explain Afghanistan. It didn't allow for here.

"I meant, are you a spy here?"

"On you? On the others? No!" Ned giggled again. "I have important friends, and obviously I write to them and tell them what's going on. I try to help."

Slaney's spine shimmered, because suddenly he remembered several things that the men had talked about in the hut, ways to improve service life in this new air force, and several of those changes had been implemented, albeit weeks or months later, following directives from Delhi and London. It could be just coincidence—the changes were minor, basic stuff—but what Ned said was true: he did have powerful friends.

"It's all right," Ned reassured him. "I don't write reports on what Rogers says about officers, or how many times Cameron goes to the brothels in town."

Slaney's feelings for Ned, already deep, intensified. A small part of Ned suddenly made sense to him. Whatever his reasons for being here, he realized that Ned cared deeply about the erks and their welfare and was prepared to do something to improve their lot. If only more officers were like Ned.

An awful memory assailed him. When Harold was sent to France, Slaney had gone with his big brother to say good-bye. A thousand men in uniform were gathered at the station with their loved ones, most going to their death. By then the war had stalemated, and slaughter was the only news that came from the Western Front.

"Cannon fodder," Harold had said. "That's all we are."

As often happened, Ned understood Slaney's dark mood. "The men are too important to me," he said. "I lost two brothers to the war, and there is nowhere, not one square inch of soil, that is worth an English soldier's life."

It was said with a sudden, vehement bitterness, and it was the most shocking thing he could have said, and the most redemptive. Slaney was moved almost to tears, because it was true, nowhere was worth Harold's life, except, perhaps, England. If Ned understood this, perhaps he could communicate it to his powerful friends, perhaps a change could be wrought. Slaney was filled with a flooding gratitude. Ned had given up everything to espouse the cause of the men, one of them and not one of them, an extraordinary man who only wanted to be ordinary and who thought all men considerable, no matter their station, no matter their class. If Ned ruled the world, concepts like cannon fodder might cease to exist. If Ned ruled the world, Slaney would ride beside him, his guardian and protector. If Ned ruled the world, Slaney would ride into any battle, without question, even unto death, and would consider it a life well spent.

Ned had shared with the others the triumph of Lawrence of Arabia, of riding in glory into Damascus at the head of a victorious army, but he had just given Slaney a hint of the tragedy. There was something else.

"Why did you tell them that?" he asked. "Tonight. About Mrs. Shaw—about you . . ."

"I don't know, it was stupid," Ned said. It had been very stupid, and very unnecessary. In truth, he had done it for Slaney's benefit. The friendship was becoming increasingly dear to him, and he wanted Slaney to understand. He hadn't known how else to tell him. "I wanted them to know something about me, to understand me a little better, perhaps."

"But that—that's personal, that's private." Slaney had been shocked and puzzled that Ned had chosen to reveal this aspect of himself.

"Yes," Ned said. "I believe a man's seed is sacred, it is holy," he whispered. "I believe it is the source of his masculinity, his manhood, his power. I believe it should be saved for his beloved. I believe that it is a divine gift he can give to his beloved. In giving it, he gives himself."

It was said softly, intimately, and Slaney found it intensely moving. Harold had told him this same thing, less eloquently, so many years ago. Slaney made a silent vow to the moon to keep himself pure for his beloved. He guessed he would fail though; the urge was irresistible sometimes, but the promise was meant when it was made.

He knew Ned was staring at him, and he turned to look at his friend. It was a melding moment.

He is astonishing, Ned thought. He is dark and dour, and carries a granite loneliness with him. He is moors and mists and secret places. He is Heathcliff. He is not Dahoum. But he might be John Bruce.

"I was wrong. It was a bad thing to do. I suppose I'll have to pay for it, one way or another." His voice was caressing, almost pleading. He looked like a schoolboy admitting a sin, accepting of his punishment, perhaps desirous of it. "I should be beaten for it."

Slaney thought the price was extreme for so small an error, but he did not want the moment to end, because it was so intimate. He had never felt so close to anyone, except Harold, and the feeling was fulfilling and warm and wondrous. He realized how very lonely he had been for so many years, and he never wanted to be that lonely again. He thought he should say something to Ned, if only thank you, but he knew words were irrelevant. He wanted to stay there forever, in this whisper-quiet tropic night, standing side by side with the man who was his friend. He could hear his heart beat, and gratitude surged through him, making him light-headed with an emotion that was so intense he felt a sting of tears in his eyes.

It was also deeply disturbing to him because it was so intimate, so seductive, as if he had ventured into a dark, beguiling place where demons dwell. He wondered if he dare go forward and what he might find if he did, but suddenly he became frightened that what he would find was unfathomable to him, and he drew back from going on.

"We should get back," he said, and turned away. "Be lights-out soon."

15

I have just killed a man!

I think I have.

He's twenty yards away, sucking on his wounded hand, from which blood is pouring, and howling like a banshee. Only a dying man could make such an infernal noise.

Thinking my copper watch gold, he tried to rob me. I was dozing by a pretty brook among straggly olive trees. Then he was there, grabbing at me, tearing the watch from my wrist, breaking the strap and shouting for money. I grabbed my gun and warned him, and he backed off but would not go till he had money. I told him I had none, to leave or I would shoot. He advanced again, guessing that a fair lad like me was not a crack shot.

I pulled the trigger. The explosion rattled me, but not as much as his almighty scream. I saw the blood and thought I must have killed him.

But no. He lives. He curses me up hill and down dale, calls all the wrath of Allah on me and scrambles to his donkey.

This is adventure!

This is the life!

From first landfall in dusty, ruined Egypt, I knew I was home, or nearly. It is not here, but close; I can feel it, sense it, smell it, hear it ringing in my ears, taste it, almost touch it. It might be over the next terraced hill, or just around a minaretted corner, or on some plain of the forgotten battles of Ozymandias that I may find tomorrow.

It will not be in hectic Port Said—that was merely the gateway to here and to my manhood. From there we sailed to lovely, clean Beirut, and that was the end of Europe for me. I set foot on Levantine land and found myself face to face with the glorious past and my unwritten future. My clothes are tattered, my boots are porous and my body smells from lack of bathing. My hair is matted, my skin is apricot. I have walked hundreds of miles, or ridden on donkeys, or hitched in carriages, from Phoenician Sidon to Nazarene Galilee, from bustling Haifa to converting Damascus, and every step of the way has been a revelation. As

Saul became Paul, so I have become another me and cannot be the me I was again.

I have sought shelter in stone huts where Mary might have sung the Magnificat, slept in cheap hotels and incense-burning monasteries and villages of biblical antiquity, and have been fed cumin-laden goat stews by Orthodox monks and thin bread, yogurt and boiled wheat by kind, inquisitive peasant folk. All subscribe to Arab rules of hospitality; the request for shelter is a sacred thing and must be granted, the stranger made an honored guest.

I have seen bedizened strumpets ride by in gaily painted carriages, escorted by small armies of dragomen in scarlet fezzes and gilt-encrusted uniforms, and I have seen fat merchants trot on suffering, spindly legged donkeys through cobbled, crowded streets. I have tasted sticky sweetmeats, and I have seen and smelled, but not yet tried, hashish.

I have seen marriage ceremonies where boys younger than I are wed to girls younger than they. Children and women clap and sing, and men dance and fire their guns into the air. I have held babies in swaddling clothes and watched quaint funerals with open coffins. I have bargained with garrulous, turbaned traders for Hittite seals, and I have found pieces of Canaanite pottery and marveled at Alexandrian coins and Mameluke glass.

I conduct myself in French and ever-improving Arabic, have talked with simple, saintly men who have made the hajj and been to Mecca and Medina, and I have met Jews who have wept at the Wailing Wall. I have seen old rabbis with curly ringlets bob the Talmud and heard aesthetic choirs of black-robed, bearded, high-hatted men chant ancient hymns in the churches of Byzantium, under domes glistening with golden mosaics.

I have been sick and sunburned, blistered and bloody, footsore and exhausted. I have been alone, but never lonely. Here I walk with Caesar's centurions, where Saladin's horses prance, and stand on hills where young shepherds sit with harps and flutes, as David did, in love with Jonathan.

I have taken photographs of the living past and been robbed of my camera.

I have been attacked and beaten; I have learned to yell louder than the rest and weep and laugh and create such a spectacle of myself that all my wishes are granted, for my fine performance, or, more simply, out of fear that I am mad!

I have talked with scholars whose minds span two great cultures, East and West, and have been to universities where algebra was formed, and talked with philosophers who do not understand the confining horizons that an insistence on Christian morality can put on thinking, but can see beyond the limit of their sight.

I have learned verities from the simple act of living each moment as if it were my last. Seize the day takes much too long—grab the moment!

I have done all these things and shall do more, I can never go home again, no matter how many times I return to England.

I shall visit all the seven cities that are the pillars of wisdom, the cradles of civilization (Damascus is my first), and I will dwell in, or near, one of them.

I am myself here. I can do—and be—anything I want.

Perhaps I can even love myself.

And—perhaps—be loved.

16

IN SPRING OF 1928, Wing Commander Aubrey Stapleton was removed. Transferred. Sent back to England.

The depot breathed a collective sigh of shocked relief and then sucked its breath in again and held it, wondering what the successor would be like.

The new CO, Wing Commander Bone, had a distinguished record of service and an easy authority. It was a considerable change for the better, Hawkins thought, but he could not rid his mind of a recent meeting he had witnessed but not heard between Ned and Sir Geoffrey Salmond, and the sneaking belief that Stapleton's incompetence had been discussed by them. Hawkins felt an odd flicker of fear of Ned, which he immediately dismissed as unworthy, of himself and of Ned. The change in CO was welcome, however it was achieved, and Hawkins dismissed his suspicions as petty.

The depot had no doubts. Military men thrive on rumor, they flock to it as crows to carrion, feed on it, stripping the flesh until the bones are clean, then whirling on to fresher kills. This particular furphy provided an enduring feast. It was accepted as a given that most commanders were blinded by the scrambled egg on their caps and that only an airman could reveal to them the indignities that the ranks belligerently claimed to suffer. And since officers only listened to their own, and since Ned was obviously one of their own, however disguised, it followed, as night follows day, that Ned was the man who had brought sight to unseeing eyes.

It puzzled the men of the hut that Ned did not share the general mood. He seemed worried about something, something important. He became, if anything, even more insular, more isolated from them, except for Slaney.

"Come for a walk," Ned said to Slaney one night. Slaney guessed that Ned wanted to be away from the others.

They walked along the perimeter wire until they came to the Moslem quarters. A group of men were gathered around a small campfire. They greeted Ned cheerily as someone they knew and made room for him. Ned introduced Slaney and sat cross-legged on the ground. Slaney squatted beside him.

Slaney was puzzled. "You speak Urdu?"

Ned shook his head. "No, we talk in Arabic. It is the language of the Koran and crosses national borders, like Catholics speaking Latin." He giggled. "When they speak Urdu, I have no idea what they're saying."

It didn't matter. For an hour they sat listening without understanding, mostly ignored, except when coffee was made. Occasionally, someone would speak to Ned haltingly, in a language that wasn't Urdu, and Ned would reply, but otherwise the two airmen were left alone.

Then Ned began to speak, softly, in English, to Slaney, as if to rid his mind of worry.

He spoke of the fall of a city called Troy, and of a brilliant and cunning man called Odysseus who was the architect of the Greek victory and condemned by the vengeful gods not to find his way home. He told of Odysseus' epic journey, shipwrecked on enchanted islands, imprisoned by one-eyed monsters, bewitched by beautiful sirens, and of a constant wife who waited through twenty long years for reunion.

Slaney thrilled to the tales, and dreamed of one day finding a wife as faithful as patient Penelope.

"They make the gods jealous," Ned said. Something in his voice tugged at Slaney's heart. He knows, he thought, he's met someone like that. Was there some faithful someone, somewhere, waiting for Ned to come home?

"Are these real people?" Slaney wondered aloud. "Did they really exist?"

"As real as the Bible," Ned replied. "As are their gods. If you believe in Noah and Joseph and Ruth, you must believe in Zeus and Athena and Apollo."

"They're pretty fond of putting curses on people," Slaney ventured.

"Yes," Ned said. "They are."

Ned's stories of these ancient Greeks were as grand, as thrilling as any adventure of Arabia, and he made people who perhaps had never lived as real as any airman. Time disappeared for both of them, and Slaney imagined they were sitting under a goatskin tent, three thousand years ago, listening to gossip of families that he knew, of old rivalries born and old enmities healed.

Slaney thought that Ned existed in two time frames—the ancient past and the recent past. The epic tales of Homer were no more fantastic to Ned than his own exploits in Arabia. Slaney realized how very little he knew about Ned, the domestic trivia of him. He knew of Ned's famous friends and of a cottage somewhere in Dorset called Clouds Hill; he knew Ned had a mother and a brother who had been in China, but of a wife and family, if such existed, he knew nothing. There was nothing of Ned in present time except an anonymous airman. He determined to find out more, but not now. Nothing mattered now except the journeys of the King of Ithaca, son of Laertes, who was kinsman to Zeus.

Eventually, Ned drifted to silence. The fire had died to embers, some of the Moslems had wandered away, and a few had lain down to sleep.

Slaney, cross-legged on the ground, had seldom been so happy, utterly relaxed in the company of the man who was his friend. He could not guess how long they had been there, or how long they sat in tranquil silence. His eyelids grew heavy, and he would have dozed, but then Ned looked at him.

He is content, Slaney thought. Perhaps he is even happy. The ice in Ned's blue eyes had melted and there were only liquid pools of sapphire, tranquil oases.

"'And thou, beside me in the wilderness,'" Ned said softly.

Slaney did not understand the words except as he heard them, that he was beside his friend in the wilderness, and it was enough, more than enough. The wilderness was, at that moment, everything that he desired.

"Do the men blame me for the Stapleton business?" Ned asked Slaney.

Slaney was stunned.

"Blame you?" Slaney said. "Christmas, no! They love you for it."

"I wish they wouldn't," Ned said. "It complicates things."

Ned was aware of the difficulty of his position. At the recent meeting of the big brass—the scrambled eggs—to discuss the air route from Britain to India, Ned had spoken to Sir Geoffrey, the air vice-marshal, about Stapleton because Sir Geoffrey had asked him. He had not expected such a swift or emphatic response. He guessed that his few comments only added to the general opinion of Stapleton held by his superiors, that his remarks had been a link, not the whole chain, but it was dangerous. With Stapleton gone and Bone in command, Ned vowed to lie low, to keep his head down and tail up. He would do his erkly duties and translate the *Odyssey* in his spare time. And nothing more.

It was too late, however; the damage was done. Many of the officers believed the rumor too, and their attitude to it was antagonistic. If a lowly erk could get a commanding officer removed, then none of them was safe. This angry fear was seldom voiced, or obliquely expressed, but it was unmistakable. "Letting down his class" was the general opinion.

The new CO had expressed nothing but admiration for Lawrence of Arabia and was sympathetic to Ned's need to be in the ranks, which he thought sprang from an extreme but probably justified case of shell shock. So it came as a surprise to Hawkins when Bone said that Ned's present position was untenable and had to be resolved.

"In what regard?" Hawkins asked. Bone had invited Hawkins to dinner at the club, in Karachi.

Bone's attitude was simple. If Ned wanted to be an erk, let him be that, but he could not be both an erk and a powerful influence on the running of the base. How could a commanding officer maintain discipline and efficiency if any unpopular order was subject to the whim and whispers of A/C 2 Shaw?

"They are only rumors," Hawkins protested.

"The point is that the men believe them," Bone insisted. "What if Shaw makes some objection to the way I run the show? Will he run to his friends in Delhi and London? Can *I* expect to be replaced?"

Hawkins remembered again the conversation between Ned and Sir Geoffrey, and the subsequent removal of Stapleton.

"What shall you do?" he asked.

"For the moment, nothing," Bone said. "But if he gives me grounds, I'll lay the jump on him." He raised his glass in a small toast. "I hope it doesn't come to that."

His position was fair and reasonable, but Hawkins knew how much Ned needed the RAF, if not why. Stapleton, an incompetent officer, had been no serious threat to Ned, but Bone was efficient and highly regarded and could arrange for Ned to be transferred at the stroke of a pen. This in itself would not result in dismissal, but Ned's service contract was coming up for renewal, and black marks on his conduct sheet, added to his age, would count against him.

At the very least, Hawkins believed he had to alert Ned to the present danger, and he thought he had a solution to the problem. The job in Afghanistan was still open.

"You would be very useful there," he urged Ned.

"It wouldn't be safe," Ned said.

"But nobody would know you there," Hawkins persisted.

"I would be known anywhere," Ned said. "I can't escape the man I was. And there would be too many temptations."

"Temptations?" Hawkins was puzzled.

"To be that man again," Ned explained. "The situation—the political situation—there is too"—he searched for the right word, and giggled when he found it—"enticing."

Hawkins understood. Here, in the ranks, Ned functioned under British rules and was made secure by lack of contact with the outside world.

"There" the rules were different. "There" the political situation was volatile, with the Moslem fundamentalists in almost open war with the ruling revisionists. "There" was a mass of unruly tribesmen violently struggling to achieve some cohesion, with a king who was pulling in directions they didn't want to go. "There" was a country with alliances with many colonial or expansionist powers and allegiances to none. There the British, the Russian Soviets, the French, the Italians, the Persians and a dozen others, even the Americans, were in a constant rivalry.

"There" was an Oriental bazaar. How could a man who was expert at haggling be immune to the thrill of involvement? And, once involved, not find a cause? "There" was very dangerous indeed. But "here" was not safe either.

Hawkins could not let it rest.

"Even so, I wish you would change your mind," he said. "There, you would have few enemies."

Ned's eyes narrowed, as if in sudden alarm. "What enemies?"

Reluctantly, Hawkins told him of the conversation he had had at the club, although without revealing the identity of the officer. For just a moment he had the feeling that he had hit Ned hard on the chin and delivered a knockout punch. The man seemed to sag, as if all the stuffing had been knocked out of him.

Then there was that curious, challenging change again. Ned stared at the floor, then pulled his head up and his shoulders back. The blue eyes sparkled. And he giggled. "Well," he said. "That's torn it."

"So you see," Hawkins insisted, "Afghanistan makes sense."

But Ned shook his head. "It makes no sense at all."

There was a small silence.

"What shall you do?" Hawkins asked.

"I don't know," Ned said. "Something will turn up. It always does."

There wasn't much else to talk about. Ned saluted and left. Hawkins got up and went to the window. He saw Ned leave the building and stand outside by the garden, on the edge of a desert. He looked as if he had nowhere to go and no reason for going there.

Hawkins cursed himself softly. No matter how good his intentions, no matter how necessary it had been to tell Ned what he had heard, he felt that he had cut off a lifeline. Then, to his surprise, the little, lonely man suddenly looked chipper. He walked smartly away, and Hawkins was sure he was whistling.

Slaney and some others were in the hut when Ned came in, whistling.

He greeted them cheerily, went to the gramophone and put on a record, a thunderous Beethoven. He sat on his cot, took out his pad and began writing a letter.

Slaney wondered what had happened to cause this change in mood, but Ned only shrugged in response to his questioning look and went on writing. When the letter was done, he put it in an envelope, sealed and stamped it, and left it on his bed while he went to the latrine.

Jones, in the next bunk, did what they all wanted to do. Leaning over for a look, he whistled. The letter was addressed to Air Vice-Marshal Sir Geoffrey Salmond, in Delhi.

None of them had any doubt that they were intended to know to whom the letter was addressed—it had been too obvious. In half-whispered conversations, they wondered what Coughdrop was up to now, and if any of them were mentioned in the letter. They could not know, short of opening the envelope, that the letter was a request for a transfer.

For the most part, for the next week, Ned ignored the other men, and only half remembered Slaney, who spent that week in an odd anxiety, an anticipation of loss. Ned was waiting for something, and Slaney began to believe that it would not include him.

Whatever it was came at the end of the week in the form of a letter from Delhi and another summons to the adjutant.

When he returned, it was another Ned. He had an air of departure about him, of going, of leaving them, but he was not unhappy.

He packed up his gramophone and gave it to Slaney.

"Look after it," he said. "I won't be needing it anymore."

The airmen looked at each other in surprise, and then they all looked at

Slaney, who shrugged. Ned was rifling through the pile of records. He pulled out one, the Sophie Tucker.

"This has seen better days," he said. "I'll get Charlotte to send you a new one."

An astonishing sense of loss, coupled with a bitter feeling of betrayal, assaulted Slaney. He thought he was standing on the edge of a terrible precipice, and that at any moment he would fall into the awful abyss of loneliness below. "What's up, Ned?" he asked.

"Just a little spring cleaning," Ned replied. Why not? It was spring, and a journey was in the offing. He would not need a great deal of baggage.

He picked up a pile of paper, the book he had been working on.

"Do you have any matches?"

No one spoke, because no one was sure what to say. Slaney fished in his pocket, found matches and threw the box to Ned.

"Ta," Ned said, chirpily. "I'll bring them back."

He walked out, the manuscript under his arm.

Nothing was said, but everyone looked at Slaney again. Burning with anger, flushing with hurt, Slaney got up and followed Ned outside. The others fell in behind him, or went to the windows to see what was up.

Ned was standing on a patch of clear ground near the hut, lighting a page of the manuscript. As it burned, he let it fall to the ground, and then, one by one, added the other pages to it until a bonfire blazed, and then Ned dropped all the remaining pages into the flames.

The airmen were shocked. They knew how much the manuscript meant to Ned; he had been working on it for as long as they had known him and obviously for some time before that. Yet Ned seemed calm, almost happy. They watched the ritual from a respectful distance; only Slaney had the courage to stand close to Ned.

Ned could not bring himself to look at Slaney; this moment had happened too many times before. If he looked at Slaney he would see in the young man's eyes too much hurt, too much regret, too much reproach, too many promises of friendship, broken. And this symbolic immolation was in itself a lie, like so much else. A copy of the manuscript he was burning was safe with Charlotte, in London.

It was a gesture, perhaps, but it was something more. It was the gentlest way of saying good-bye, if any farewell can be kind.

It did not help Slaney.

"What are you burning?" Slaney asked, tears smarting in his eyes. He told himself they were caused by the smoke from the fire, but he knew that wasn't true.

Ned stared at the flames.

"My life," he said.

17

May 1928

So—close to the end of the world wasn't far enough. I have to go farther— right to the very edge.

And if that isn't far enough, if that doesn't work, why then I'll just—

—fall off.

(I shall miss Slaney, though.)

London

—⚬⚬⚬—

(Charlotte and Sarah)

1928

18

CHARLOTTE SHAW WAS ANGRY, very angry. She was angry with the world in general, she was angry with Martha, her maid (for being overly solicitous), she was angry with GBS (for being so wretchedly right, as always), and she was angry with Ned (how could he be so naughty, so careless of his reputation?).

Mostly, she was angry with herself, with her weak, frail body, and her weaker, frailer mind. If she had a true faith, like Nancy Astor, she could, by faith or by sheer willpower, force her body to resist these recurring ailments.

Knowing she had to get better, she prayed for a little of Nancy's faith, summoned up some of her own not inconsiderable willpower and attacked her malady with logic. There was no point in being angry with the world at large, or railing against the direction in which the world was heading. Change was the order of the times, and Charlotte was already doing her level best to advance those changes for the better. Not as hard as some, of course, but the others didn't have GBS to look after, which was a lifetime's sheer slog for anyone.

Charlotte longed for a better world, a more equitable society. For most of her adult life she had been aware of the injustices that society wrought on much of humankind, and those injustices pained her. For years, she had, in her own words, "flailed about" looking for some way that she might try and set right the manifold wrongs.

As a young heiress sojourning in Rome, she had thought that the philosophies of the philanthropic doctor Axel Munthe were her key to effecting change, that if the physical—that is the medical—condition of the lower classes could be improved they might look forward to the future with some optimism.

Of course, there had been whispers that Charlotte's passion for the underclasses was simply a sublimation of her unrequited passion for the gorgeous Dr. Munthe. Charlotte did not deny her idolization of Munthe, but the revolutionary flame that burnt so fiercely in her breast had been kindled long before Rome, in her youth, on her father's estate in Ireland.

After Rome and Munthe's careless (callous?) rejection of her love, she flung herself into charitable work in London. When she met the Fabians Beatrice and Sydney Webb in London, and through them GBS, she became convinced that it was not simply the health of society that needed to be improved, but that the entire system had to be changed.

Previously, she had thought of herself as a philanthropist. Now she regarded herself as a quiet revolutionary.

She was not unaware of the whispers, the snickers behind her back, that it is all very well for her, worth millions, to espouse the cause of socialism, but if she was a true believer, why didn't she give her millions away? Charlotte had a simple answer. If she gave all her money away it might make a few lucky souls happy for a while, but the essential poor would still be poor, and Charlotte would be poor as well and could do no good for anyone.

Besides, her inheritance was a sacred trust from that blessed man, her dear father, who had suffered so much in life but who had been kind and thoughtful to his two daughters and had ensured that they should never want for anything in their lives, unless, of course, they squandered his patrimony.

So she adopted the world's cause and put a solid portion of her income (although not her capital) toward working for a better world. What vexed her was that the world couldn't see the sense of it. Even Nancy could be particularly obtuse on this point, but then she was an American and married to one of the wealthiest men in the country, and Charlotte suspected in her heart that Nancy didn't really want change, merely superficial improvements.

Charlotte didn't want violent revolution as in Russia, she wanted change by common sense. Beatrice and Sydney had persuaded her that economics was the key, so Charlotte gave money to Beatrice and Sydney for their school of economics in London and helped pay for the school building by renting an apartment on the upper floors. She had also endowed some scholarships for young women who wanted to become doctors, and on good days she felt that she was doing all she could, but on bad days like this, despaired because her efforts didn't seem to be making any difference at all.

She turned her attention to her specific irritations, to come to terms with them, lay them to rest.

Martha, her maid, was only doing her best. Martha had been with Charlotte for years and, usually, her understanding of Charlotte's needs was flawless, but today it was all out of kilter. Charlotte knew the fault was her own, but she had lost her temper with Martha. Well, well, she would make it up to her on the morrow with some little trinket and some carefully judged words of praise and apology.

Then there was GBS. He was always at his most annoying when she was mildly unwell (as opposed to being at his most endearing when she was truly ill), and her sick headaches were the butt of many of his cruelest jokes.

GBS thought any sickness was because the mind had allowed it, whereas Charlotte believed that impure thoughts, "sin" in GBS's gross oversimplification, could cause a physical manifestation. She knew that he laughed with friends about her "sick headaches," saying that Charlotte was wrestling with the devil to conquer him, while ordinary mortals would merely take a pill.

But Charlotte didn't believe in "sin" as such. She believed in some higher spiritual authority, and she had spent many years wondering about the nature and manifestations of God. She had long since strayed from the path of the Church of England, had flirted briefly with Rome and, for an even shorter period of time and under GBS's influence, had espoused atheism, but she could not bring herself to believe in nothing.

So she had turned, like a lotus to the rising sun, to the East, to the non-judgmental philosophies and the complex simplicities of Oriental mysticism. And she had turned at the same time to the West, to some of the more interesting theories of religion that were emanating from America. Somehow, it had all jumbled together in her mind to bring her to a religious truth that she understood but could never adequately explain to anyone else. In that truth, spiritual and physical well-being were utterly intertwined. If the mind was disturbed, so would be the body.

Which is why she had been so cross with GBS. He had popped in early in the morning, bubbling with his usual confounding energy. He had rattled through their social calendar, which was as hectic as ever, and then charged off to do battle with the world.

He bounced in again just before lunch, when she was at her worst, toying with some beef tea and dry biscuits. He made some unkind comments about her carnivorous habits (beef tea was, of course, meat) and insisted that a good bowl of porridge (she couldn't stand the stuff, but he lived on it) was what her body needed. He then suggested that the real reason for her sick headache was her coming appointment with Sarah Lawrence. He darted off to a healthy luncheon of nut rissoles with some friend at Shearn's, leaving Charlotte in a ferment. It was then that she had lost her temper with Martha.

Of course it was her meeting with Mrs. Lawrence that was upsetting her, but only GBS had the sense, or impertinence, to point it out!

Still, that was GBS, and she loved him, even though on this and many other occasions he drove her mad. In her frail condition, she didn't want his brittle iconoclasm, she didn't want his chirpiness, and she certainly didn't want him putting his finger right on the heart of her anxieties. She wanted—love?

Love, the love they had agreed on, the love that kept them together, was what he gave her. What he had not given her, never gave her, was romance, or not in any accepted form. Their whole relationship, their courtship and marriage, was intensely practical, but in her present frail condition she didn't want energy, she wanted Byronic stupor. She wanted to contemplate beauty as an unattainable ideal, not an achievable reality. She didn't want aggressive Wagner, she wanted lazy Brahms. She didn't want Ibsen, or Tolstoy, she wanted Keats and Shelley, or even, heaven help her, Tennyson. Or even that other Shaw, Ned.

The silly thing was, GBS's lethally accurate diagnosis of her illness was making her feel better. Was that love? Surely so, but hardly romantic.

She wasn't sure if GBS was even capable of that other kind of love. Charlotte was quite aware of the other women in her husband's life. He'd always had a reputation as a formidable womanizer, had had flagrant affairs before (Ellen Terry) and during (Mrs. Patrick Campbell) their marriage. Charlotte could not swear that he wasn't lunching with Mrs. Pat today, but if so, it wouldn't be nut rissoles on the menu. Mrs. Pat was a voracious meat- and man-eater, and Charlotte guessed that skinny GBS was only a crunchy snack to her.

Charlotte was not unduly disturbed by his philandering because she knew, or believed, that the affairs were never consummated in any real and physical sense and that with GBS it was only the outward trappings of passion that mattered. It was his ego that needed to be fed. Or it was the Irish in him, or perhaps because he had been blessed with such an extraordinary brain, his libido was tiny by comparison. Whichever was fine by Charlotte.

To her he presented an errant boy—himself—to be coddled and fussed over and cherished and admonished. To her he gave a sense of place and of belonging in a world in which she previously had thought she had no place and did not belong. To her he offered responsibility for the nurture of his body and thus for the well-being of his mind. Thousands of women might envy her this gift, for it was she who provided the domestic circumstances in which his genius thrived.

Still, sometimes she needed something more, just as GBS did. They teased each other about this, and he had been right on target today. Today she was to meet, for the first time, a woman who had rival claims on the object of Charlotte's affections.

Today she was to meet Ned's mother.

Mrs. Lawrence, with her eldest son, Bob, was back in England after years of missionary work in China, and they were to take tea at the Savoy that afternoon. Charlotte, after a restless night, had woken in great distress, with a high temperature and a splitting headache.

She knew that Ned's feelings toward his mother were highly ambivalent, which is how Charlotte felt about her own mother, but today she was to meet the woman who, more than anyone, had shaped the man whom Charlotte considered to be one of the greatest men she had ever met. (And, at this particular moment, a very naughty one.)

Charlotte had heard the rumors about her own relationship with Ned. "Poppycock!" she said out loud. "Twaddle! Yes, I am old enough to be his mother, but I am not his mother, nor do I want to be, nor would he let me be." But she knew she mothered him.

At their first meeting, in the summer of 1923, Charlotte had not been impressed. She remembered a small, shabby man with fair hair and electric blue eyes, intensely polite but with an occasional cheeky irreverence. And giggly. In particular, she remembered his rather high-pitched giggle.

He had come to visit with a mutual friend and then had sent GBS a manuscript, which he gave to Charlotte. Well, well, writers came in all shapes and sizes, and it would be wrong to judge this rather effete young man's talent by his unprepossessing presentation of himself, cockily shy. What astonished her was that this young man was, supposedly, Lawrence of Arabia, the fabulous hero of the war. If it was true then, based on first impressions, Lawrence of Arabia was very far from being all he was cracked up to be.

She approached his manuscript cautiously, warily, ready to believe the worst of it and its writer. It was a hefty work, but within pages she found herself swept up by it, wrapped up in it, dazzled by it. In the pages of that manuscript, she found a remarkable writer and believed she had met an extraordinary man.

His use of language beguiled her, sweeping, highly descriptive prose that gave her an absolute sense of being there, with him, on his desert campaign. If it was occasionally overwrought and self-consciously clever, it was a first draft, and every writer had his foibles. His sense of history impressed her, but there was something more.

Charlotte was no stranger to documentations of the vagaries of the human heart, or of the human sexual condition. Celibate herself, she was fascinated by the sexual behavior of other people and by their passions. She had translated some plays, from the original French, which were honest depictions of human nature. One, about a young woman "damaged" by an illicit sexual relationship, was considered so shocking it was refused a license for public performance.

Nor was she unaware, as were many women of her acquaintance, of the breadth of human sexuality. She knew exactly why Oscar Wilde had been sent to prison. She knew precisely what the British government had secretly whispered about Sir Roger Casement, she even knew the obscenities that were in his supposed diaries. But she had never encountered anyone who was prepared to discuss, especially in print, this unspoken side of human nature. Until now.

Up until the chapter dealing with Ned's flogging at Deraa, Charlotte had thought the book to be splendid. After reading that chapter, Charlotte became consumed with curiosity about the man. She did not believe him to be "queer" (how she hated that word!) or an "invert" or "one of those," whatever the fashionable phrase was, or if he was, she did not care. He had written of an experience with other men, no matter how awful, no matter how violent, that became sexual. It fascinated her, because despite its apparent honesty, it was also highly ambivalent. There was something missing, something about which the man had not been honest. Charlotte couldn't imagine what it was, but she was determined to find out. A correspondence began between Charlotte and Ned, who wanted GBS's help in publishing the book.

They met again and became friends. They met once more and became more than friends. They both adored Ned, she and GBS, but Charlotte held him in especial affection. She wanted to nurture and cherish him, wanted to hold him, bathe him, feed him, caress him and sing lullabies that would take all his hurt away. She worried about him endlessly.

In those days, Ned had no job, almost no income and no formal address. He was lodging in a friend's attic, and then on someone else's sofa, and there were nights Charlotte was sure he slept in the park. She knew he seldom had enough to eat and relied on friends and acquaintances for sustenance.

She gave him freedom to call whenever he wanted, and then she would feed him, make sure his washing was done, sit him down by a warm fire and talk with him for hours upon hours about anything that came to mind. He opened new worlds to her and would speak of things most men would not discuss in front of women, but coyly, in gracious terms. What made her heart sing was that he took so much from her — not material things, they were as nothing to him—but things that mattered, opinions and memories from dark corners of the heart.

He asked her frequently about her childhood in Ireland, and when she talked of it his eyes would grow dreamy, as if she were talking of his home. He admitted the truth of his parentage to her, that his mother and father had not been married, but that if they had he would have been Irish and would have inherited land there, land that came to his family from Sir Walter Raleigh. He questioned her at length about her relationship with her parents, and Charlotte revealed things about her family that she had never told anyone else. He nodded and said that he understood and told her of his difficult relationship with his own mother and his intensely ambiguous feelings toward the woman.

To Charlotte this was a revelation. She had hated her mother, but believed herself to be in the wrong and had tried to obey the commandment. She had thought herself to be unique, alone in her misery, and yet here was someone else, someone she respected, loved and admired, who shared a similar burden.

They talked of ever more intimate secrets. Other than GBS, he was the only man with whom she could discuss her denial of her sexual self, because he was denying his and their reasons were similar, based on a detestation of their parental situation. Their common celibacy bonded them, and even though Ned admitted to occasional failure, the attempt was everything in her eyes. He would not discuss what had happened at Deraa; what he had written in the book was everything, all there was to know, he told her forthrightly, so that she very nearly believed him.

She came to love him but was not fooled by him. She relished his impudent, schoolboy humor and knew him to be a teller of tall tales. If she caught him out in fibs, she scolded him for an infernal liar but forgave him because he was a writer and all writers told tall tales. GBS told lies of giant size, but always with a twinkle in his eye. Just like Ned.

She had helped him with his book, editing, correcting, suggesting, typing, and her signed copy of the private edition, when it finally was published, was a dear possession. Her heart sang for him when he got a job at last, when he was accepted into the ranks of the Royal Air Force, although she did not understand why he needed so desperately to be there. She wept for him when the discovery of his identity caused him to be thrown out of the service.

Friends in high places got him into the army, the Tank Corps, and she prayed for him during those awful years, and read, in grief, the harrowing letters that came from him, each one bleaker than the last. She met one of his few friends from the corps, the granite John Bruce, and thanked him for being Ned's friend.

"I love him, lady," John Bruce said. "He is more than a brother to me."

She and others pleaded Ned's cause in the highest places, and GBS launched formidable campaigns on his behalf. When the glad news came that he was accepted back into the air force, she did not care who had wrought the miracle. Ned was happy again, and that was all that mattered to her.

She had no patience with the vociferous negatives she sometimes heard about him at smart dinners from fuddy-duddy colonels ("traitor to his class"), because they were easy to dismiss. But sometimes at bohemian parties in Chelsea, from bright young things, she heard other, hurtful whispers: he was the son she had never had. He was the child that she and GBS could never have. He was their secret love child from before their marriage. He was GBS's son by another woman. They hurt because she wished that one of them, at least, were true.

When Ned was posted to India, she tried to make his time there as civilized as possible with frequent packages from Fortnum and the latest gramophone recordings. She thought he was content, if not happy.

And then one day, out of the blue, came the bombshell. The new book.

The book, in manuscript form, was a record of his earlier sojourn in the Royal Air Force. She read it in wonder. It was a ground-breaking work, the daily lives of simple servicemen as seen by a crystal-clear eye, told in dazzling prose, with blistering honesty. The ordinary working man was put down on paper just as he was, complete and entire, flawed and ugly, beautiful and great, and always observed with piercing honesty and sudden, flashing outbreaks of love. Now, she thought, his reputation as a writer, if it had ever been in doubt, was secure.

Which is why she was so cross with him. He contended that he did not intend to publish it, at least not in his lifetime.

After reading the book, Charlotte believed she had divined the real reason for Ned's monasticism. If she was being unduly fanciful or overtly romanticizing the man, it didn't matter, it was what she truly believed. Born to one class, he had jumped downwards to another, of his own volition, and he was determined to bring to his adopted class all the benefits of his talent and his intelligence. He had given away fame and riches to a nobler cause, that of a more equitable society. He was the possible future of a greater Britain. Others, herself less so, but GBS, Beatrice, Sydney, all their friends, were working to change society. Ned had already effected that change. He was the living revolution.

And today she was to meet the woman who had borne him.

The prospect of a face-to-face meeting with Ned's mother had unnerved Charlotte to the point of illness, yet from this woman she might learn so much, the answers to so many of her questions, for while Ned was honest with Charlotte, she knew he never told her the whole truth about himself. She forced herself to think of Mrs. Lawrence as her own mother and determined that on this occasion she would not let her mother win.

She felt much better.

She got out of bed, rang for Martha, sat at her mirror and inspected her straggly hair. Well, she had to look her best, and there was work to do. She no longer felt nervous about meeting Mrs. Lawrence, because she held a secret truth. She knew Ned better than his mother did. She wondered what she should call him. Did the family use Ned or Tom?

She smiled, for the first time that day, as at some private secret. She and Ned shared so much, not least a multiplicity of names. Her socially ambitious mother had twice embroidered the family name: Charlotte Frances Shaw, formerly Charlotte Frances Payne-Townshend, previously Charlotte Frances Payne-Townsend, had been born Charlotte Frances Townsend.

The smile faded only slightly when she remembered that Mrs. Lawrence's name had not come to her by legitimate birth, and the man she called her husband, but to whom she was not married, was not Thomas Lawrence at all, but really Thomas Chapman.

What should she call Mrs. Lawrence, she wondered, who wasn't really Mrs. Lawrence at all, not in the eyes of the law?

19

THE SAVOY WAS quite the wrong choice, Charlotte decided. The stern Mrs. Lawrence was completely out of place in these sophisticated surroundings.

Her unease had been evident from the moment Charlotte had first seen her, in the grand foyer. Mrs. Lawrence stood at the edge of the room, as if unsure of herself, and held her son's arm, as if needing his protection. She was dully dressed in a plain hat, a shapeless, dark serge overcoat, lisle stockings and sensible shoes. Her skirt, showing beneath her coat, was unfashionably long. Her only jewelry was her wedding band and a tiny gold cross pinned to the lapel of her coat. Bob, her son, wore a cheap, well-pressed suit and tired raincoat. His hat was clutched in his hand.

There was no need to have them paged. Charlotte knew them at once, and her spirit failed her slightly. They looked so out of place. Well, well, they are missionaries, Charlotte told herself sharply. They have little money, they have dedicated their lives to good work, God's work, and have suffered much. They deserve a treat.

She went to them and introduced herself. They were polite and overly formal. They were not nervous, just—out of place. It occurred to Charlotte that she was daunting to them, the wife of one of the country's public figures. Here, in these alien surroundings, with her, of course they were uneasy. She led them to the lounge. As they entered the enormous, darkly paneled, chandeliered room, Charlotte decided she was being silly. There were half a dozen cheap tearooms in the Strand where they would be much happier. Just as she was about to turn around and take them somewhere else, Marcel, the headwaiter, recognized her, greeted her, and led them to a good table by a window.

"Will you take tea?" Charlotte asked, as she settled into a comfortable chair.

"That would be very nice," Mrs. Lawrence replied, sitting on the edge of the sofa. Bob perched beside her.

Charlotte ordered the high tea, wondered what to say next and prayed that the afternoon wasn't going to be a waste of time.

"It's so nice to meet you at last," she began. "I've heard so much about you from Ned."

"Do you have news of him?" Mrs. Lawrence asked.

"Why, yes, of course, he's still in India, somewhere on the North West Frontier." She tried to be jolly. "Quite a wild place, I gather. Has he not written?"

"He's usually very good about it," Mrs. Lawrence said. "Once a week, at least, when the mail comes through. But we haven't heard from him since we've been back. We've been quite worried, haven't we, Bob?" Mrs. Lawrence looked at her son, who took her hand reassuringly.

"You worry too much, Mum. Ned can look after himself. Look at all he's been through." Bob's voice was calm and reassuring.

"You must be very proud of him," Charlotte said, meaning Ned, although Bob was a son to be proud of as well. A good man, a caring son, guardian angel to the God-struck woman.

"Proud as punch," Bob chuckled, blatantly puffed when speaking of his younger brother. "Always have been. But he does get into some scrapes!"

"He's been a good boy," Mrs. Lawrence agreed. "Although I don't understand why he's in the ranks. They're not his sort of people at all. And how can they accept him among their number? He was a colonel, you know, in the war."

She sounded as if she needed the reassurance of his previous rank.

"As long as he's happy, Mum." Bob's voice was calm, soothing; again the reassurer. "After all he's been through."

"Yes, as long as he is happy," Mrs. Lawrence said to her son. "I'm never sure. He never really says very much in his letters. Oh, he goes on a lot, about silly things, but he doesn't ever tell me what he really thinks or feels."

"Now, Mum," Bob said, squeezing her hand. Mrs. Lawrence looked at him gratefully.

There was another tiny silence.

"He is a very wonderful writer," Charlotte said to break that silence. "*The Seven Pillars* is one of the finest books I've ever read."

Mrs. Lawrence inclined her head slightly, regally, as if in thanks, and then looked down at her hands.

"Goes on a bit," Bob said.

Mrs. Lawrence looked up again, directly at Charlotte. "Why did you want to meet us?" she asked.

Charlotte was flustered by the directness of it. "Because I admire your son so very much," she said. "And his work. I wanted to meet his family. I'd like to know more about him . . ."

"What is it that you want to know?" Mrs. Lawrence was still staring at Charlotte, and there was a hint of antagonism in her tone, or of challenge.

Charlotte met the stare. "I don't have a list," she said.

She tried to think of some of the things she wanted to know, but she *didn't* have a list. She wanted to discover them less directly, by conversation and discussion, not by question and answer. But she had been asked, and so she had to find a question. She came—unexpectedly, because she had not planned to mention it—straight to the heart of the matter.

The published version of *Seven Pillars* contained a dedication, "To S. A." It was a blatant love poem, it seemed to justify and explain all of Ned's actions in Arabia, and gave his reasons for doing what he did. Nowhere else, in the book or in his other writing, did Ned mention S. A., and Charlotte had no idea who S. A. was, but she had made an educated guess. Robert Graves had suggested that the initials weren't of a person at all, but a concept, *son altesse,* which was poppycock to Charlotte. Bobby Graves could be very pompous, sometimes. Or very obtuse.

"Do you know who S. A. is?" Charlotte asked Mrs. Lawrence.

Straight to the heart of it. Mrs. Lawrence didn't even blink, she continued to stare directly at Charlotte, but all the light faded out of her eyes, and Charlotte thought she saw the woman flush.

"No," Mrs. Lawrence said, and Charlotte knew she was lying. "I have no idea at all."

She reached for Bob's hand again, and he squeezed hers again, as if to encourage her, or to forgive her the lie, and he began sterling salvage work. "Someone he met out there, we think," he said. "He met lots and lots of people, not only in the war, he was in Syria for three years before that, you know, and those Arabs have funny names. Some woman—"

He stopped, as if he didn't want to go on. It was his mother's turn to rescue him.

"I've kept every one of his letters," Mrs. Lawrence said. "Every one, since he first left home."

Charlotte was thrilled. "That's marvelous," she said, "I'd love to read them. They must make a remarkable diary. Perhaps they will be published one day."

She was surprised by the vehemence of Mrs. Lawrence's reply.

"Not in my lifetime! They're private. Family matters. Written to me." She glanced at Bob. "To us."

Charlotte knew she was going to say the wrong thing, but couldn't stop herself. "But the public would be fascinated . . ."

"The public knows too much about him already, if you ask me," Mrs. Lawrence retorted angrily. "And about us. Private things, things that should never be talked about, written about. It is shameful to me. And to Bob, and to Arnold."

Arnold was the youngest of the surviving brothers, and Charlotte wondered which Mrs. Lawrence loved the most, her eldest, Bob, or her youngest, Arnold. And where did she stand with Ned?

"Ned should be ashamed of himself," Mrs. Lawrence said.

Well, that's it, thought Charlotte, that puts the kibosh on that. Of course she means Deraa. She is offended by what he wrote, horribly, painfully offended. Perhaps there are other secrets in those private letters, revelations of self, of the sacred secrets of the family. Charlotte knew there was no point in asking any more questions. Mrs. Lawrence was not in a mood to give answers. Well, they would know in time. She was fairly sure the letters would be published eventually, if not in Mrs. Lawrence's lifetime. Already American universities were paying handsome sums for Ned's letters, and Charlotte had no doubt that the interest would increase. Ned was that kind of man, a deeply private, public man.

A small procession of waiters arrived, three or four at least, bringing the tea and sandwiches and cakes. Charlotte offered to be mother, and, as she poured the tea, she racked her mind for some subject of conversation that might occupy the next little while.

"How was China?" was the best she could come up with, but it sounded frivolous.

Happily, she had chosen well, the change of subject worked a small miracle. Mrs. Lawrence and Bob were happy to talk about themselves and their work, as if it was a relief not to have to talk about Ned. True missionaries, they gave a long lecture about their work in China, the difficulty of saving Chinese souls for Jesus, and of the dangerous uprisings that caused them to flee the country.

Charlotte listened with apparent attention, nodding at appropriate points, but in her mind she was trying to make sense of the woman who had given birth to Ned and who reminded her so strongly of her own mother. It was difficult to find in this stern evangelist the passionate, amoral creature she must once have been, the home wrecker who caused a respectable man to forsake his wife and family, his hearth and country, all for love.

I know so many of her secrets already, Charlotte thought. I know that she has never been married, despite her wedding band, and that none of her five sons was born in wedlock. I know that she is living a lie. What other secrets can there be, more powerful than that? What has Ned done that she is so ashamed of? Is it only Deraa? Or something more?

Does she love Ned? she wondered, then answered her own question. Undoubtedly, as any mother loves her son. But she has had five sons, and two are dead in the war, William and Frank, and her eldest and her youngest are her darlings. Where does she stand with Ned? Does she love Ned? Undoubtedly, as a mother must love her child, but she despises what he has done, or what he has become. She wishes he had never been famous. She wishes with all her heart that he had never left home, that she might protect him from the world, from himself and from the devil. She doesn't want to understand his demons—she wants to exorcise them. She wants to save his soul. She wants him to embrace God and her, to accept her authority and guidance. As Bob has done.

Charlotte stared at Bob, and a ghost appeared in her mind and made her shiver. The ghost of what she herself might have become. If her mother had not died, Charlotte would have looked after her for the rest of her life, out of duty, as Bob was looking after Mrs. Lawrence. I could have been him, Charlotte thought, living the rest of my days as my mother's shadow, never leaving home, never escaping the maternal embrace. Mercifully, her mother *had* died. Blessedly, Ned had left home.

"Mrs. Shaw?" Charlotte heard Bob's voice and found herself in the lounge of the Savoy Hotel, not in Ireland or China, or in a distant desert with Ned. "We really should be going."

"Yes, of course," Charlotte replied. "So very kind of you to spare the time . . ."

She ushered them out of the hotel, and they exchanged pleasantries of good-bye, but to Charlotte's surprise, they didn't leave. It was as if Mrs. Lawrence wanted something from Charlotte but was afraid to ask. Or afraid of the answer.

They stood in silence outside the Savoy. A light drizzle of rain began. "In his letters to you," Mrs. Lawrence said eventually, "does he ever write about God?"

I have to say yes, Charlotte thought. I cannot bear to hurt her with the truth.

"Yes," she said. "He writes about God very often, in many questioning ways. I think his faith is not easy for him."

She saw the relief in the mother's eyes. "Faith is not easy for any of us," Mrs. Lawrence whispered, but she had heard what she wanted.

She said good-bye again and walked away. Curiously, Bob didn't follow her immediately. He waited until his mother might be out of earshot, then looked at Charlotte. She thought he was going to say something of consequence and hoped it was about Ned. But she was wrong.

"Thank you," he mumbled. He turned away, almost hurried away, as if embarrassed by what he had said. He caught up with his mother, took her arm and rested it in his own, as a good son should.

Charlotte watched them go, wondering what Bob had meant and why he had seemed embarrassed. He wasn't thanking her for the tea, they'd both done that, several times, inside the hotel. He wasn't thanking her for her company, she was sure.

Was it gratitude, perhaps, that she hadn't pushed too hard about the identity of S. A.?

She wondered why there had to be so many lies between such truthful people. Why had she lied to Mrs. Lawrence about Ned and God? Why did Ned lie to his mother every time he wrote to her, putting on a cheerful face and never revealing the torments of his soul? Why had Charlotte lied to her mother, so often, in so very many ways? What was so frightening about the truth? She went back into the hotel, to the lounge, and ordered a large gin and tonic. She didn't drink alcohol very often (GBS wasn't keen on it), but she needed a cocktail now.

So many secrets, she thought. So many frightening secrets. But what power can they have if they are brought out into the sunlight?

Why had Mrs. Lawrence lied about S. A.? Charlotte was convinced that

Mrs. Lawrence knew who S. A. was and that she was determined that anyone who didn't know wasn't going to find out. Bob knew too, but would never tell. Why was S. A. so alarming to them? What power could S. A. have now? Charlotte was certain that S. A. was dead. Toward the end of *The Seven Pillars*, Ned had given four reasons for his adventures in Arabia. The most compelling of these was his affection for a certain Arab who was now dead, and when that was read in conjunction with the dedication, it made absolute sense to Charlotte.

She sipped her drink and stared out at the evening and the drizzling rain. Not for the first time since she had met Ned, and in fact because of him, she found herself in an uplifted state of emotional pleasure, with a feeling that she was close to something extraordinarily beautiful.

Ned had undertaken the Desert Campaign to free the Arabian people from Turkish domination, but if what was written in the dedication was true, then Ned's real purpose in Arabia beggared the imagination.

Ned had loved S. A., and because of that love had attempted to do something few men had ever dared even to dream. He had taken upon himself a quest of heartbreaking magnificence—foolish and foolhardy, perhaps, even misguided, but grand in scale, pure in its intention and profoundly moving.

Ned had attempted to give unto his beloved S. A. the priceless gift of a people's freedom.

And Charlotte yearned to know what human being on earth could have been so splendid, so inspiring—and so lucky—to have been so loved.

20

"HE IS LOST to the devil," Sarah Lawrence said to her friend. The room was empty, she spoke only to God.

The meeting with Charlotte had disturbed Sarah profoundly, had awoken in her painful memories of things she would rather forget.

Sarah had loved being at the Savoy, but she hated Charlotte for giving her this tiny glimpse of something she could never have. The stylish luxury and Charlotte's absolute ease with it all only served to remind Sarah, too sharply, of her own less fortunate circumstances. Charlotte, married to a godless atheist, had money, position and privilege, and had never done a day's work in her life—not real work, slaving as a skivvy in a freezing house from dawn till dusk for an ungrateful master, as Sarah had done in her youth.

Even in her adult years when she was with Thomas, life had not been easy. There had never been enough money, and bringing up five boys and worrying about their eternal souls was a labor of Hercules, all done under the stigma of adultery and illegitimacy.

She felt a small surge of triumph that Charlotte didn't know the truth, about Ned or S. A., and would never find out from her. Then she was downcast again, because whether Charlotte knew or not didn't matter. The truth of it was all, and the truth was that Ned, like Sarah, was a damned sinner, lost to the devil.

She had hardly spoken on the way back to Norwood, where they were staying in a bleak house with austere missionary friends. Bob had not asked her what was wrong; he knew. Bob always knew. As they waited at the bus stop in the drizzling rain, tears of despair had smarted in Sarah's eyes. Bob didn't say anything, but he hugged his mother and wiped the tears dry with his handkerchief.

"It'll be all right, Mum," he said. Sarah had nodded, but only to make Bob feel better, because she knew he was wrong. It wouldn't be all right. Not ever.

At the house they had shared a light supper with their hosts, then Bob went off to a mission meeting and Sarah retired to her cold room. Rebelling against frugality, she put some pennies in the meter and lit the gas fire. She sat beside the warming fire, feeling wretched, and talked to her most constant companion, God.

She prayed briefly for the soul of the dead man she had called her husband but to whom she was never married, prayed that God had been forgiving of Thomas on his Day of Judgment. She prayed for the souls of William and Frank. She prayed for Bob, who, she was sure, found favor in the Lord; and she prayed for little Arnie, that he might be spared punishment for the sins of his mother and father.

She did not pray for Ned. Ned had always been different. What a man he might become, she had thought when he was younger, and she had shivered in fear of the potential.

She used to pray for Ned when he was young, had prayed hard for him, prayed fervently that she was strong enough to beat the devil from him, and had prayed for herself and for Thomas, for they had visited this affliction on the child. It was they, the parents, who lived in perpetual sin; why could not the child be saved?

Oh, he is a vengeful God, a wrathful God, a cruel God. The Bible speaks true.

Sarah had known since she was a young girl that her body bore a damning fire. From her earliest memory she wanted to be held, yearned to be comforted, dreamed of her father, but no man, when she was young, took her to him and held her and made her safe. When she was older and pieced together the truth of her own illegitimacy, it only increased her loneliness and her conviction that she was an outcast in the world.

She had been taken in by an uncle, James, a minister in Perthshire, a furiously forgiving man, dour and lean, relentlessly in love with the New Testament, constantly, aggressively, turning the other cheek. Sarah was raised in an atmosphere of ungenerous charity.

It was a hard life, especially during the bleak Scottish winters. Aunt Mairie, who had a fundamentalist belief in original sin, was not liberal with warm clothing.

They could sniff out a sinner, actual or potential, this barren couple, and it soon became clear to them that Sarah's soul was in peril, and they almost drowned her in the blood of the Lamb, urging her to Calvary without any real hope of her arrival.

"The devil will out," was Aunt Mairie's constant estimation of her niece, and it terrified Sarah that she was right. But try as hard as she might she could not quell the longings that burned within her, the warming, dangerous fire.

She did mighty battle with her demons, praying to God, Jesus and the Holy Spirit with all her heart that they might keep her from these exquisite temptations, but since she was not sure of a place in Paradise she began to believe that any victory over lust was Pyrrhic, and that the battle was a waste of time.

Sarah loved the kilt. Jamie Farr wore the kilt. Jamie Farr told her he loved her. Jamie Farr, a soldier who could make his kilt flick, flick, flick behind him in a way that drove Sarah mad, wooed her with urgent whispers and probing kisses, and his mouth seemed to melt like warm honey on her own.

Jamie Farr held her in his arms while she cried her fear of the future. Jamie Farr made promises he would never keep. Jamie Farr put his hand to the place that brought her comfort. And Sarah surrendered to ecstasy.

She didn't become pregnant, Jamie had been careful, but she could not disguise her guilt, nor silence Jamie's boastful whispers. The triumphant wrath of her aunt and uncle was awesome. Damned and damaged goods, they sent her away to keep house for a distant cousin on the Isle of Skye, banished to the remotest spot they could imagine.

Ariadne chained to a bleak rock, Sarah could not come to terms with her banishment. She spent her modest allowance on stamps to answer advertisements for help in the newspapers. She had endured her exile for two years when apparent salvation arrived, in the form of a letter in response to one of her own, offering her employment as a governess to a wellborn family, the Chapmans, in Ireland.

Thomas Chapman was the second son of an aristocratic Irish family, and his uncle was a baronet. Thomas had grown up with no expectation of the title, but the baronet died and his unmarried son succeeded him. Thomas was now second in line, after his brother, William. Shortly afterwards, William passed away, also without issue, and suddenly all of Thomas's circumstances changed, the survival of the title rested with him.

He went to England to find a bride and came back with Edith Wharton. If she was a little sharp of tongue and quick of temper, the dowry she would bring with her would palliate any of her minor shortcomings, and in any case, she would be his wife, not his mistress. Thomas thought it was an ideal contract.

He was to be bitterly disappointed. English to the core, Edith never mixed with the Irish, except for necessary discourse with her servants and on fruitless missionary expeditions to the village to bring the heathens from their impiety. She became known as the "Vinegar Queen," a willing prisoner of the mansion with God as her jailer.

Just as Edith could not understand anyone not loving her God, Thomas could not imagine that there were people who did not enjoy sex. The marriage night had confused him utterly; he was confounded by Edith's cries of pain and her refusal to participate in any but the most basic terms of duty.

He learned to find his pleasure elsewhere and settled into a comfortable life of hunting, shooting and fishing. The dark cloud of his existence was that his wife gave him daughters but no son, and this made him the last of his line. He and Edith lived separate lives except on formal occasions, when they visited each other as stiffly as acquaintances.

Sarah Madden was the tempest that wrecked Thomas's tranquil ship. Freed from Skye, Sarah was all sunshine and even melted some of Edith's frost. The girls adored her, Edith was charmed by her; Thomas fell in love with her, and she with him, and it was beyond her ability to control. She knew it was wrong, she knew it was a sin to covet another woman's husband, but the knowledge was meaningless.

Yet both fought their need. The possible spiritual consequences, if not the material ones, of their mutual passion tormented them. Abstinence only made the desire greater, and after a year of torment, on a tranquil summer evening, they both gave in and were lost to the world they had known.

Sarah gave notice to Edith, claiming illness of a relative in Scotland, said a fond farewell to the girls, a curt one to the master, took the train to Dublin, to some rooms rented by Thomas as their love nest.

Thomas had no immediate intention of permanent infidelity, but he made no allowance for divine disposition. Edith discovered the arrangement. Her faith demanded that she forgive, but her price was formidable. If Thomas left Sarah, she would allow the marriage to continue in name only. Thomas would live in his own apartments and have no access to his daughters. He would sign a document admitting his infidelity, and if there was any further philandering, Edith would leave him, and Ireland, but she would never divorce him.

The cost of leaving Edith was even higher.

To leave Edith and live with Sarah would make Thomas a permanent outcast from society. To his peers, he would be a dead man, and would have died dishonorably. He could never marry Sarah because Edith would never divorce him. He would be financially impoverished. After making provision for Edith and his daughters, he would be left with the annual income of a prosperous tradesman, which was adequate for the tradesman, but ludicrous for a gentleman. On his death his estate would go to Edith if she outlived him, and if not, to his daughters.

Love won. Love for Sarah, and astonishing love for the baby son she bore him. The first time Thomas held Bob in his arms, the prospect of spending the rest of his days with a woman he had come to despise, and never again to see the woman and the son he adored, was the difference between winter and summer to him.

He made a proper settlement on Edith and his daughters, gave himself a modest annual income and set off for a new, uncertain life.

They left Ireland, settled in Wales, living as man and wife, and took the name Lawrence. They seldom went out or encouraged friendships.

Another son, named Thomas Edward, was born to them, a kicking, yelling boy, boisterous and constantly crying, as if he knew what the world had in store for him. Restless with guilt, they moved to Scotland, birthplace of a third son, William, and then to the Isle of Man, before settling in France.

Ned, in particular, flourished there, and spent happy days exploring the medieval castle or pretending to be a pirate who used the bay as home port. But Sarah was unhappy in France, although they called their fourth son Frank, so they moved again, back to England, to a house in the New Forest, and pretended it was home.

Sarah's dislike of the French had a simple cause, she thought them to be immoral. To Sarah, it seemed the French used the confessional as an outrageous, hypocritical safety valve that let them enjoy the pleasures of the flesh during the week and be forgiven their sins on Sunday. They seemed to have very little guilt, especially about carnal matters, and guilt, especially about carnal matters, lay on Sarah like a shroud.

Sarah's best hope for her sons was that they, like Ruth, would go where she went and live where she lived, that she might protect them and try to shepherd them to the Kingdom. When Sarah realized how deeply Ned carried the stain of her multiple sins, she despaired of the Lord.

Sarah was convinced that Ned dwelt in the city of Sodom, or was a frequent visitor there, lost to the flesh and to the devil. He had been found with another boy at school, committing an abomination. It all came to the surface one dreadful night when Sarah, hoping to shock the boy to a realization of his imperiled soul, told him the truth about her relationship with Thomas and their sons' illegitimate state.

The resulting argument was vile and violent, but desperate circumstances demanded desperate actions, and in any case, her sons had to know the truth sooner or later. Still the devil confounded her. Ned ran away from home, and it was only in the days of his absence that Sarah understood that her final assault on Ned had been futile. Instead of returning to righteousness, he ran to the seductive world. Gone from her protection he could never be saved, and Sarah was never sure which pain was greater, the loss of his physical presence or her understanding of the scale of her failure.

Sarah thought she might not live, the mother's pain was too intense. She could not bear to think of Ned lost and lonely, cold and hungry, or harmed. She came to understand that she loved him living, just as a deformed puppy can be the darling of the litter. She prayed to God that He bring Ned back to her and swore that she would love and comfort him in this life, and let Ned concern himself with the next.

But the days of Ned's absence became weeks, and hope for him faded from Sarah. He must be dead, and Sarah began to doubt even God. How could He be so cruel?

Almost as soon as she denied Him, God relented. On a blessed day, a telegram arrived from Ned. He was in the army and deeply unhappy. The effect on Thomas was immaculate. For the first time in months, he put his arms around Sarah and was affectionate with her, but firm.

"I will bring him home," he said. "And you will be kind to him."

Sarah assented. She was too tired to fight anymore, and God, by answering her prayers and bringing Ned back, had revealed His presence to her and had restored her faith in Him.

The homecoming was jubilant, and even the conditions that Ned put upon his return were accepted with relief by Sarah. The responsibility for Ned's soul was no longer hers. When he came home, Sarah saw a man, not a boy. His experiences had changed him, made him more sure of himself, and Sarah felt old before him, and, for the first time in her life, weaker than he. She turned to God and found comfort.

The years that followed were among the sweetest of her life. The truth of her relationship with Thomas was known to her sons, and although the matter was never discussed, she no longer felt the need to lie and pretend to them. Thomas, in his profound gentleness, forgot or forgave whatever bitterness he had felt and loved her sweetly.

Ned, lost to sin, flowered as man, and Sarah tried hard to show him love, despite his perdition. He studied hard and won a scholarship to Jesus College where his mind exploded like a garden in a riotous spring. His professor, D. G. Hogarth, became his mentor and led Ned in provocative, antique directions. Ned's friends were a predictable lot, worldliness and vice hung about them, but they behaved well in front of Sarah and were kind to her. Each summer, Ned went away on bicycling tours to idolatrous France and then to infidel Arabia. This was especially hard for Sarah, because she still worried about his soul, but Ned was so exuberant and his relish of life so contagious that Sarah found herself enjoying her lost son.

Nor did he seem ignorant of God. His letters were full of humbling glories, the wonder of Chartres Cathedral, or Crusader castles. On his return from these adventures, he was enchanting, nut brown and rock hard, eyes shimmering, and he would tell them tales that left his brothers open mouthed and his father chuckling. But he never told Sarah that he had missed her or that he loved her. She always had to ask.

Her other sons were beyond reproach. Bob was determined on a missionary life, and William and Frank were fearful of the Lord. Arnold was gorgeous, molded somewhere between Bob and Ned, but without the danger she had always sensed from her second born. Her most stringent regret was that none of her sons had yet found a suitable bride. Sarah became acutely conscious of her passing years and was increasingly lonely. She yearned for grandchildren.

It never occurred to her that she had raised her sons to be wary of women. Only William had ease in their company. He was especially fond of Janet Laurie, whom Sarah had thought might marry Bob. Sarah, getting lonelier with each passing day, encouraged her relationship with William.

So she was thrilled when Janet, sipping tea one pleasant afternoon, grinned saucily and told Sarah she had had an offer of marriage.

"You and William make a splendid couple," Sarah said.

"It wasn't from William," Janet said, enjoying the moment. "It was from Ned."

Sarah was so shocked she almost dropped her teacup. Truly, Ned was strange, she thought. It was so like him, so utterly unpredictable, so theatrical—and so very silly. "What did you tell him?"

"I laughed!" Janet was laughing now. "Can you imagine me with Ned? I mean, I like him a lot, but he's so . . . so . . . queer."

Sarah wished that Janet had used a different word.

William and Janet never married, Sarah was not sure why. They always seemed on the verge of union but never quite got there. Then the war came and ended the possibility altogether. William was killed in the war, and Frank. It was then that Sarah closed the door to her house and her heart, and for some years it appeared she would never mix in the world again. It was Arnie who brought Sarah back to life, by marrying a lovely bride and presenting Sarah with grandchildren.

Bob never married. Bob remained pure and loyal and, all his life, dedicated to his mother's welfare. Ned never married, and Sarah knew why. Despite her occasional doubts, her suppositions and worst fears were exact. She found out for sure when Ned came home for a holiday from Syria, where he was supervising an archeological dig, and brought with him two Arab friends, an older man and a younger one.

She was grateful that even Ned had been sensitive enough to bring the older man as chaperone, because she understood at a glance Ned's feelings for the younger, whose name was Selim Ahmed, but who was called Dahoum. Sarah knew the look of love. She had seen it, years ago, in Thomas's eyes. She saw it now in Ned's, every time he looked at Dahoum. To a small extent, Sarah was grateful that Ned had found some sort of love. Although the idea of that love was repugnant to her, she did not want him to be lonely.

Besides, Ned was damned already, like herself, and beyond her powers of redemption. She dedicated herself to the spiritual welfare of her other sons, those who survived, and when Thomas was dead she went among the heathens in China. There, like an old pirate who has the treasure map but is too frail to reach the island, she spent the rest of her days seeking converts to her cause, offering to those small few who would listen the precise coordinates of heaven.

NWFP

———— ⁓⁓⁓ ————

1928

21

I have fallen off the edge of the world and landed on the roof of the world.

Sometimes I think I am in Carchemish again, and I want to stay here for the rest of my life. Or at least until I go back to England.

A tiny hill at the end of the world, surrounded by nothing. An old Waziri fort at the top of the hill, and here we are, the smallest air force station in India. A thick-walled keep with tiny arrow windows, in which we mess and sleep, a central courtyard and enclosing walls with sentry towers, all built from local stone. A tiny, stony strip just big enough for the buses to land and take off, and all surrounded by barbed wire, and searchlit at night, to keep out . . .

Alexander's armies?

We look out from our mountaintop to the west, to Afghanistan, ten miles away. To the north and south are mountains. To the east, a pass among the hills and then, in the distance, the massive Himalayas. On clear days—and every day is clear—we can see forever, and there is nothing but the empty, pristine, far-off mountains and clean, fresh air.

There is nothing else, not even the nearby tiny town of Miranshah, which we cannot see. It is tucked away around some corners, down a rocky path that winds among the hills, an invisible town—to us, nonexistent. Yet every morning, mysteriously, out of nowhere, small groups of Waziris straggle to us from that unseen town, to seek what small employment we can give, to wash and clean for us, blanco our belts and webbing, polish our brasses, and, when special visitors come, sweep our dusty courtyard and paint the marking stones of our pathways in whitewash. They bring the few supplies we need, fresh vegetables and fruit, milk and, sometimes, newly slaughtered meat. Beef, they insist, but I remember camel steak.

Of a full (British) complement of twenty-six, we are only a permanent five in number, we Miranshah Irregulars. The CO, Brodie, is the best (and the kindest) I have ever encountered. Higgins, the Stores Corporal, barters with the locals fluently in the local tongue and abuses them in Cheapside argot, which they think funny compliments, for their prices. Baxter, a corporal, runs the place with meticulous efficiency in the absence of an adjutant. There is an armorer, Mitchell, whom we seldom see, lost daily to us in his store of guns, checking, cataloging, polishing, cleaning, knowing every weapon intimately, loving each as any devout librarian might love his shelves of books. And there is a clerk.

Me.

There is a company of Indian soldiers, who are our friends and fellow out-casts. They do the work that keeps us all in comfort; they parade in brilliant shiny boots and hard starched uniforms. They have their own barracks, and eat their own food, and they are British to the core, and adore an English king. By day they are our guardians, by night our sentries on the walls, guns ready, searchlights blazing, to protect us from . . .

Genghis Khan?

Or occasional small caravans of Afghan merchants, for we are situated on the antique silk route. We see them coming when they are miles away, appearing on the hilly horizon and disappearing behind another hill. Then closer again, and gone again, until they come upon us, greet us cheerfully, camp outside our fort, make tea and pretend to show their wares. Sometimes they have pretty things, some silver rupees from Victoria's reign, or cloths bright with tiny mir-rors stitched to them, or sandalwood and cedarwood and sweet-smelling myrrh. But they never show their real treasure—the guns hidden in their rolled-up car-pets, or the hypnotizing poppy juice—for these are contraband and will fetch extravagant prices in the marketplaces on the plains below.

We look ridiculous, my fellows and I, in our puttees and long shorts, our too-crisp shirts—pounded to submission on river stones and then overly starched to bring them to order—and our forage caps and bright, gleaming flashes of brass and, in the winter, greatcoats. We parade once a week, before the flag, with a gramophone playing the national anthem, and we stand at attention and salute the red, white and blue. We are Albion, madly transported to a deranged land-scape. Outside is the alien land.

None of us is high, bright youth. I am not the man I was. Mitchell wears pebble glasses, Higgins (who is trying to grow roses in a scrawny, struggling garden) is getting bald and Baxter is tubbier than he should be.

I am safe. There is no danger among them—no punisher, no John Bruce, not even a Slaney.

(Oh, I was cruel to Slaney. But I didn't take him where he might not want to go, so maybe I was kind.)

To give us purpose and bring us up to strength, a flight comes in each two months (some aircraft and a score of airmen), in rotation from the five neighboring distant squadrons. We make the men welcome and cherish their aircraft, and we become acquaintances, but they are visitors to our lonely country, and think us mad, gone doolally in our isolation, and avoid us as much as they are able. They spend their time here longing to be back in Peshawar or Quetta or Mardan, comparative civilization to them (although they curse those towns as white men's graveyards when they are there) after this windy, isolate outpost. We think of this fort, this hill, this land, as ours and run it so, despite the bimonthly change of commanding officer, who has rank and status over us but does not know our routine and leaves us to our own devices.

Sometimes, and often at night, small groups of Pathans find us, or we hear them, or their guns. They are the warriors of these mountain passes, protecting their borderless territories as they have done for centuries, in age-old ways until we came and brought them guns.

These are not the stick people of Karachi. These are sturdy desert men, first cousins to my beloved Arabs, proud and strong, careless of everything but their honor, superb horsemen, brave warriors, crack shots and, sometimes, unbearably handsome. They love to visit us, they sit for hours outside our perimeter, making tea, flocking round the planes when they have landed and begging to be taken to the sky.

Sometimes we do take one up, if a plane is empty and the pilot generous. And then he is a king unto his brothers.

They make my heart ache for another time and place, and can cause sharp tears to sting my eyes—and my heart to sing that such creatures still exist.

They are the only danger, for sometimes one of them will smile at me and almost pierce the impregnable defenses I have built around my heart and make me think, if only for a glittering moment, that I am in Carchemish again and I have found Dahoum.

I write of them each day, not as themselves, but as other men from another time. They are my Telemachus and my Antiphos, my Laertes and Leodes, my Iphitus and my Diomedes. Those young men of ancient Greece might have been these Pathans, and some of these young gods might be Greek, for Alexander's army passed nearby, and remnants of them I sometimes see now, dark skinned with startling eyes, the blue of Macedon.

And I?

I am Odysseus, trapped on Circe's island, careless of the passing time, oblivious to the future, forgetting to wonder when I might find home.

The old Greek letters fall to my translation, the pages of the Odyssey *pile up* on my desk, a hillock now, soon a tiny mountain, filling me with a sense of achievement and no fear of potential failure. Who will read my Odyssey, anyway? Some few scholars, perhaps, and those who do will know what I am trying to achieve. My only loyalty is to them and to some long-dead poets who called themselves Homer. And to myself, of course. Who else would care?

Perhaps we have gone doolally, lost our marbles. Certainly, we are eccentric. Each of us is a world unto himself, lost in his own mind, free to dream whatever he will. We do not talk to each other, except to pass the time of day. Sometimes, at night, just for companionship, we make speeches at one another, but none is really interested in the other's ramblings. It is simply that each man understands the other's occasional need to talk, and we bear it as an interruption to our solitude.

Do we serve any purpose? None. We are the tiniest, loneliest, lowliest outpost of the Empire, but because we are only a small country away from the Russian masses, the Bolshevik bear, we are sometimes made to feel important. Sometimes, though not very often (once in the months I've been here), some bigwig will fly in from Delhi or Karachi or Bombay, to show the flag and mutter, "What a godforsaken dump," get drunk that night with that night's temporary squadron leader, and fly off to comparative civilization in the first light of dawn. If the Russian hordes burst across Afghanistan and pounded at the gates of India, our armies would concentrate in Peshawar and Khyber and Karachi. We would be allowed to fall without a moment's pause on Whitehall's part, sacrificed to the greater cause, having been only a warning of war.

We are here only because we can be here, to show the flag. Nothing else matters.

I live in careless isolation here, surrounded by a thousand miles of nowhere.
In Circe's sweet embrace.

22

"AFGHANISTAN," THE PILOT SHOUTED above the drone of the engine. Of his two passengers, one, a relieving CO, was asleep, and only the other, an engineer, heard him.

That engineer, Slaney, was staring out of the window, his face pressed to the glass. He had seen Afghanistan from the air before, but never closer than this, and was entranced, though he was only looking at the edges of it from half a mile high in a flimsy wood-and-canvas biplane. He had reached the end of the British Empire, and beyond was an unknown country, and beyond that, Bolshevik Russia. To Slaney, it was like seeing the pyramids for the first time. He had a thrilling sense that he was close to something utterly fascinating and completely alien, some wild, majestic kingdom where the rules were different, where exciting things might happen.

He had known since he first fell in love with the idea of flying that such exotic vistas would be available to him if only he could get into the sky, and although he was an engineer, not a pilot, this was enough. He was flying. He was everything he had ever wanted to be.

He could hardly remember how much he had hated Karachi, and looked upon his time there with a certain affection. Everyone who was lucky enough to be based anywhere in the North West Frontier Province, the NWFP, shared the feeling and looked upon Karachi as a purgatory that had to be endured before the treasures of heaven could be revealed to them. They talked about Karachi in the mess, laughed about it, heaped derision on it, but fondly, because after Karachi there was this.

Slaney had heard stories of other magic places but had no real desire to visit them because he did not believe they could match what he had found. He heard of Jaisalmer, the fort city built on a hilltop in the desert of Rajasthan, the home of Aladdin, a city from the Arabian nights, a city such as Baghdad must once have been, forgotten and perfect in its sandy isolation. He heard of the Hunza hill towns, high up in the mountains, the gateways to the Himalayas, peaceful villages close to the infinity of God. He heard of the mountain kingdom of Tibet, locked away from the rest of the world, forgotten by time, existing only for the contemplation of the infinite.

But none of these mystic places were as enticing to him as Peshawar, where he was now stationed, the frontier post of the Khyber Pass, the track that wended through forbidding mountains to the forbidden country, Afghanistan. Peshawar was wild and lawless, every visit to the marketplace was a journey back in time, to a world of brigands and smugglers. Any man of consequence wore astonishing and unnerving decorations, incomplete, as a man, without at least two rifles and several bandoliers of ammunition. Shops in the marketplace sold every weapon available in the world, while the shop next to it sold fruit, vegetables and bunches of Indian hemp, and next to that might be a dark café, with darker back rooms where drugs darker and deadlier than hemp might be enjoyed, while on the other side of the street the bakery sold sweet-smelling bread. At any moment, a dozen men on horseback might come galloping through the market square, guns blazing, in celebration of some tribal event, a marriage, the birth of a son, or a small war won.

The RAF station on the edge of Peshawar was a secure haven, and between the old city and the base was a hotel that thought itself grand and was the best in town. On Saturday nights the airmen would go there for dinner and a dance, and mix with the local dignitaries. Slaney was surprised that so many locals could afford the hotel. He doubted they had made their money from agriculture and speculated that their wealth must come from drugs or gun smuggling. So it was a constant amusement to Slaney that as he walked in through the marbled foyer there was a sign demanding that all weapons be checked with security, and a couple of heavily armed guards frisked every customer before they were allowed inside.

He had hated the whiningly aggressive people of Karachi, but the men here were different. These were sturdy mountain men of magnificent physiques and exuberant personalities. Among them, Slaney felt no fear for his own safety. He would wander the back streets of the old market town for hours, reveling in its sense of living antiquity. He loved its narrow lanes with the high, wooden, many-shuttered houses. He thrilled to the occasional glimpse of veiled women peeping through those shutters and, on high holidays, the little groups of those women, brilliantly dressed but still secretively veiled, making their way daintily along the muddy streets to some festivity. It fascinated him that the clothes of the men were of a design a thousand years old, brilliantly embroidered jackets and cloaks and baggy pants. Slaney was adept at negotiating the crowded thoroughfares, engulfed by the East, but with some sense of chaotic order, unlike the pure anarchy of Karachi traffic. He didn't mind the crush of people, or the fast-trotting, overburdened donkeys, or the placid, pacing camels, and he laughed when he saw an occasional motorcar slowed to a halt in that menagerie, the driver yelling abuse at the world because the transportation of his important passenger was being delayed.

It wasn't England, and he didn't want to live here for the rest of his life, and he found some things simply silly, however exotic. He hated to see the poor women laboring as beasts of burden, for he had an old-fashioned sense of the place of women and thought these abused. He heard rumors that women guilty of adultery were stoned to death in public, and he prayed with all his heart that he might never see such an execution. He had no sympathy with adultery, but he did not believe that women should be treated in such a way and wondered what punishment befell the man who had caused her fall. He had been present once in the market square when a thief had his hands cut off for stealing. It had made him sick to his stomach, he thought it barbaric, but as he walked away he knew he had seen something rare, and more, a piece of something that fitted into a pattern of life, something he would never see in Sunderland.

I'm right in the thick of things here, he thought.

Sometimes they would fly from Peshawar to a hill town or fort, high up in the mountains, or to a plateau of desert. The planes were tiny and carried cargo or important local passengers, and only the bravest, or most foolhardy, pilots would fly without an engineer. They flew in all weathers and landed on all sorts of ground, and many an engine had to be fixed by the engineers somewhere out in the middle of nowhere. They all carried guns, because it was not unknown for a band of rebel tribesmen to hold up or hijack a downed aircraft.

Slaney had a sense he was living on the edge of fabulous and enticing danger; his young blood tingled, and he was filled with a constant sense of expectation. He understood that if ever he was to have adventure in his life, it was now, and he believed that the adventure had begun. It wasn't around the corner, just over the hill, on the other side of the mountains. It was closer. It was what he did every day.

"Miranshah!" the pilot yelled again, and Slaney leaned across the small fuselage and looked out of the starboard window. They were coming down, banking sharply, and at first all Slaney could see was the hills surrounding the base. Then he saw the landing strip, a couple of Bristols parked to the side of the field, and tucked among the hills, the fort and its outbuildings. It was to be his temporary home for two months, as relieving engineer, and Ned, he knew, was at Miranshah.

Slaney could not guess what his reaction to seeing Ned again would be. He remembered the man and their friendship with affection, but he still felt a sense of betrayal at the manner of Ned's abrupt departure from Karachi. Time and separation had lessened the hurt, and Slaney began to feel that he was being uncharitable, that Ned could never be judged by conventional standards. Still, he was wary.

The pilot laughed. "Cricket match!" he yelled. He circled the strip at a hundred feet, and Slaney could see that two teams of men, one white, one dark, were using the landing strip as a cricket field. The scorekeeper waved at the plane.

"Damn disgraceful," muttered the relieving CO, Squadron Leader Smythe-Clarke, who had awakened.

"We should let them finish the over," the pilot said. Smythe-Clarke was about to protest, but the plane was already banking, and a countercommand would be a waste of time.

The pilot circled again while the over was played out, each man on the plane straining to see the game. A white spin bowler bowled a curly one that the batsman couldn't shield and the makeshift wickets went flying. There were cheers and a desultory move to clear the strip, and the plane came in to land. The cricketers moved casually to the side and waved them welcome. The landing was rocky but safe, they taxied to the fort and were guided to park by a batsman wearing flannels that had once been white. Once the engine was shut down, the cricketers gathered round to greet the newcomers.

"Who is in charge here?" the squadron leader demanded as he jumped down from the plane.

"I am, old chap. Brodie," the spin bowler called cheerily, moving up to greet his replacement. Brodie was going on leave for six weeks. "Good flight?"

"Smythe-Clarke, 4th Squadron, Peshawar," the replacement introduced himself, shaking hands. "Bit of a queer thing, cricket on the strip. We couldn't come in." It was as close as he would come to a reprimand, because Brodie had the rank.

"Not a lot else to do," Brodie parried. "First time here? You'll soon get used to the hang of things. Got another bus coming in?"

"Engine trouble, they'll be here before nightfall," Smythe-Clarke explained.

"Oh, bad show, we'll have to stay another night, then," Brodie said blithely. Smythe-Clarke was puzzled. He would have thought the airmen would be anxious to get back to their home base, Quetta, however much they might disparage it when they were there.

The two officers wandered off to the officers' mess, oblivious to the rest of the world, chatting about cricket, the news of home and the amenities of Miranshah.

Among the other airmen, the usual camaraderie prevailed. Pilots greeted pilots and talked about buses and the flight. Engineers talked with engineers, and the native soldiers unloaded the plane. Slaney looked around at what was to be his base for the next two months.

Well, it could be worse, he thought, loving it already. Here, for the first time on the ground, he could still see Afghanistan, only ten miles away.

And he heard an old familiar voice.

"Hello, old thing, where did you spring from?"

Slaney turned in the direction of the voice and recognized Ned immediately, even though it was a different Ned from the one who had left Karachi. That Ned had been a dead man, this Ned was alive, vibrant with energy, eyes sparkling with sapphire luster. His hair was golden from the sun, his skin a healthy bronze. He was dressed in an ill-fitting white shirt, regulation khaki shorts and boots.

"Best I could do for cricket," Ned laughed, with no sense of apology. "We've no QM here, and even if we did, I doubt he'd have ducks."

Slaney was astonished at the warmth of the feelings that engulfed him. This was Ned as Slaney had always wanted him to be, and the hurt of Karachi was, for now at least, forgiven, if not forgotten. They shook hands and stood grinning at each other.

"You don't play cricket," Slaney said.

"No, but they needed the numbers," Ned said, laughing. "So they made me eleventh man, and we declared at the first innings. I never got to hold a bat, can't catch a ball for the life of me and snuck away to do some writing. They didn't miss me. They never do."

They were still holding hands. Slaney was surprised, because he knew that Ned tried to avoid physical contact with anyone.

"You're looking well," Ned said.

"All this country air, it's doing me good," Slaney said. Slightly to his relief, Ned released his hand.

"Close to heaven here," Ned agreed. "Come on, I'll show you your digs. You're in with us. It's quite comfortable, but Mitchell snores rather badly. Just kick him, and he shuts up. The fellows will bring your kit."

He glanced at Slaney's solar topee, the pith helmet that all the airmen were supposed to wear as protection against the sun. "You won't need that here."

"Regulations," Slaney said.

"Not here," Ned told him. Slaney looked around. None of the Miranshah airmen was wearing a pith helmet, only the new arrivals, and they looked out of place. Slaney took his off and tucked it under his arm.

Ned led the way toward the fort, talking as if he hadn't spoken to a living soul for a year. He pointed out the sights. There weren't many, just the empty, endless land, but Ned seemed to know every dale and mountaintop and had a name and a story for each. He introduced Slaney to the Miranshah Irregulars, as he called them. Baxter was harried by the demands of having two squadron leaders on the base at the same time. Higgins was vainly pruning roses, and Mitchell, on a rare outing from his armory, was headed, as always when he left his beloved guns, to the kitchen.

"He's a Sussex man, so he loves suet puddings," Ned explained. "Bacon pudding, golden pudding, jam roly-poly. Cannonballs, for the most part. He sent for recipes from his ma in Bognor, but the local cook can't get the hang of it, and suet's in short supply. We don't get much beef."

He led the way into his own tiny, cluttered office. "And this is me," Ned said. "Keeping the paperwork in order and sending and receiving signals. It's a cushy number."

"Better than Karachi," Slaney said.

"A thousand times," Ned agreed. "What are you doing here?"

"I got fed up with that dump," Slaney said, "same as you. So I applied for a posting and got Peshawar."

"You'll be a regular visitor then," Ned murmured.

"Hope so," Slaney said. "Doing some writing, I see?" He nodded at the pile of paper on Ned's desk.

"Yes," Ned agreed, but didn't elaborate. He led Slaney outside. "You'd best get to the shower block early," he explained. "It's always busy on changeover days, and we don't have a lot of hot water." He laughed. "We're desert men here, a layer of dirt helps keep us warm."

Ned took Slaney to the shower block and left him to his ablutions. He had to make sure that everything was in order for the departing flight, but the second Bristol from Peshawar didn't arrive until sunset, which was too late for the Quetta planes and crews to leave, so Miranshah was crowded that night, and they had a party.

Or rather, they had four parties, which melded into one. The officers celebrated in their mess, the white NCOs and erks in theirs and the native NCOs and erks in theirs. And outside the perimeter, lit by searchlights and watched by a few disgruntled sentries (grumbling because they were missing the celebrations), a hundred or so of the local tribesmen had gathered, for they could hear the revelry. They lit their own fires and roasted their own meat, and sang and danced their own dances.

At any base of decent size, the NCOs would have had a mess separate from the erks, but Miranshah was too small for such segregation, so they all shared the same large room and pretended to conformity, the NCOs at one end, the erks at the other. It was a spacious room, with comfortable furniture—sofas and chairs—and a small library. Smythe-Clarke had expressed surprise when he had been shown it, on his earlier tour of inspection.

"Don't they smash it up?" he had wondered aloud, and Ned, who was there because he was the librarian, took up the erks' cause.

"Why should we, sir? To those of us who live here it is home, and we treat it as we would our own homes."

Smythe-Clarke looked at Ned steadily, wondering if he had grounds to put him on a charge for insolence, but Brodie pulled him away, to show him the rest of the fort.

"Jolly interesting chap, that," Brodie said to Smythe-Clarke, and told him Ned's true identity. Smythe-Clarke, who had not been in India long, was astonished.

"To all intents and purposes, he runs the place," Brodie continued. "At any rate, it's all in tip-top order, and the men adore him."

"But he's an A/C 2!" Smythe-Clarke spluttered.

"Yes, now, but he was a colonel once, remember. And he's done a jolly lot of stuff. For most of the men, us and the natives, he's a bit of an education." Brodie chuckled. "A sort of reference library."

Smythe-Clarke wondered if he hadn't, like Alice, stepped through some invisible looking glass into a topsy-turvy world. He looked around and saw that none of the men was wearing a pith helmet, except himself. That was it, then. They all had a touch of the sun.

"Why is no one wearing a pith helmet?" he asked.

"That's Lawrence again," Brodie explained. "Sorry, Shaw." He was leading the way toward the edge of the encampment. They passed by a wretched garden plot of tired, struggling roses, and Smythe-Clarke glared at it impatiently. The man responsible for that garden knew very little about roses. He, Smythe-Clarke, would have to take charge. Damned erks couldn't even be left to run a garden properly.

"He says they never wore them in the desert, and he can't find any medical value to them." Brodie was still rabbiting on about pith helmets. It was a waste of time; pith helmets were required by regulations, and Smythe-Clarke would see that the regulations were enforced. He couldn't do anything until Brodie left, but after that, pith helmets would be the order of the day. "The sun doesn't get strong enough here, except in the middle of the day, in summer, and then sensible chappies don't go out. Or wear their forage caps. In a way, it's a relief. Damned uncomfortable things, pith helmets. Sweaty."

He stopped and looked at the distant mountains. "Beautiful, isn't it?"

Smythe-Clarke had to agree, the landscape was very beautiful. It was harsh and remote and arid, but the sun was well past its zenith and was casting purple shadows on the mountains. Somewhere behind him he could hear the men's voices, and the odd one, Shaw, giving a gentle order that was more like a sensible suggestion. Obviously, the station was running efficiently, and Smythe-Clarke felt no urgent need to investigate. He was in wonderland, he decided. An enchanted dominion, where erks were kings.

"You get used to it, you know," Brodie said, as if reading his thoughts. "Shaw's a jolly good chap, and the others are salt of the earth. You won't have much to do."

He saw in the distance unseeable things, and his voice was soft. "Gives a chap a chance to think about things."

For just a moment, Smythe-Clarke wondered if Brodie had been sampling the local drugs and if some had been put into his own tea. He felt odd, a stranger, although not out of place. He was a good officer, enjoyed his authority, took his duties seriously and loved the structured ranking of the service, the absolute and, in his mind, rigid and proper chain of command. But he felt the stress of being responsible for so many men, not to mention the aircraft, and even though he could always refer a problem to a higher authority, he tried, as far as possible, to solve all those problems himself. Tried much too hard. Worried far too much. He was still a young man, but at his last medical he had been told that he might have an incipient ulcer and that his blood pressure was too high.

Now, standing beside Brodie, looking at a fabulous vista, miles from anywhere, a seductive peace visited his soul. The idea of spending two months as CO of an irrelevant station that was effectively run by an A/C 2 who had once been a colonel and one of England's greatest heroes was very attractive. A great weight lifted from his shoulders, and he breathed in deeply.

He took off his pith helmet. "Wonderful air," he said.

"The best," Brodie agreed.

Smythe-Clarke couldn't think of anything else to say, because anything he said would be irrelevant in this idyllic setting. There was a vastness, a peacefulness about the empty country that made him think of roses. And of heaven. And even God.

They stood side by side in silence, each man lost in some sweet, private wilderness, and out of the silence Smythe-Clarke heard a perfect sound. Somewhere, distantly, an unseen muezzin was calling the faithful to prayer.

Neither man moved. Somewhere, Smythe-Clarke knew, desert men were answering the call to the desert God, and the world seemed to make sense. He thought, just for a moment, that if he stayed here long enough, in this topsy-turvy paradise, he might find answers to things that had been puzzling him for many years.

The prayer of the muezzin faded to nothing, and then there was only silence. A limitless, infinite silence.

There was the sound of laughter from the fort.

"Well," Brodie said. "Feeling peckish?"

Smythe-Clarke was feeling decidedly peckish, and that was not the least of his surprises that day. Ever since his last medical he hadn't been eating well at all, too worried about his health to be worried about his appetite. He ate to live. But now he felt an old and once familiar feeling. It was like greeting a friend he hadn't seen for years. He was peckish. More than peckish. He was damned hungry.

The dinner suited his taste exactly, as if someone had written to his mother to find out all his favorite things. A splendid mulligatawny soup, not too spicy, just enough pepper to make him sweat a little, a silly fish course of canned sardines on toast, which Smythe-Clarke loved, and then enormous servings of corned beef and mustard sauce, with boiled potatoes, carrots and cabbage. The topper was the pudding, a jam roly-poly (for once Mitchell and the harried Indian cook had got it right), with lashings of thick, sweet custard, and hardly any lumps.

"It's just like being back at school," he chortled to Brodie as he helped himself to another thick slab of the suet pudding. His school days had been the happiest days of his life.

The cheese was adequate and the port tolerable, better than he had expected so far away from any decent wine merchant. He allowed himself to get more than a little tiddly and decided that if this was what happened when erks were put in charge, then a lot more erks should be put in charge of things. He was to be CO of an excellent ship that was running the way he wanted it to be run without any effort on his part.

Things were just as cheerful in the NCO and other-ranks mess. The few NCOs sat at one end of a long table and the fewer erks at the other, to maintain the charade they had separate messes, but the imaginary wall between them was irrelevant and had long been breached. They were one big and very happy family, the Miranshah Irregulars the expansive hosts, and the visiting airmen their grateful and responsive guests. The menu was the same as the officers' (minus the sardines), and there was a plentiful supply of beer, local stuff, but good.

Slaney, sitting beside Ned, was on his third bottle of beer and was feeling no pain. He thought that Ned looked thoroughly at home, sitting at the head of the table, conducting the conversations, as if he were giving a dinner for his la-di-da friends at some smart house in Knightsbridge. Yet none of the men felt out of place; Ned never confounded them with brilliance or belittled them if he corrected false knowledge. He made sure each man was included in the general talk, and ensured that no one voice dominated the table. Higgins was allowed five minutes on the difficulty of raising roses in this arid climate, Baxter was given as long on his topic—he was an acknowledged expert on the local carpets—and Ned led the praise of Mitchell's jam roly-poly. Every other man at the table was encouraged to discuss his hobbies or vent his irritations with the service, but only mildly, and even Slaney had given a small speech on the beauty of the Lake District in England, which made everyone dream of home. Jokes were enjoyed, the bawdier the better, and tales were told of life at Miranshah, and how only airmen, of any rank, could appreciate its wonders. Civilians, no matter how well born, couldn't understand it, and soldiers, the scum of the earth to airmen, were oblivious to its civilization.

"The army—crikey, they're a wonder," Baxter told them. "We had four of 'em 'ere once, remember Ned, the army signalers?"

Ned and the other Irregulars nodded and laughed at the memory.

"Pigs, they are," Baxter explained, "can't hold their drink. They was 'ere to practice signaling from the air, and they was a bloody disgrace. Got roaring, fighting drunk, right 'ere, in this very room, spewing their guts up everywhere."

"'Ere, the barracks, everywhere," Higgins confirmed. "Didn't even try and make it to the lav."

"Wild beasts at Ephesus," murmured Ned.

"'E's got such a way with words," Higgins told the others. "I could listen to 'im speak for 'ours."

"Well, Ned fixed their goose good and proper, didn't you, Ned?" Baxter looked at Ned, who laughed. "'Ad a word with the CO, Smethan, it was then, wasn't it?"

Ned nodded. "Thankfully, he had a sense of humor." He was staring at Slaney in a way that unnerved the young engineer. His eyes seemed to ask a question to which Slaney did not know the answer, or did not want to guess what the answer might be. He looked away.

Well, well, thought Ned, he wants adventure. I was cruel to him, but now I will be kind. I will show him what I was, what I can be.

Baxter was still telling the tale of the soldiers. "Took each one up, the CO did, half an hour each he give 'em, and he rolled the bus all over the place. Bankin' left and right, nonstop for 'alf an 'our, even give 'em a victory roll at the end of the flight."

"Green as clover when they came down," Higgins agreed. "Spewed their guts up everywhere. We 'ad to 'ose the machines down after, but it was worth it, weren't it, Ned?"

The sense of well-being was contagious among them. They were airmen, an elite. They understood the joke against the uncouth army.

More beer arrived, and they toasted the king, and then it occurred to Slaney that the only man who had not talked about himself was Ned. Queer bastard, he thought affectionately, glad that the two of them were friends, no matter how curious that friendship was.

He remembered how it had begun, in the empty barracks in Karachi when they had talked for the first time, and Slaney had first felt a stirring of affection toward this lonely, many-friended man. Not really affection though—it wasn't quite that, or not by any definition of the word that Slaney knew. It was a sense of wanting to protect a man who had survived untold dangers, of wanting to make him understand that what he had done was loved and appreciated.

Slaney could not say that they were still friends, but surely they were not strangers, and just as surely, more than acquaintances or messmates. For those last few months at Karachi, they had been almost inseparable, yet at the same time separated by some invisible barrier of Ned's self-protection that Slaney knew he would never penetrate. Ned was an unexplainable man filled with awesome demons, struggling to survive. And, Slaney believed, failing.

Despite Slaney's bitterness at the way Ned had organized his departure from Karachi, his heart sang to see him here in Miranshah, apparently so very happy. Or, if not actually happy, at least a very long way from being unhappy, a long way from Karachi and Farnborough. Ned had laughed and joked and even eaten well, unlike Karachi, avoiding the meat, of course, but having two helpings of the vegetables.

But, Slaney wondered, how will he be when he has to leave this place? He still felt this need to protect Ned, even here, but had realized that here, at least, Ned would survive without his protection.

He also realized, with surprise, that Ned had left the table, was gone from the room. No one else seemed to have noticed his absence, for when Slaney asked, they all looked about in surprise.

"'E was just 'ere," Mitchell said, pouring more beer. "Well, 'e's a queer cuss. Never know what 'e's up to."

A native soldier came in with a message. "Sahib Shaw says to come outside."

The Irregulars, and those who had spent time at Miranshah, were used to doing what Ned said, and even the visitors were already under his spell, so they went outside. Some soldiers led the way, not in any formal order, but just because they seemed to know where they were going, and the white men drifted, in twos and threes, officers and men together, expectantly, toward the perimeter of the airfield.

The gates of the fence were open and there, just outside, a campfire burned. Squatting around it were some tribesmen, tribally dressed, a hundred of them, and Ned.

A different Ned, one whom none of them but Slaney had seen before. The desert Ned. Ned, dressed in a flowing white robe and a headdress, talking to the Waziris as to his friends, struggling only a little with their language, but accepted by them as one of them and part of their company. They danced and sang, they leaned on their rifles and sat on their rugs or camel saddles and stared at the fire and drank coffee and told stories of the tribe, and Ned was at the very heart of it. A few of the young bucks, inflamed by the dancing, got excited and fired their guns into the night, louder than any fireworks, if not as colorful.

The sky seemed infinite, the stars and planets brighter than diamonds, and the moon shone down on a mystical scene. The men watching had seen such festivities before, but seldom in such a setting or in so benign a mood, and never in the company of Lawrence of Arabia. They were not of this place or time anymore, but in the land of legends, in another desert a thousand miles away, ten years ago, soldiers in an unlikely army that had swept in triumph across the Arabian Peninsula, through the holy cities, Mecca and Medina and Jerusalem, even to Damascus, vanquishing the Turks and returning home as glittering heroes.

Their souls tingled as the cares and tedium of the modern world fell away, and they were carefree boys again, or golden youths, unsullied, unconquerable, triumphant.

And none more so than Slaney.

23

September 1928

I am on the very verge of seeking what I despise myself for needing. I want to feel the pain again. It hasn't been so strong since I've been in India, I thought that I would never feel such an urgent need, a desperate need, an overwhelming need as this again. I thought that part of me had died, like the rest of me, but as I come back to life, in Miranshah, that other me revives as well.

Or Slaney brought it with him.

Or Umar made it happen.

(You do not know about Umar. He is part of the secret me. He is Dahoum if he had lived. He is strong and handsome and brave, as Dahoum was. He is noble and honest, as Dahoum was. He flirts with me, outrageously, as Dahoum did. When I am with Umar, I am myself again, in Carchemish.)

Slaney is dark, stern, intense like a sharp winter, so loyal, but so capable of being offended, outraged, by what I need, that if he were to deliver the punishment, his wrath would be completely cleansing. That mighty arm of his could chasten me to purity again, rid my body of that which I cannot release myself.

I think he will not do it. Rather he would estrange himself from me and tell the world what a foul creature I am, and then even the hope of him would be gone, temptation gone, salvation gone.

But the dreaming, oh, the dreaming. The dreaming is enticing danger. I can't resist the dreams, but I must resist him. I must resist myself. I will not think of him again (but, of course, I will). I shall lose myself in books and letters, write to friends, translate my Greek and never go outside again. I will resist Slaney. And I will resist Umar.

There are too many secrets.

24

SLANEY WAS COMING TO the end of his time at Miranshah. In a couple of days he would be back in Peshawar, and he knew he would be homesick for this dotty place. He had loved this dotty outpost, right from the moment of his arrival when he was greeted by the happy Ned.

As Brodie had suggested, the base at Miranshah was superbly run by the Irregulars, and Smythe-Clarke had spent most of his days in happy consultation with Higgins, cultivating roses until the bushes flourished in the barren soil, and leaving the men to their own devices.

Always lonely since Harold's death, Slaney loved the isolation of the country and the tumbledown fort. Ned sought his company even more than in Karachi, and the two spent long hours together. As always, Slaney was a willing student to Ned, the amiable pedagogue, and would sit in the wireless cabin with Ned, reading books he otherwise would never open and watching Ned translate an ancient language. Slaney deferred to Ned as a man who had experience of life that Slaney could only imagine, but Ned had an ability to make Slaney feel that he was the stronger of the two, the senior partner in the friendship. They joked and laughed and chattered and bickered, and when Mitchell suggested that the pair of them were carrying on like an old married couple, neither Ned nor Slaney took it amiss. When Slaney came back to the barracks covered in oil, greasy from tending engines, Ned would insist he bathe and had tea waiting for him when he was done.

Now an expert engineer, Slaney sometimes took the aircraft up on his own, to check the sound and vibrations of a repaired engine. Up there in the limitless sky, looking down on land that hardly knew the twentieth century, Slaney felt himself to be king of a tiny country, and when he came down to earth the landing never seemed sudden, because Ned was always there, asking him how the flight had been, or how the engine had behaved, or how it felt to be master of the flying machine.

"Why did you never learn to fly?" Slaney asked him once.

"I never really had the chance," Ned said, a little wistfully. "I grew up in places where there were no aircraft, and later I always had too much else to do." He giggled. "Besides," he said, "you have to be a man to fly a plane, and I'm not sure my balls have ever dropped."

Slaney laughed with him. It was an old, occasional joke. Ned, who had been brave beyond daring and had experiences beyond imagining, always deprecated his masculinity, giggling that his balls had never dropped.

It wasn't true, they both knew that, but it sounded good to Slaney when he said it, a compliment which somehow suggested that Slaney had balls of iron. It made him feel strong and manly.

Tempered by the memory of Karachi, Slaney labored under no misapprehensions. He knew that others, in England, had greater claims on Ned's loyalty, that Ned and he were friends only because they were here, but it was enough. He knew there was a part of Ned he would never understand, and another part of Ned he would never reach. He would never sit at a dinner party in London and hold his own with Ned's brilliant, powerful friends, but he knew that he gave Ned something that those others could not, and Ned gave to him, gratefully, something special in return. And sometimes, rarely but sometimes, when they were alone on quiet evenings, he would talk to Slaney about the place called "Kargemish."

Then Slaney's heart swelled, because he believed he was the only person, perhaps in all the world, to whom Ned told these secrets. He didn't care what had caused Ned to open a small part of his heart that had previously been locked. He accepted Ned for what he believed him to be—a lonely man, like himself, looking for someone to be his friend. And he had found Slaney.

Partly it was the security of this friendship, and partly it was the strong reminders of "Kargemish" here at Miranshah that caused Ned to allow himself to remember the man he had been. After Arabia, after Paris, he had sworn he would never get mixed up in tribal politics again and he had kept that oath. It had been easy in Karachi; he never went out, he never met locals and the politics of that city were urban, not tribal. It was difficult here in Miranshah. He understood these desert people intimately, their complex loyalties and needs, their alliances and rivalries, their territorial ambitions. He had felt himself drawn to them, as iron is drawn to a magnet. He had fought against it, knowing that to surrender must somehow, in some way he didn't understand and couldn't prophesy, destroy him.

That very danger was part of the attraction. He flirted with it, frolicked at the edges of it, darted close to it and then away again, believing himself immune to its seduction and then realizing, when it was far too late, that he was caught, inexorably entangled in it, unable to resist involvement.

All because of Umar. A prince of the desert. How many princes could the desert whelp?

It had begun so simply, as easily as slipping on his galabia, and as sweetly soft. From his first days at Miranshah, he had greeted the local workers in their tongue, not their mother language, Urdu, but with the words of Mohammed, the unifying language of Islam.

They had opened their hearts to him, as a brother, thinking him a Mussulman, and he had accepted their invitations to sit, at the end of the day, on either side of the perimeter wire and talk about the world and God. No one on the base thought it strange that Ned should be so involved with the locals, knowing his history, and it seemed proper that a man who had lived a desert life should be so familiar with desert folk.

He became their friend and sometime counselor. When they had problems with their employment by the British bosses, they would come to Ned, and he would advise them or intercede on their behalf. And no one thought it strange. They would ask his advice on tribal differences, and he would give them his opinion, and they would accept it or not, as seemed fitting to them. And no one thought it strange.

When important visitors or pilgrims came to the town of Miranshah, they would be brought to meet Ned, the white Mussulman, the onetime Prince of Damascus, who had visited the sacred cities of Mecca and Medina and Jerusalem, had seen the holy places, and who knew as a personal friend the Keepers of the Faith. And when they had celebrations they made Ned their guest of honor, and he would go to that forbidden place, outside the perimeter, and dance and sing and talk with them. And no one thought it strange.

So when a truly important man came to Miranshah, a fugitive with a price on his head, fleeing both his native country and his uneasy exile, plotting rebellion, they all agreed that he must talk to the wise white man up on the hill, who had once helped to lead a revolution that had destroyed an empire.

Sardar Mohammed Umar Khan was an Afghan prince of the blood royal, nephew of the deposed Amir Yakub Khan, and son of the daughter of Qazi Nur-uddin Khan, who was once the chief minister of Kandahar. A wealthy and well-educated young man of traditional Moslem values, Umar had dedicated his life to reclaiming—not necessarily for himself—his family's usurped throne.

The country called Afghanistan was a wild, mountainous territory, peopled by warring tribes whose loyalties and allegiances shifted as constantly as the country's borders. Kabul, the capital, was the key. The family that controlled Kabul controlled the mountain passes and the few fertile plains, and the city had changed hands countless times over the centuries, as ambitious princes made their grab for power.

Kabul was also a hotbed of diplomatic intrigue, because Afghanistan was of profound strategic importance, the cushion between the empires of Britain and the tsar—and latterly, between Britain and the Bolshevik expansions. From the time of Peter the Great, the Russians had sought an overland route to the treasures of British India, and twice the British had invaded Afghanistan to thwart those Russian ambitions, but the Afghans resisted both them and the Russians. An uneasy balance of power developed. Until ten years ago the ruling family had been sympathetic to the British, while maintaining a fragile entente with the Russians, but the success of the Bolshevik Revolution inspired a young khan, Amanullah, to grab the throne in Kabul after a series of bloody coups. Umar's uncle, the amir, was killed, and the boy Umar had been spirited away to his family's mountain retreat, to be raised as a prince should be and instilled with a lust for vengeance.

The new king, Amanullah, was no socialist. He ruled as an absolute monarch, claiming divine guidance, and in his ruthless attempts to modernize and secularize the country he alienated the devout mullahs. Likewise, the brutality of his secret police and his many personal foibles enraged a people unused to peace, and now his throne was under siege. Umar was a prime mover in one of the failed uprisings, and he had escaped to India, where the British, reluctantly, had given him protection. He lived under surveillance in Allahabad, but had found it easy to escape his watchdogs. A small caravan of merchants had brought him, in disguise, to Miranshah, and allies of his family had hidden him. It was they who brought him to Ned.

They disguised Umar as a peasant and one morning took him to work at the fort, as a cleaner. They waited until Ned was in the wireless cabin alone, then two of them brought Umar in and introduced him. Ned was charming at first, but when Umar's identity was revealed, he tried to avoid further conversation. Umar, however, made a persuasive speech.

Umar had listened to his friends talk of Ned and felt a stirring of his blood. If this man who had led the conquest of the Turks and had helped set up Feisal's kingdom in Iraq could be enlisted to his cause, then anything was possible, and the throne of Afghanistan would return to his family.

He was excited to meet Ned, would have borne any disguise, no matter how lowly, to do so, and his young blood sang when he was taken into the wireless cabin. Then all his high hopes came crashing down, and he was sure he was wasting his time. He could not believe that this small, meticulous, methodical bookworm was any warrior prince. It must be some mistake. Surely Ned was a liar who had put about a legend to aggrandize himself. There was more. Umar guessed, instinctively, at least one of Ned's secrets.

But Umar was a young man with a mission, for he believed himself a victim. Determined to restore his family's name, he could not resist presenting his case, even to the most insignificant audience. His two friends absented themselves that the leaders might talk in private. Umar began to speak, at first almost casually, as if Ned were irrelevant to him.

As he spoke, he saw a change happen in Ned, and that wrought a corresponding change in himself. It is his eyes, Umar thought. Those blue eyes that were empty and disengaged can hear me, and the eyes are the window to the heart. His heart is listening.

Umar had been blessed with many gifts, not the least of which was a strong and righteous personality. He bore himself as a true prince, he looked the part and had the manner of leadership about him. He may very well be kingly material, Ned thought. He was what Feisal was when young. He had another compelling attribute as well—the physical beauty of a darkling Adonis. He was what Dahoum might have become. Ned stared at Umar and saw in him Dahoum. The young prince's grievances made sense to him, and as he listened, something of the old Ned, the man he had once been, came back to him. He who was once a triumphant colonel could not resist giving advice to a headstrong young soldier. Aware of the potential danger, he kept a sharp rein on himself, counseled caution in all things and kept his advice as theoretical as possible. He knew that Umar wanted more, but believed that what he was giving him was enough. More might be dangerous. More might be destructive, not to Umar, whose fate was in his own hands and Allah's, but to Ned, whose fate had been decided long ago, by himself.

It was thrilling to Umar. As he talked he began to feel the room must surely explode with Ned's presence, and he knew that at least part of the reason for this was flattery. He beguiled Ned with talk of honor and a cause, he impressed Ned with the justice of his case, he fired Ned's blood for war, and he seduced Ned, quite deliberately, with his beauty.

He sat near him on a stool, he looked deep into Ned's eyes, finding there a pathway straight to Ned's heart. He took off his headdress and let his brown locks fall free. He caressed his neck with his hand while he spoke, and pushed up his sleeves that Ned might see the muscles, sculpted, alert, ready for action. Then, as if unable to contain his energy, he sprang from the stool. Like a lithe and graceful young tiger, captive in a too-small cage, he paced the room, all vibrant energy, until Ned thought he must break free from his unkind bondage and wreak havoc on the unsuspecting world. He was youth, young and magnificent.

Slaney came in without knocking, looking for Ned. Startled, Umar stopped in mid-speech, glared at the intruder and then at Ned.

Slaney, Ned's self-appointed protector, immediately realized that this was no ordinary cleaner but a man of formidable strength and ambition. He could not imagine what the two had been talking about, but he was sure it was a subject greater than the dust of Miranshah, because, at the moment he came in, he had felt fire—the flames of potential violence.

They stood staring at each other, Slaney and Umar, each defying the other and each denying the other's right to be there. There was a silence that might have been a small eternity.

And then Ned giggled. They are jealous of each other, he thought. They are like two rival suitors, each assessing the other's attractiveness to me, and I am the desirable object of their competing affections. My twin temptations, each vying for the honor of my fall.

So he giggled, and the giggle broke the silence, if not the rivalry.

"Sorry," Slaney said. "Didn't know you had company."

"That's all right," Ned assured him. "Umar was just finishing up."

He turned to Umar.

"I enjoyed our little chat," he said in English. "I'd like to talk with you again."

Umar, still angry, glared at Ned and nodded. The wireless cabin was small for two, uncomfortable for three, so Slaney excused himself to wait outside.

Thus he did not see the flick of eyes that Ned gave Umar, to the broom and cleaning rags that lay discarded on the floor.

Slaney stood basking in the warm summer sun and reflecting on Ned and Umar.

"If he's a cleaner, I'll eat my hat," he told himself. But what was he to Ned? When Slaney had burst into the wireless cabin and seen Ned in intense debate with a passionate and fiery young man, when he had felt his flesh tingle because the atmosphere in the room was combustible, he had experienced a new emotion, one he had not felt before to any remarkable degree.

He was jealous.

He smoked a cigarette, waited for Ned and tried to come to terms with a curious, burgeoning anger.

Umar came out of the cabin. He glanced suspiciously at Slaney and then walked away to the perimeter. He was carrying a broom and rags, but he didn't fool Slaney. He didn't have the bearing of a man who spent his working life stooped over; there was nothing obsequious about him.

"If he's a cleaner, I'll eat my hat," Slaney said again.

Ned came out a few moments later and suggested they eat. They had walked a little way to the mess before Ned spoke. "Curious chap," Ned said. He didn't identify which chap because there was no need; both of them were thinking of the same man. "He turned up out of the blue, said he was a cleaner and made a big speech about the injustice of life under British rule. One of those Indian nationalists, I suppose."

Slaney grunted noncommittally, but he was bitterly disappointed, because Ned had lied to him.

There were very few Indian nationalists here; there was very little need for nationalism here. Theoretically, the British ruled the NWFP just as they ruled the other British provinces, but no one was ever sure quite what it was they ruled. A collection of disparate tribes, all battling it out amongst each other for territories only they could define, paying only lip service to British laws and judgments, oblivious to British punishments unless they went to the city and did something especially silly. For the most part, the hill tribes regarded the British as some benevolent uncle who had come to stay for a while and didn't show any signs of wanting to leave. On a practical level, the tribesmen used the British as referees of minor disputes (major ones they solved among themselves, usually by blood) and enjoyed the fringe benefits that British civilization brought them.

The true nationalists were much farther away, in true India, and there the disputes were as much between the Moslems and the Hindus as they were with the British. Down there, in the cities, there was a strong and strident cry of India for the Indians and a resentment of British laws and taxes. Up here, no one paid much tax (most of their income was illegal and there was very little bookkeeping), and there were no large cities (Peshawar was only an overgrown village) and thus few attendant slums, the real hotbeds of nationalism.

Unless some young Freedom Fighter with a mistaken sense of place and order had come up here to incite the locals to revolt—an almost futile task— or unless some nationalist had escaped to here after throwing a bomb in Delhi, in which case Slaney would have heard about it, Umar could not be what Ned had claimed.

In which case Ned had lied, and that knowledge disappointed Slaney and tinged his jealousy a darker shade of green. Still, he tried to be fair. He could not abandon the protectiveness he felt toward Ned, and if he was mixing with unsavory types, or involving himself in local politics, he could get into real trouble, and Slaney was determined to save Ned from that.

Ned, to his frustration, however, didn't appear to want to be saved. He wouldn't answer questions about his visitor and wouldn't be drawn into discussion of his attitude to the local politics. On the surface, nothing between Slaney and Ned had changed, but in Slaney's mind, at least, there was a difference. They went about together much as they had before, they appeared to enjoy each other's company as much as before, but a veil was drawn over part of Ned's life here, much as Slaney tried to draw that veil aside.

Instead of being with Ned, he was watching Ned, following him everywhere he went, keeping an eye on every local to whom Ned spoke, wary lest the cleaner who wasn't a cleaner appear again.

This night he had. During the afternoon, Slaney had seen Ned talking to some of the locals at the wire, glancing about as if he did not want their conversation to be overheard. Slaney vowed to be vigilant that night. After lights-out, the men settled themselves for sleep. Slaney said good night to Ned, then rolled over and closed his eyes. He would not go to sleep until he was sure Ned had as well. It didn't happen. He heard one of the visiting engineers relieve himself with his hand, struggling to keep his orgasm quiet. He heard Mitchell's snoring. Baxter farted once or twice. Through it all, Slaney knew Ned was still awake.

Slaney woke suddenly, realizing he must have nodded off. He looked at his watch. He could only have been asleep for a few minutes, perhaps only moments, but he looked to Ned's bed and saw that it was empty. He cursed himself, got up, slipped on a pair of shorts and made his way outside.

He knew exactly where to go. The fence was lit by searchlights each night, but there was a point on the wire that the searchlights couldn't reach, and it was there, out of light's way, that occasional assignations were made. Slaney had heard that at least a couple of airmen with a taste for Indian hemp had bought it there from the tribesmen. He had heard the joke that once there was a nancy airman, a bum boy, who had been shafted at that very spot by a couple of the local lads. And it was there that, even in broad daylight, Ned sometimes had conversations with the locals.

He got to the wire in time to see Ned, but too late to stop him. Ned was already on the other side, and in the company of someone who, in the moon-light, looked remarkably like Slaney's rival. They moved into the night and were gone. It was useless to call out; that would give the game away. It also was useless to follow them; there was only ambient light from the quarter moon, and Slaney knew he would soon be lost.

He cursed himself again—and Ned—and went back to the barracks. He lay down on his cot, determined to stay awake until Ned came back. His emotions were mixed and running high, and Slaney rehearsed in his mind all the things he would say to Ned.

He was only dozing when Ned returned, and immediately was awake. It was nearly dawn, and, thinking the men to be asleep, Ned, silent as a cat, came into the barracks and moved softly to his bunk. He sat down, rubbed his tired eyes and stared at Slaney. He didn't seem to notice that Slaney's eyes were open and staring back at him. Or if he did notice, he gave no sign of it. He doesn't see me, Slaney thought. He isn't here.

Ned knew that Slaney was awake and that he must explain himself, if only to deflect suspicion. He had met Umar at the wire and they had walked into the desert, sat under the stars and talked for hours about the strategy of rebellion. Umar had a simple view, his grievances so strong they outweighed his sense of logic. He believed his cause to be just and that if he merely raised his standard, others who hated Amanullah would rally to him. He believed that by sheer force of numbers they would win.

Ned took a general's view. Yes, the cause was just, and doubtless Umar and his friends could rally an army, and maybe they would win. But what happened then? The cause alone, no matter how just, was not enough. Alliances must be formed and promises made, and the eventual distribution of power must be decided on before the battle if the outcome of the battle was to have any meaning. In a few short hours he gave Umar a crash course in military strategy, and something more: he gave Umar the benefit of the bitter lessons he had learned at Damascus and at Paris.

It was like nectar! To be able to prepare a young commander for the future, the time after his war, when all the games of power would assail him—from friend and foe alike—was balm to Ned's mortally injured soul.

Once, when young, he had thought a just quest was enough. Once, when young, he had imagined that triumph was victory and victory was power. Once, when young, he had believed all the false promises his military and political superiors had made to him. Once, when young, he had offered Damascus to a desert prince, but all he gave him was Baghdad.

Everything was a lie. Every promise that was made was conditional upon the political need of the moment. Every government was at the mercy of every competing power. Every victory on the field only created new battles in the strategy rooms.

As for the quest, the pure and noble quest, the one honest reason for all that Ned had tried to achieve, that was simply a waste of time. Because when the glittering prize was within his reach, so close he could almost grasp it, only a few weeks and miles away, all of his dreams had faded like a mirage in the high, bright light of reality, because the beloved, for whom the prize was intended, had died.

For all these years, Ned had nursed this venom in his system, this poisoning bitterness at what he had failed to achieve, but now, tonight, he was able to give the antidote to someone possessed of his own lost innocence.

He knew he was playing with fire. If caught off the base, he would be punished. If he was discovered aiding and abetting a known fugitive, he might be court-martialed. If it was thought that he was plotting rebellion, he might be banished from this sanctuary forever. But he had been unable to resist the dazzling redemption of the young prince, whatever the price might be.

He stared into Slaney's eyes. Wine dark, like Homer's sea, he thought, in which I could easily drown. Fathomless eyes, that pulled him in. Ambiguous eyes, because he could not imagine what Slaney was thinking.

He smiled a little. If Umar was the temptation outside, then Slaney was the temptation here, inside, where he thought he had been safe.

"Still awake?" he asked softly.

"Waiting for you," Slaney whispered.

Ned turned away, heartsore. Someone else was waiting for him somewhere, in a place to which he dared not go.

"You've been outside," Slaney said. It was not a question. "You'll cop it if you get caught."

"Yes," Ned agreed.

"Why?" Slaney asked. "What's that bloke want?"

"Just to talk," Ned told him. He paused for a moment and looked at Slaney again. "I hope my uncle never finds out."

It came out of nowhere, Slaney had never heard Ned talk of an uncle, and it didn't seem to have any relevance to the conversation.

Ned, whose lust for danger was tingling since his talk with Umar, led him gently. "I was poor, dirt poor, before I joined up." He talked so quietly that Slaney strained to hear him. He thought it was because of the sleeping airmen, but there was more to it. His whispering and his tone were deeply intimate.

"I should have been rich when my father died, but I couldn't inherit, I was"—he seemed reluctant to say the word—"illegitimate."

Slaney didn't look at him, the confession was too private.

"I tried to keep myself alive to write my book, but in the end I had no choice. I had to go to the moneylenders. I fell into their clutches like a newborn babe, and before I knew it I owed them hundreds. I had no way of paying them back, not in a million years. I couldn't bear to disgrace my mother by being sent to prison. It would break her heart. So I went to my uncle, who had inherited my father's estate."

There was another small silence. Slaney was fascinated. This was something of Ned he had never known and that touched unused banks of sympathy in Slaney's heart.

"My uncle was brutal." Ned's voice trembled, as if the memory was too painful for him. "He called me worthless, wasting my life on a book, when I could have had a good career. But for my mother's sake he agreed to pay back my loans. On one condition—one condition . . ."

Slaney had to move closer to hear Ned. Touchably close.

"He made me promise to enlist. He made me promise never to do anything wrong, ever again. And he made me promise, made me agree—"

Something in his look, his voice, disturbed Slaney. He sounded—what? Husky. Excited. Sexual.

"—that if I did do anything wrong, I would be beaten for my sin. He would decide on the number of strokes, and he expected a report from the beater. Only when he was satisfied that I had been punished enough would he continue the payments."

Ned looked at Slaney.

"So I have to be beaten when I have been bad."

Slaney had no idea what to say. His heart ached for Ned. How could the old man be so cruel? How could Ned bear the pain? It was a bargain with the devil. It explained so much about Ned's behavior, why he had enlisted in the ranks, why he kept to himself so much, why he seemed to carry an awful weight on his shoulders. He longed to take Ned in his arms and hold him until all the pain had gone away.

And yet . . . and yet . . .

And yet he could not touch him. Nor could he explain to himself why he could not. He only knew that he must not. The room seemed pin-drop silent.

"I'm really sorry, Ned," he whispered. "If you need a few quid, if that'd help—"

"It isn't money my uncle wants," Ned said. "It is my pain."

The silence lingered, drowning out the noise of sleeping airmen. Slaney had to end it, quickly, suddenly, make it stop. "He'll never find out you've done anything wrong from me," Slaney promised Ned. "I swear to that." He inched away, gently as he could, and lay back on his own cot.

"And I'll kill any bastard who tells him," he said more aggressively, to reinforce his promise.

Ned nodded, but Slaney thought he was disappointed.

The bugle sounded; the night was over. Ned moved away to go to the bathhouse as the airmen roused themselves. Slaney lay on his cot, trying to come to terms with what he had been told.

He hated Ned's mysterious uncle with an intensity that made him punch the wall.

"Poor bugger," he said to himself, thinking of Ned and the dreadful scars he bore. Was that it? Did that explain those livid weals on his back? Did they all come from his punishment at Deraa, or from some other beatings? What must it be like to have to undergo that torture, just to satisfy a rich old fart's whims and pay back a few bob to the moneylenders? Was it worth that to stay out of debtor's prison? Did Ned's mum mean so much to him?

Floods of protectiveness washed over him, and he understood, at last, why he felt this almost violent urge to shield Ned from harm.

And yet . . . and yet . . .

Why had he not been able to touch Ned when he knew Ned needed to be touched? Something had stopped him, some knowledge that if he had touched Ned he would be drawn into something that was repugnant to him.

He was leaving Miranshah and had not been looking forward to his departure. Now he was glad to be going. Much as he wanted to look after Ned, he needed to be away from here, to be alone, to come to terms with something greater, darker, more violent than anything he understood. He was in over his head in waters much too deep and drowning. Because he was certain, as sure as he had ever been of anything ever in his life, that at that moment, Ned, who hated to be touched, wanted to be held.

Or to be struck.

Some weeks later, back in Peshawar, Slaney was sent on a flight to Allahabad as escort to a political prisoner who had been captured in the Hindu Kush, arrested for inciting revolution in Afghanistan.

The prisoner was Umar.

At last, Slaney knew who Ned's mysterious visitor was and what he was up to, and he despised Umar for reasons both personal and patriotic. Slaney believed in an absolute order of things, a constancy of government, and if the British government had reason to arrest Umar, then Umar was some kind of traitor to Britain. Yet that same traitor was Ned's friend.

Slaney's faith in Ned, already under considerable siege, was suddenly, ferociously, dented.

As for Ned, even before he heard of Umar's arrest, he knew, from the coolness of their parting, that he had pushed Slaney too far, too fast. He cursed himself for a fool. Miranshah had provoked too sharp a remembrance of the past, of Carchemish. Vanity was his enemy, and lust, that foul serpent, was his downfall. He wept himself to sleep for several nights, cursing his bitter fortune, dreaming of himself when young, longing for the joy he had once known, briefly with Slaney, momentarily with Umar.

And always with Dahoum.

25

Autumn 1912

I am twenty-four years old—a man, not a boy—so I can be very clear eyed about this, hardheaded. I do not want you to misunderstand me. I do not want you to think me a besotted fool, bedazzled by exotic beauty, lost to an ingenuous infatuation which I mistake for love.

I am acutely aware of the differences between us, of race and class and breeding, of birth and rank and education. I do not foresee a lifetime of conjugal bliss; I have other needs than him, and he has other needs than me. I do not imagine that we will live forever together in the wildwood, in a cottage garlanded by roses, we have no suburban longings. I know that we will not always be together. I know that he will marry one day and have children—it is the nature of him—but I also know that he will never love anyone else as much as he loves me.

We do not need to be together every second of the day, or of our lives, but even when we are apart, each inhabits the other's mind and heart and soul, because we are one being, two separate halves that only when together make a complete whole.

I want you to understand my precise feelings for him.

I adore him.

Dahoum is the rest of me. He is my opposite and my exact other self. He is Earth and I am Air, I am Autumn to his Spring. He tempers all my longings and incites all my desires. He is simple, I am complex; he is the present, I am the past; he is practical, I a dreamer; he is innocent, I am sophisticated; he is lecherous and I am chaste. And sometimes we reverse ourselves. Sometimes he will vault to the peak of Olympus and see angels that are invisible to me, and I, grounded, lust for him.

Or sometimes, when I am lost in reverie, gazing on the battlefields of King Hattusilus, who once ruled Carchemish, and seeing in my mind's eye armies that conquered the Assyrians and made alliances with Egyptian pharaohs, he will ask me where I am, and when I tell him, he will grin, or shrug, and go to his friends and drink arak and dance dances that his people have danced since time immemorial. He is the living past, and I am the remembered past; he is the vibrant present, and I the puzzling scholar.

Later, drunk, he will come back to me and smile or shrug, and yawn and snuggle down beside me, needing no confirmation of my love, because it is never said or spoken. He requires only the security of my presence, in whatever antique pasture I might be, and he will sleep an innocent, exhausted sleep, near me, with me, safe in my protection.

Sometimes he gets too cheeky or forgetful of his duties, and then I have to scold him, or threaten to send him away to live with the women. He pouts and sulks and will not speak for a while, but then he comes to me with a tiny gift—a sharp, green orange, or a cheap mat, or, once, a valuable seal he had stolen from the site—to beg my forgiveness and swear he will never neglect his duties again for fear I will cease to want him. Of course I forgive him (how could I not?), and he smiles and is himself again.

Sometimes, he is angry with me. If I have been away on a visit to Aleppo or to the mission at Jebeil, when I come back he shouts at me and calls me faithless, then weeps because I do not like him anymore. It is my turn to ask forgiveness and swear I will never go away again. After considerable consideration, he, graciously, cheekily, agrees to forgive me, to give me one last chance, and he smiles, and we are ourselves again.

He doesn't always understand me, doesn't always comprehend my future aspirations, because the future, to him, is now and whatever his God disposes it to be. When I try to tell him of the grand plans I am shaping, of the dreams I will make reality, he looks at me in wonderment and giggles and marks me as mad Ned, the crazy English, who has come to him from an alien land, speaking a ridiculous language and with fantastic, impossible enterprises swarming inside his head.

"Inshallah," he will say. "If God wills it."

Sometimes we talk about God, but it is a limited conversation. He believes, and I do not. Only when I talk about the old gods, the wayward family of Zeus, do we find a common ground. He wants to hear all the myths, but most of all, he loves to hear about the Hittite gods, their guardian deities, for he might be descended from those people, and the stories have resonance for him and connect him with his forebears.

Sometimes he goes away from me to his other life, to his own village, to see his friends and family and to make them laugh with stories of the silly things the English do, digging in mountains to discover unnecessary artifacts, remnants of a long-dead people, his most ancient ancestors, who live now in himself, the sum of the generations that created him. He will give his mother the pennies he has earned, to buy food and the pots that, when broken, she will throw away, so that after more millennia others like me will come to find them, ponder on the people that once used them and wonder who they were.

Yet sometimes, and at surprising moments, when we uncover some long wall and there are carvings of forgotten warriors, or when we unearth statues of the Weather God, he will stare at them and nod in recognition of them, as if these stony images have meaning for him. The distant past becomes the immediate present and the unknowable future—all in a single moment, all in a young man's comprehending eye.

Let me get business out of the way. I have attained my majority, I am a man. We are at Carchemish on the plains of northern Syria. It is the site of a city conquered by the Hittite king Suppiluliumas in the thirteenth century B.C. For five hundred years, Carchemish was a Hittite vassal city state. The absolute monarch ruled from Hattusus, in mountainous Cappadocia, and the satellite cities had their own kings, or viceroys, and functioned with considerable autonomy. Carchemish, far away from the capital and on the camel routes between the Mediterranean and the Persian Gulf, was a rich city of cosmopolitan culture, but its gods were the Hittite deities, benevolent guardians, to be loved and placated, but not to be feared, not wrathful and jealous in the way of the God of the Old Testament. Over time, as the royal bloodline thinned, the Hittites lost their empire, and eventually even mighty Hattusus fell into decay. We don't know yet why Carchemish was abandoned, but we intend to find out.

Small parts of the ruins have been uncovered by previous Oxford expeditions (two led by Hogarth), but there is a mound of intriguing interest, and we are digging it away. We are a few miles from the modern town of Jerablus, and we are beside the Euphrates, the river that once watered the gardens of Babylon, three hundred miles away. Just outside Jerablus, nearer to us, a contingent of German engineers are building a railway bridge across the river, for a line that will stretch from Berlin to Baghdad. We have an uneasy relationship with them, friendly or otherwise, depending on our mood, and theirs.

Our relationship with the Turkish authorities is more complex. We have all our papers and approvals from Constantinople, but any bureaucrat loves to parade his power, and they are constantly denying us things their superiors have granted, or questioning our licenses or the limits of our area. We have to swagger a lot with them, and sometimes offer small bribes or extravagant hospitality. Once, bored with their pettiness, I got my way by waving a gun.

We have two digging seasons; the first is spring to midsummer. When it gets too hot for comfort, we English retreat to England for leave; then we come back in late summer, to work again until the end of autumn. These are variables, for we rely on funding from the British Museum, and we are not their first priority.

We used to live in tents between the river and the dig, but then we built a house, a simple thing—two rooms and a flat roof—that is cold in winter and hot in summer, but is functional and prettily decorated with fine pieces scavenged from the site. It is my home. There is a small village (descendants of the ancient population?), but it does not provide enough workmen for our needs, and so we import gangs of men, up to two hundred, from other places.

A local man, Sheik Hammoudi, is our foreman and liaison with the gangs, and two other villagers, Hajj Wahid and his wife, Fatima, look after us, and she cooks for us. They have a little house near ours.

Hogarth was in charge the first year and gave me my head, but now we are led by the archeologist Leonard Woolley. Len's a good chap, but he's only here in the digging seasons. He goes back to England the rest of the year, but I stay if I can, or go hunting for antiquities, because this is home. I am happy here.

My duties are light—an assistant supervisor to Len—and mostly I am in charge of cataloging what he has found, or piecing together scraps of pots or seals or statues and organizing the gangs of local workmen at the dig. We make games of it, or I divide them into competing teams, offering rewards to the ones who remove the most dirt, and laugh with them and urge them on in competition, and they love me for it and will do anything I ask them.

I have a lot of free time to do what I will, to read or study, or explore the country, or befriend the locals, or chat with the women, or take photographs, or learn the language, or—in summer—swim, or entertain our many visitors.

(They're not always friendly. Several other archeologists came to inspect our site the first year and complained to Hogarth because my methods are somewhat unconventional. Hogarth put Len in charge the next year, and I was sent to Egypt, to learn a few lessons from Sir Flinders Petrie. What an old poop he is, and all the other Egyptologists! They can't see beyond their own Upper and Lower Kingdoms and don't understand that our Hittites were once much stronger and grander, and that their death-obsessed pharaohs sought our life-affirming alliance. And they have no sense of humor! Sir Flinders got very tetchy about the way I treated his mummies, as if there weren't enough of them.)

Oddly, Sir Flinders thinks better of me now, for he has suggested to Hogarth that I lead my own dig in Bahrein. Bahrein? Why would I want Bahrein, when I am here? I have no cares here, only careless rapture. Here, they love me, even while they laugh at me. I don't care! They can't understand that I'm not married, I'm older than their oldest bachelor, and I parade my virgin state before them, wearing huge tassels on my belt that indicate my innocence of women. They giggle and point and hide their smiles behind their hands; they present young women to me as potential brides, but as a joke, because they know I won't get married. They know who it is that I love and do not care that I love him. They care only that I am loved.

The moment of our meeting is burned indelibly in my mind. It is during our first season, I am at the site, and Hammoudi, our foreman, is yelling instructions to a young man I haven't seen before, his nephew from his village. The young man is startling, handsome, blazing with vitality, but straining to shift a stubborn donkey, and does not take kindly to his uncle's orders. I ask who he is, and Hammoudi introduces me to him, proudly, and calls him by his proper name, Selim Ahmed. But everyone calls him Dahoum, "the dark one," because his skin is olive, and his hair is raven. He looks at me shyly because I am the English effendi, and shakes my hand, and his eyes are ebony pools in which I might drown!

I think in that moment I know—both of us know—that we will be more to each other than servant and master. He stares at me. I am the first fair-haired man that he has seen. He stares at me, and I at him, and then he smiles.

I feel, in the pit of my stomach, something I have never felt before, as if my guts are turning upside down. His face is open, flawless, his teeth are perfect white, dazzling against his skin, and his lips are full and firmly outlined. Hammoudi makes him promise to be a good worker and not embarrass his uncle and his family. Dahoum promises; and how could anyone not believe him? I giggle and do not let go of his hand, even though I have held it for too long. Hammoudi and some workmen are staring at us. Someone whispers something mildly obscene. I know what it is, and I don't care, because at that moment, Dahoum does something devastating that no one else can see.

His hand still clasping mine, with his right index finger he tickles, ever so slightly, the palm of my hand, and sticks out, ever so slightly, the tip of his tongue, wet with glistening spittle.

Oh, the wicked tempter! My serpent leaps to attention. I giggle again and drop his hand and turn away to hide my hardness, which is pushing at my shorts, as if to announce my serpent's presence to Dahoum and to the world. I blush, and Dahoum sees me pink despite my sunburned skin and knows that I have answered him and that I have said yes.

But not yet. I am shy with him and glance back at him, flirting with him slightly. The others laugh again and make jokes about us, but kindly. One even makes a rude gesture, and Dahoum leaps to my defense, shouts that they are all dirty old men and do not understand a young man's fancy. How can he be so bold?

Fear grabs me. They must not, cannot, know the secret me! How can I give orders to men who know I am not manly? They would destroy me, beat me, call me names! I speak sharply to them, send them back to work, order Dahoum to get about his business. They disperse, and I turn away. But I know he is still watching me.

I see him every day, but when I see him I find some busy thing to keep me occupied. He is always there. He carries earth away from the site, in woven baskets on his donkey's back, and then returns when the baskets are empty to fill them up again. I watch him slyly. He is stripped to the waist, muscles rippling, sweaty skin shining in the sun. He stands, knowing, I'm sure, that I am looking. He rubs his hand over his hard stomach, pushes at the loose belt of his pants and scratches at a velvet hint of hair.

For a mad moment, I am a drop of his sweat, trickling across his hard, full chest and down across his belly to be guided by his caressing hand, ever downward, to his groin, to a bushy mass of prickly hair that guards his fat, thick, resting serpent. I am a tiny libation to his manhood, his godhood, which even though I have not seen it I know must be magnificent.

Am I bewitched? Has the sinful creature taken possession of me? I would, at this moment, do anything that he commanded!

It cannot be. I will not let it happen (although I know that I am powerless). I feign a sickness and stay home and do not go to the site for several days. But I see him from a distance, the donkey boy Dahoum, making his journeys to and from the site, and when I see him I look away, but only after a moment, only after our eyes have locked, and he has waved and smiled and chipped another piece away from my poor heart.

I shall sack him! I shall dream up some pretext and have him dismissed, sent away, back to his village and his family, out of my sight, never to taunt me, tempt me, again.

I don't do that, of course. Instead, I avoid him. I stay in, inside the house to nurse my feigned sickness. There is a tap at the door, and he comes in. He looks at me most seriously and begs to inquire after my health. He wishes to be forgiven, but he has some food that is good for me and will make me better. I accept his gift. He smiles, and I can't think of anything to say. He sits, humming some small song until he hears Hammoudi call his name; it's time for him to eat. He bustles about and straightens my rumpled bed and says he hopes I will be better soon. He goes, and I wonder why I think he is disappointed with me.

It is late summer, under a blazing sun, but I am burning with another heat to which I can't give a name. I go to the river, to bathe and bring some coolness to my raging lust. The clear water, tumbling down from the Taurus Mountains, fed by snow and ice, is calmer here, a magical swimming hole. I splash about and dive for tiny, startled fish, but this is not Lethe, the river of forgetfulness, and does not wash him from my mind. These are the waters of sinful Babylon.

Then he is there.

I stand waist-deep in the river, staring at him on the bank. He has been watching. He has seen my naked frolics and been driven to the unthinkable. He comes to the water's edge, ten feet from me, and puts aside his garment, pushes down his baggy pants. Oh, I was right—he is a god, monstrous, glorious, unde-niable. I stare in wonder as he caresses himself and stares at me as if transfixed, eyes glazed with need, mouth slightly open, tongue seeking mine, so far away, hand coaxing, stroking, urging. I cannot move. I cannot go to him; I cannot go away from him. I am hypnotized by him. My serpent is begging for attention, but I will not do his bidding.

It doesn't matter. The cool, engulfing water has become his body, and I am lost within him, drowning, until I hear him cry, just once, and see his seed, and I waste mine in the water, and it is carried away, gone forever, swept down-stream to Babylon.

He stands, for an eternity, I think, alone on the riverbank. Then he looks at me, and I see only disappointment and regret. Because I was waist-deep in water, he could not know that I have done what he has done, and even though we were separated by an unbridgeable gulf, we were for that time united. He can't know this. He thinks me cold, unmoved by him, or angry.

Like a puppy who has just been spanked, he hangs his head, then rearranges his clothes and walks away, and I, who cannot move, stare after him and beg him to come back. But silently, of course—I say nothing. I do not even call his name.

This is madness! What if someone had seen us? What would they think of us, of me?

But he is gone! For several days after that, I don't see him again. I am insane with loss of him! Is he avoiding me? Is he angry with me? Did he reveal too much about himself, and did my distance infuriate him so much he wants nothing more to do with me? I cannot eat, I cannot sleep, I am desperate with need of him.

I call Hammoudi. "Where is Dahoum?" I ask him, point-blank.

"He is gone." Hammoudi shrugs.

"Where, gone? Why?"

"It is the end of season, English." Hammoudi shrugs. "We are laying off men."

"Why him?" I cry, my heart aching for want of him.

"He thought he had offended you," Hammoudi says. "He came to me and said he was not happy because he had displeased you, because you never speak to him. I tell him that a great effendi will never speak to a donkey boy like him, and he called me names for it. He is an insolent wretch and needs to be taught some manners. I boxed his ears and sent him home."

"Bring him back!" I'm shouting now.

"He is very rude; there are many better workers than he," Hammoudi says, and I begin to wonder if he is taunting me, deliberately provoking me, to see how far I will go, anxious for me to reveal what my true feelings are.

"It doesn't matter! Bring him back!"

"Yes, English," Hammoudi says, as if he is puzzled at my insistence. But do I see, or think I see, a smile tugging at the corners of his mouth?

It is two days before he comes, two endless days, two days of my life wasted pining for him, two days of sleepless nights.

"What's up, old chap?" Len Woolley asks.

I can't tell him.

Dahoum comes back with Hammoudi. It is nighttime. The oil lamps are lit. Len and I are sitting outside our nearly finished mud hut. Hammoudi walks up to us, with Dahoum a few paces behind. Dahoum is angry, or disconsolate, and keeps his eyes on the ground. He will not look at me.

"I have brought him back, as you demanded," Hammoudi says. Len looks up in surprise.

"I told the devil that you are angry with him and will punish him," Hammoudi says.

"Why would I do that?" I ask.

"Because he has offended you," Hammoudi says. "Or has not pleased you."

"He has not offended me," I reprimand Hammoudi sharply. "Except by his absence. I have had need of him."

Does Dahoum look up and glance at me?

"It's the end of season," Len says. "We're letting chaps go."

I'm going mad! Are they both in on this? Have they set up some elaborate game to trap me?

"I'm not leaving," I decide on the spur of the moment. Or have I been planning this all along? In truth, I have, for two days, anyway.

"I am staying here for the winter," I explain—to him and to Hammoudi, and to myself. "To finish the house for Mr. Woolley, next season."

I know that Len is staring at me, astonished by my stupidity. We always go back to England for the winter.

"Look at me, Dahoum," I order.

He looks at me. Arrow straight, those black eyes find their target in my soul. Is he reproaching me? Entreating me?

"I am staying here for the winter," I tell him. "I have need of someone to help me, to learn to take photographs, and to fetch and carry for me. Would you like to do that job?"

"You are very gracious, effendi," Hammoudi says, but it is not his answer that I want to hear.

Dahoum considers his reply for a while. He looks at the ground, scrapes at the dirt with his toes, sulkily.

"Will you speak to me sometimes, and tell me what you want from me?" Dahoum asks me, and I know that he is hurt because I have hardly spoken to him since the day of our first meeting.

"I will speak to you," I swear.

"What will you do if I am forgetful of my duties, or if I am not to your liking?" he asks. He's staring straight at me again, and there is a challenge in his eyes.

I'm stunned by his audacity. He is demanding a public declaration of my intentions! I dare not look at either Len or Hammoudi. So I look at him.

"If you are forgetful of your duties, I shall beat you," I tell him, trying to look stern. "But I shall always like you because I think you have a good heart."

Now he looks cocky, and I can't let him get away with that. "But if ever you do anything that causes me not to like you, I shall ask your uncle to beat you—"

That's no threat to him! He grins at that, as if it were a sexual invitation. Has the wanton creature no shame?

"—or I shall send you home to your mother and tell her to keep you among the womenfolk until you have remembered your manners."

He doesn't care! I could threaten him with the cruelest punishments (and having him put away with the womenfolk is as cruel as I could be), and he would suffer them gladly, because I have ordered it. He does not speak. Instead, his eyes are shining, and he smiles. And whatever fragments of my heart are left are smashed to smithereens.

"Yes," he says at last. "I will look after you."

I can't say anything, or even smile, for if I did they would all know me for what I am: a mad fool, lost, in love. Perhaps they know anyway.

"What on earth do you see in him?" Len asks, later.

Dahoum and Hammoudi have gone, the uncle giving the nephew a noisy lecture about how hard he must work, and that the protection of the effendi is entrusted to his care. But Dahoum knows that already. Len has stayed silent, puffing on his pipe and staring at the eastern stars, but then asks the one thing that is puzzling him.

"What on earth do you see in him?"

I don't know what to tell him. What on earth do I see in him? How can I explain that when I am near Dahoum I am happy, and when I am not near him I am not happy? What intrigues me is that the question implies an understanding by Len that Dahoum is very much more to me than a simple servant to guard my house.

"I don't know," I say, embarrassed by the public revelation of myself that I have made.

"Well, he seems to be a good lad, and Hammoudi will be here to keep him in check," Len says.

He sits in silence for a moment, but I know he wants to say more.

"Do have a care, old thing," he says, after a while. "It's different out here in the middle of nowhere, but chaps at home would never understand."

It's a good and gracious warning, and sensible, but I am too far gone to turn back now, for going back would be a greater distance than the journey I have made.

"He amuses me," I say, and shrug.

26

WET, COLD, MISERABLE and wondering if his number was up, Slaney hung on to the gun ring for dear life and thanked his Maker that his pilot, Bats, was such a buccaneer. They were coming in for a landing on the muddy strip at Kabul, the Afghanistan capital. As they had flown over the city, Slaney saw smoke rising from several buildings bombed by the rebels and heard bursts of gunfire from the mountains around the city. Their plane had been fired on several times during their flight; there were bullet holes in the canvas fuselage. Among Slaney's various prayers was that he had remembered to bring his ransom note with him.

Even in his parlous circumstances, Slaney could see the irony of his prayers. Usually, as they came in to land, he would be cursing Bats loudly and with all his heart.

Bats, Wing Commander Peter Belfridge, held an enviable position in the air force. A man of impeccable breeding and authority, of noble family, he had fallen in love with flying as a young man and made the Raf his life. Because his older brother had married well and fathered several sons, Bats was unencumbered by any obligations to the family title, and his personal wealth gave him the freedom to indulge his whims. He had been a daredevil since boyhood, obsessed by speed and danger.

Bats had been posted to India ten years ago and had spent eight of those years here, in the NWFP. Adored and admired by officers and airmen alike, Bats had fallen in love with this wild country and had made it very clear to his superiors that he had no interest in desk jobs or advancement. Because his family had highly placed friends in Whitehall, his superiors had acquiesced to his demands, and Bats functioned as a virtual one-man show. An aircraft, a D.H. 9A, was permanently assigned to him, and an engineer for that aircraft. Presently, that engineer was Slaney, who thought his job a cushy number most of the time. Bats lived in a splendid, well-guarded bungalow outside Peshawar, paid lip service to his orders, flew the missions that were demanded of him—usually no more than two a week—and, once away from the base, did exactly as he wanted.

It was the confidence of his class, Slaney thought, and wondered why Bats had chosen him as his only crew. He was first assigned to Bats in the usual way, by roster. He had heard the legends of Bats's takeoffs and, more especially, his landings, but Bats's calm, upper-class courteousness at their first meeting belied all those rumors. He had all the clichéd failings of his class: he was almost chinless, and his *r*'s all sounded like *w*'s. He was completely disarming on the ground, but in the air, Bats was another man, a wild, death-defying man, and the plane was an extension of his heroic self. But he was not fearless. Slaney quickly realized that every flight was, to Bats, a test of himself, of his ability to defy gravity and the elements in his rickety machine, and the harder the test, the more it was spiced by the possibility of mortal failure, the greater was Bats's triumph. At least one engineer had wept after one of Bats's landings and refused to fly with the man again. He was in no danger. After the tearful display, Bats would not have had him as engineer if he were the last on earth.

Slaney, on his first flight with Bats, knew he was being tested just as surely as Bats was testing himself. A British missionary woman had been taken ill, high up in the foothills of the daunting Himalayas, and Bats had volunteered to fly her out. The journey there was bad enough. Dodging through mountain passes, they were caught by unexpected wind drafts and almost dashed onto the craggy slopes. Slaney, in the cabin, resigned himself to death, strapped himself in with rope and closed his eyes that he might not see his coming destruction. Landing, though welcome, was almost worse. There was no real strip at the mission—only a track of partially cleared, rocky land, surrounded by steep hills.

"Hang on to your balls," Bats yelled. "Could be bumpy." Slaney couldn't conceive that it would be any bumpier than the flight, and he had been hanging on to the struts for an hour.

The landing was bumpier, but not as frightening. Having survived the journey, Slaney knew he was in expert hands, and that if disaster befell them, it would be simply bad luck. Bats circled the mission twice, to take stock of the strip and gauge the weather, and then came in fast and furious, as if to outrun the wind, or perhaps to crash through it. Inches from the ground, Slaney thought it might all be over. It was a peculiarity of the aircraft that it was sensitive to longitudinal trim, and if the tail was too high on landing, the propellor would dig into the ground and flip the plane over. At the exact, critical moment of potential disaster, Bats pulled the nose up and set the wheels down. They bounced back to heaven a few times, then settled to earth, and suddenly it was all over—Bats was taxiing the plane to the missionaries who were waiting at the edge of the field. Slaney, who had kept his sphincter muscle tight the last few minutes, felt suddenly wonderful, filled with a vibrant sense of life after having just survived the possibility of immediate death, and to his astonishment he found he had an erection.

"How was it?" Bats called as he jumped from the cockpit.

Slaney stuck his head out of the cabin and looked the man straight in the eye. "Could've been smoother," he said, poker faced.

Bats looked at him steadily, as if he had guessed Slaney's somewhat guilty secret about his state of sexual arousal. "You'll do," he said, and turned away to meet the missionaries.

Slaney knew that he had just been paid the highest compliment of his life.

A couple of days after they got back to Peshawar, Slaney had been told that he was permanently assigned to Bats—and so began an extraordinary period of the young engineer's life. All the dangerous assignments came to Bats, either because he volunteered or because, by tacit agreement with his superiors, there was no one else who could do the task.

Mostly, for Slaney, it was a snip of a job. The flights were always interesting, and the time on the ground was comfortable. As one of the few men who could tolerate Bats's flying, Slaney was accorded ungrudging respect by the other men, and even the vagaries of the aircraft made the job a constant and interesting challenge to him.

He even found a way to cope with Bats's landing bravado. The bumpiness, the dicing with death, didn't bother him, the manner of the dying was his nightmare. He had a fear of being burnt to death. If the plane tipped over during a landing and caught fire, Slaney, trapped in the cabin, would have no hope of getting out. His solution was to climb out on to the gun ring as they came in to land and hang on for all he was worth. There was an obvious risk of being thrown from the plane, but a broken back was infinitely preferable to death by conflagration.

The NWFP was the most turbulent province in the British Empire, and Bats's idea of heaven.

"A couple of hundred years ago—that was my time," he said to Slaney once.

"A man could do wonderful things then, discover Australia, or fight beside Clive. Too late now. It's all been discovered now. All the fun's over now."

When he wasn't flying, Bats was prone to melancholy, and only talk of exotic adventures and adventurers cheered him up. Often he spoke about leaving the air force and going to live among the headhunters in the treacherous jungles of Papua or New Guinea, or Irian Jaya.

"Be a bit scary," Slaney said. Being burnt in a plane crash was bad enough, but being roasted alive for someone's dinner was something else. At least here he had a chance if they were forced down. All the men who flew dangerous missions were given ransom notes, and three times a day Slaney checked that his was still in his wallet. It was his security blanket.

"Lord love you, duckie, I'd be scared," Bats confirmed. "But better that than being bored to death."

It occurred to Slaney that Bats had no fear of dying, only of being bored.

"You were at Miranshah—ever run into that fellow Lawrence?" Bats said one night. He and Slaney were billeted for the night in the only bungalow at the remote station of Landi Khotal, and both were getting drunk.

"Now there's a chap," Bats said, staring into his glass. He giggled. "He's got the desk wallahs in Delhi hopping mad."

"The desk wallahs" were the viceregal government officials. Slaney was puzzled. How could Ned, secure in a desert fortress, be upsetting Delhi?

Bats shrugged. "There's talk in the marketplace that he's stirring up another revolution, like he did in Arabia."

Slaney stared at him, his stomach lurching.

"He's going AWOL for weeks at a time, trotting off to Afghanistan, disguised as a Moslem holy man." Bats's eyes were sparkling, and Slaney thought he saw a hint of envy. "He's spreading the word that Amanullah Khan's a heretic, an agent of the devil, and they should get rid of him. A lot of the Afghans agree."

Slaney had known there was trouble in Afghanistan; they were so close to the border it affected all their lives. The marketplace in Peshawar and all the border towns were unusually volatile and dangerous; they went to sleep lulled by gunfire, and there was a constant sense of political unrest. Little things made a greater picture—political prisoners such as Umar escorted to Delhi, missions flown to remote stations to supply them with guns and aircrews, ransom notes upped from seven hundred and fifty rupees to a thousand.

But this news was different. This involved Ned!

Slaney got up and poured them both another drink. He was on the edge of unknown and unpredictable territories. He had wanted adventures and he had them with Bats, but Ned and revolutions was something else. Tipsy, he giggled. What would they call him, he wondered, "Shaw of Afghanistan"? He knew he should not be surprised by the news. He had believed Ned was a spy in Karachi, and he remembered Ned's meeting with the political prisoner, Umar. Still, he didn't understand Delhi's present anger, and, to a small degree, he was hurt that Ned had not given him any indication of what was afoot. Plus he felt foolish because he had doubted Ned.

"That's all gossip," he said, wanting to hear more. "He'd never get off the base."

Bats shrugged in agreement, but then added, "Where there's smoke, there's fire."

It made absolute sense to Slaney, and confused him utterly. He knew because he was there when it had happened that Ned sometimes left the base at Miranshah dressed as a local, but how could Ned go AWOL for weeks at a time, even under the most lenient CO? And why would Delhi be bothered? Slaney had only a limited knowledge of Afghan politics, most of it learned from Bats, but he understood that the amir, Amanullah Khan, the present ruler of the country, was modern in his thinking, but pro–Soviet Russian and anti-British. A revolution might bring to power a ruler who was more amenable to the West, and Delhi should be pleased.

"Whole thing's a balls-up," Bats said. "Delhi wants a revolution, or wants Amanullah out, but doesn't want to be seen to be the *provocateur*. Doesn't want a war with Russia," Bats explained. "Bit too bally late, if you ask me. The Commies are already raging."

Suddenly, drunk, he started to laugh. "What a chap," he said, admiration and envy in his tone. "What did you make of him?"

Slaney had no idea how to answer, because he didn't know what he made of Ned anymore. After the incidents with Umar, Slaney had thought Ned to be some kind of traitor, if only because of the company he kept. But if Britain wanted a revolution in Afghanistan, why did they arrest the revolutionary Umar? And if Ned was fomenting that revolution, why was Delhi so cross? Was Ned working on his own, or for the British—as opposed to the Indian—government? Slaney knew there were constant territorial and policy squabbles between the government of British India, which considered itself virtually autonomous from London, and London, which did not have the same opinion.

"Bally politics," Bats said gloomily, his speech slightly slurred. "String 'em all up, I say, fornicating politicians. A chap never knows where he stands with 'em, stuff up a chap's life good and proper."

He rested his head against the back of the threadbare sofa and stared at the ceiling. Moments later, he was snoring.

Slaney stared at Bats and saw Ned. No one is what they seem. There were hidden depths to Bats, some things in his past that might explain his present, just as there were with Ned. What was Bats doing here, in this self-imposed exile? Why did he never want to go home? Did his family prefer to keep him out of England? What was this bitterness about politicians that he had revealed? Why had he never married?

Slaney was getting drunk himself, and his mind wandered into exotic territories. He was in exile too, lost in a wonderland of adventure and mateship and danger, almost deliberately removed from the company of women. Why had he, Slaney, never married? The question was as valid, but Slaney had the answer to it: he had never found the right woman. Sometimes, though, he admitted the real truth and confessed to himself that he was slightly scared of women.

All Slaney knew of the opposite sex had been learned from his faithless mother, his brother Harold and the foul talk of other men in the service. He didn't understand women, but he desired them and believed he would get married one day, when his adventures were over. He wondered if that was why he was so happy here on the frontier, where there were so few white women.

In the rough barracks he had learned of men who shagged, or were shagged by, other men, but the idea of touching another man intimately was repugnant to Slaney, unfathomable. But was that true of Bats? Or of Ned?

By Ned's own admission, he had been buggered by some Turks in Arabia. Slaney excused that incident as a form of rape, because he could not conceive that anyone, no matter how debauched, could get pleasure from having something, anything, stuck up his arse.

It didn't add up. He knew that Ned, who could be a cocky little braggart, was also deeply lonely and desperately unhappy. There was no evidence of any sweetheart or loved one of either sex; Ned had no photos, as all the other men did, of anyone special in his life, apart from famous friends and the Arabs in the war, nor did he ever talk about anyone who might have been special to him at any time in his life.

Slaney was certain of one thing. On that last night he was with him in Miranshah, Ned had wanted to be held, to be hugged. Slaney had never seen such naked loneliness. If it had been only that, Slaney might have obliged, because he felt tender toward Ned. But there was also this conviction that Ned wanted, in some way that Slaney didn't understand, to be hurt, physically hurt, to be hit, to be beaten, and that contradicted the need to be held, and was, to Slaney, instinctively repugnant because he sensed it was sexual.

He hated to think about that because the implications were too disturbing to consider. Instead, he tried to concentrate on the news that Bats had given him.

What was Ned, who had been a hero, doing in Afghanistan, disguised as a Moslem holy man? If caught, he would be chucked out of the service, and Slaney knew that to be Ned's paramount fear. Why was he so deliberately provoking the wrath of the politicians in Delhi and Whitehall?

Or was it all just gossip? Was everyone assuming that Ned was involved, just because Ned was there? Was "Lawrence of Arabia" still so famous? Or so needed?

Within days, Slaney had the opportunity to find out the answers to at least some of his questions. A number of the austere, fundamentalist Afghan tribes revolted against the modernist, reforming, pro-Soviet Amanullah Khan. Bats and Slaney had to fly several rescue missions, to bring out Westerners who were in danger in Kabul and some of the other cities.

It happened thus that Slaney, wet, cold and miserable, was hanging on to the gun ring outside the plane, hoping devoutly that his ransom note was still in his wallet, and thanking his Maker that Bats was such a formidable pilot. For only Bats, Slaney was sure, could bring them to a safe landing in Kabul.

27

He moves in with me that night. He tethers his donkey outside and comes in with his rolled-up blanket, in which he keeps his few possessions, and asks where he will sleep. Fortunately, Len is still sitting outside, writing a report on the day.

I tell him that Len and I have cots in the bedroom and that he can sleep in a corner of the main room. He looks disappointed, and I glance outside. Surely he must understand?

Yes, he understands. He looks outside at Len, looks back at me and winks, and sets about making a comfortable pallet of straw for himself in a corner of the main room. For the next three weeks, while Len is still here, he behaves with perfect propriety. He works hard and well, keeps his distance and only occasionally looks at me. Late at night, when the flickering lamplight makes him appear even more handsome than the garish sun, he looks at me, his dark eyes filled with yearning, or with sauciness, or some seductive combination of the two. I put my finger to my lips, commanding him to silence, and glance at Len, and Dahoum nods his understanding. But he does not stop staring at me.

The sun has lost its furnace heat, the nights are getting cold. The workmen are dismissed. The site is silent. Len and I spend his last day inspecting our achievements, and when Len wanders off to say a private good-bye to the antiquities, Dahoum and I walk together to a temple and entreat our guardian deities for a mild winter.

Hammoudi organizes the carriage to take Len to Jerablus. We shake hands and say good-bye, and wave until the carriage has turned the corner and Len has gone back to his other world and we are left in ours. Hammoudi watches us, then looks at the sky and says it will be a hard winter. He leaves us, and we are alone.

Dahoum goes to finish the small stable he is building for his donkey, and I stare out at the village that is my principality, in perfect contentment.

Then I hear Dahoum shouting at his donkey, or cajoling her to eat, or singing pretty songs to her, and I smile.

Oh, he amuses me!

That night there is a crisis. Now Len has gone, Dahoum wonders again where he will sleep, and the glint in his eye is almost irresistible. I must resist him. We are not loose and base, we have to prove our love before we can indulge our senses. I tell Dahoum that he can bring his blanket and his sheepskins into the bedroom and sleep in the corner. He's very disappointed, but does not contradict me. He shifts his things into the bedroom, but I know the subject is not done with yet.

We are tired and make ready for bed. He comes close to me and tries to touch me affectionately. I sit on my cot and try to explain to him that we must sleep apart. He goes to his blanket and snuggles under his sheepskins and thinks I have rejected him. I turn down the lamp and get into bed. We lie in silence, several feet apart, and although I hear his heavy breathing, I know he is not asleep.

It is pitch black, there is no moon. I do not see him get up from his corner and walk to me. I see only blackness. I feel that he is near me, I feel the warmth of him. I hear his breathing. I know what he is doing to himself and inviting me to do.

I cannot! He means too much to me! But I am hard, and the sound of his pleasure is enough for me. I hear him cry out, and I am lost, to him and to myself. Without my even touching myself, my serpent strikes and I cry out. I cry out his name!

It is enough for him. He is satisfied. He does not understand me or my reticence, but he accepts my demanding rules, and it is enough for him that we were together and that I cried out his name.

What do I see in him? I see everything in him, all that I have ever wanted my beloved to be. And he is my beloved, and I am loved, in the only way that I think it is possible for me to be loved, and he is my beloved, and this is the only way that I know how to love. Of course, he wants more from me, and in the fullness of time, when I am worthy, I shall give myself to him, but at the moment it is enough that I cried out my need of him.

And so it goes, all through the changing seasons. He sleeps in the corner beneath his pile of sheepskin rugs, happier on the floor because he has never known a bed. With Len gone, I am free to be my other self, and I move my blankets, and my sheepskins because the nights are very cold, from the bed to the floor, close to Dahoum but far enough away to keep our purity. Yet near enough to stare at him on moonlit nights, to watch him as he slumbers and to be astonished that this trusting, simple soul can be content with me.

He makes my coffee in the morning, grinding the beans with his own hand, and wakes me with silent surliness, for he does not like the mornings. He does not cook—Hajj Wahid's wife, Fatima, does that, and she is fond of him and clucks about him like a second mother. Fatima is old and has her own family, so Dahoum helps her clean the house and folds my things, and I go about my business until, his duties done, we can be together.

The workmen have gone back to their wives and families, Hammoudi is visiting his wife's relations. Only we small few, the villagers, are left, and we make ready for the coming snow. Dahoum cuts firewood and tans with salt the skins of new-killed sheep and goats, making more blankets for our cold nights, and I fix doors and window shutters and pitch the roof, making safe our shelter from the elements.

Often, and for long periods of time, Dahoum and I do not speak, we have no need, each secure that the other is there, or nearby. I teach him to take photographs or make paper squeezes of reliefs, and he's a good student. Sometimes we walk into Jerablus, to shop for household items, or watch the camels being sold, or to see if the bookshop has received the books I ordered months ago. We go to the market and sit at a café and drink our tea and watch the world go by. We are content. We walk back, chattering about our day, and when we get home he makes a fire. We sit beside it, staring at the flames and letting our most private thoughts drift to the surface of our minds.

Sometimes we have visitors, but not many in the winter, and we are pleased to see them and entertain them properly. Dahoum never intrudes if they are foreigners, but sits on the floor at my feet, pretending to understand what we are saying. Or, if bored with that, he goes down to the well, where other men have built a fire and someone has made coffee, and sits with his own people and talks about the things important to him and them.

He is a formidable gossip and comes home laden with well-told tales of trivia, or of some nastiness the Turkish police have done to an acquaintance, or news of a marriage, a birth or death, or of a blood feud started, or how fat Azizah fell over the other day, on her back, with her legs flapping in the air and her skirts up around her thighs, so everyone could see her bloomers. It is the stuff of village life. If our guests turn in early, I will wander down to join the men and listen to the stories and laugh about fat Azizah. Or perhaps the young men, the hot-blooded youths, will turn to talk of war. Perhaps some Turk policeman has been rude to their mother, or insulted their sisters, or stolen from their father. Or they have been beaten by the Turks for insolence. This winter, while a Balkan War rages, there is talk of a Kurdish uprising. Now is the ideal opportunity. Turkey is distracted in the west by Bulgaria's aggression, and we hear wild rumors of Kurds marching on Aleppo, or even Alexandretta.

Blood up and ready to march with the Kurds, our young men curse the Turks who govern them and convince each other the day will come soon when they will rise up with avenging swords and guns and wreak havoc and bloodily dispatch all Turks to death, thereafter to live in freedom, governing themselves. They have no concept of a country—Syria is too vast for them. They see a city-state, like ancient tribes, and the more fanciful imagine our village, or Jerablus, as its capital. Most accept that far Damascus would be the seat of government, but even that's too distant. They want to rule themselves.

If energy and passion could bring it about, they would be free tomorrow. Their war cries, sharp, aggressive songs, curdle the peaceful night. It was like this in Sparta, when the young men trained for battle and passed their evenings dreaming of their victories. It has always been like this, forever and forever. It was like this at Ilium, when forty young men, silent inside a wooden horse, could not sing their coming triumph, but each man dreamed of victory. It was like this for Odysseus on that same night, when the blood-reddened morning would bring the end of ten years of war, and then, at last, he could go home.

It was like this for the Medes and Persians, and Darius. It was like this in Macedon and Gaugamela. It was like this for Joshua at Jericho. It is any young man's birthright and every young man's need. And it is mine.

Because I am not a harsh Turk, and because I have some immunity from Turkish authority (only some), and because I am the sole representative of a great foreign king, and because I am one of them and not one of them, and thus impartial, the villagers come to me with their grievances. Like Solomon, I arbitrate on the proper allotment of a contested scrap of land, or tell a young girl she has treated her aged mother unfairly, or decide who is owner of a sheep that has strayed into someone else's yard. Dahoum sits beside me while I hear the cases, I the judge, he the advocate for both parties and the counseling jury, whispering his opinion of the merits of each case, and we are an essential part of a tapestry that has been woven from the beginning of time, first defined by Hammurabi, and will be woven until the end of the world, the unrecorded, richly intricate history of village life.

Sometimes my decisions are easy, because the grievance is simple, and my adjudications are accepted with laughter and good grace on all sides. But sometimes they are of moment, and then my petitioners hang on my words, and sometimes my words offend a guilty man who believes himself innocent. My judgments are argued about for days on end—there's little else to talk about—and I have to be studiously careful not to make enemies, or too many overt friends.

Is this what it is to be a king? To have the responsibility of their lives thrust on me? Am I their king, elected by their own authority, regardless of who claims to rule them? Do my credentials and my seasonal authority and my apartness make me monarch?

I am not king, I have not been prince for long enough, I have not served my apprenticeship, I make mistakes, I have not earned their total fealty yet. I have not proved myself in war.

But I will be their king one day, when I have earned my crown, when I have proved my wisdom and my bravery and soldier's spirit. When I come to them a conquering hero and bring them rich and worthy gifts, they will acclaim me king. And I, Ned the wise, Ned the brave, Ned the good, will govern my contented people, my gorgeous consort at my side, a new Hittite king, a true descendant of a noble line.

When it is late we go back to our mud castle and sneak into our room (if there are visitors, they sleep in the outer room) and lie together, side by side, two feet apart, and giggle and whisper our secrets. We are happy, but we do not encourage visitors. We have no need of them.

We have a festival to celebrate the harvest and our coming hibernation. The women sing and clap the rhythm, and the men dance, and Dahoum is the nimblest of them, the star of the show, leading the swaying line of men with graceful energy. He comes to me, holds out his hand, and I, who cannot dance, accept his invitation and join the others, men like me and not like me, for I am one of them and not one of them, but I dress like them and speak like them and dance like them, and they cheer my participation in their lives.

We roast goat meat, or sheep, or camel, over open coals, and eat with our fingers, squatting in a circle round a central platter heaped with rice and sour milk and sultanas, and the women wait their turn until the men are sated, and the children wait until the women have fed, but everyone gets their portion. We are not greedy, we are desert people, open and generous, and each dependent on the other for survival through the winter.

The cold strikes with a vengeance. The sweeping wind cuts through the thickest sheepskin, numbs the brain and chills the fingers. We do not go out then. We lock ourselves in our refuge, light the lamps and long for blue skies and a sunny day.

I catch a cold. I am feverish and grumpy, and for the first day he is my attentive nurse, but then he catches that same cold and sulks because I don't cosset him, and we nurse each other and our grievances, wrapped up and sweaty, pregnant with self-pity. We are fed mutton broth by the local midwife. The only physician that we have nearby, she believes her soup will induce the inhabiting viruses that swell inside our bodies to a premature delivery. She's right. Three days later our bodies are purged, and we are our thinner selves again.

And always, he amuses me. He's slow to anger but has an explosive temper when something maddens him too much. He curses all the world then, but it doesn't last long because suddenly he will see the funny side of whatever had frustrated him, and he will laugh and shake his head and settle down to his contented self.

Sometimes I am moody, lost in thought. He will ask me what is wrong, and I will shake my head, and he will shrug and move away to sit by the fire and wait until my good humor is restored. Sometimes the local Turkish authorities will come to visit and parade their wretched authority, for even the lowliest Turk thinks himself important by virtue of his country's domination. It makes me mad, and I protest their cheek and violence. They dare not harm me, but Dahoum is patient and advises silence. They dare not harm me, but they can do what they like with anyone from the village.

We don't celebrate Christmas. It isn't a festival of his religion, nor mine, whatever religion I may have, but our German neighbors come to visit, trudging through the snow, and we have a party. They bring their own food— sausage and sour cabbage, and lots of schnapps—and they get drunk and sing songs of piercing nostalgia for their homeland, for they are shipwrecked, stuck here not by choice but by employment, and lonely for some other, different company. They give each other presents, and I, because I am sentimental, give a small trinket to my beloved, and he, because he has heard about these things from an Orthodox family in the next village, gives me a huge, brightly wrapped parcel, a camel saddle he has carved himself, working the leather and decorating it in brass, badly, but it is the most beautiful, and touching, Christmas present I have ever received.

But mostly on winter nights we are alone and snug, Dahoum and I. We talk about our families. He tells me of his village and his plump, adoring mother and scrawny, overworked, farmer father. He talks of his pretty young sisters and his older brothers, one married with children, one gone to Aleppo to find his fortune. He speaks of poverty and scratching a living from an undernourished soil, but he also talks of warmth and generosity. It is a happy picture, and he is puzzled that it saddens me.

I tell him of my father and my brothers, but I do not talk about my mother. He asks me why. I try to explain in simple terms my complex feelings for that woman. I explain her faith in a vengeful God, I explain her belief in damna-

tion, but he shakes his head because he thinks his God would not be so cruel to a dead being. I tell him of her punishments, of how she beat me, hurt, degraded me. He laughs and says all mothers beat their boys, and fathers too—it is part of being a boy.

"But you love her very much," he says, as if it is an obvious fact.

I don't answer. I don't know how much I love my mother. Or if I love.

"How can you not?" he asks me, his eyes wide with astonishment. "She gave you life."

Yes, she gave me life. She gave life to the boy and tried to kill the man. She has succeeded with Bob, she has emasculated him, cut off his balls. (Does she keep them somewhere, mummified or pickled, a trophy of her victory?) Will she do the same with William or Frank? Neither of them is married, nor shows much interest in the idea, and neither has found a love as I have. And little Arnie? What will become of him?

But she has failed with me! I am a man, and Dahoum is the living proof of it! She has to know! She has to see my victory! She has to be shown that she has lost! I will take him back to England and present him to her and revel in her gall.

Spring comes, and blue skies and sunny weather. We throw open the shutters and windows of our house, to air it out, and make ready for the coming summer. We wash and clean the pots and furniture, dump the rubbish of our seclusion and paint the walls anew, to rid them of the soot of fire. And cleanse ourselves.

We go down to the river. We strip naked and plunge in. The water, fresh from the icy mountaintops, is stinging cold. We caress each other with soap, rinse each other of impurity, and wet together, we embrace. We lie down together on the bank by the waters of Babylon and let the weak sun dry our bodies. We put our robes on. Hand in hand, we walk to the site, to the temple, to the Weather God, to thank our guardian deity for bringing us safely through winter.

Then, still hand in hand, we walk home again. And because it is spring, and because I love him, I want to celebrate him and I carve a statue of him, naked, from local limestone. It isn't a very good statue—I don't carve very well—but he stands with his shirt off for hours in the barren patch we call a garden and seems oblivious to the giggles of the passing boys. The young women keep clear, because their mothers tell them it is a sin for them to gaze upon a seminaked man; instead they peep at him from hiding places. We do not care what anyone says about us, because we are unique unto ourselves, and I want to parade him before the world, that all the world will know that I am loved.

I take him home with me to England, to show Mother the man she has made of me and the man who makes me happy. Of course, I have to be a little careful of what others will think, and so I take Hammoudi with us. It would be unseemly for us to travel in England without a chaperone, because these things are not done there. We would be destroyed in England, if England guessed my secret.

But Mother knows. She knows as soon as she sees him that she has lost, and I have won, and that Dahoum occupies a place in my heart that is forbidden for her to enter. It is a sweet revenge for all that she has done to me.

I am a conquering hero who has ransacked Ali Baba's cave, arriving home with a glittering sackful of Oriental trinkets—brass lamps and gleaming coffeepots, bright brocades and shining filigrees, camels carved from olive wood and huge, curved knives in silver sheaths bestudded with sparkling colored glass— and even my father nods and laughs at the fun of it and says that he is proud of me. My brothers are entranced by my silly souvenirs, and fascinated by Dahoum and Hammoudi, in baggy pants and flowing robes, the first Moslems they have ever met. Bob's a bit pi, of course, because they are infidels to him, and he tries to convert them. They are courteous but will not be drawn to talk of God, his or theirs, and eventually even Bob gives up and shakes his head and goes back to his Bible, leaving the rest of us to our fun.

Father is at his most gracious then, and takes Dahoum and Hammoudi on tours of Oxford, chattering to them as if they understand every single word he says to them. Bill and Frank and Arnie and I tag along behind, giggling, and listen to Hammoudi practice his erratic English, which confuses Father utterly, but he is too polite to admit that he has no idea what Hammoudi is saying. Then I step in and help, and my brothers are open mouthed at my command of the language and beg to be taught some words.

Dahoum thinks England wonderful; he loves to be the center of attention, and he causes quite a stir in Oxford, or anywhere in England. (The boat trip scared him—he got sick and never found his sea legs—but the train was a miracle of mechanics to him. Sometimes, at night, he will squat on the floor, legs akimbo, and rock from side to side and make choo-choo noises and pretend to blow a steam whistle, until it gets so tedious that Hammoudi slaps his head and tells him to stop.) They are agog at the sights, and we take tea at Grantchester and eat hot buttered muffins, and visit Hogarth and the colleges and dine on Mother's steak-and-kidney pudding, and everything is an exotic adventure, the impossible dream of a lifetime made real.

If we are tourists in the daytime, we are ourselves at night in my little bungalow at the back of the house. We clear the two small rooms of furniture and squat upon the floor and pretend we are back at Carchemish. We all three sleep in sleeping bags in the other room. It confuses poor Mother. She is convinced that I am lost to Sodom and thinks Dahoum my evil seducer, that he and I indulge our vice together every night, while Hammoudi keeps guard in the other room, against the prying eyes of strangers. (Or perhaps, in her overheated imagination, she thinks Hammoudi joins us, in bacchanalian orgy.)

Poor Mother, she does not understand. We are not profane. We are not lecherous Sodomites. We do not invade and violate each other for reckless pleasure. One day, when I am worthy, I will give my body to him, but it will be my ultimate gift. When I dazzle him with glory, so that he will never want anyone but me. When I come to him as a great soldier, bringing a priceless treasure. His eyes will be shining in gratitude for my worthy gift, and for love of me, and he will conquer my body as he has my soul. And I will have the very best of him.

But that is not the basis of our love. We are the Republic and the Symposium. We are Babylon, but we are also Nineveh, and we are Troy and Macedon. We are Alexandria and Rome. We are the Spartans of Leonidas, and we are life-affirming Athens. We held Thermopylae against the eastern invasion and gave our blood at Marathon. An army of us could conquer the world, because I would not be disgraced in battle before my beloved, or let him be, and I would give my life for him, and he for me.

Poor Mother. She who is a damned sinner, lost to carnal flesh, but denying it, does not even begin to understand that what I have with Dahoum is not of lust but of the heart, not of passion but of the soul. She cannot fathom that we can be lovers even if we do not lie together, that the majesty of our love is in that purity, not in carnality or physical expression, in its virtue, not its vice.

We are one being, Dahoum and I. We are soul mates, on earth as we will be in heaven, or any hereafter. On the fields of Elysium, or in the brimstone halls of Hades, or in those meadows that are reserved for those who are neither good nor evil.

Even in the void, if that is all there is, we will be inseparable.

28

"I'm afraid you will have to fend for yourselves," Lady Humphrys told Slaney, without apology. "My first responsibility is to the women and children."

She glanced around, and Slaney thought he saw a flicker of annoyance in her eyes. The building was full to overflowing with potential evacuees, expatriate families trying to make their dire circumstances tolerable. In every corner there were makeshift cots and bunks, blankets draped between them to provide some small privacy, and water was being boiled in tin mugs over kerosene lamps. The kitchen had ceased to function—many of the staff had fled—and the larders had been raided by the refugees.

Lady Humphrys turned back to Slaney. "I need a strong pair of shoulders," she commanded.

It was an order, not a request, and Slaney spent the next little while lugging beds and cots from the storeroom for the refugees, under Lady Humphrys's direction.

Bats had landed safely, if tempestuously, at the Kabul airfield, heralded by gunfire from opposing armies who were not firing at the planes but at each other. They had been greeted by a loyalist captain and his unit who escorted them to the British embassy, which also served as the ambassador's residence. Light was failing, and they would not be able to take off until morning. Bats was taken to the ambassador, Sir Francis Humphrys, and Slaney was left to organize their accommodation, which was difficult because the embassy was now functioning as sanctuary for expatriates. A rather prim and austere Englishwoman appeared to be in charge, so Slaney had asked her for help and soon found himself dragooned by Lady Constance Humphrys, wife of the ambassador, into helping with beds.

They turned the library into a makeshift dormitory. Lady Humphrys hardly spoke to Slaney while he worked, except to give him orders, but he began to feel a certain kinship toward her. They were both, in Slaney's mind, in the same boat.

"Perhaps the child's cot is too near the window," Lady Humphrys said. It was not a suggestion, but a sensible order, and slightly chilling to Slaney. If the residence was attacked, the windows might be broken, and a child sleeping in the cot might be injured by the glass. He moved the cot away from the window.

"Well done," Lady Humphrys said of his labors. "I think we both deserve a cup of tea."

She called a name, and one of the few remaining servants appeared.

"Tea," Lady Humphrys ordered. "Just for the two of us."

The servant was clearly fearful of the guns and of remaining in the house while the war raged, but clearly was even more fearful of Lady Humphrys. He nodded and left. Lady Humphrys turned to Slaney. "You're an engineer," she said. "Do you enjoy your work?"

Slaney's uniform proclaimed that he was not an officer and therefore not a pilot, but that Lady Humphrys should recognize this and then make the correct association of his rank to his function was surprising to him, but only for a moment. Of course she knows, he thought. It is her job to know. Slaney had never before met her like, a woman of the upper class who said what had to be said, as clearly and simply as possible, and did what had to be done. She seemed to have no fear of the civil war raging outside her garden gate, but went about her business as if she were organizing a rather chaotic fête at home. Her authority and her sense of domestic order changed his opinion of women somewhat. Without the women, he thought, the Empire would be impossible. Men might win the wars, but when it came to the housekeeping afterwards, the women were in charge.

"First time I've been in a revolution," he volunteered cheerily, as he heaved a horsehair mattress onto a bed.

Lady Humphrys was sorting through blankets. "It's all so very unnecessary," she said, "but, I suppose, inevitable."

The servant brought the tea. Lady Humphrys ordered a break, and, to a symphony of gunfire from outside, Slaney settled on a bed to sup with Her Ladyship and thought himself a very lucky young man.

During their year in Kabul, Sir Francis and Lady Humphrys had both reached the reluctant conclusion that revolution against the amir was not only inevitable but probably desirable. When he was first given Afghanistan, Sir Francis was disappointed. He had hoped for something more glamorous, but he discussed it with the ever-constant Constance, and, both being old-time

Empire builders, they agreed that Kabul, while a tough and challenging post, was vital to British interests. They would do battle with it and bring it to submission. As a reward, they might be given one of the smaller Caribbean islands in their later years.

They had arrived in Kabul as befitted their station, by an overland motorcade of a dozen cars, led by the embassy Rolls-Royce and attended by troops of the Indian Army. For their entrance into the city, the embassy staff organized a spectacular parade led by those Indian soldiers, supplemented by colorful local tribesmen. It was unfortunate that most of those who participated were from tribes hostile to the amir. The new ambassador and his lady were greeted by small legions of cheering, gun-firing, horse-riding men. The amir, Amanullah, recently returned from an extravagant trip to Europe, watched contemptuously from the palace windows. The circus was yet another example of British arrogance and colonialism, gunboat diplomacy. Three times the British had fought wars to gain control of Afghanistan, and three times they had lost. It was clear to Amanullah that Sir Francis was the vanguard of another coup, which, he determined, would fail as surely as the rest.

Sir Francis went to the palace to present his credentials in full court dress—gold braid, knee breeches, plumed cocked hat—and was shocked by what he saw. There was a complete absence of anything Eastern in the court. A gramophone was playing "The Entrance of the Peers" from Gilbert and Sullivan's *Iolanthe*. From the amir to the lowliest page, all the men wore Western clothes. Officials in frock coats greeted each other by shaking hands, and, most shocking of all, there were women present, including the amir's wife and daughters, dressed in the latest Paris fashions and not wearing the veil.

Sir Francis smelled trouble, and not for himself. Outside the palace the old, Orthodox Moslem order ruled. When Sir Francis gently taxed the amir with his modernism, Amanullah was furious and denounced Sir Francis as a paternalist and a colonialist. No foreign power had a proprietary right to the advantages of the twentieth century, which should be available to all countries and all races, not as some imperial largesse. He praised the people's revolution in Russia that had deposed a corrupt monarchy and brought freedom and equality to the suffering serfs, and he was determined to achieve the same for his own country.

He lauded those in neighboring India who were fighting for independence from Britain and boasted that he subsidized anti-British propaganda on the frontier, in the tribal areas of the Khyber Pass and Hindu Kush, and that he refused to extradite criminals sought by the British who found refuge in his country. Very little of this was news to the well-briefed Sir Francis, but the vehemence of the speech shocked him, and he was aware that the Russian ambassador, seated in a place of honor near the amir, could scarcely contain his smile.

Sir Francis returned to the residence nursing the conviction that the amir was hell-bent on self-destruction and might very well lead his country into civil war. Constance reminded him that they had not expected their posting to be easy. Together and separately, they cultivated the other families and tribal leaders of the complex Afghan society and learned from them and from their embassy spies that the amir was on the verge of an alliance with the Soviets, which would give Moscow a formidable base for operations against both British India and the precious Persian Gulf.

Every day, it seemed, brought a new and ever more dangerous decree. Amanullah's photograph was to be hung in public buildings, which was blasphemy to the fundamentalists. No one was required to kiss the amir's ring, which was shocking to the traditional families, an affront to their own authority. The veil was no longer required of women, and girls were ordered to attend school. Polygamy, sanctioned by the holy book, the Koran, was forbidden to government officials. The Sabbath was to be celebrated on Thursday, not Holy Friday. The mullahs, the fount of all religious teaching, the Keepers of the Faith, were stripped of their positions of power and packed off to remote monasteries. Even the atheist Russian ambassador, a hard-liner when it came to social reform, was shocked by the audacity and range of the social changes and cautioned his government against too much generosity to the amir.

"It must explode," Sir Francis told Constance. "All it needs is a match to the fuse."

The fuse was lit, but it was a slow one. Young hotbloods from the Shinwari family, enemies to the amir, allied themselves with other malcontents and attacked several military outposts. Success brought legions, and other disgruntled tribes rallied to the Shinwari cause. Kabul was besieged. The amir, who might have won the battle if his troops had been paid regularly, capitulated to the rebel demands. He had little choice. His own underpaid soldiers were selling their guns to the Shinwari to buy food.

"Back to the primitive," the amir announced bitterly. "As you were!"

He reversed all his decrees, created a council of mullahs, and conceded to his army's demands for regular pay. Everyone went home, and at the British embassy Sir Francis and Lady Humphrys sighed in relief and began to prepare their Christmas card list.

But chaos was come. An effective political vacuum existed, abhorred by man and nature, and rumor rushed in to rule.

Sir Francis and Constance were astonished at what they heard. Every adventurer, every soldier of fortune from the East and from Europe had supposedly arrived in Afghanistan. Trebitsch Lincoln was there. It was possible, of course. Lincoln was a disgraced politician, a German by birth who had once held a seat in the British House of Commons. When Sir Francis had last heard of him, he was a Buddhist monk in China, but it was known that Lincoln, for reasons of his own, was desperate to get to Tibet, and Afghanistan was a possible back door to that country. Dr. Francis Havelock was there. Havelock was a well-known medical missionary, a mischief maker and an advanced social climber. If he really were in Afghanistan it was probable that he would have presented himself at the embassy. Umar Khan was said to be there, a prince of the Shinwari tribe, nephew of the deposed Yakub Khan, and a potential future king. He had been imprisoned by the British in India to avoid exactly this circumstance. This rumor, at least, was likely true. More than once, Umar had escaped his captivity, and Sir Francis had recently received advice from Delhi that the man was loose again.

Most shocking of all was the whisper that Lawrence of Arabia had turned up in Afghanistan disguised as a Moslem holy man, Munshi Shah, and was inciting revolt, as he had done in Arabia years before. This last rumor was the most persistent, and Sir Francis had telegraphed Delhi for clarification. The formal reply assured him that Lawrence was in India, as an airman, but reassurances did nothing to quell the rumor. The Russians believed it, and *Pravda* published furious editorials denouncing his chicanery. The amir believed it. Certain that the British were plotting against him, believing his Russian friends, he ordered the arrest of T. E. Lawrence on sight.

Perhaps it was this paranoia about malign British influences that distracted the amir, preventing him from discovering the real agent of his destruction, Bacha Sakau (which means "Water Boy"), a pockmarked peasant who was ambitious beyond realistic expectations and called himself Habiballah Khan, the "Darling of God." He led a small band of desperadoes, and during the Shinwari revolt he offered his services to the amir. Amanullah, grateful for any allies, even gangsters, accepted, and financed and armed Water Boy—who double-crossed him. With Amanullah's money, he raised a larger army, besieged the palace and proclaimed himself king.

The country fell into a state of war. Sir Francis decided that the remaining British, except himself, his wife and his most immediate and loyal staff, should be evacuated, and he sent to Delhi for help.

Bats and Slaney were the first to arrive, leading four other aircraft, and thus it was that Slaney, who had expected to run airborne missions of mercy, found himself shifting beds. But Lady Humphrys was grateful and found space for Slaney and Bats in the laundry. Slaney, by dint of some healthy bribes to the few remaining domestic staff and elaborate flourishing of his ransom note, managed to get billets for the other airmen, then went to scrounge food. It was during this quest that he was press-ganged into service by another woman, a forthright American, who brooked no argument.

Mrs. Carol Isaacson seldom brooked argument, especially when her cause was her husband. Married a year previously, she and Allen Isaacson had decided on an eccentric honeymoon. Wealthy beyond avarice, they had wanted to see the world before settling down. They bought a motorcar in Paris and decided to drive on the old silk route to China. It was a dangerous and primitive journey, but Allen was a crack shot, Carol was self-sufficient in domestic and toilet matters, and they hired local bodyguards to ride with them through the more turbulent places. They had the time of their lives. They fell in love with the East, reveled in the nomadic life and were invigorated by the constant perils of their journeying.

Innocents abroad, they had arrived in Afghanistan and thought the country magnificent, the high point of their travels. They hadn't heard news of the real world since leaving Persepolis and had no idea, nor did they care, why the road to Kabul was so spectacularly peopled. Here was the adventure they had been seeking. They thrilled to the troops of horse-riding, gun-firing tribesmen and the heavily veiled women who walked at their side. They arrived in

Kabul to volleys of gunfire, and from the few other guests in the hotel learned of the reality of their circumstances. They spent their first night under guard at the hotel, and when Allen went out to see the fun he was wounded in the leg by a stray gunshot. Carol, rushing to be at his side, was grazed in the arm by another bullet. They decided that discretion was the better part of valor and took refuge at the British embassy.

Lady Humphrys took pity on the couple, although she regarded them as foolhardy. It was so typically American, she thought, to rush in where angels would have paused. She put them up in the second-best bedroom, sent a boy out in futile search of a doctor, did her best with their wounds, gave Carol instructions on nursing and went to attend to the needs of British mothers and children. Carol Isaacson went looking for soup, and a servant to help change the bloody sheets, and found Slaney.

Slaney had never met an American woman before and fell immediately to her assault. In awe of her resourcefulness and self-confidence, he helped her change the bloody sheets, showed her to the laundry, put the sheets to soak and then went with her to the kitchen.

Carol Isaacson was a kind woman with strong opinions and unshakeable convictions, and her thoughts on the situation in Afghanistan were ingenuous but implacable. Most of what she knew about the country and the present crisis she had learned over a meager dinner at the hotel the previous night, but this didn't stop her from espousing a radical view. In her eyes Amanullah was a great, reforming king brought low by infidel traditionalists, and most of her sympathy went to the women of the country. Her knowledge of the Islamic order was superficial, but what she had been told shocked her, and she tarred all Moslems with the same brush. She thought the veil monstrous, polygamy an affront to the wives and the general place of women in the society to be intolerable. Since her only immediate audience was Slaney, she gave him the full benefit of her strident views.

"They have no rights, you know," she said as she boiled water for soup. She had paid a local boy an outrageous sum for scrawny goat meat, and Slaney was cutting it up under her direction.

"They can be divorced like that," she said, snapping her fingers. "All the man has to do is say 'I divorce thee' three times in public, and it's all over for the poor woman."

She was furious that the amir's decree ordering girls to go to school had been rescinded, and she was contemptuous of Afghani men. "Sex maniacs, every man jack of 'em," she snapped.

Slaney blushed. He had never heard a woman talk like this. "No self-control at all. They're so foul they satisfy themselves with each other until they get married, and then their favorite thing is to take their women from behind."

Slaney dropped the carving knife he was using. He bent down to pick it up and to hide his scarlet face from this brazen woman.

"They can't do it any other way, of course, because the women are mutilated." She glared at Slaney. "You know what they do to girls?"

Slaney shook his head, silently praying that she wouldn't tell him.

"They circumcise them, when they're only six or seven, with no anesthetic."

Slaney, mortified, was also confused. He couldn't imagine how a woman could be circumcised.

Even if she had been aware of Slaney's embarrassment, Carol wouldn't have stopped. The night at the hotel had rattled her more than she cared to admit. She was worried about her husband's wound, and her own, and their situation. In her fear and anger she blamed men for the world's ills, and since Slaney was the only man in earshot, he was getting the brunt of her anger.

Night had fallen, and Slaney thought it would be the longest night of his life, trapped in a kitchen with this relentless, shameless creature who spoke of things no woman should know about, and certainly not speak about in company, mixed or otherwise.

"And you know who's to blame for it all, don't you?" The soup was bubbling in the pot. How long does this soup take to cook, Slaney wondered, how long before the hour of my release?

"Your Lawrence of Arabia, that's who!" Carol told him. "He's to blame for all this, he's the one behind the revolution! He's the one trying to bring down the amir so the country can go back to its barbaric ways!"

It was only gossip, hearsay, picked up at the hotel, but it made sense to Carol. Since the cause of the amir was so patently right, a devil had to be found, and Lawrence fit the bill, along with the British in general. True, Allen had British ancestry, and although Carol was wary of denigrating his background and offending her hosts, still she needed to personalize her demons. She told a fantastic tale of Lawrence's adventuring, and because he was the only hero the West recognized from the Arabian Campaign, so he became the leader of the Afghan revolutionaries.

"I think the soup's ready," Slaney said hopefully.

Carol glanced at the pot. "Yes, that'll do," she said. She ladled some soup into two plates and headed for the door. "Help yourself," she said. "I don't think there's enough for everyone."

She went to nurse her husband, and Slaney breathed an enormous sigh of relief. Hungry, he helped himself to a bowl of soup and sat in the kitchen, eating and thinking about Ned. Where there's smoke, there's fire, he decided.

Gunshots sounded close by, and moments later Bats stuck his head in the door. "There you are, Slaney," he said casually. "There's trouble; got a gun?"

It was an order to follow, and Slaney trailed Bats into the garden, to Sir Francis, who was staring at the night sky. Beyond the compound, distant fires blazed as buildings burned. Bullets whizzed over their heads, a battle raging in the street outside. Slaney was ready to duck for cover, but neither Sir Francis nor Bats moved.

"Tricky," Bats said to Slaney, loving it. "We're right in the firing line. Government troops on one side, rebels on the other. Presently, we're the meat in the sandwich."

"What are we going to do?" Slaney wondered aloud.

"Oh, Sir Francis will sort it out, he's a good man," Bats said casually. "But if you believe in God, a prayer or two might help." He looked at Sir Francis. "I speak the lingo, sir, if that's any help."

Sir Francis nodded, without a word accepting the offer of help. He cocked his gun and went to the garden gates.

"Iron balls," Bats said approvingly, and went to the ambassador's side.

Lady Humphrys came out of the house. "See to the women, my dear," Sir Francis told her. "They'll be scared."

"Godspeed," Lady Humphrys said, and went back inside.

They all speak a common language, Slaney thought; it is their class and breeding. He put his hand in his pocket to check that he had his ransom note, sent out a few alarm calls to God and watched in amazement as Sir Francis ordered the servant to open the gates, then went out into the night with Bats, to stand between the opposing forces. "Bloody mad," Slaney muttered.

He couldn't see Sir Francis and Bats anymore, but he could hear the firing. Then, miraculously, the sound of gunfire stopped, and he heard Sir Francis speaking clearly and loudly in English, Bats translating for him, in Pushtu, and urgent, blood-lusty voices replying. Then there was comparative silence.

Slaney sensed that something of moment had happened, and his curiosity got the better of his nervousness. He crept to the open garden gates and looked out into the street.

Sir Francis and Bats were squatted on their haunches, negotiating with the leaders of the two warring parties, surrounded by gun-wielding Afghans. There was very little light, but Slaney was sure that the leader of one of the warring armies was Umar.

An agreement was reached, and the negotiators stood up and shook hands. The Afghan leaders called to their respective forces, and amid gunshots and cheering, the two sides vanished into the night.

"Jolly well done, sir," Bats said, as if he had played no part in the business.

"The gold sovereigns did the trick," Sir Francis said, dismissing the compliment. They came back into the compound and gathered the refugees to them. Lady Humphrys stood at her husband's side.

"We're safe for tonight," Sir Francis said crisply. "They've agreed to have their battle somewhere else. It will be uncomfortable, but I believe I have secured your physical welfare. I want the women and children to be ready to leave at dawn. Aircraft have arrived from India, and you will be evacuated there. I shall stay, of course, as will my wife."

Slaney doubted that Lady Humphrys's husband had ever asked if she wanted to stay. It was natural that she should be beside him, to the end, if that was what the fates had planned.

It *was* an uncomfortable night, but Slaney and Bats, used to discomfort, each dozed for a while in the laundry. Before they slept, Slaney told Bats of the rumors of Ned.

Bats giggled. "Told you so," he said. "Even Sir Francis has heard of it. Damn annoyed about it too. He's old school tie, thinks that chaps should know their place and not meddle in things that don't concern 'em." He yawned and settled for sleep. "Iron balls," he said as he drifted off.

Slaney, who had troubled dreams, woke early, and stared out at the stars. At least the sky was clear; they would be able to take off.

His mind was filled with thoughts of Ned. There had to be truth in the rumors, they were too persistent. Then there was the presence of Umar, obviously an important soldier and a friend of Ned's. Somehow, in ways that

Slaney didn't understand, Ned was responsible for their present circumstances and for this revolution. Horrified by what the American woman had told him of the life of women here, he had started to think of this revolution as a despicable thing. He was sure she spoke the truth. During his time on the frontier, he had seen how women were treated, and although he had accepted it as part of the culture, Carol Isaacson had awakened him to the inequities. Why would Ned do battle to sustain this awfulness? It all seemed wrong.

None of it made sense, none of it added up, but all of it had a kind of aberrant logic. He wanted to see Ned, to confront him, to find out the truth. Whatever his feelings about Ned after that odd night at Miranshah, Slaney, in his present circumstances, only remembered the gentle, lonely side of Ned and was worried for his welfare.

He woke Bats, as he had been requested, an hour before dawn. Immediately, Bats looked to the window.

"Clear," Slaney said. "We'll get off."

"I don't think it's a good idea that we all fly in convoy to Peshawar," Bats said. "Too easy a target."

He paused for just a moment and grinned at Slaney. "Shall we go to Miranshah? It's close—and safe."

It wasn't a question, he had the devil in him. Slaney knew exactly what was in his mind.

"Besides, I wouldn't mind meeting this Lawrence chappie," Bats said, his eyes bright with adventure. "Find out what he's been up to."

Slaney was thrilled and wondered if Bats, among his many other skills, could read his mind.

"If he's there, of course," Bats added.

29

We hate the Turks. Look what they have done to us!

Safe, in Carchemish, I hear rumors of treasure. I hear from a German bridge builder who has a love of the antique world that near a village to the north of us there is a statue of a lion goddess, or of a woman seated on the backs of two lions, probably Hittite. Unusual. I have to see it.

The village is beyond the Syrian border, inside Turkey proper. My letters of commission will be irrelevant there, so far outside our territory. It is dangerous, but I want to see the statue. (And we are bored, Dahoum and I, with our seclusion and each other. We need adventure.)

We decide to go as Bedouin man and wife. I am fair and blue eyed, pale from the winter, and will be a veiled woman to disguise my coloring, because even the foul Turks will respect my female modesty. Dahoum will be my husband, taking his bride home to show his family. We are like a pair of silly schoolboys, giggling at the excitement and the daring of our plans.

I borrow clothes from village women. Dahoum helps me dress, distracted briefly by my nakedness until I slap his exploring hand and tell him we have work to do! I wear all-encompassing black and a flowered veil of muslin that completely covers my face. I make a respectable woman, and Dahoum seems to stand an inch or two taller, as befits my husband. We take my camera, hidden in a bag; I want to photograph the statue. We pack some food and set off. The village laughs and cheers us as we leave.

We walk the miles north side by side, but when we see strangers, Dahoum is sharp with me and orders me to walk a few paces behind, as befits my station. Oh, his head is swollen with pride, because he is young and lusty, with a pretty bride. (Only he knows how pretty I am, because only he has seen under my veil, but anyone would know, from his proud bearing, that I am beautiful.)

We know when we have crossed the border, although it is not marked, and walk more warily now. The villagers here know nothing of us or who we are, but they disregard us, or treat us with the curiosity of strangers: we are the only distraction to their day. We sleep in a tiny barn, and Dahoum is very difficult, demanding that I fulfill my wifely role. I giggle and slap his hands again, and he chases me around the barn, but I'm too quick for him. I hide behind some hay, but he discovers me and springs upon me. All hope is lost. I get cross with him and tell him I have a headache. He says he doesn't care about my head! I know that I will get no sleep until he has something of his way with me, and so I allow him his pleasure, but circumspectly, as befits a virtuous woman.

I remove my veil (but not my robe) and pull up my skirt to reveal my legs and let him gaze upon me while he does what he needs to do to himself. My being a woman has a remarkable effect on him, and it's all over very quickly, although, at his peak, he demands a wifely kiss, and then I am driven to distraction by his hot, fat, wet, probing tongue, his harsh chewing lips and his stubbly chin scraping my flesh, his teeth grinding into my mouth until I nearly lose my virtue and abandon myself to him. But I don't. I have more self-control.

Afterwards he lies beside me in the hay and is soon asleep, whispering pretty things to his beautiful wife, but I lie awake, wrapped in his arms, too thrilled by the wonder of the adventure of him to sleep.

In the morning, the farmer gives us bread and laban (kindness to a young married couple) and directs us to where we want to go, and by the second afternoon we have arrived at the place of the statue.

What a disappointment! It isn't Hittite at all, just some miserable Roman thing, eclectically combining several legends. I lose my womanly grace and stomp around in anger, but we've come a long way, so I take photographs of the vulgar thing. It has naked breasts, which Dahoum caresses, looking slyly at me, and he points to her bulging buttocks and points to mine and, giggling, makes his want of that certain part of my body very obvious! He has a peasant vulgarity that I adore.

We start for home and are accosted by three Turkish policemen. They demand to see our papers. Dahoum gives them his, and they see he is a Syrian. They are abusive and tell us that we shouldn't be here. They ask about me and don't seem convinced by my disguise or by the papers he gives them for me, bad forgeries we made at Carchemish. They threaten me and tell me to remove my veil and cloak. Dahoum curses them and calls them blasphemers to doubt his word and insult his wife's integrity, but two hold him while the other strips me and sees I am a man.

They question my fair hair. I tell them I am a Circassian, going home to see my family and disguised against bandits. They don't believe me, they think we are deserters from the army. They find the camera. Now they call us spies. Dahoum tells them that we stole it.

They make us go with them to their station. One of them, the smallest, ugliest, whispers obscene remarks about me and what he will do to my fair body when we get there. They tell their captain who we are, and we are kicked into a lousy dungeon. I am badly bruised, and Dahoum sprains his ankle. I tear strips from my tattered dress to bind it.

The captain comes and says he does not think us spies but deserters, and we will be sent back to the army. So I am to become a Turkish soldier! But he tells us we must be punished for our desertion. We will spend a week in the cells and then be sent to training camp.

We are alone and in despair. How will we escape our enforced enlistment? How will we get home again? We squat in separate corners, cursing our misfortune, pining for Carchemish.

I have money, I remember. I sewed two sovereigns into a secret pocket of my garment. I fish them out. I go to the door and call the guard. The small Turk comes. I demand to see the captain.

I tell him who I am and that the British government will be very angry when they hear how he has treated me. He shrugs. There's nothing he can do. Britain means nothing to him, Britain has no authority here, and it is unlikely that Britain will go to war for the sake of one Englishman who was where he shouldn't be and might be a spy. He laughs. I will be the first English to fight in Turkey's army, and, if there is war, I will have to fight against my own countrymen.

But something is left hanging in the air. I know it well. I learned it first in Egypt, that unfinished silence which means that anything can be arranged for a small present of gold, a little backsheesh.

The only good that ever came out of England is gold, he says, gold sovereigns.

So the deal is done, but it is a Byzantine bargain. They have not had their fun.

Two of the three who arrested us bring us a mean meal, and the small one, the ugly one, the one who is fascinated by my white skin, makes cooing words of love to me. He comes close to me and touches me and plays with himself and tells me what he is going to do to me.

Dahoum goes mad and attacks the Turk. They subdue him, although he scores a bloody mouth on the stronger of the two. One holds him while the other punches him. I call out my distress, and the small, ugly policeman giggles lecherously.

We are man and wife? They'll show us! They call their friend the sergeant, and he brings a cane. They strip me naked, handcuff me to a bar of the window.

But the punishment is of Dahoum. They push up his robe and pull down his pants and make him bend over. Two hold him while the other whips him. I beg them to beat me in his place, but they laugh, and the sound of the cane striking his flesh is harsher than any of my mother's chastising rods, because they will not beat me, but I feel every cut that hurts Dahoum.

He does not cry out, though I know the pain must be intolerable, because I have felt it, can feel it, my serpent begs for it now. He flinches every time the bamboo snaps on his bare rump, but he stares straight ahead. At me. Only at me. I realize that he is staring at me, concentrating on my naked body to distract himself from the pain.

I cannot contain myself, because I want that blistering pain, I want to feel it on his behalf that he might be spared, because I know, more surely than I have ever known anything, that he is using his lust for me to endure the agony. I know, because I can see it, that he is hard. And I know, because of his glazed eyes and heavy breathing and his straining godhead, that in a moment he will spend himself. The small Turk knows it too, and is fiddling crazily with his crotch.

I cannot contain myself! My serpent spits, and I moan in degradation. It is the climax of the punishment and the only time that Dahoum makes a sound. I hear the small Turk grunt in satisfaction.

Twelve lashes were enough. Twelve vicious strokes of the cane.

Now they are done, they are disgusted with us. They push Dahoum, bloody and exhausted, to a corner and shout abuse at me, shower me with spittle. Two leave us to our despair, but the small, lascivious third stays for a moment and grins at us, a coconspirator. He unlocks my handcuffs that I might be with Dahoum.

I creep to him and hold him close. I use my ragged dress to mop his blood. I cannot bear to see his flawless, chunky buttocks so despoiled, and kiss his wounds that they might heal, and he holds me in his despair, and we swear vengeance on the Turks.

They kick us out before dawn. Dahoum is limping badly but refuses to admit his pain, which is more than a sprained ankle, much more than his wounds of beating. They disgraced him in front of me, and the insult is offensive to his manhood. But I tell him, because of them, I disgraced myself in front of him, and I am no more than he, and we are one, united in degradation.

He is angry. "What have you done to me," he cries. "Have you bewitched me with some English magic? Have you stolen my manliness from me?"

"No," I tell him. "I have given you your manliness. I was there; I saw that you were brave and I can tell the world that you did not cry out despite the fiercest pain."

He grunts and seems mollified, but limps along in silence. Only when we have crossed the border and are comparatively safe does he say anything.

"Perhaps we will not tell anyone," he says. "It is enough that we know what happened."

We get back to Carchemish, to a happy welcome for our safe return, but Dahoum will not tell anyone what happened, only that we had a great adventure, and that both of us were brave.

That night, near the well, we sit with the men and drink arak, and I fill in some few details of what happened to us, but nothing of our torture, only that we were imprisoned and that we got out.

"He is being modest," Dahoum says, eyes bright, tongue running with the liquor. He begins a fantastic story, a version of our captivity that owes only the smallest fraction to the truth. We were imprisoned, beaten, tortured! We fought our way out! With our bare fists we bested our cruel guards, broke free from jail and fled into the night.

The other men are speechless with admiration. They cry out their hatred of the Turks and vow revenge and beg to hear the tale again. This time, we were almost raped, and in our fury we broke several jaws and left our captors bloody and defeated!

The men are enraptured. "Oh, how we hate the Turks," they shout, and each tells the other what he will do to the very next Turkish soldier or policeman that he meets, and each begs to hear the tale again.

This time, we battle together side by side, Dahoum and I, against a small army of Turkish soldiers firing guns, dodging their bullets and grabbing any weapon—logs or their own swords—and cutting them all to pieces as we fight our way, inch by inch, body by mangled body, to freedom!

"You are the greatest warriors, English and Dahoum!" the young men chant, and they start to sing and dance a song of triumph that celebrates our victory! We are heroes, and we hate the Turks.

The story grows and swells in each retelling, becoming more unlikely, more preposterous, but eagerly believed. I do not put a rein on Dahoum's babblings, because I am caught up in the thrill of the moment, and I find that I do not exactly remember what happened, and his versions are as good as any because they are, in essence, true. We were arrested, and he was beaten, and we got away. If we were not quite as magnificent as we are in Dahoum's lurid recounting, does it matter? Besides, how can I disappoint him with the truth, how dare I call into question the fabulous legend that he weaves about himself and me. How can I call him liar? How can I belittle his manliness?

I watch as he tells the story, time and time again, and love him, because we become great heroes—fighting at each other's side, we are one, we two brave soldiers, fending off a formidable army—and we are triumphant. And if it isn't exactly the truth, but only a small fragment of a truth embroidered and elaborated into a story that will be told by the storytellers in this village for many years to come, for lifetimes—what does it matter? We have become part of a history that they need. We are legend.

What does any truth matter anyway? Who cares? There is only one truth that matters to me, and it is this: I am a man in their eyes and in his, and Dahoum is a man in their eyes and mine.

When he tells the story he holds my hand and looks to me for corroboration, and I give him that because he gives me something so much more. We are lovers, in the purest sense, two valiant warriors who have sworn an oath of love and loyalty and have been tested in blood and battle. We are Alexander and Hephaestion, and it doesn't matter which of us is which, because together we are one.

I watch him as he tells the story, and I see the breathless wonder on the faces of the adoring young men. Their cheers rend the night, and I accept their celebration of us.

I look at Dahoum and think that he has never been happier in all his life. The donkey boy is lost forever. He regards himself as a total, tested man, with me beside him: I was there at his trial and can vouch for him. I am the proof of his masculinity.

The women are trilling our victory, and the men are shouting and dancing and firing rifles in the air, and I know that when I look at Dahoum again his eyes will be shining.

30

As THEY CIRCLED TO LAND, Slaney, shivering on the gun ring, thought that Miranshah looked a world away from revolutions. Snow had fallen during the night, and although the landing strip was being cleared, the fort and the parked aircraft were almost invisible to the naked eye, lost in a landscape of white against which the dark ants of the ground crew were scurrying around to get the strip ready for them. There were four aircraft already parked on the ground, the number temporarily enlarged because of the trouble in Afghanistan, or so Slaney assumed.

Slaney was numb with cold. They had passengers being evacuated from Kabul, and there was no room for him in the cabin. He'd spent the entire flight on the gun ring, bundled up in Afghani sheepskin coats and a blanket. It had been a long flight and a longer day. They had left the British embassy at first light, and their convoy of cars had traveled uneasily from the city to the airfield, with loyalist troops to protect them.

Carol Isaacson, leaving under protest because her husband was staying in Kabul, had jumped into the car beside Slaney, unwilling to travel with the other women. She kept up a steady barrage of complaint about the involvement of renegade British troublemakers, such as Ned, in the Afghan troubles, and of the parlous position of women in Moslem countries, until Slaney was sick of the sound of her voice. He couldn't restrain a grin when a pilot sitting beside her in the car told her that she had no idea what she was talking about and that women were honored in Islam. The rebuke did nothing to stem her flood of complaint. By the end of the short ride, Slaney agreed with those of his friends who thought the Americans would one day take over the world. They'll wear us all out with righteousness, he thought.

There had been some small skirmishes at the airfield during the night, but all the buses were safe. Bats had given Slaney money to find security guards for their plane, and the two men had made themselves comfortable inside the aircraft. Well armed and locked in, they only opened the door when Slaney agreed to beef up their promised two sovereigns pay to three.

As they readied for takeoff and the evacuees were assigned aircraft by Lady Humphrys, Slaney whispered to Bats that he didn't think they should tell Carol, who was complaining about her allotted space in another plane, that they were going to Miranshah. If she knew that Ned was there, she'd demand his execution. Bats winked.

"Lord love you, duckie, no," he whispered in agreement. "We should drop her over the border in Russia. She'd sort the Commies out." He looked at the gun ring. "It's going to be cold," he said.

Slaney shrugged. "I've been cold before." He wasn't looking forward to the flight; it would be freezing up there, outside the plane in this winter weather.

Bats was genuinely concerned for his welfare. He went away, fishing in his pocket for silver rupees, and came back a few minutes later with a couple of brightly embroidered sheepskin coats, bought from tribesmen. Slaney and another airman started the engine, then Slaney donned the coats, climbed on to the gun ring, tied himself into place and let Bats drape a blanket round him.

"A sort of Eastern Father Christmas," Bats said, inspecting his handiwork. "Do take care."

Slaney knew he looked ridiculous, but it was preferable to freezing to death. The other airmen cheered his appearance and called out good wishes, and Slaney waved back to them as Bats taxied to take off.

Bats hadn't told anyone he was flying to Miranshah, which was not in his orders. If anyone complained, which was unlikely, he could always say that engine trouble or bad weather had forced him to change plans. Not that anyone would complain, as long as he delivered his passengers to safety. It was generally believed that Bats was somewhat more than an eccentric, albeit splendid, pilot. A number of his superiors were convinced that Bats's vagaries had a specific purpose—to gather information for the government or, to put it bluntly, to spy—and he was accorded suitable leniency.

Bats was not a spy, at least in the accepted sense of the word, any more than Ned or D. G. Hogarth had been. Like many adventuring men who turned up in odd corners of the world, they had friends in high, obscure places, dark corridors in Whitehall. All were patriotic, loyal to their country, or certain causes of their country, and in letters home or over quiet dinners in London they would report on all they had seen, which information, if it was thought to be of value, was relayed to the proper government departments.

But Bats did have a mission in Miranshah, which was both personal and professional. That mission was to meet and evaluate Ned.

On a personal level, Bats simply wanted to meet a man who was a legend among adventurers, and since Miranshah was so close and so accessible, it was too good an opportunity to miss.

Professionally, he had been asked, in cryptic cables from Whitehall, to try and establish if there was any truth to the rumors that Ned was involved, in any way, in the troubles in Afghanistan. The rumors of that involvement were causing problems among the Indian nationalists, and the desk wallahs in Delhi, who had become increasingly unhappy about Ned's posting to India, wanted to know the truth, or wanted ammunition to get Ned out. Lawrence of Arabia was not regarded affectionately by the government of British India. No one in that government really believed that a man of his past achievements or reputation could really be happy as a simple A/C 2, and his very presence in such a volatile area was a thorn in Delhi's side.

More truthfully, the desk wallahs were piqued because they had not initially been asked about or advised of Ned's posting, and they saw it as an affront to their sovereignty. Ned's few advocates—Sir Hugh Trenchard and Sir Geoffrey Salmond—had protected Ned's position assiduously, but now, with the Russians raging that the British were fomenting revolution in Afghanistan, several of Ned's enemies sensed victory for their cause.

Bats, no lover of the desk wallahs but extraordinarily protective of Britain's position in the world, had no opinions one way or the other as to the truth of Ned's activities. A true pilot, Bats seldom speculated about anything, but instead concerned himself with facts as he found them. Foul weather was foul weather, and good weather, good. It was pointless complaining about the difficulties of an approach to an airfield until you had personal experience of what those difficulties were. And it was ridiculous to imagine that an A/C 2, under constant supervision, was able to flee his base at will and go wandering about Afghanistan disguised as a Moslem holy man. It was the stuff of heated imaginations and lurid novels.

Still, stranger things had happened, and Bats had his orders. Besides, a side trip to Miranshah made an interesting excursion, he could not imagine that a meeting with Lawrence of Arabia would be dull, and anything was better than being bored.

Conscious of his engineer's precarious position on the gun ring, Bats made as smooth a landing as was possible, and as he turned off the motor he barked instructions that Slaney be got down as a first priority. Higgins and Mitchell climbed up to Slaney, gave words of encouragement and freed him from his icy perch. Higgins called for tea, and Mitchell massaged Slaney's aching limbs.

"Long time no see," he said, and in that unemotional but caring greeting Slaney knew he was back in a world that he understood. Lips blue with cold, he tried to smile but almost fainted. Mitchell gave orders for help, and men lifted the freezing engineer to the ground. Higgins forced him to sip tea, then built a small fire within feet of the aircraft.

"Bugger the bloody buses," Higgins said, as Slaney tried to point out the possible danger. It was that personal warmth, as much as the fire or the tea, that revived Slaney.

Bats, sure that Slaney was in capable hands, had seen to his passengers and had reported to the CO, who greeted their arrival. Officers took charge of the refugee women and children and led them to the fort. Bats, as was proper, came to see that Slaney was faring well.

"Good show, Slaney," he said, and went with the other officers. Officers looked after officers, erks looked after erks. Everything was in order, as it should be. Except for one thing. Most of the men based there, permanently or temporarily, were on the field to help or to hear news of the flight or the troubles in Afghanistan, but Slaney couldn't see Ned.

"Gone troppo," Higgins said in answer to his question. He looked at the snow, aware of the silliness of claiming a tropical affliction in this wintry weather. "Doolally," he said, more accurately. "He'll be pleased to see you."

Ned was not mad, but for the last few weeks he had been giving the appearance of it. In October he had been summoned before the new temporary CO, the Honorable Jocelyn Fraser. Ned knew it was trouble.

Fraser came straight to the point. "Are you aware of what is happening in Moscow?" he asked.

"No, sir," Ned lied. He was aware. In charge of the wireless cabin, he had seen the incoming messages. He had been tempted to destroy them, to protect his position among the other airmen, his position in the RAF, but fear of the consequences stopped him. He was fearful now.

"The Communist newspaper *Pravda* has accused you of inciting rebellion in Afghanistan," Fraser said. "I have to ask you if there is any truth to these charges."

"No, sir," Ned said, as innocently as he could. It was ridiculous, a trumped-up Soviet fantasy of Imperial aggression. They were threatening to put Winston Churchill and some others on trial for treason against the Soviet state.

"Why do you think the Russians are convinced of it?"

"I am known to be friends with Winston Churchill," Ned said, and could have bitten off his tongue. Fraser had not mentioned Churchill. It was a tiny slip but could reveal a bigger lie, or a suspicion of one.

"Do you leave this base for periods of time and go into Afghanistan among the natives?"

"Not possible, sir," Ned said. "We are locked in at night." That was true. They were locked in at night, for their own safety, but barbed wire had never stopped Ned. He excused the lie to himself, because the occasional nocturnal meeting with the villagers, or even Umar, were not in Afghanistan.

"Do you speak Pushtu?"

"No, sir," Ned said honestly. He knew a few words of the Afghan language but could not speak it.

"Pushtu is very similar to Arabic, I believe," Fraser said. "And you are fluent in that language."

Similar, but not the same, Ned wanted to correct him.

"In what language are the books you are studying written?"

"Ancient Greek, sir," Ned said, "I am translating the *Odyssey*."

"In your own hours, I trust," Fraser chided, but gently. He was a lover of Homer, and Ned thought he saw, or hoped he saw, a twinkle in the man's eye. If it was there, it was the first lightness in the interview.

"Entirely in my spare time, sir," Ned confirmed.

Fraser looked at him keenly, sure that there was something more behind all this talk. Delhi, alarmed by Moscow's strident claims, had instructed him to question Ned, to try and arrive at the truth of the matter. Fraser knew it was hopeless. What man, unless mad, would admit to revolutionary activity? What man, unless mad, would confess to such flagrant breaches of orders and discipline? What man, unless mad, would put himself in such a provocative situation?

Of course, there was always the possibility that this airman who called himself Shaw *was* mad. This was, after all, Lawrence of Arabia, who had been a young man's idol to Fraser. Only madness could explain his presence in the ranks, his acceptance of such lowliness, his complete fall from such a lofty pedestal.

"You are obviously a very intelligent man," Fraser said. "Yet you are still an A/C 2, you do not seek advancement in the service."

Ned almost relaxed, he was on familiar ground at last.

"Not educationally qualified, sir," he said, unable to resist the urge to flippancy. He cursed himself as he said it. It had been his undoing before and might be again. Surely it was the wrong thing to say to Fraser, who had tried to be generous. The man's eyes lost any sign of a twinkle and were frosty.

"I am aware that discipline has been lax here," he said, "and it appalls me." Whatever charms Miranshah had for others were lost on him. He was a man of action, and nothing ever happened here. If there was to be a revolution in Afghanistan, the RAF would be involved, but Fraser could not expect to play any significant part in it, stuck here in charge of this remote desert outpost, even though close to the trouble. This was the fringe of the world, and Fraser wanted to be at its center, in Peshawar.

"I must warn you to be very careful," he ordered Ned. "The political situation in this part of the world is volatile. No matter how innocent any of your actions may be, you must consider how they will be interpreted by others. You should keep a very low profile. The Raf is not a place for errant individualism."

That's what I want, Ned screamed inside! I want the lowest profile in all the world, I do not want to be noticed, I am not fit to be remembered, I want to be forgotten!

"Yes, sir," he said.

He was dismissed and went back to the wireless cabin, where he stared at the wall and cursed his fate. Why was he so seductive to attention, why would notoriety not abandon him? He had done nothing—or very little—that defied the regulations. He had talked at night with a possible revolutionary about theories of war, and that was all! Was that so much? Was that enough to get him dismissed the service, to exile him again from home? Or was it the ghost of the man he once had been, that dead man who haunted his every moment, which endangered him?

Was this home? Where was home? Earthly home was whatever base the RAF assigned him to—and Clouds Hill. Spiritual home was Carchemish and the wilderness of Zin. But the wilderness was lost to him, and the RAF—and Clouds Hill—was all he had, the only place in all the world where he had some chance of sanctuary. Had he, by his own foolishness, his vanity, put even that at risk?

He did not move for hours. He stared at the wall for the rest of that day and determined on flawless behavior. He had been warned but not dismissed. If he was obedient and disciplined, if he obeyed the letter of the law as well as the intention, perhaps they might be lenient with him. Trenchard would always intercede on his behalf, would always do his best to protect him. But if the sin was too great, if the notoriety was too extreme, not even Trenchard could withstand the political pressures. He must do nothing provocative.

He did nothing except the most necessary of his chores for days on end. The *Odyssey* lay abandoned, despite the siren song that lured him to distraction with its insistent beauty. Ancient Greek was dangerous, too liable to misinterpretation by others. Homer was his enemy, for those inspiring poets spurred him to action, like Odysseus seeking Ithaca or Elysium, to search for home, for Carchemish and Zin, and to find the man he was before the war, who died outside Damascus.

His friends, Higgins, Mitchell and Baxter, worried for his physical welfare and mental state and kept watch on him. They encouraged him to his duties, to eat and sleep, to walk about the fort and to be Ned again, but while he went through the motions of existence, he was lost to them, curt, unfriendly and removed. He never giggled anymore. They did not call him Tee-Hee now.

"He'll be pleased to see you," Higgins said to Slaney, who was known to be Ned's friend. "He needs to talk to someone."

Slaney, when he had bathed and changed and was warm again, found Ned in the wireless cabin and was shocked by what he saw. The man was there, but the spirit was gone. This was not giggling Tee-Hee, or chipper Ned, or even sad, disconsolate Shaw. This was some other man, a shell of a man, lacking the luster of life.

"What's up, Ned?" Slaney said.

Ned turned to him and stared. To Slaney's relief, after a small eternity, he saw recognition in the vacant, sky-blue eyes.

"Not much," Ned said.

They talked for a while, but Ned revealed nothing of his feelings about himself. Because he believed that Ned could be lulled back to reality, Slaney recited his adventures in Afghanistan, making them as exciting and as humorous as possible, but Ned hardly reacted.

He listens but he does not hear, Slaney thought. He told Ned about Bats, but that only seemed to make Ned more suspicious. "What does he want?" Ned asked.

"Just to meet you," Slaney said reassuringly. "You'll like him, he's a corker bloke. We're off to Peshawar tomorrow, just here the night."

There was silence. "It's good to see you," Slaney said.

Ned shrugged but said nothing, expressed no interest in Bats or his adventures or Slaney's. At last Slaney ran out of things to talk about.

"What's up?" he said.

Ned stared at Slaney again, and now his look disturbed the engineer and reminded him of their last meeting, that awful night when he was sure Ned wanted to be hit, to be hurt.

"It's all my fault," Ned said. "I have only myself to blame. I need to be punished."

The intensity of it, and the disturbing potential, frightened Slaney. He was suddenly in an unknown country, wild and unpredictable, and he did not want to be there.

The tension between them in the tiny room was electric, almost palpable, as if both had just touched a naked socket. It was broken by the arrival of an orderly, summoning Ned to the CO.

"It'll be Bats," Slaney said. "I know he wants a chat."

To his surprise, he saw fear in Ned's eyes again.

When Ned was gone, Slaney sat alone in the wireless cabin and wished he did not feel so alarmed—and so vulnerable.

Needing the company of others, he went to the mess. Higgins and Mitchell greeted him cheerily, gave him a beer and demanded to know all his adventures. They did not ask about his meeting with Ned. Although they were curious, and concerned for their fellow airman's welfare, they recognized the necessary secrets of friendship.

They listened to Slaney's vivid retelling of the hijinks in Kabul, laughed and shook their heads and added their own wild rumors of the revolution. They had heard the tales of Ned's supposed activities as Munshi Shah and laughed.

"We're locked up in 'ere every bleedin' night," Mitchell scoffed. "'Ow's Ned supposed to get out, that's what I want to know?"

All well and good, Slaney thought, but Ned's been out before.

"That Trebitsch Lincoln, he's the real bugger," Higgins opined. "Effing traitor, that bloke."

For a period of time, before any of them were posted to India, Trebitsch Lincoln had been a star of the gutter press, a strange and unpredictable man, a traitor to his adopted country and a refugee from justice. His name still popped up in the papers from time to time, in unlikely and unpredictable situations.

These were all the same old stories that Slaney had heard in Kabul and from Bats, tales of improbable but feasible mischief in a remote and mysterious country, less than an inch away on the maps, wrought by mountebanks and charlatans and scoundrels—and Ned.

Always Ned. Even though the Miranshah Irregulars defended Ned to the hilt, the temporary airmen thrilled to the idea of being in the company of Lawrence of Arabia and were convinced that a man with such an illustrious and swashbuckling past must be playing—or have played—some small role, at least, in the present ferment.

There was no sign of Ned all evening, and they turned in. Slaney, who had tried to drown himself in beer, was only slightly tipsy and lay on his cot, trying yet again to make sense of it all. Reason told him that Ned had never ventured farther outside than yards from the perimeter wire, that he was innocent of all the many charges laid against him, but his charged imagination told him otherwise.

He woke, realized he had dozed, and saw Ned sitting on his cot staring at him. He could not guess how long Ned had been sitting there but knew it was more than minutes. The loneliness and fear surrounding Ned, and again, that strange, indefinable need, caused him to shiver.

"How was it?" he asked.

Ned shrugged. The meeting with Bats had dragged on and on, over dinner, which they had eaten in a private room, through port, to Bats's bleary drowsiness. Yet Ned did not believe that Bats was drunk, he thought it was an act, as if Bats, in his cups, might hear from Ned secrets that would not be given to a sober man. To a large extent, it was a repeat of Ned's interview with Fraser. Although Bats had tried to disarm with casualness, the same accusations lay under everything he said, and the same denials were given by Ned.

If anything, the session with Bats was more alarming to Ned than a formal interview, for Bats was playing his own game. Ned believed that truth could be discovered in gossip; it had been his formidable ally at Carchemish and in the Desert Campaign. In chitchat, in good-humored company, in talk about the trivia of family and friends, critical secrets of loyalties, allegiances and alliances could be discovered. Ned was certain that Bats was trying to discover a truth that did not exist, and the casual persistence of the questioning convinced him that his position in the service was under immediate threat.

Finally dismissed, he had walked the perimeter wire for an hour, shivering in the cold because he had no coat, but impervious to it because of the fear that froze his heart.

He wanted a friend, someone to talk to, someone to whom he could reveal his most secret self, someone who would hold him in his arms, even if only for a moment, and tell him that he was of value. But since he was not of value, and since to be touched, to be held, was impossible, there was only one feasible alternative. He had to rid himself of demons. If he was to survive, he had to trust Slaney.

Could he trust Slaney? Wasn't it easier just to duck under the perimeter wire and walk out, thinly clothed, into the desert, march for miles into the freezing nowhere, then lie down and go to sleep and wake up in his beloved wilderness, comforted by the only human being who he was sure had ever loved him?

He couldn't do that. Once, in the heat of the moment, in the black night of his soul after Deraa, it might have been possible. Once, when his fury with the mischief of the gods made him wild enough to challenge them, he might have died by another's sword in a bloodthirsty rampage, and then there would not have been this aching void called life. But the fury had passed, shocked out of him by the violence he had discovered in himself, and now there was only the fear that he was wrong, and that if he died there would be nothing, no pretty waters to lie down beside with his beloved, no happy wilderness in which to roam. No heaven, no hell. No seraphim. No angels. No Dahoum. Only an empty void called death.

DAVID STEVENS

He dared not run the risk of a disappointment of such magnitude, so instead it had to be life. And Slaney.

"I have done something very wrong," he whispered. "Can we talk?"

Slaney nodded, and Ned got up and went outside. Slaney knew he was supposed to follow, but he was scared to go. He did not want to be alone with Ned, somewhere in the dark, away from the company of others. But he did not know how to say no, and it was also a chance to learn the truth.

"I have to be punished," Ned said.

They were in the wireless cabin.

"Why?" Slaney asked. He clung to the hope that it was all quite ordinary and aboveboard, that Ned had revealed the secrets of his Afghan exploits to Bats and was to be dismissed the service. He could not imagine a greater punishment for Ned than that.

There was a stick on the desk, a sort of small whip. Slaney had never noticed it before. Ned picked it up and offered it to Slaney.

"My uncle demands it," he said.

Slaney, dumbstruck, stared at the whip in revulsion.

"Do what my uncle wants. Beat me," he pleaded. "Beat the devil out of me."

Slaney felt sick to his stomach, he thought the ground was moving beneath him.

"Beat me," Ned urged, moving close, whispering, as if it were love he asked for. "There's money in it."

Slaney's mind exploded. He knew it was a sexual demand, that it was filthy, unclean. He knew there was no sadistic uncle—only Ned's desire. Everything he had ever been sure of fell away from him. The tiny, pathetic, urging man before him revolted him. And even worse was that Ned thought him, Slaney, capable of such vileness, that he would accept money for it, as a common whore. Bereft of comprehension, he submitted to his dominant passion and took recourse in the only weapon available to him, his fists.

He punched Ned hard, iron hard on the jaw, and knew he had drawn blood. He punched him again, blind with fury. Ned fell to the ground. Slaney, who wanted to leave, could not until his victory was absolute.

"Yes!" he heard Ned say. "That's the ticket! Harder!"

Shocked to comprehending impotence, Slaney felt the uncharted precipice on which he stood crumble beneath him. He realized that Ned was

228

in a high state of sexual arousal and might at any moment, certainly if struck again, come. Not to hit him was impossible, but to give him what he wanted was inconceivable.

"You fucken queer bastard," he shouted.

"Beat me!" Ned cried.

It was the last thing Slaney ever heard him say.

31

Spring 1914

He lies beside me, sleeping now, exhausted, spent. His body is heavy against me, but I feel no burden, wrapped in his embrace. My head is nestled in his shoulder, and his steady breathing ruffles my hair. We're sweaty under sheepskins, wrapped up against the cold and wet.

Our bedroom is a cramped hole in a rocky ledge, high up on a mountain, where, at the summit, Aaron, the brother of Moses, is buried. Our ceiling is a pitch-black sky. The stars and moon are hidden by the clouds I cannot see but know must be there. Then suddenly, as I watch, the clouds part, and there is a star!

We are north of Aqaba, southeast of Beersheba and Gaza, and west of our destination, Ma'an. We have no money, and to get from Ma'an to Aleppo I will have to borrow our fares from someone. I don't know who. But I also don't care. I could wander here forever, with my beloved.

We have been away from Carchemish for six weeks, surveying the wilderness of Zin (some call it the Negev). A few days ago, in Aqaba, we were told that our commission had been withdrawn and we could not survey the area anymore. Newk, an army man, takes it on the chin, but I make a fuss. The Turkish Resident is angry.

"We know what you've been doing," he shouts. "We know you are not Bible people! We know you are spies!"

It's a vile accusation (even though it's true!), and I am very huffy, but Newk calms me down. He's been on the wireless to Kitchener, who told him to accept their decision with good grace and pull out. We've already achieved most of what we came for anyway.

Lord Kitchener, in Cairo, sees wars round every corner (they're his bread and butter—and lifeblood) and is worried sick about the Suez Canal (as he should be). The Turkish front line is scarcely more than a hundred miles from the canal, their border with Egypt running from the Mediterranean just outside Gaza in a straight line south to Aqaba, bisecting the wilderness of Zin. One good push by the Ottomans would have them on the eastern banks of the canal and threatening the Empire's most vital artery.

It's true that under an old agreement we hold much of the Sinai Peninsula, but we don't have an army there, and we don't really know the Turkish military strength on their side, or even the geography or topography on either side of the border. Most of the exploration of the wilderness (what little has been done) has been by Bible people. This is Old Testament country. This is Exodus. This is where Moses wandered with his people for forty years. The Bush burned here, and the Golden Calf was worshipped.

The Turks, of course, will not allow a military survey, so Kitchener asks Hogarth's help, and he comes up with a brilliant notion. Len and I are trained archeologists of impeccable credentials (well, Len is), and we are known to the Turks. Oh, we've had the odd skirmish with them at Carchemish, and we've told a few of their petty bureaucrats to jump in the lake, but we've kept our noses pretty clean. The Turks know there's nothing much to do at Carchemish in winter, so they might allow us to survey the biblical wilderness sites. (The Turks are cautious about offending Christians; the American missionaries in Jerusalem get very aggressively American if they think they're being denied access to what they regard as their provenance!) Thus, Len and I can make our maps, and Kitchener can send a few army chaps along "for our protection."

It's a good scheme; it bluffs the Turks, and the British Museum jumps at it. They have to keep us on half pay in winter, but if we're away on a military mission, the army foots the bill. Len is keen on the idea. He's bored here at Carchemish this winter. (Why did he stay? Was it to protect me? Spy on me? Save me from myself—or from Dahoum?) It's cold and he's looking forward to some southern sun. Dahoum and I are thrilled to go. Len staying here for the winter put the kibosh on the happy solitude we were anticipating. Dahoum got the grumps when I told him, sulked through the days and ignored me at night. (As he should. Even if Len, or anyone, guesses what Dahoum and I have together, no one must ever know. They would destroy us. They would think us "queer." Well, I'm not "queer." I love another man, but I'm not "queer." What Dahoum and I have is age-old love reborn. The world doesn't understand that.)

We sail from Beirut, all three of us, because I refuse to go without Dahoum, so the army coughs up his pittance. We meet with Newk, a surveyor of the Royal Engineers, at Beersheba, and he's shocked by our appearance, expecting us to be a couple of old professors. He's cheerful, fun and dazzlingly efficient. He has five teams of men working already and knows at any moment of the day where every one of his teams is, though the desert here is trackless.

We buy camels, hire guides and pass some pleasant evenings listening to Newk's news of the world. At first I thought him pukka sahib and I was wary, but he's kind and caring, and very jolly when you get to know him, and we invite him to visit us at Carchemish next season (we've added more rooms to the house and even have a proper sitting room; the interior is quite splendid!). Newk says he'll come if he can find a military purpose so that Kitchener will pay for it, and Len tells him that the German railway line could be interesting. Newk is intrigued. To my relief, he makes friends with Dahoum. (Does he know, or guess? Do I care? Yes. Why do I care? Because I do not want the world to misunderstand us.)

He goes about his military business, and we, our own. Even though we're only a cover for a more serious purpose, we're excited—we are men dedicated to discovering the past. There's nothing here for us, and it was foolish of us to imagine that there would be. The old tribes led by Moses were nomadic, tent-dwelling people, and this wilderness is not conducive to construction. I think between Beersheba and Aqaba there are but three solid buildings, and those are modern outposts.

The rest is only wilderness, and it is beautiful, wild, primeval wilderness. Not flat desert, but all hills and rocks and limestone cliffs, and great ravines where ores of undiscovered metals dazzle the eye. We bump along on wretched, humping camels, lost in time and space, for we are nowhere, and there is nothing but the manuscript, unedited by man, of a landscape changed only by weather since the first day of Creation.

Len's miserable. He's not a nomad like us and longs for a proper bed and running water. He wants to find something, anything, that will spark his interest: Aaron's rod or Moses' staff, or even a few coins or shards of pottery. But there is nothing. Not a single trace of a mighty flight from Egypt, or the journeys of the Josephs, or Joshua's armies. No civilization has left man's thumbprint here, for what is there to conquer? If we do find ruins—and once or twice we do find some—they are tiny, straggly, miserable things, as if the builders came here with high hopes, endured the desert for a season, then went home defeated, leaving the wind to work the few stones of their dwelling places to inconsequence.

Dahoum and I ride apart from Len, ahead of him, away from him, because, unlike him, we are happy. We have fun doing nothing except making maps and reveling in the glory of this undiscovered land.

With our maps made, we come to Aqaba and are disbanded by the angry Turks. Newk hotfoots it back to Cairo, and Len is to Aleppo gone, to proper beds and running water.

But I want more. There is a small Crusader castle here, on Pharaoh's Island, not far offshore. The Turks won't let me go there (why? do they fear I will dis-

cover Saladin's defenses?), but "can't" is the wrong word to say to me. We make a raft, Dahoum and I, from some old ten-gallon drums, and paddle out to the castle, while the Turks, who have discovered us, jump up and down and call us back, and when we come back—after we have achieved the castle, of course—we are expelled from Aqaba.

Who cares? There is more to the world than Aqaba, and much, much more to see.

The Turks don't trust us (perhaps they're not such fools) and give us an escort, a lazy lieutenant gone soft with idleness, to bring us to the railway at Ma'an. Our escort complains enough for twenty men, and once we're out of Aqaba, we easily give him the slip. He has no inclination to find us again, the country is too rough for a man from Adana who hates Aqaba and wants nothing more than to be with his wife and family, in familiar surroundings.

At last, we are alone, Dahoum and I! Unguarded, unguided, left to our own devices, we roam at will, insanely, but always headed sort of north. We camp with hospitable Bedouins at night. We find the routes of ancient armies in the day. And we see Petra.

If there is any other place in the world that I would live with my Dahoum, other than Carchemish, it would be Petra. The old Nabatean city itself is fabulous, carved out of the living, rose-red rock, but, oh, the situation! We ride into a small, narrow ravine, dark and claustrophobic, trudging on forever, and then through a narrow gap before us we see the first sign of man's hubris and achievement, the Treasury. We stand in awe before it, then explore the rest, and slowly as we pass the baroque, carved façades of the huge caves that constitute the buildings, going ever up through timelessness, we come to a plateau that gives a breathless vista. Who were these people that built this place? Where did they come from? Where did they go to? Who cares? It is enough that they were here and left a legacy more stunning than anything Michelangelo could envisage.

We are weary and cold. We have no money. We should go home to Carchemish. But I want more and find it.

Like Aaron, we never see the promised land, but at the summit of the mountain where he is buried, we find our own fulfillment. We climb all day, wet and miserable, cross as bears, but urged on by expectation. There are no bones at the top of the mountain, no tombstone to mark Aaron's burial place. But there is a view like paradise. We, on a high mountain, gaze down at a valley that is a thousand feet below sea level. Farther than we can see, to the north in that same valley, is the Dead Sea, and beyond that the holy river, and beyond that the lake where Jesus walked on water. To our right, on one side of the great rift, there must be a statue of salt, a woman who disobeyed God. Beyond her, the castle of the Crusaders, at Ajlun, guards the Jordan valley. To the left, hidden in mountains that are beyond the horizon, is the city that is sacred to three religions, one of the seven cities of wisdom, and a village with a manger where a Messiah was born. And even if we cannot see these places—because of the weather or the limit of our sight—we know they are there, and that we, two tiny, shivering, rain-sodden men, wrapped in each other's arms for warmth and comfort and for love, are looking at the story of the world.

The soaking rain has stopped, the sun breaks through the clouds, the wind chills our bones, but still we sit together, side by side and silent, because silence is the only possible response to what we see.

It will be dark soon, the rain threatens again, and we are hungry. Dahoum shoots a partridge, and we make a miserable feast, fire lost to the recurring rain. We find a rough shelter, snuggling together in a hollow in the rocks. We hold each other to keep warm. Because we are so discomforted we find the only comfort that is available to us. I feel the fire of him, and then my own. His face is inches close to mine, his hot breath on my cold lips. I feel his strong heart pumping, his blood surging. He does not ask, does not entreat me with his eyes, for he already knows my answer, knows that I don't care, and if I did, I think he would not care, not here, not now, for he is driven by a deeper need, and so am I, and so I welcome him upon me.

He is harsh and hard, not gentle or coaxing; he is urgent. His lips chew mine, his tongue invades my mouth, his stubble scrapes my chin. He climbs astride me, fully clothed, it is too cold for nakedness, we do not need it, this is enough and more. He wrestles me, and I fight back, not to make him stop, but drive him on. I am smothered by him, engulfed by him. I feel the furnace of his groin pumping against mine, and I push as hard, upwards, against him. Our two rods, molten metal, iron hard, battle each other, armored only in cloth. He hugs me so hard to him I think I cannot breathe, and forces his tongue down into my mouth so deeply as to seek my heart. I taste salt. His teeth have gashed my lips, but I am careless, wanting wounds. His mouth falls on my neck and leaves a vampire mark of blood. His hands encircle my narrow waist and pull me harder to him, and he throws back his head, and he cries out, and he cries out my name, and I cry out, and I cry out his name.

He lies beside me, sleeping now, exhausted, spent. His body is heavy against me, but I feel no burden, wrapped in his embrace. My head is nestled in his shoulder, and his steady breathing ruffles my hair.

The black sky is clearing, there is a star. The silver moon is peeping from a ragged cloud. I shall never leave this place or his embrace. I will lie forever with him, here in this wilderness of Zin, for I am in the company of angels, guarding his slumbers and singing him lullabies, and I see fantastic enterprises.

I have found what I have been searching for all my life, and it is he. I move my head, ever so slightly, so as not to wake him, and look to the edge of the world. Here from this ancient mountain I see a limitless land, pale with the coming dawn, and I have found my quest. I know what I must bring him now, to prove my worth.

It isn't so impossible. Two years ago the Bulgarians threatened Constantinople, and though they withdrew they proved the Ottomans are not invulnerable.

Not far from Carchemish, near to Aleppo, in the soft and vulnerable armpit of Turkey, the unarmored access to its heart, there is a port, Alexandretta. A small force could take that port, and armies could be gathered there, and from there legions be sent out to split the beast asunder. Let them keep Anatolia, let them hold Cappadocia, let them rule Byzantium—I don't care, for my path is east and south. From Alexandretta we could free Aleppo, Hama, Homs and then Damascus, and we could take Jerusalem. We free Mecca and Medina, severed from the capital, cut off from supply, give them back to their rightful rulers, and all Arabia is grateful.

Wars won, I ride in triumph to Jerablus, and I go home to Carchemish. I bring with me the most precious gift, his people's freedom and his own, and he and they acclaim me worthy king, and I, descendant of a noble house, an avenging Hittite, put on my crown and, with my shining consort at my side, rule with wisdom and benevolence a tiny kingdom that is my only home.

Is this a lover's fancy, the foible of a madman? Perhaps, but it is not unachievable. I do not know the place or time, but I will make it happen. I can see it clearly in my mind's eye, as surely as the coming day, and that dawning day gives proof of it.

The sun is peeping over the edge of the world, and because there has been rain, there is a rainbow. The seven-hued spectrum arcs down to the pristine land, the grail at the end of it is in my grasp and I have made a covenant.

32

"WHAT'S UP?" Bats asked him.

"Getting drunk." Slaney shrugged.

"Not like you," Bats said.

Slaney didn't feel like talking. "Yeh, well, a lot of things have happened," he said, wishing Bats would leave.

Bats didn't. "Trouble at home?" he wondered.

"No." But he found it difficult to be rude to an officer, especially Bats. "Just—things . . ."

Bats motioned to the red-bearded Pathan behind the rickety bar, ordering more drinks. He sat down at the table beside Slaney.

"Getting drunk helps, sometimes," he said. "But the problem doesn't go away."

It was a small, dingy tavern in a dark street of the old city of Peshawar. A dangerous place frequently declared out of bounds to British servicemen, but it was said that anything was possible there. Guns could be bought in a room upstairs, as well as drugs for those who wanted them. And for those who had the money and said the right things to the staff, there were women.

Slaney wanted a woman. He needed to prove to himself that he was a normal man, that his desires were completely conventional, that he could do to a woman what real men are supposed to be able to do. In the two days since his experience with Ned at Miranshah, Slaney had been beset by a persistent fear that he was, in some way he didn't understand, unmanly. There must have been a reason why Ned had chosen him as his vile collaborator, and Slaney had to prove to himself that Ned was wrong.

It was Friday night, but the rules of the Moslem Sabbath didn't apply in this dive. Slaney had resisted the urge to come here; the narrow streets were unpredictable, and he had heard that the available women were dark skinned and pox ridden, but the intensity of his need overcame his reservations. He had been sitting at a table for an hour, drinking and wondering how he should go about losing his virginity. He felt unclean.

He was surprised when Bats showed up, and resentful as well. He didn't want to talk to anyone, and especially not to Bats, who had been at Miranshah and might have heard what passed between Slaney and Ned. It was unlikely, because Slaney surely had not spoken about it, and he couldn't believe that Ned would, but anything that reminded him of Miranshah picked at his suppurating grievance.

He had walked out of the wireless cabin, leaving Ned on the floor, and he had blocked his mind to what Ned might have done next, when alone. Not knowing how to restore his sense of self, his dignity, and needing to release his furious energy, he hit a wall several times until his knuckles bled and pain replaced some of his anger. He wrapped a handkerchief around his fist and felt achingly tired, but he couldn't go to his billet. He couldn't look any of his fellows in the eye, and there was always the probability that Ned would turn up later, to sleep, and he didn't want to see Ned, ever again.

He saw the plane parked at the end of the strip, and he had the key. He went to the aircraft and climbed in. Blessedly, his blanket and sheepskin coats were still in the cabin, and he wrapped himself up against the cold, settled on a seat and stared out at the snow.

For a long time, he couldn't sleep. The awfulness of what had occurred was vivid in his mind, and he kept imagining Ned, naked, bloody and bruised, cowering before him, but smiling, leading him to abomination. At one point he felt salt tears sting his eyes, and he cursed himself and hit the metal struts of the plane, because crying was weak and despicable, and surely he had nothing to shed tears for, except a burdensome sense of failure as a man. It was then he decided he must have a woman, for only in the proof of his masculinity would he find self-respect again.

He avoided Ned the next morning or perhaps Ned avoided him—and didn't speak to anyone, not even Bats, except as a curt answer to a direct question. He accepted his position on the gun ring with bad grace. Why should he, the engineer who kept the plane airworthy, have to endure this privation, while others traveled in comparative comfort? It didn't matter that the passengers were women and a child, there were too many for the plane, and it was typical that a lowly erk should be bottom of the ladder. He even resented Bats, because Bats came from the ruling class, and Slaney thought of Ned, because of his accent and manner, as a debauched toff, preying on less-fortunate victims. He spent the unhappy flight alternately cursing the class system and berating the air force for letting someone so decadent as Ned run rampant among the decent working men.

When they landed at Peshawar, Bats had asked what was wrong, and Slaney had shrugged. That night, Bats had sought him out in the mess and again asked what was wrong. Slaney still said nothing, but wondered why officers were allowed in here, when he couldn't go to their mess. They hadn't flown on the Friday, and Slaney spent the day on his cot, nursing his grievances and planning his deflowering.

He never asked how Bats knew he was at the bar, but he wondered if Bats guessed what had happened at Miranshah and had been keeping tabs on him, to laugh at him, or report him, or sneer at his manhood. The truth was more charitable. Bats was concerned about Slaney. He had a high respect for his engineer and was puzzled by his present, atypical foul temper. He did not follow Slaney to the old city; he was there because he was bored with his own company and tired of telling other officers his tales of Kabul. At least in the native quarter something interesting might happen, and his hope was justified when he glanced into the bar and saw Slaney. It was odd that Slaney was there, and odder because Slaney was getting drunk, which he very seldom did, and so had the potential to be mildly amusing. Or, at least, not boring.

They drank in silence for a while, and then Bats began to get irritable. "Have I done something to offend you?"

"It isn't you," Slaney said. "It's the whole bloody system."

"Looking for a woman?" Bats wondered. "If so, there are better places than this."

"Not for erks like me," Slaney said.

So that was it, the old working-class prejudices coming to the surface in drink. Bats was disappointed. He had expected more of Slaney. "Well, there you are, that's how it is," he said. He got up to leave. Slaney could stew in his own self-pity.

"What did you make of him?" Slaney asked, as if he really needed to know the answer to something that was baffling him. It came out of the blue to Bats, but he knew exactly who Slaney meant.

He smiled. "I think he's a terrific impostor," he said, and sat down again. Perhaps something interesting might transpire after all.

"Bloody bullshit artist," Slaney said, and Bats was surprised at the level of hostility in his voice.

"That too," he agreed. "Or perhaps—"

Slaney looked at him, keenly.

"When I say he's an impostor, I mean he is not the man he was," Bats explained. "Whoever he might have been once, he is not that man now. I suppose I can't really call him an impostor. He's not pretending to be anything more than he is"—he smiled—"a lowly erk."

He used the last phrase deliberately, to see if it would offend Slaney, but the man accepted it for what it was, an apparent statement of fact.

"It is we who want him to be more," Bats said. "It is we who want him to be Lawrence of Arabia, but that man is dead. Perhaps it is our need for heroes."

Bats had been disappointed by Ned. The oddness of Ned's present circumstances suggested to Bats that he was not going to find Lawrence, but he expected something more than a secretive, defensive monk, a frightened rabbit caught in the headlights of an approaching car, a man who still could be impudently cheeky, but whose overriding concern was that he not be chucked out of the service.

"I almost think he wants to die," Bats said.

It caught Slaney's attention, because he had thought that once, of Ned.

"Life no longer has any real meaning for him," Bats continued. "What does he have to live for? What do you do after you've been to the top of the mountain? But he is too scared to do anything about it. In that way, he is an impostor, living a lie of a life."

"Fucken queer is what he is," Slaney muttered.

"That too," Bats agreed.

He ordered more drinks, and there was another small silence. From somewhere upstairs the sickly, sweet smell of hashish drifted down to Bats, and he envied the smoker.

"Of course, that depends on what you mean by queer," Bats prodded gently, and was gratified to see Slaney blush. He wondered if Slaney and Ned were more than simply friends, but as quickly dismissed the idea. Slaney, he was sure, was a sexual virgin. It had occurred to Bats that Ned was homosexual—there was a certain softness about him, and that high-pitched, nervous voice was unfortunate. But people laughed at Bats's voice, too, and he knew better than to judge others by their appearance. His only interest in Ned's sexuality was as an explanation of his odd behavior, and because he was an inveterate gossip. He learned so much from others' indiscretions.

"Just queer," Slaney said. "Doolally." He couldn't tell anyone the truth about Ned, because in doing so he would have to reveal too much of himself.

Something's got his goat, Bats thought, watching Slaney carefully. Something has provoked a need in him that he is embarrassed to define. He wondered what that something was. "Are you a virgin?" Bats asked him.

Slaney was furious. Was it that obvious?

"Bet you are," Bats said to his silence, with a silly-ass grin.

Slaney looked down at his glass.

"I know better places to lose your cherry," Bats said.

"Where?" Slaney asked in a whisper, not looking up.

"Nowhere in Peshawar; they're a raddled lot," Bats said.

"I want to fall in love," Slaney whispered.

It was predictable to Bats. Slaney was a good fellow, but he had bourgeois longings. Love, the way Slaney used the word, was respectability. It was the past, and another country. Bats had never been bothered by respectability. His desires ran in dusky directions, which might be obsessive and could be loving, but definitely were not love.

"Well, there are the hill resorts," he said. "Dozens of lusty, pink-fleshed secretaries, all panting for a handsome soldier. Or an airman. But nobody goes there much at this time of the year. And your need seems to have a certain urgency. Delhi is probably the answer."

"Yeh, and pigs might fly," Slaney grunted.

"Oh, I don't know." There was a tinge of relief in Bats's voice. Something might come out of this yet. Helping a young innocent to his deflowering might be amusing.

"I can probably dream up a reason for needing to see the desk wallahs. And I was going to get you something for Christmas. Let's call this your present."

Slaney looked at him now, in disbelief.

"Takeoff at dawn?" Bats suggested. "Better not get too drunk tonight, there's a good lad. Keep yourself nice for tomorrow."

They flew to Delhi the next morning. Bats took rooms at the Imperial Hotel, a good one for himself and a second-class one overlooking the kitchen for Slaney.

He advised a nap, then later took Slaney in a car to a house in a pleasant part of town, quiet and secluded. There was a long, high wall and a closed gate. Bats rang the bell.

Looking crisp in a newly starched uniform, Slaney was nervous. It was all a little clinical to him, and he wasn't sure what was going on behind that wall.

A dark, heavyset young man in a turban opened the gate and greeted Bats as someone he recognized.

"This is Mohan," Bats said to Slaney. "Mohan, this is my friend, Sahib Slaney."

Mohan nodded a greeting, motioned them inside and shut the gate behind them. There was a large, pretty garden and a house with a spacious, open verandah. There were sofas and tables on the terrace and in the reception room inside the house, but no sign of other people.

Mohan showed them to a table, and they sat down. Bats ordered Johnny Walker.

"Don't worry about a thing," he said to Slaney. "This is all on me."

"What do I do?" Slaney asked, feeling foolish.

"Whatever you want to do," Bats said.

Two young women came from the house and sat with them. Bats asked their names and introduced himself and Slaney. Mohan brought the whisky, two glasses and an ice bucket. The young women did not drink.

"Bottoms up," Bats said, raising his glass to Slaney. One of the young women giggled.

They were very light skinned Anglo-Indians, and in this lamplit garden, both looked beautiful to Slaney. Still he felt no desire for them. The very ordinariness of the surroundings, however charming, mitigated lust. He asked a few simple questions, the young women responded, and slowly Slaney relaxed. He thought it unlikely he would achieve what he wanted here, so he decided on simply having a good time.

A bell rang. Mohan appeared and went to the gate. He ushered in a well-dressed white man, probably an officer in mufti, who glanced at Bats and Slaney, and sat at a table some distance away from them.

"A few may find it odd that you're not an officer," Bats whispered to Slaney, "but you're with me."

Two more young women came out of the house and went to sit with the newcomer. Then an older woman came out to them, smart and well dressed

and charming. She greeted Bats like an old friend and was courteous and wel-
coming to Slaney. She was an unlikely courtesan in a striking black silk sari
and flawless pearls. Her name was Mrs. Windsor.

"Not her real name, of course," Bats chortled, "but she has regal aspirations."

The officer in civilian clothes got up and disappeared into the night with
one of the girls from his table. It all fell into place for Slaney. At first he had
thought that Mrs. Windsor was giving some kind of eccentric party, but now
he realized that this was indeed a brothel, and probably the best that he would
ever visit. Amused by the whisky, the company and his situation, Slaney began
to relax. He found it easy to talk to these women, and the protective arm of
Bats was always, tacitly, there.

He decided that perhaps he would be able to sleep with one of the young
women, and wondered which of them, but still felt no urgent longing for
either. They were too sophisticated for Slaney's taste. He became aware that
Bats was whispering something to Mrs. Windsor, and it was about him, he
knew, because she glanced at Slaney and then went into the house. She
returned a few minutes later, bringing with her the prettiest creature that
Slaney thought he had ever seen. She was darker than the others, dusky but
still light, and had perfect, almond-shaped eyes, softly rimmed with kohl.

"This is Doreen," he heard Mrs. Windsor say. "Doreen, this is Slaney."

Doreen sat beside him on the sofa, and the two other young women and
Bats took their leave. Slaney remembered Doreen's name, but little else of the
next half hour, which was spent lost in a world of feminine grace, exactly
where he wanted to be.

Doreen was perfect, shy yet knowing. She took care of Slaney as in his
erotic dreams, pouring his whisky for him, caressing his hand, staring deep
into his eyes as if every word he said had meaning for her. He felt no timidity
in her company, no sense of being a novice, no fear that when the time came,
as he now knew it would, for him to take her, he would not be worthy.

The time came, but it was she who took him. She whispered coyly in his
ear that he should lie down and relax for a while, and Slaney, warm and lazy
with whisky, but vibrant, nodded. She led him by the hand to a candlelit room
where there was a large and beautiful brass bed, canopied by a flowing mos-
quito net.

She made him sit on the bed, and she caressed him, her touch light as swansdown. It was a while before he realized she had unbuttoned his shirt and taken it from him, and his chest was naked. She unlaced his puttees and took off his boots and socks. Then there was the cooling splash of water. She was washing his feet from a basin.

She giggled shyly and told him to stand up. Slaney, unembarrassed by the strident erection that threatened to pop his fly buttons, obeyed. She undid his belt and pushed down his shorts and underpants, and he stood before her in what the other men sometimes called their glory. Now she touched him there, washing him and looking carefully at him, as if inspecting him for disease. He loved her for that. She was clean and careful, concerned about him and herself.

She kissed him, there, and used her tongue in ways that Slaney had never imagined. She took him into her mouth, but that was something outside his limited knowledge, and he was alarmed by its surprising and exciting novelty. He loved it, but it wasn't what he wanted, it wasn't what he was here for.

He pulled her up to him, but although she resisted his urgent roughness, she let his tongue explore her mouth. He had to have her soon, or burst his seed upon her, he thought, and laid her on the bed and climbed astride her. Still she was calming, cajoling him to patience. Her breasts were tiny, but flawless, he thought, and as he lay on top of her, caressing them, nibbling them, he could feel his cock between her legs, slipping into moistness.

Then he was inside her, and the hot, wet, yielding firmness of her enveloped what had become his total being, and he thought her limitless. She pulled him into her and led him quickly, inexorably to a climax that was more consuming than anything he could possibly have imagined, intensified by the fears that Ned had caused in him.

Afterwards, he eased himself from her and lay beside her, stroking her midnight velvet hair and whispering things that she had heard a hundred times before but were, from him, newly minted.

He was drowsy, and she hummed a pretty song to him, a gentle lullaby. He drifted to sleep, with her beside him, safe in his strong arms.

In the morning, he knew what he had to do. He was a man, young and virile and mated. All his doubts about himself had been resolved, and he felt a furious anger that Ned had caused him to have those doubts, when the answer was so simple, so easy and so natural. Ned's vice was against nature, frightening in its perversion, and he wanted to hurt Ned, hit him hard, in a way that had some meaning. Since to physically strike Ned was futile, Slaney had decided, in his slumbers, on another course.

He knew how to hurt Ned in an effective and surprising way. He said good-bye to Doreen, and promised to write, or to see her again. He gave her money, although he knew it was unnecessary, because Bats had told him so. He didn't look for Bats; they would meet again at the hotel. He walked out of the house, hailed a rickshaw and asked to be taken to the cable and wireless office.

There he spent some time composing telegrams. He sent one to the *Times of India,* the others to newspapers in London, describing every rumor he had heard of Ned in Afghanistan, and embroidering the stories with details that were only available to someone who had been in that country. All the wildest tales made sense to him. Fabrications or not, he envisaged Ned in Kabul, riding beside Umar, challenging the mandate of the amir.

He let his mind run riot, let Ned's own tales of Arabia color his imaginings, and although the cost of the cables was high, he would gladly have spent every penny he had to bring about his vengeance.

Ned's greatest terror was of being kicked out of the RAF. This, thought Slaney, should cook his goose.

33

January 1929

It isn't fair!

In the words of Higgins as we said good-bye, it isn't bally, sodding, effing, blinding fair!

I'm going mad, I know I am. It isn't my fault, this time. I didn't do anything wrong, not this time.

Or did I? Did the old serpent lead me into confounding temptation yet again? Did it cause my downfall, my exile from my quiet asylum?

Was it for lust? Was it my lust for Slaney? Was Slaney my accuser, my betrayer? Was I so wrong about him, blind to trust him? Was he the one who broadcast all the rumors to the press and forced me from my hiding place as a ferret does a fox? I was a fool to trust him. I thought him bigger, like John Bruce, massive in his simplicity, giant-size in loyalty and solitude and loneliness. But I was wrong. I should have guessed that my demanding demons were too affronting to his narrow soul. How could I have been so wrong, so careless?

In any event, I am betrayed, or I betrayed myself, or gave the serpent charge of me.

(I shall conquer him. I will command him to obedience. I will not march to his base commands, for then what will become of me?)

Or was it Bats? Despicable Bats, who has everything that should have been mine: a second son, honestly born, with all the advantages and security that legitimacy bestows. Careless Bats, who couldn't know what treasure I had found in my seclusion and thrust the priceless thing before the world.

Or was it Fraser, or Stapleton, or all the others whom I so offend? Or Higgins, or Mitchell, or Baxter, or Pravda, or Burlington bloody Bertie from bally, sodding, effing, blinding Bow?

Or was it me, only me, was it all my own doing? Am I hell-bent on self-deracination, restless, rootless, lost? Was I too alarmed that I had found some quietude, and that monster guilt, that other Caliban, could not abide my wise government of his discontent and thrust me into exile from my secluded, magic island?

There was a mighty shout, a scream from Fleet Street's Grub Street gutters, a dickens of a fuss, which burst upon me like a cyclone. The newspapers in London found me out and published things that are not true—their own hysterical longings, wild hearsay, tales of my other self, newborn and rampant, the scourge of despots—vile rumors so wantonly colored that they destroyed my chances of surviving them.

Munshi Shah! A holy man! Me!

Instigator of the Afghan revolution! Me!

Cause of Amanullah's downfall! Me!

A British Imperialist, acting against the best of British interests! Me!

That I am not fit to live a simple life, forgotten in the ranks, dangerous because of who I was, not who I am! Me!

The governments could not withstand the pressure—not India, which has always hated me, nor London, which does not know what to do with me, as I do not know what to do with myself. GBS could do nothing, Winnie couldn't help (he's cast in the same mold, adored for what he might have been, despised for what he is now). Trenchard tried to save me but was powerless before the onslaught. They'll kick me out of the RAF for sure, just as they have banished me from my seclusion. I was plucked from my mountain hermitage, thrown into Karachi and, within hours it seemed, on my way home.

But where is home, and what will I do there? Home is the place where you are loved, and I am not loved in England. I am adored for what I was and despised for what I am, and now, not anywhere is solitude available. I am to stay in the air force, but who knows for how long and doing what. It is, they tell me, my last chance, but will I be given that chance? Will the voracious appetite of the hero-needing masses let me live out my time in seclusion? Will I, or my old serpent, allow it as well?

So here I stand, on the deck of SS Rajputana, *a smaller ship of the P & O line, at anchor in the Bitter Lake, staring out through the night to the only place in all the world where I have been truly happy. I can see it, in my mind's eye, only a hundred miles away, but further than another galaxy. But what's the use? Unless I could travel back in time I would be alone there too, and the memories of what was would drive me mad! Are making me mad! I am going mad!*

I stand here on the edge of my beloved wilderness, and I cannot get to where I want to be, except by the route I am too cowardly to take.

I stand here all night, alone at the rail, and I know that the others are watching me, talking about me, giggling about me, calling me a queer bastard.

Well, I don't care anymore what they think of me. I shall stand here all night, because it is the closest I will ever come to home.

Imperceptibly, the sky lightens. In the distance, I can see it now, a strip of sandy land, and I hear a muezzin calling the faithful to prayer. Oh, my unworthy soul, what balm that is to my unquiet, and yet so full of painful resonance it makes my body ache to die. It is the sound of him—his threnody, his elegy, his requiem. It is the hymn of the desert as the camel bell is its metronome, the song of Carchemish, the call to thoughts of God. Sunrise, sunset, morning, noon and evening, five times daily, he abandoned earthly matters and turned to eternal contemplations. Five times daily, he forgot me, and yet I was always in his prayers, as he in mine. Yet he believed, and I do not, and he found peace, and I have not, and I am condemned to hell because I was faithless, and this thing called life is purgatory.

The stars disappear, the moon is gone. The ship stirs. The engines throb, the anchor is hauled from the sea and we set sail again, and I am carried away from even a glimpse of the place where his spirit still lingers and, I pray, waits for me to come and join him.

I want to go there! Now!

It would be so easy. All I have to do is fall over the side of the ship, just a little slip, so easy. Easy to drown in bitter waters and trudge over burning sand until I come to the last obstacle and entrust myself to the ferryman—he knows I have paid the fare!—and he will row me across the Stygian river to a golden morning, and Dahoum will be waiting on the other shore.

And his eyes will be shining, even though I have failed and do not bring him the long-promised freedom—he found that years ago, without my help. He will be angry with me that I have kept him waiting for so long, and shout his grievance at me. But then he will smile, and it will break my heart, and he will see that I am crying, and, because he cannot bear to hurt me, he will hold me in his arms again and forgive me, and I will be happy.

I want to go there now! I will! I shall just. . . . slip away—my hand is on the rail—slip over the side of the ship . . . away . . .

But what if he is not there?

What if he knows of my faithlessness? What if he has discovered my unworthiness? What if he is in some other place that is forbidden to me, some place where I can never find him? Or what if there is hell, as my mother tries to convince me, and I am consigned there, while he sits with seraphim in paradise? Or what if there is nothing? What if there is no afterlife? No God, no Lucifer, no redemption or damnation, no angel's trumpet, no fire, no brimstone, no Elysium, no Tartarus, no Zeus, no Hades, not even the meadows of Asphodel? What if there is only nothing? What if all these years of dreaming of his constancy have been only a terrible illusion, a false hope that I have clung to because I cannot bear to think that there is no resting place for his sweet soul?

What if there is only an empty void called death?

I'm going mad, I know I am!

Still I stand clutching the rail until all hope of anything is gone, and I am crying.

We steam along the narrow canal until we come to Port Said. I have not moved. The passengers gather on the decks to watch the scrum of bumboats gathering about us, laughing at the cries to purchase every waving of bright-colored cloth and cheap, shining brass, every brandishing of badly carved camels. It is stinging salt in my open wounds, because this is the gateway to my other self, the path back to the man I was, to youth, to life, to shining, bright adventure.

And I cannot go there.

I am not allowed to go ashore. I am confined to the barracks of this boat because my presence on dry land is too provocative. They will not even let me visit Newk. They will not let me wander in this gaudy city, they will not allow me even one tiny glimpse of remembered happiness, for fear I cause revolutions!

Me!

Well, I will provoke them! I will give them something to chew on! I will let them know I am still me and do not accept their churlish abuse of me easily!

I go to the galley. No one stops me, they do not know my plan, and in any case, they are slightly in awe of my determination, my madness.

I find a crate of canned soup, second-class stuff as befits my station. I take it back on deck and start a war.

I pelt the bumboat boys with the cans, and they retaliate, throwing all the rubbish of their boats at me, and iron bars which they keep for the purpose; and for a while it is wild and fun and crazy, and I am mad with energy and frustration and adoration of these tempestuous people, and they are furious with me, and scream abuse at me, as befits my awful self, but they love me too, because I am a vivid distraction from a life scratched out of poverty, and the cans of soup they try to catch and dive in the water to recover are more to eat than they will earn in a week of selling souvenirs.

For just a moment, all care is forgotten, except of the moment.

A few other passengers cheer me on and even throw a few cans. Most are *appalled by my behavior, however, and by my profligate waste; I'm showing off, they say quite loudly, but I'm used to that, in everything I do.*

Who cares?

Finally, there are no more cans to throw, and I am tired. I wave good-bye to the bumboat boys, who might have been my friends, acknowledge the applauding few passengers and crew, ignore the sneering many and go below to my cabin.

I lie on my bunk and wait for whatever is going to happen next and dread the future.

I cannot imagine what will become of me.

London

—⟨⟨⟨⟩⟩⟩—

(Charlotte and Feisal)

1933

34

A DENSE FOG, a London pea-souper, had descended on the city. His Majesty King Feisal of Iraq stared out at the river that he knew was there but could not see. Melancholy foghorns sounded their warnings, and occasional misty lights shimmered in the gloom. The sound of traffic was dulled to a whisper, the clatter of horse-drawn carriages the only sharp noise, or the occasional tooting of a motorcar horn. The city went about its business muffled, smothered in a grimy eiderdown.

Feisal loved London in every weather but especially in the fog. It was all so very different from Baghdad, his capital, his seat of government, the place of his tedious throne.

He should have had Damascus, not Baghdad. Damascus was like London on a smaller scale, a city of surprises, a sensuous city, a walled, protective city, a city of secrets and intrigues and redolent with history. An Aramaean, Hittite and Assyrian city; a Persian, Greek and Roman city; a biblical city; a Moslem city, once the capital of the caliphate; a Crusader city; briefly a Mongol city and, until recently, a Turkish city. In Damascus, Feisal might have been happy.

Damascus was what he had wanted from the beginning. He had dreamed of it in the waterless wastes of the Hejaz, and he had won it in battle. It was his by right of conquest, and if it hadn't been for the French it would still be his. He would have had Damascus instead of dreary Baghdad.

Yes, Baghdad had oil, a limitless sea of it, but that was about all it had.

There was a tap at the door.

"Come," Feisal said. He knew it was his private secretary. It was time for the meeting he didn't want to have.

"Mrs. Shaw is here, sir," the secretary said.

"Yes." Feisal nodded, without turning away from the window. "I shall be there directly."

The secretary bowed and left. Feisal stared at the fog outside. He was meeting Charlotte Shaw at Ned's request, a favor to an old friend, but he wasn't looking forward to it. He had hoped that George Bernard Shaw would come with his wife; his was a mind to parry with, and they could talk about socialism and Russia. Feisal believed in knowing as much as he could about his enemy; there were a number of subversive groups in Iraq—republicans and small cells of Communists financed and encouraged by the Russians—and he did not intend to have his reign, or his life, or that of his son, cut short by any kind of coup.

But no, Mrs. Shaw was on her own, and Feisal was disappointed. He assumed that she wanted to talk about Lawrence of Arabia, and he was weary of that legend.

It had been so different when the promise was made, the debt first incurred, at Feisal's camp near Medina, soon after the start of his father's war against Turkish domination of his land.

Before the war, the vast Ottoman Empire of Turkey encompassed the Arabian Peninsula. Feisal's father, Sherif Hussein ibn Ali el-Aun, emir of Mecca, guardian of the holy places, was the hereditary ruler of that territory, but he governed at Turkish pleasure. The libertine Turks were heretics in the eyes of the austere desert Arabs, and when Turkey sided with Germany in the European war, rebellious Arab nationalists saw a chance. With tacit British support, Feisal's father began a war for the independence of his lands, or, at the very least, to capture the holy cities of Mecca and Medina.

The reclusive Hussein sent his sons into the field. Mecca was taken, but Medina was heavily fortified and garrisoned. Feisal was forced to accept that an assault on the city would be costly and futile. He made camp, tried to keep his motley, grumbling, ill-supplied Bedouin army inspired and wondered how to proceed.

A good general but an impatient son, Feisal strained against his father's leash. Born to authority, he did not know what it was he would rule. The desert was large enough for all four sons to inherit a goodly slab of it, but Feisal didn't want to be a king of sand without a city of any consequence. His dreams drifted north, to Damascus.

It was impossible, of course, and Feisal put away his secret dreams and contemplated immediate battles.

And then there was Ned.

Like an aberrant angel, a young, fair-haired, blue-eyed, junior British officer appeared out of the desert. Insolent and arrogant, but full of vim and vigor, he was fluent in Arabic, with a strong Syrian accent, he had a surprising knowledge of Arabian affairs and was brimming with ideas as to how the campaign should be conducted. At their very first meeting he had struck Feisal's rawest nerve.

They were at dinner in Feisal's tent, with several of his lieutenants, seated on carpets and eating from a central platter of rice and mutton. Thankfully, the young British officer was comfortable and knew how to eat with his fingers. Feisal tried to make his guest feel welcome, asking polite questions about the officer's journey and what he thought of the encampment.

The officer, who had introduced himself as Ned, looked straight at Feisal. There was a challenge in his eyes.

"I like it well," he said. "But it is a long way from Damascus."

There was a shocked silence, broken only by a hissing disapproval from several men present. All eyes turned to Feisal.

Feisal was furious. It was open rudeness and a direct challenge. Damascus, so far away, the center of the Arab world, was a fantasy, an enticing mirage. If Ned had been under Feisal's command he would have ordered him to be punished for his insolence. But he was not under Feisal's command. Ned's position with Feisal's army was vague—some sort of adviser—but his orders came from Cairo, and Feisal did not intend to offend the British. He tried to be charitable but couldn't, and settled on a vague generality. "Praise be to God," Feisal said, "there are Turks much nearer to us than that."

They met again and clashed again. Ned seemed to have some urgent, private motive for reaching Damascus, and he was always chock full of plans, overflowing with energy. Despite his reservations, Feisal found himself drawn to this odd, unlikely man.

"Medina is irrelevant," Ned said. "It cannot be taken, not yet. Let us secure the coast, so that we can be supplied, and then go north. There in the unguarded desert we can cut the beast in two. We can wreak havoc on the railway line and keep the Turks busy repairing one section while we destroy another. We will inch to our goal and achieve what both of us want."

It made absolute sense to Feisal. It was guerrilla war, and their only chance of success, but he was puzzled. "What is it that you want in Damascus?" he asked Ned.

"Freedom," Ned said simply. "It is my quest." And then whispered, so quietly that Feisal almost could not hear: "I have made covenants with rainbows."

Feisal wondered if Ned was one of those wild Englishmen whose insanity cannot be contained in England and who come to the East to be some kind of king. History was littered with them—dotty, fearless, improvident adventurers seeking open spaces to claim as their own. Or was he obeying secret British orders for some obscure Imperial purpose? Or was it for personal fame or riches? Was Ned's "quest" a search for gold? And if freedom, from what? Ned was not conquered.

Ned insisted he had no orders, secret or otherwise. He was a free agent sent to advise the Arabs in their revolt. He was not an explorer; he claimed to have found already the country he had sought. Fame, he said, was odious to him, and after the war he intended to retire to a lost Hittite city near Aleppo. He despised money, he said, and had no need of it.

He was a provocative and inspiring adviser, and Feisal abandoned Medina and headed north, to the impossible dream of Damascus.

Ned was no great soldier—too many of his ill-considered missions ended in disaster and defeat—but he was brave, sometimes foolishly so, careless of his physical welfare, of pain or personal hardship. He was honorable, he knew and understood the Arab code of chivalry, of loyalty to friends and vengeance on enemies. He was considerate of friends and unforgiving of treachery. He had formidable stamina, always driving himself, and others, beyond reasonable endurance.

And he was chaste.

Ned loved to be among the young warriors, as reckless as they in boasting, as exuberant as they in play. After a pitiless march across an anvil desert, or jubilant at the blowing up of a Turkish train, or beset by the emotions a bloody battle aroused—of life or death, of victory, of the loss of a loved friend—after these times the young men would gather at an oasis, strip naked and cleanse themselves of the day. Some few might rid themselves of another need, for survival of imminent death is an almost irresistible sexual stimulant.

Always, at these oases, Ned was there, watching, chatting, advising. Singing with them if they were happy, comforting them if they were sad, a boy amongst them, like them, zesty for life. But he never sought another's intimate company, at least, not to Feisal's knowledge.

They inched north, first to Aqaba, then to Ma'an and Deraa, toward seductive victory and destructive doubt. All were valiant, all had extravagant ransoms on their heads, but the glory came to Ned. Aqaba fell to Auda Abu Tayi's audacious assault from the land, not the sea, but the Western world gave the credit to Ned. Journalists came and made him a legend. Ned failed at Ma'an; others took the town, but the world did not hear of that. Allenby took Jerusalem, but Ned was the liaison, and Feisal was disregarded, as Ned's native lieutenant.

It dawned on Feisal that it didn't matter how brave he was, how strategically brilliant, how valiant his conquests, the West would always look to one of their own as the hero. He had been naïve to suppose otherwise. How could white men, bogged down in an unwinnable war in the miserable, muddy trenches of France, accord victory to a brown-skinned Bedouin? In British eyes, Feisal realized bitterly, he was a wog. It was a fact of the European need for supremacy, and he had allowed himself to be blind to it, or to forget it, or think he could overcome it.

Well, he would show them! He would win Damascus!

And he did! And he got Baghdad!

The British broke up old Mesopotamia, and, after the French exiled him from Syria, gave Feisal the biggest chunk of it, flowing with oil, and expected him to be grateful. They did not understand that it was not his by birth or battle, neither inherited nor won. He had not fought for oil, for money, but to be king of something of value, and now he was a puppet, not a man, kept on his false throne by foreign masters.

And always, there was Baghdad.

Feisal could not understand how a city with such a vivid history could be so dull. There was nothing here of Babylon, the ruins of which were only fifty-five miles away. For a short time, under Harun al-Rashid, Baghdad had been one of the most important cities of Islam, but after it was sacked by Mongols it never recovered its vitality. The only real reason for its existence now was as an oil head, and the city lay there, a lazy, ugly strumpet sustained by Western need.

The sloth affected his people, who went about their business dully without the sparkling bustle of Damascus. The summers were unbearably hot, the winters overcast, there was hardly any rain, and only for a few weeks in spring and autumn was the weather pleasant. The architecture was functional and uninspiring, and the Tigris River, the city's lifeblood, was muddy here, and torpid.

It was only on the banks of the river that there was a tiny flash of color. Feisal had never lusted for young men, but he knew that some of his friends found substitutes for women in other willing youths. Sometimes these relationships could last for years, even beyond eventual marriage. Feisal had never been attracted to the idea, or perhaps he had never found a young man whom he thought desirable. He had indulged himself occasionally with arranged women, in Cairo and in Europe, but nothing of any consequence. Then he married, and he was content.

But they would gather, these questing young men, in a park on the banks of the Tigris to seek each other out. When partnerships were formed the couple would promenade together, and the one who took the passive role would carry a single red rose to indicate his submission to his more dominant partner.

It was a silly and simple thing, disgraceful to many, but it amused Feisal. It indicated that at least some of his people had a spark of bravado. In his more cynical moments, he sometimes thought that those few red roses were the only splash of individuality in all his sandy kingdom.

Baghdad? The name meant "Given by God" in Persian, but Feisal thought that was simply the foolish optimism of its founders.

He smiled to himself, because he had to face a truth. When all his bitterness was stripped away, he was, ultimately, a realist.

Better Baghdad than nothing.

35

CHARLOTTE WAS SLIGHTLY NERVOUS, and cross with herself. She fretted about her appearance. She wasn't happy with the plain, blue serge suit she had chosen for the audience—there was a small stain on the sleeve—her corset was tight and uncomfortable, and a wretched lock of hair wouldn't stay in place. She pushed the hair up under her hat, and a bobby pin fell out. She tutted in annoyance, then fished in her bag for a handkerchief. She didn't want to shake hands with Feisal if her palms were moist. She wanted to make a good impression.

Because of Ned. She was about to meet a man who had been one of Ned's closest confidantes, a companion in battle and a friend. A man who knew as much about the other Ned, the legendary Ned, as any man alive. She was not nervous of the man she was going to meet; she had met royalty before, and the King of Iraq was hardly the most illustrious of monarchs. She was nervous because she was about to be in the presence of the mystic, mysterious past.

It was hot in the formal sitting room of the hotel suite; someone had turned the heating up till the room was a furnace, and she was uncomfortable, perched on the edge of an enormous sofa. It was all so infuriating. Why didn't he come? Why had she been left alone like this, to fuss and fidget and worry and wonder what on earth she was going to ask him?

It was all so very different at Buckingham Palace. There, you were never left alone, an aide or secretary was always with you, chattering on about nothing to make you feel relaxed. Then suddenly King George was there, with only a small fanfare of announcement, and was charming and asked all the right questions. Charlotte was never nervous when she went to the palace.

This was all so—foreign. The dark-haired, dark-eyed secretary had greeted her formally, asked her to sit and offered her a drink. Charlotte had declined, and he had gone, disappeared somewhere, and she was all alone. Then the secretary came back and said His Majesty was detained for a few minutes, and did she want to change her mind and have a drink?

Charlotte did change her mind. He mixed a strong one, gave it to her and left. Charlotte sipped the drink, but there was too much gin and not enough tonic, so she put it down. Really, this was intolerable; she'd been there for nearly half an hour. Why didn't he come?

It was like waiting for Nancy Astor. She liked Nancy, they were friends and Nancy could be very kind, but she was American, even though she knew how to use a knife and fork, and very imperious. She had a forceful personality and strident opinions, necessary in a politician, perhaps, but she always made Charlotte feel like a silly schoolgirl for a few minutes, every time they met. Nancy was very witty, and sometimes cruelly unkind, but that wasn't why she and Nancy had drifted apart recently.

Left to her own devices in the formal sitting room, waiting to meet a king who had been one of Ned's dearest friends, Charlotte realized something awful. She was jealous of Nancy, not for her wealth, for Charlotte was not poor, nor for her self-assurance, because when Charlotte got over her initial nervousness, she was quite prepared to tell Nancy she was talking twaddle.

She was jealous because Nancy was stealing Ned from her.

Charlotte was horrified, because as soon as she had made the admission, it was obvious to her that she had been feeling this way for some time but had denied it, or pushed it to the back of her mind. She disliked herself for it. She thought of herself as generous (to a fault, GBS always said), and dozens of people claimed Ned's friendship. But no other woman. And not now. Ned needed Charlotte now.

Was this why she had come to see Feisal? Did she want to learn something about Ned that Nancy did not know? Was she being so petty? Well, she would deal with that later. She gave herself a short, sharp telling off, picked up her glass and had another sip of gin just as the doors burst open. The secretary came in followed by two burly bodyguards; he announced His Majesty, and then he was there.

He was charming, and every inch a king. He was small of stature, but he had a personality that filled the room. She would have known him at once, even if he had not been announced, as someone of importance. She would have known him anyway, because in his flowing robes he looked exactly like the man in all the photographs she had seen of him, and her heart fluttered. She was in the presence of a man who had been there when Ned was that other man. She was in the company of legends.

She instantly felt completely at ease. She put down her glass, got up and gave a bob of a curtsy. He took her hand, said something nice, and they sat. They chatted about the weather, or the fog, for a few minutes, and Feisal asked after GBS. Then there was silence.

"It is so very good of you to see me," Charlotte said. "You must be very busy."

Feisal wasn't all that busy. There was the usual round of embassy receptions and formal dinners and meaningless conversations with secretive men in Whitehall who kept telling him how to run his country. And shopping, of course. His wife and daughters went shopping every day, in Bond Street or at Harrods, and Feisal went with them sometimes, but apart from that he was at a bit of a loose end and slightly bored. It was why he had immediately agreed, at her request through Ned, to meet Charlotte, and then, as immediately, regretted it.

"I assume you want to talk about Ned," he said, managing to bring a twinkle to his eye. Might as well get the ball rolling.

"Yes," Charlotte said. She didn't know how to proceed. Her mind was full of questions, but they all seemed suddenly trivial. "Was he happy in Arabia?" seemed point-blank silly, but what did you ask to get an insight into a man's soul?

Honesty flooded her. "I am so very worried about him," she said, and a tear came to her eye. She was cross with herself, but there it was, it couldn't be helped, it was how she really felt, deep down at the bottom of her heart.

"If I can be of any help . . ." Feisal said kindly, fully aware that there was nothing he could do to help Ned, except financially, and he knew Ned didn't want that. Ned was his own man, struggling with his own demons. He knew that Ned was deeply unhappy, but he never did anything to help his own cause. That silly book hadn't helped. It was Ned's stab at literary immortality, but it was also a gigantic fueling of the Lawrence legend that Ned claimed to despise. Why feed your own monster?

"What has happened to Ned that is causing your distress?" Feisal asked Charlotte.

Charlotte shook her head and wiped her eyes with her handkerchief. She had to be clear-headed, but she was upset because she didn't see much of Ned anymore. He was stationed at Cattewater, near Plymouth (Nancy Astor's electorate!), and although they still wrote to each other, his letters were less fulsome than before, as if he had closed off part of himself from her. As if, having revealed much of himself but not everything, he had drawn back, fearful of what he might tell her or what she might learn.

She had seen him on his return from India and was shocked by the change in him, although it wasn't surprising. No one should have to suffer the nonsense that Ned had endured. She had first become aware of the furor when GBS showed her that outrageous article in the *Empire News* claiming that Ned was almost single-handedly responsible for the revolution in Afghanistan. The international press had taken up the banner. The Americans were howling, the Russians were brandishing sabers, and the Indians were passionately aroused. Ned had been burned in effigy at Tower Hill by Indian nationalists, and the Indian newspapers were screaming for his head. The government was forced to remove him, with indecent haste, from Miranshah, from India. This, Charlotte was sure, had broken his heart, because he had been happy there, at Miranshah. Or, if not happy, as close as Ned would ever come to some kind of personal well-being.

Still the press was not satisfied and hounded him as an old-time imperialist desperately searching for vanished glory. No one could believe that he was content to be a simple airman in the ranks. When the ship bringing him from India docked at Southampton, the throng of besieging reporters was so large and so aggressive Ned had to be removed from the ship by subterfuge. In London he was called to the House of Commons to give an account of himself, and no one but a few loyal friends championed his tale of innocence.

Charlotte had seen him the evening after his appearance in the House, and her heart bled for him, all the sparkle gone, no smiles, no giggles, no Tee-Hee, no bright flashes of the other, funny Ned, or the intense moody insight from the dark Shaw. He was a shell of a man, and not even GBS could rouse him to any vitality. Ned was determined to live out his days in the RAF utterly unnoticed, doing exactly what he was told, fearful that even his mere existence was offensive, and bitter beyond reasonable measure.

Later, when Charlotte visited him once at his cottage, Clouds Hill, he seemed to be back on a more even keel, but Charlotte sensed that she had lost someone dear to her and had but a shadow of him, an impostor, in his place.

John Bruce was with him at Clouds Hill that day, and Charlotte blessed her cotton socks that John, at least, was loyal. He was an odd one, but his brooding personality, his Scottish dourness and absolute protectiveness of

Ned made her think that at Clouds Hill with John, Ned was safe. She was worried that Ned might do something drastic, something awful, something final, but she was sure John Bruce would not let that happen. Charlotte had made certain educated guesses as to the truth of Ned's relationship with John, but she couldn't know for certain, nor did she care. She only wanted Ned to be happy. Or at least, not unhappy.

"What really happened at Deraa?" she asked Feisal. She hadn't prepared the question, it came out of the blue. Or perhaps out of thoughts of John Bruce.

Feisal was shocked. Obviously, the woman had read the book and was prepared to discuss things that most women, and many men, would prefer to ignore or would find offensive. But why had she asked the question? Did she not believe what she had read?

How could she believe it, when it didn't make sense? Feisal hadn't seen Ned until some little while after the incident at Deraa, and he hadn't quite believed what Ned had told him, even then. The tale changed, however slightly, in Ned's subsequent retelling of it to others, and changed again, however slightly, when he wrote it in the book, but in none of the versions did it ever make sense, it had no logic to it. Ned was severely beaten at Deraa—Feisal knew that because he had seen the wounds—and it was possible that he was raped. It was not an unusual thing for Turkish soldiers to do.

But Ned claimed that the Bey, the Turkish commander, had told him that he knew who Ned was, and if that was true, why did he let Ned go? There was a price of ten thousand pounds on his head, a fortune to a Turkish officer, unbelievable wealth to a Turkish soldier. Moreover, if the Bey was loyal to his country, which was certainly the case, why would he let Lawrence of Arabia escape?

Part of the story, at least, was easy for Feisal, turning on a nuance of the language. When the Bey had said, "I know who you are," if he had said it at all, he probably meant, "I know what you are," meaning a catamite, a fancier of men. Ned was blond and blue eyed and tiny, and sometimes oddly feminine, and to a dark Turk intensely desirable in the way that a fair woman is attractive in Arabia, or a black man much sought after in Scandinavia. Ned went on to admit that he was punished for refusing the Bey's advances, beaten to a bloody mess, then raped by several of the soldiers, and that it brought him to sexual climax. Possibly so, but while the Turks had a reputation for bisexuality, not every Turk was a sodomite, and there were no rumors of especial depravity at Deraa, by the Bey or by his men.

And why publish that story at all when Ned knew it must call his own sexuality into question? Was the beating and rape at Deraa meant to explain his disillusion with the war? To mark the turning point, the moment when it all ceased to be an adventure? Or was it more complex? Was the publication of the incident intended to suggest a truth about Ned? Why mention it at all, especially in such lurid terms, unless it was intended to suggest—or mask—something else?

"I don't suppose we shall ever know exactly what happened at Deraa," he said to Charlotte. "We only have what Ned has told us."

He saw at once that Charlotte didn't believe him. She continued to stare at him as if he were privy to some knowledge that she didn't have and was desperate to acquire, but he sensed that she felt fobbed off.

"I am quite sophisticated, I have experience of the world," Charlotte said tartly. "I am not shocked by what he wrote, except for the violence done to him. I am puzzled."

For just a moment, Feisal felt like a naughty boy before his scolding mother and would not have been surprised if Charlotte had rapped his knuckles and sent him to bed without any supper.

"As are we all," Feisal murmured. The woman was tougher than he had thought. Where would she go next?

The secretary glanced at his watch, and Charlotte saw him do it. If she didn't have a lot of time, she was going to make the most of it.

"Did you know S. A.?" Charlotte asked.

Feisal's respect for her grew. It was an obvious question for someone close to Ned, because of the dedication in the book, "To S. A.," and the extravagant love poem that followed. People had puzzled about the identity of S. A. since the book was published, and some ludicrous speculations had been made. For a moment, Feisal was cross with Ned. Why coyly put that dedication in the book when it would have been so much easier simply to tell the truth? The simple truth would have ended so much speculation and laid to rest so many ghosts.

The anger was momentary. The political Feisal knew that if Ned had been honest about S. A., he would have been hounded and vilified by his puritanical countrymen. But was that so very different from what was happening to him now? This woman knew the truth of it, or was guessing. A remarkable woman, a modern-thinking woman. He would not try to fob her off this time.

"No," Feisal said truthfully. "We never met."

"But you know who he was?"

She knows, Feisal thought. The use of the masculine pronoun means that she is not persuaded by others' speculations. But she does not know it all. She does not know who he was, she cannot give him a name. "Of course," Feisal said.

"And did not meet him?" She was bordering on impertinence. He had said not.

"He was at Carchemish," Feisal said. "I never went there."

Charlotte continued to stare at him. The secretary looked at his watch again and coughed, but Charlotte did not see or hear him. She had learned more than she had hoped for, although not as much as she wanted. She was almost grateful, but not quite, not yet.

"What happened to him?" She had to know that much at least.

"He died," Feisal told her. "Of typhus, I think."

"When?"

Straight to the very heart of it. Was she guessing? Or had she pieced it all together? Had Ned told her? If she was guessing, there was no harm in giving her one more clue. If she had pieced it all together, she might as well know the truth.

"Sometime after Deraa. Before Damascus."

At last she stopped looking at him and looked down at the floor.

"Were they happy?" she asked, very softly.

"I was never at Carchemish," Feisal said, almost as softly. "I never saw them together. But I believe—yes. They were very happy."

It was what she wanted to hear and exactly the right thing to say, and it was true, although Feisal had never been to Carchemish, had never seen Ned and Dahoum together. Much of what he knew of their relationship, he had pieced together. Or learned from spies. It was important to know as much about your friends as your enemies, because you could never be completely sure when one might become the other.

The secretary moved forward. "Mrs. Shaw . . ." he prompted. Feisal flicked him a glance of annoyance, an order not to interrupt again. Let the old woman have what she needed. If only he knew what that was.

"Yes, of course," she said. "I've taken up too much of your time."

"Not at all," Feisal responded.

Charlotte seemed uncertain if she should stay or go.

"What did you think of him?" she asked. She spoke so quietly that he strained to hear her.

"I told you, I never met Dahoum," Feisal said, and almost laughed in shock because of the triumph that flashed into her eyes.

She had trapped him, exquisitely. Now she knew his name.

It was a mistake to underestimate British women. They were adept at presenting a fussy, emotional exterior, but underneath they were dragons. It was British women who kept the Empire running. It was they who carted children around the world and fretted about their welfare, suffered unlovely climates and coped with alien societies and lived in dangerous situations, all to keep the house running for the men. Or perhaps the same was true of any woman anywhere. He began to understand what the formidable GBS saw in this fussy lioness, which had been incomprehensible to him before.

"I meant Ned," she said.

Of course she did. She didn't care about Dahoum, except as he affected Ned. Ned was the focus of all her attention. Chastened, Feisal gave an answer that was certainly diplomatic, but less than the complex truth.

"I admired Ned very much. He was most valuable to our cause. I have reasons to be profoundly grateful to him."

It was not what Charlotte wanted to hear. "Yes, but what do you really think of him?" she asked again, a hint of reprimand in her voice.

Feisal could see she was searching for something, but he was not sure what. He assumed, wrongly, that it was praise. "Many of my people—the people who were with us then—" He corrected himself, because the Iraqis he ruled were not the people he had fought to govern. "Many of them say that he is a man without equal and we will never see his like again."

That, surely, must make her happy, he thought, and he was astonished that he did not see pleasure in her eyes, but rather enormous disappointment. He sought to end it. He leaned toward her and whispered, as if they could be intimate and could discuss anything.

"What is it you really wish to know?" he asked her gently.

Tears welled up in Charlotte's eyes again. She held his hand, hard.

"I want to know why he is so very unhappy," she pleaded, even more softly than before. "So very, very lonely."

Feisal understood, or thought he did, and cursed himself for not understanding before. But surely she did not harbor romantic hope for Ned?

Then again, why not? We all have the right to an expectation of love. But looking at her, this aging, slightly shapeless, slightly untidy woman with wayward hair, and knowing what he knew of Ned, that hope seemed patently unrealistic. Better to be kindly.

"I think he was a man who found his exact place in time," he said. "And in so doing, lost himself."

He wasn't sure that what he had said made sense, and he did not want to be cruel to her. "And the place and the time were Carchemish," he said. "He was happy there, with Dahoum, and never so happy again."

It did the trick. She clutched his hand even harder than before, and a smile suffused her face, radiant, a sensible woman foolishly in love.

"Yes," she whispered.

She took his hand to her lips and kissed it, and he realized that he was wrong again, that her love for Ned was not nearly as simple as he had supposed. She was thanking him as a grateful mother might thank her king for kindness to her son.

"Yes," she said again.

His Majesty King Feisal of Iraq did not sleep well that night. The
audience with Charlotte Shaw kept whirling in his mind, for she had reminded him of something about human behavior—and perhaps about himself—
that he had always known but had carelessly forgotten.

Beset with his own boredom, he had misjudged Charlotte, or prejudged
her, and was not prepared for the passion she harbored for Ned. It was one
thing to have been wrong about an aging Englishwoman who was irrelevant
to his throne, but what if he had made the same mistake about one of his subjects, who, angry about a grievance, passionately aroused to action, might do
something drastic for his cause and conspire against—or kill—his king?

Oh, he had spies and bodyguards aplenty, but was that enough? It was easy
to dismiss rumors of peasant or nationalist plotting when the plots seldom
came to anything, or the plotters could be instantly arrested, but it was com-
placent to assume that every plot against him was discovered. It was better to
be constantly sensitive to the reasons for the discontent, to hear the grievances
before they exploded into action. Iraq might not have been Feisal's choice of
kingdom, but it *was* his, and his heirs', and he did not intend to lose his
throne to a disgruntled rabble or a lone fanatic.

These were dangerous times. Many Iraqis were resentful of an unwanted
king foisted on them by a foreign power, and the spectacular rise of National
Socialism in Germany and Italy was a fearsome and unknown quantity that
had the potential to sweep away established forms of government, bringing
havoc to an untidy world. It was foolish to imagine that the Middle Eastern
kings and sheiks were immune because they were possessors of the lifeblood
that kept the West alive.

Oil. The West would cease to function without it, and yet most of its
oceans were Arabian. If any single power controlled the Middle East, they
could, would, control the world. Feisal's present allegiances were to Britain
and his inclinations, autocratic. Both those things could change.

Feisal got up from his rumpled bed. He slept alone, used to it from the desert and an austere life. He poured himself a brandy and stared out at the foggy river.

What he said to Charlotte Shaw, intended as a comforting platitude, was truer than he realized at the time. We are each given our moment in time, but it is up to us to recognize and seize the opportunity, for the moment is ephemeral and can blow away as easily as sand across a desert, never to be in the same place again.

Feisal had thought it must be, for him, Damascus; he had wanted it so much. But Damascus proved to be only a beguiling chimera. His destiny was in Iraq, in Baghdad. Well, so be it. He would keep Iraq, he would not let Baghdad slip from him.

Ned had been given his moment in time, and for whatever reason—a failure of self, of inner strength, of personal conviction, or because of innate weakness—it had slipped through his fingers and now was lost to him, and he to it, never to be himself again.

Or was it fate, or cruel chance, or simply the will of God? The loss of Ned's moment had happened somewhere between Deraa and Damascus, and Feisal grieved for his old friend and longed to be of comfort, but could do nothing to help. He didn't believe Ned's claims that all he ever wanted was a quiet life. Ned had exulted in the revolt too much for that, but he did believe that Ned's primary reason for it all was to live in the wilderness with his love.

The slightly crumpled Charlotte Shaw had reminded him sharply of this, and he knew why. He had been in the presence of love and he had misunderstood it, or belittled it, or thought of it too conventionally. He had thought she wanted to know about Lawrence the legend, when in fact she was only concerned with Ned the man.

He should have recognized it sooner. She was a wealthy woman of some position in society, and she was married to an undisputed genius. Great men were breakfast to her; she was not in awe of celebrity. She saw through cant and sought a truth. For all her occasional tetchiness, she was clearly a woman of massive heart, and he had no doubt that she loved Ned.

But it was naïve to dismiss her as a woman harboring romantic illusions about a wayward man some years her junior, or as a childless woman who had found, in Ned, a son. It was that, but it was very much more. The love that had radiated from Charlotte for Ned astonished him with its purity. He had no doubt that it had moments of failure—complaints of fickleness and faithlessness, of jealousy and possessiveness—but what had burst upon him was that the paramount need felt by the lover was that the loved one be happy.

Had Ned ever been happy? Oh, yes, there was no doubt of it, but poor Charlotte, who needed to know that for a fact, could only guess at it.

Feisal knew the truth. When Ned first came to them, in the desert, Feisal had accepted him for what he appeared to be, an adviser or liaison officer assigned by Britain, or even perhaps a spy sent to discover Feisal's merit or intentions—it amounted to the same thing. It was enough that Ned hated the Turks.

Later, when Ned became so much more, when he became one of them yet not one of them, when his relentless insistence on Damascus became the metronome of the revolt, Feisal had needed to know more about him. He made subtle inquiries and sent out spies, and he arrived at a conclusion that was so ridiculous, so romantic, that he would not have believed it had it not been the only explanation that made sense of everything Ned was and did. The man himself had said it, and Feisal had not understood. But slowly the pieces came together and made an extraordinary whole.

It was a quest, an epic, chivalrous quest, Arthurian in its majesty. Ned didn't want Damascus in itself, he wanted much, much more. He wanted freedom. Just as Saint Joan had led the French to rid themselves of the ruling English, Ned had taken it upon himself to rid Arabia of the occupying Turks, to secure the freedom of Damascus and of Syria to give as a gift unto his beloved, to prove himself worthy of the adored one's love.

The scale of his quest beggared Feisal's imagination, and the glory was that he came so close to achieving it, and the tragedy was that at the very moment of triumph the beloved had died, and the extravagant purpose was lost.

Somewhere between Deraa and Damascus, Dahoum had died, not gloriously in battle, which might have been something, but prosaically, of typhus, and all of Ned's noble ambitions, all of his valiant sacrifices of bodily need and personal comfort, all of his abject privations, all his hopes and desires and dreams became meaningless, a waste of time.

Somewhere between Deraa and Damascus.

Of course it was unrealistic to imagine that the death of a Syrian peasant had blighted Ned's life to such a remarkable degree, but Dahoum's death was the last in a series of calamities that had turned Ned's world upside down—the straw, as it were, that broke the camel's back.

After Allenby's capture of Jerusalem, Ned, who should have been jubilant, became moody and downcast. Feisal now believed that Ned had learned the truth, from Allenby in Jerusalem, as to the division of the spoils after the war. Palestine and Mesopotamia were to be British. Syria would go to France, no matter who conquered Damascus.

Perhaps Ned had known about it all along—it was an old agreement—or perhaps he believed he could change it, but now, scarcely a hundred miles from the prize, Ned was forced to accept that he could change nothing. That all his dreams of Arabian freedom, and his promises to the Arabs, were meaningless. That the Desert Campaign had been a charade.

"I have been very bad," he said to Feisal one day, moodily. "I must be punished." But he would not elaborate, and Feisal had no desire to pursue.

Feisal knew what had happened at Deraa, however disguised or embroidered by Ned. There was no reason for Ned to go to Deraa; spies could as easily learn what Ned might discover. He went there deliberately, as a test of himself, perhaps even hopeful that some awfulness might happen to him for his false promises.

The punishment was worse than he could imagine, and it found him wanting.

At Deraa, Ned, who had been keeping himself pure for his beloved that he might come to him with the priceless gift of his virtue, had allowed himself to be raped. He thought he could withstand any pain, but he had failed to find the strength to stop the violent invasion of his integrity. So he became unworthy of his beloved.

It was a romantic notion, and a foolish one perhaps, but almost from the beginning Feisal had known that Ned was not a man who lived in the modern world. He dwelt in ancient kingdoms, he was governed by Homeric laws, by archaic codes of chivalry. He was Galahad in search of the Holy Grail—that was both sweetly charming and frightening in its innocence and intensity. Noble beyond reason, brave, gallant and, at times, slightly ridiculous.

Feisal was sure that Ned's illegitimacy had something to do with it. He constantly paraded his bastardy as if it were irrelevant to him, a thing to be joked about, but it was obvious it rankled him beyond all proportion, had stripped him of a sense of his own worth, and his only path to his redemption was in Olympian labors.

In the end, he proved to be everything Feisal had thought him to be from the beginning. He fit the legends. He was, after all, one of those insane Englishmen who cannot live in England and will suffer any privation in desperate efforts to prove their own value. And he was a man who, out of sorts with his own class and overwhelmed by his own intellect, draws comfort from the brute simplicity of donkey boys. One of those strange and lonely men who thinks the world well lost for love.

It wasn't as if the beloved was anything special. Dahoum was not a prince or the son of a mighty sheik, not remotely well born, not wealthy or educated, not even all that handsome. Feisal had been shown a photograph of Dahoum once and couldn't believe that this was the object of such breathtaking adoration. A donkey boy, a peasant boy, a rough and uncouth lad with dirty feet and broken fingernails. There was something about him, though, that even Feisal found appealing. It was his smile that was so engaging, even in the faded photograph, a smile that might break a heart.

And somewhere between Deraa and Damascus, the quest, already failed, proved worthless because the beloved died. Ned's fury had been monumental then, the anger of Achilles mourning Patroclus, the death-defying grief of Troy. A Turkish troop had raided a small village and massacred the inhabitants. Ned, mourning Dahoum, his Patroclus, went in vengeance. It was butchery, the Turks were mercilessly cut down, and Ned the avenger waded through rivers of blood, careless of pity or remorse, as if seeking his own annihilation or challenging the gods to destroy him. He should have died then—it would have been a mercy—but the cruelty was that he survived, and his punishment was that he was condemned to live.

It wasn't only Dahoum who died somewhere between Deraa and Damascus, it was Ned's soul. But the living shell of the man survived.

His Majesty King Feisal of Iraq was tired, the cognac had done the trick. He climbed back into bed and composed himself for sleep. That was all the past, tomorrow was the future. Besides, there was his son: he was everything to Feisal, the sun and moon, the planets and the stars. He would inherit the kingdom, and Feisal was determined it would be a fabulous patrimony. He prayed for strength and wisdom, and worried that he lacked the stamina to see it through. He was thankful that he, unlike Ned, had something to look forward to, and he was grateful that Ned, or Lawrence of Arabia, had helped to shape that future. He was sorry for his old friend's unquiet mind, but there was nothing he could do about it. Each man was responsible for his own fortune, his own future, his own destiny, based on his own strengths and weaknesses and all the forces that had shaped him. Paths might cross, others might help or hinder, or fate, or the gods, or chance might be capricious or favorable, but in the end what each man made of his life was his own doing.

Or was it all the will of God?

37

"POPPYCOCK," CHARLOTTE SAID angrily to the saucepan of milk.

"Twaddle," she said, turning away so that the pot would be unwatched and boil.

"Damn!" she cried as she turned back. The foaming milk had bubbled all over the stove. She grabbed the pan, burnt her fingers, put the milk on the table and used a wet cloth to wipe up the mess.

Not far away from the Savoy Hotel, Charlotte was passing a restless night. Unable to sleep, she got up to make a cup of hot chocolate, thinking the milk might help her sleep, but her mind was racing. The tiny kitchen was dark and quiet, the rest of London was safe in slumber, why not she? GBS was fast asleep—she knew because she had looked in on him before she went to bed.

Wretched man! How could he just nod off like that? His antic mind must surely be whirling, even in dreamland, cavorting with Methuselah, or more likely Mephistopheles, and there he lay, smiling, gently snoring. She turned off his bedside light, adjusted his covers and, satisfied that her boy was safe, she retired herself.

But she could not sleep.

His Majesty King Feisal of Iraq was the focus of her wrath. What poppycock, she told herself for the hundredth time since leaving the Savoy. How dare he try to fob her off with such arrant nonsense, such platitudes, such evasions of the truth. She had not been seeking state secrets of Iraq, merely reassurance about a mutual friend!

Still, he was a king, and kings had to be careful; and she was a woman, and the things she wanted to know were not usual for women to ask, and he had, toward the end at least, been more honest.

He knew more than he had told her, Charlotte was sure. But what rankled her most was that clearly he had jumped to those tedious conclusions about her that were common, if whispered, currency. She found them insulting to her.

She didn't "love" Ned! She didn't harbor silly, illusory, amatory desires for a man many years her junior who wasn't all that fond of women, had sworn himself to celibacy and didn't intend to get married. Charlotte had found her love in GBS. She was married and happily so, to a great man, and if that love was complex, if it didn't conform to conventional concepts, it didn't matter, it was still love.

Nor did she want to "mother" Ned. She cared about Ned deeply and wanted to look after him, just as she looked after GBS. Or any of her young male friends. That bitter pain Ned carried with him like a constant cross wounded her. She wished with all her heart that she could take that pain away, but she didn't want to be his mother.

Childless by choice, Charlotte had gathered to her a number of young men whom some called her surrogate sons but who were, to her, simply her darling boys. Most were not at case with their own families, and many of them were attracted to their own sex and sang the love songs of lonely men. They flowered in Charlotte's company as even the most wayward vine is nourished by the kindness of the sun.

She fretted about them, lectured them sometimes, went out with them, when GBS was busy or when they needed a woman on their arms. She looked after them, sent them presents and was attentive to their emotional well-being. They, in turn, were kind to her. They kept her company when GBS was away. They took her out, made her laugh, shared naughty secrets with her and made her feel like a person in her own right, not just an illustrious man's dreary wife.

It could be argued that GBS was one of her boys. Surely GBS was an odd one, though just as surely he was very far from "queer." Quite the reverse, if anything. His relationship with Charlotte might be nearly virgin pure, but with a few other women GBS had a schoolboy's fervid, fetid interest in sexual matters, and, Charlotte was sure, had gratified at least some of them.

Yes, it was true, she "mothered" GBS—that was part of the bond between them. She kept his home running, and his life, she fussed and fretted and made sure he changed his socks and underwear, because if she didn't, he wouldn't, he was so careless of his person. He, like a wayward, naughty boy, allowed her this and encouraged her protection of him that he might be his complete self, unfettered by domestic trivia. She mothered him, but she didn't want to *be* his mother.

So it was ridiculous of people to think that she wanted to mother Ned, but she knew that Feisal had thought it, because if she was going to be honest she had encouraged him to believe it, just as, to be even more honest, she had allowed him to speculate that she was in love with Ned.

It wasn't easy being married to a genius, a dazzling firework of a man who exploded into a room rather than entered it and kept people agog with his gunpowder intellect and wit. From the beginning, Charlotte had known that she couldn't compete with him, and so she had not tried. She accepted her role as his protective, organizing guardian, knowing that she was regarded as the fussy housekeeper who had to be tolerated because the pyrotechnic GBS had found in her some value that most could not imagine.

She encouraged this assessment of her and used it to her advantage. She could afford to dress well, but she thought it wicked to pay a king's ransom for a gown by Worth, so she bought all her clothes ready made, off the rack.

"Charlotte, dear, you're such a frump," Noël Coward had said to her once. She didn't like Noël; he wasn't one of her boys. He was too catty, his humor too cruel and his interest in his young male conquests much too predatory, but his assessment of her appearance was true. Charlotte had found that looking like a frump disarmed people ("What on earth does GBS see in her?") and gave them a false sense of security about her so that they gave away secrets they might otherwise have concealed.

As had Feisal. She felt a tiny surge of remembered triumph. She'd bested him! She had gone to battle against a king and she had won! Her carefully constructed dowdiness, her wayward bobby pins and her second-best suit, her tetchiness and her artful honesty had persuaded the wary, careful Feisal to reveal more than he intended. She knew S. A.'s real name at last, knew that all her guesses had been correct and that with Dahoum, Ned had been happy. What else was there to know?

Just this: if he had been so happy then, why could he not be now? It was one thing to remember a first love as a golden glory, but perverse to let that memory blight a life. Charlotte's youthful adoration of the doctor Axel Munthe was the peak of passion in her life, however cruelly unrequited, but she had kept her heart open afterwards and had found GBS. If what she had with him was not passion, it was, perhaps, something more, something greater, grander, more fulfilling.

There were young men in Ned's life, she knew, but she was fairly sure that those friendships were platonic. About his friendship with John Bruce she was not so sure; it had an essential, underlying darkness that frightened her. She couldn't imagine anyone having fun with John Bruce, and whatever comfort both men found in each other, it didn't seem like a fulfilling relationship. Was that because Ned believed he could never again find what he had lost?

Dahoum had died between Deraa and Damascus. Was Dahoum's death part of the reason for Ned's abject sense of failure, of lack of worth? Was it all tied up with the flogging and rape at Deraa and the realization that Anglo-French political chicanery would never allow Damascus to be a triumph for the Arab cause, no matter how great the victory?

What did a man do if he spent his life planning the conquest of unclimbable Everest only to find when he got to the summit that the mountain was just a mirage, that all his hopes and aspirations had been a waste of time? What did he do then? Much as Ned had done, perhaps.

Ned had said it once in a letter, that his life was "all a ruin," and that was written when he was back in the RAF, the bleak days of the army behind him, and when he should have been happy. But no, his life was "all a ruin"; the words still stung in Charlotte's mind.

In the distance, Big Ben chimed four. Was it so late already? Really, she must go to bed. But would she sleep?

She went up the stairs to her bedroom, took off her dressing gown and climbed into bed. The springs under the old mattress sighed, and the feather counterpane settled around her. She wasn't angry anymore, only tired. She turned off the light and settled to sleep.

Somewhere between Deraa and Damascus Dahoum had died, and Lawrence of Arabia with him. And Ned? Everything Ned did, from seeking obscurity in the ranks to hiding in a forgotten fortress in a distant land, only served to keep the legend of Lawrence alive. Was the need of him so great?

Was Lawrence all things to all men, everything anyone wanted him to be? A crusading angel to the Arab cause, a demon to the Turks? The keeper of the flame of Imperial glory to those who believed that Britannia should rule the waves, the epitome of colonial aggression to the yearning nationalists in India? The one unsullied hero of the Great War to the war-weary, disillusioned masses, an archaic hegemonist to the burgeoning socialist cause?

Some said Ned could have almost any job he wanted, from running the country's defenses to governing the Bank of England. Others would not even allow him to be forgotten in the ranks.

She was drifting to sleep, and although she would be tetchy in the morning at being woken early, her anger had dissipated and she was filled with a thrilling sense of what once had been.

And Nancy Astor? Well, well. It was wrong of her to be jealous. If Ned heard some quieting or provocative music in Nancy's strident drum banging, so be it. Let him find what he can and let him be happy.

Nancy picked people up for a while and then moved on to others, and Ned would come back to Charlotte. Nancy knew how to alleviate boredom but didn't know how to comfort pain. Charlotte did. The true test of friendship was constancy, and that Charlotte had in abundance.

And if he didn't come back to her, it wouldn't matter. She would miss him and be there if ever he needed her, but if he didn't come back to her, it would be because he had found someone he needed more, someone who made him happy; and if that was the case, her heart would sing.

She had learned from Feisal what she needed to know: that once, Ned had been happy. It wasn't in the war, as everyone supposed, it wasn't as the legendary leader of the Arab Revolt. Happiness was some other place and time. Happiness was before the war. Happiness was in Arabia, but one man's life away from Aqaba.

At Carchemish.

She fell asleep at last and dreamed sweet dreams of an ancient, forgotten kingdom, half buried in the sand, surrounded by a thousand miles of nowhere, where her darling, crippled Ned had once been a gilded king. And at his side stood a simple donkey boy, with dirty feet and broken fingernails and a smile like an angel, a smile that had filled Ned's heart.

Dahoum. She knew his name at last and although she would never meet him—could not meet him, for he was gone—she blessed his soul for what he had been and what he had given to Ned and done for Ned, and knew that to him she would always be profoundly grateful.

Clouds Hill

---ᗡᗡᗡ---

1924–1935

38

I survive. I always survive. Worse luck.

I am not dismissed the service when I come back from India. My contract is renewed for five more years, and I am sent to a tiny English backwater, Cattewater, to serve out my time.

This is solid, peaceful England; there is no revolution here. The battles for this rustic tranquility were won and lost at the dawn of English history, for I can throw a stone to Tintagel, or Glastonbury, or Camelot. And even though, on pretty summer days, my faithful steed Boanerges, my motorbike, takes me to Saint Michael's Mount, no questing knights challenge me to battle, no damsels need me to save them from distress. There are no dragons here, only my own, echoing footsteps, and views like paradise. No danger, no temptation, no Umar, no Slaney. (Although there is sometimes John Bruce.) So I, freed from provocation, serve out my last five years, peacefully, if not at peace.

I lose myself in the technical world, in engines and fast boats, and avoid many of my old friends, who remind me too much of myself (I know Charlotte is hurt. I also know that Charlotte has found out—or guessed—the truth, or close to it). Nancy Astor takes me under her wing for a while, and it's impossible to think about yourself when Nancy is around, the conversation is limited entirely to her. Of her. About her. By her.

She dabbles with a forceful, authoritarian crowd at Cliveden, that gracious mansion. I spend occasional luxurious weekends with her and her modern friends. They have little interest in who I was, they are too beguiled by the new men, the modern men: Mosley, Hitler and Mussolini. (The latter made the trains in Italy run on time they say, in praise of him. But who wants Italian trains to run on time? Punctuality is Switzerland and Germany. Italy is all beguiling, gaudy tardiness.)

I have no interest in that future. I have no future.

Mostly on weekends I go to Clouds Hill, my surrogate kingdom, and there I am alone, accompanied only by music and words.

And sometimes, John Bruce.

Sometimes, when I can't block out the memories, when I can't forget Dahoum and what I set out to do and how very miserably I failed, John Bruce comes to me and bandages my broken heart with pain.

Sometimes, when I remember that I was not the victor but the vanquished, that I was a worthless liar who betrayed all of my promises, to myself and my beloved, when that anguish becomes too great, John Bruce comes to me and beats the pain away, just as the truth of my weakness was flogged into me at Deraa, and the sole purpose of my being was taken from me before Damascus.

It is because of John that I have survived, since I was Ross, and since the Tank Corps, and since India. He stopped me once from killing myself and wondered why I was not grateful. Was once enough?

So I survive, protected by John Bruce's punishing arm, in the sheltering shade of a backwater barracks and in a Dorset cottage called Clouds Hill that I pretend is a Hittite house at Carchemish.

But all things end, even survival. Within a year, my service contract will be up and cannot be renewed. I am too old.

My days are numbered.

39

NED HAD FOUND CLOUDS HILL in the autumn of 1923, when he was in the Tank Corps. The worst of it, basic training, was over, but still he was miserable, pining for the RAF. His only friend in the army was John Bruce, and his only happiness was his motorbike, Boanerges, which he drove at alarming speed.

"'E'll bleedin' kill 'imself one day," Poppy opined to a corporal nearby. The subject of his prophesy was Ned, who was careening around the camp on a brand-new motorbike.

Poppy, Sergeant-Major Peter Popplethwaite, said to have the loudest voice on any parade ground in the British Empire, knew who Ned had been, but he didn't care. Ned was a recruit, even if he was the oddest recruit who had ever come Poppy's way. A legendary colonel who had chucked it all, then joined the RAF as an erk, got chucked out of that and turned up here, at Bovington, in the Tank Corps.

All that meant nothing to Poppy. Ned was a number, a woeful piece of dog shit like all the rest, if a little older and frayed around the edges. He was good at drill, kept his nose clean and jumped when Poppy barked. He had also been wretchedly miserable, hating the army and everyone in it, desperate to join the RAF again.

"Look at 'im now," Poppy said to his mates. "'E's got a cushy job in the QM's stores, 'e's found out that life isn't all a bowl of three-day-old spew and 'e's even starting to make a few friends."

John Bruce and some other soldiers came out of a hut to watch. Ned waved at them, swerved as he almost lost control of the bike, grabbed the handlebars again and zoomed toward them.

"Learn to ride the fucken thing, why don't yer?" Poppy bawled in a voice that could be heard in Bournemouth.

Ned brought the motorbike to a skidding halt outside the hut. "What do you think?" he asked proudly.

John whistled in admiration and came over to inspect the gleaming motorbike. It was the latest model by Brough and was the snazziest speed machine any of them could imagine.

"What's it called?" John asked, longing to be invited to drive it, or be taken for a ride.

"Boanerges," Ned said, proudly. John, who seldom smiled, simply nodded. Ned's previous bike had been christened Boanerges as well. He wondered where Ned got the money.

"Want to go for a spin?" Ned asked him. Now John smiled, and jumped on the pillion behind Ned.

They left the camp and drove through the country lanes, reveling in the speed and the sunny day. Ned, wearing goggles, was leaning over the handlebars, and John was hugging close to him, his strong arms around Ned's waist, clutching him, holding tight to him. Ned hated to be touched, except in special circumstances, and John, who also held himself aloof from physical contact most of the time, often yearned to take Ned in his arms and hold him close, as he did now, and keep him safe from those private storms that surged within his friend.

Today there were no tempests; they were spent. Today there was only the chill of winter and the warmth of comradeship.

They rode for about five miles and then turned back toward Bovington. Near the camp, Ned made a detour off the road and came to a halt outside a tiny, run-down cottage. It hadn't been tended for years and was in need of serious repair. The door was off its hinges, and John guessed that the roof leaked. It was surrounded by bushes and sheltered by majestic trees.

"Home," Ned said quietly.

There was no point in being surprised or puzzled by anything Ned said or did. He had found this cottage, rented it and intended to renovate it, as his private retreat. Downstairs was a mess, almost uninhabitable, but upstairs, once the rickety boards were nailed down safe, had possibilities.

From the upstairs windows there was a peaceful view of English woods. "Clouds Hill" Ned called the place, and John understood the poetry of it.

"Where's the bog?" he asked at the end of the tour.

"The bushes," Ned told him cheerily. "We didn't have bogs in Carchemish, not the English sort, anyway."

They went to a bush and relieved themselves. Surprisingly, Ned, who could be very coy about nudity, didn't try to hide himself and even started a competition to see who could piss the farthest.

Well, he is happy, John thought. And so am I.

When he was old and looking back on it all, John Bruce would remember the times he spent with Ned as the happiest of his life, and that Clouds Hill was the best Christmas present he had ever been given—although it was not his.

A few of the fellows from the hut pitched in to help them, and within weeks they had the cottage in order. They had a party then, with cider and a jar of stuffed olives, some cans of baked beans and a lot of bread and butter and jam. The cottage was still fairly primitive—no bathroom nor much furniture, not even beds—but it had a very special atmosphere, thrilling to John, who had never known much domestic happiness.

Ned had a gramophone and would play music that most of them had seldom heard: Bach, or Beethoven, or his favorite, Elgar. Ned didn't sleep at the cottage very often, but he would go there in his spare time to work on his book, and sometimes John would walk the mile or two from camp and sit in the untended garden in the sun, or inside in one of the rickety chairs, and listen to the enthralling music.

Perverse as always, Ned had made the upstairs the living room and would work there. They seldom spoke—there was no need to speak here—but John thought Ned was as content as he had ever seen him. He knew that Ned still wanted to get back into the RAF, and that he still wrote letters to his bigwig friends beseeching them to get the RAF to take him back, but he had accepted that it wasn't likely to happen for some time, if ever, and his fever for it seemed to abate.

"What's so special about the RAF?" John asked once, because, to his surprise, he was happy in the army and here at Clouds Hill.

"I want to fly," Ned shrugged.

Visitors came from time to time—Mrs. Shaw, or that writer, Teddy Forster, from Oxford. John thought he was a right little pansy pretending he wasn't, but he was nice to John, and he and Ned talked for hours about things that John didn't understand, and it was enough that Ned was pleased.

Ned's mother and older brother came one weekend, and the open pages of Ned at Clouds Hill fluttered closed. John never understood why. Mrs.

Lawrence was starched and unyielding, and very religious, but John could see that she loved Ned and was worried about him. The brother, Bob, was a pill; he kept asking John questions about his faith in God, which John met with silence. There weren't many laughs while they were there, but then they went away, and the book of Ned opened up to him again. It was after their visit that Ned carved something John didn't understand above the front door.

"It's Greek," Ned explained. "It means 'no cares,' but I think it translates better as 'who cares?'"

To a lonely young man raised in wintry Aberdeen, being at Clouds Hill and in Ned's company was something close to paradise. Sometimes, sitting in the sun, or on winter evenings listening to the rain beat a march on the roof, John thought Clouds Hill had always been there, from the beginning of time, a placid witness to the turbulent history of England, touched by that history but removed from it.

There were times when the old blackness came over Ned. Usually it was after yet another request to rejoin the RAF had been turned down, or it had something to do with his book. It always seemed to coincide with something that Ned had done to offend his uncle, the Old Man, and when it happened, John would do what the Old Man required, then write a report of the beating he had given Ned, and soon his friend would be himself again.

John had long since ceased to believe in the existence of the Old Man, but he understood it was a fiction that Ned needed. It was because of the Old Man's supposed demands that John's unlikely friendship with Ned had become something more intimate.

They had met in 1922. Work was scarce in Aberdeen, so John had moved to London and drifted to the city's netherworld, among the dark hungers of the night. He made friends with whores and pimps and petty criminals and got a badly paid job as a bouncer at a small, dingy club in Soho. Often broke, John frequented a pub near Piccadilly, where a young man like himself could sometimes earn a few bob doing things to the bodies of richer men.

John was not brutal by nature, but inured to brutality. More than once, as a boy, he'd had to drown a sack of kittens, and he could snap a rabbit's neck with one hand. An only child, raised in the slums of Aberdeen by an unkind but not unloving family, he had a granite dourness that made it difficult for him to find friends, but he had a fathomless need for a mate, a mucker.

As a teenager he'd been sent to an institution for a month, and as a young man he'd been in prison twice—never for any actual criminal intent, but because he was young and surly and resentful of intrusive regulations, and the coppers regarded him as fair game.

In the institution, his already strong sense of survival was forged to impregnable armor. His dourness filled a room, and after he had proved his fighting skills, others avoided him. John didn't mind being left alone or merely tolerated at the fringe of a crowd. He didn't want to be lonely, but he didn't know how to make friends. What he really wanted was someone to look after, to protect and comfort and hold in his arms and love.

In the institution there were substitutes, boys who sought protection from bullying in the arms of a strong mate. It was the concept of being their protector, of looking after them, that appealed to John, and if they wanted to show their gratitude with their bodies, it was the closest he had ever come to human comfort. He never regarded sex as a casual thing, but the choice of a sex partner ceased to matter, and John became convinced that sex was not a path to love. Later, he discovered that there were older men who were prepared to give him small presents, cigarettes or even money, in return for his body. They were kind to him, and he enjoyed their kindness. A few other men, not many but some, paid better for something less, men who wanted to be beaten.

Such as Ned.

They met at the pub. Ned was different from the regulars; he didn't seem to be looking for urgent gratification. He never left with any of the young men, although sometimes, shyly, he bought them drinks and chatted for a while. John could not remember their first conversation, but after a few visits, Ned would always say something kind to John and buy him a drink. At some point, John had made his availability obvious, but Ned had not taken up the offer. Instead, when he left, John found a pound note in his pocket that had not been there before.

They drifted into a cautious friendship. Ned would stop by the pub in the early hours and chat. When John finished work they would go for a walk, to Trafalgar Square and on to the Embankment. Ned would prattle on about a million things, most of them unknown to John. He talked about great writers and of his ambition to be one himself. He talked of distant countries where he had lived, fabulous places to a lonely lad from Aberdeen, and important people he had met. He talked of the distant past as if it were the living now, and if sometimes John didn't always understand what Ned was telling him, he never felt that Ned was talking down to him, or trying to impress him with knowledge or his own cleverness.

He was writing a book, Ned told John, a difficult and demanding book about his life during the war, in Arabia, and sometimes he was happy with its progress and sometimes in such a state of despair that John worried for him. He was out of work, living from hand to mouth, but hoping to get into the Royal Air Force. John assumed he would be an officer, and it was a shock when Ned said, no, his only ambition was to serve in the ranks.

John was never sure when he became aware that Ned was someone remarkable, that he had been a legend, but it was no enormous surprise when he did realize it. Only the magnitude of Ned's past awed him, and he was filled with gratitude. For the first time in his life John felt that his existence was of moment to another human being, and the fact that Lawrence of Arabia could be bothered with someone as inconsequential as himself filled him with a sense of worth.

Ned took him to lunch one day, to a smart restaurant. John was overawed by his surroundings but, as always, relaxed in Ned's company, because Ned ignored all the pretensions and made John feel secure. Ned offered him a job, a couple of pounds a week to run errands for him, or post letters. It didn't make sense to John; he couldn't imagine how someone as broke as Ned claimed to be could afford that money, or even to bring him to lunch here, or why Ned needed to hire him, the tasks were so simple. Still, two quid was two quid, and Ned was Ned, odd and unpredictable.

Once or twice Ned talked about commissioning artists to paint pictures for his book, and the cost of it, and John was confused again. How could Ned, broke, pay for paintings?

"I've been a fool about money," Ned said one day. "I'm in a lot of trouble. I need your help."

They were in Ned's small room in Westminster, an attic in a house owned by a friend. It was early September, unusually hot and sultry for London, and Ned was sweating slightly. John thought he was nervous and excited and fearful all at once. He told a sorry tale.

After leaving the Colonial Service where he had worked for Winston Churchill after the war (it tickled John to hear Ned call him "Winnie"), Ned was broke and couldn't find a job. He wanted to write his book and, in order to support himself, he borrowed money. Now, two years later, the book was not finished and the moneylenders were at his heels. A wealthy uncle, the Old Man, had assumed the debt on certain conditions. Ned was to find steady employment in the army. Half his pay was to go toward repaying the loan. He was to behave himself properly and never give the Old Man reason to be sorry for his generosity.

"I've let him down already," Ned said. "I didn't join the army. I'm joining the RAF."

John wasn't sure why that should make a difference, but Ned insisted that the Old Man was furious.

"There's nothing he can do about it, I've signed the papers," Ned said. "But he wants his pound of flesh for my disobedience."

He glanced at a birch rod on the bed, a cane. John understood its meaning. It was a situation he was familiar with, as was an edgy, neurotic sense of sexual anticipation. He knew what was expected of him. He opened his legs a little and let his hand fall to his crotch.

"I have his instructions," Ned said, offering a letter to John.

John didn't take the letter. He caressed his rising erection. "Just tell me what he wants," he whispered. He made his voice husky because he knew that was what Ned wanted.

Ned picked up the birch. "Twelve strokes at least," he said, and John thought he was genuinely scared of the pain that he so desperately needed. John didn't know how much of the story about the Old Man to believe, but it explained a lot of things about Ned's financial situation. What did it matter? He knew what was coming next.

"There's money in it," Ned whispered again. "Three pounds."

"Better get ready," John said.

Ned giggled shyly and cast aside his clothes, almost unwillingly—like a modest bride on her wedding night—and lay facedown on the bed. John had to subdue the sudden gentleness he felt, because the sight of Ned's body shocked him. He was wiry and hard, but his back was a mass of ugly scars, and he was piteously thin. John could not imagine how he had passed his RAF physical.

"Do it," Ned whispered, and John began the punishment. At the twelfth stroke, he stopped.

"One more for luck," Ned said thickly.

John hit him again, and almost with relief he saw Ned's body shudder in something other than pain. When he turned to look at John, his eyes were bright, though stained with tears.

"Well," he said, "that should keep the Old Man happy. For a while."

He joined the RAF, and John didn't see him again for a few months. They wrote to each other, and Ned, who was calling himself Ross, said he was happy. He made occasional references to the Old Man, but mostly the letters were full of the RAF and how he had found his place in life at last, and of how well his book was going.

Queer bastard, John thought to himself. But he loved him. It was not love in any usual sense, no lusting in a carnal way for Ned's body, no expectations of romance, nor even a need for sexual release. It was simply love, affection, admiration and protectiveness, gratitude for kindness, for friendship. It was undemanding on John's part, and it encompassed all the quirks of Ned's curious self. It was love without desire, except for a companion.

He would have done almost anything that Ned wanted to prove his loyalty, and would remain a friend to Ned throughout his life. He would worry about him, guard him, join the army because of him, give him the only sexual release he ever seemed to need or want and, once, he would stop Ned from killing himself. But once was not enough.

Then one day, John got a letter filled with remorse and self-denigration. He'd done something wrong, Ned wrote, and the Old Man was furious with him. The rest of it was a babble, about how he'd been discovered in the RAF and might be chucked out, and how he would never find rest or peace anywhere, how they would not let him be happy.

John wasn't surprised to see the headlines in the papers a few days after that, screaming that Lawrence of Arabia was hiding in the ranks of the RAF, and suggesting various suspect motives. He wasn't surprised when he read that Ned was to be thrown out of the service. He wasn't surprised when Ned turned up at the pub one night a few weeks later.

He was, however, shocked by Ned's appearance. Usually, Ned was fastidiously clean and particular about himself, but this night he was scrungy and unkempt, he hadn't shaved for a few days and his clothes were rumpled. He'd been sleeping rough since his expulsion from the RAF, sometimes in the sidecar of his motorbike, sometimes at Salvation Army hostels, once or twice in the park, although it was winter.

He was in a wild state of nerves, sometimes ranting about the injustice of his dismissal and how his cherished book was worthless, sometimes filled with a manic, undirected energy then lapsing into bouts of severe melancholy. He seemed relieved and pleased to see John, and anxious, like a man on the edge of a precipice. John had had experience of men who were cracking up, in prison; and not for the first time, he began to wonder if Ned was mentally unbalanced.

The Old Man was making his sadistic demands, Ned said, triumphant at Ned's dismissal but furious at the publicity he had unleashed. Ned had to be punished. Only after severe chastisement would the Old Man be moved to help. Ned was puzzled that John seemed reluctant, and John didn't know how to explain that he had hoped he meant more to Ned than as the instrument of his flagellation.

Ned booked a room at a cheap hotel in Surrey and drove John there on the motorbike. John loved speed, but Ned's recklessness with the bike alarmed him. A couple of times they skidded on a corner, and John was sure Ned had lost control. But each time Ned proved to be the master of the machine, laughing at his success.

In the hotel room, John did what Ned demanded, although this time it took eighteen strokes. When it was done he threw the birch away.

"I hope you're bloody satisfied," he said.

Ned looked at him in amazement and said nothing for a while, but let John sulk. Then he came to him, and it was a different Ned, or an old Ned reborn.

"I'm sorry that you had to do that," he said, softly, gently, kindly. "But it was necessary."

They had a meal in a pub, and Ned was in top form. He told John stories of the past, of his adventures in the desert, and the Scotsman was enthralled. He'd heard some good jokes in the RAF that were new to John and made him laugh. He filled him with tidbits of gossip about his famous friends and made John feel important. And he came to terms with his future.

"I suppose the Old Man's right," Ned said. "It has to be the army."

John chucked his job, and for a couple of weeks they lived from hand to mouth, the two of them, and shared all that came to them. They would go for rides on the motorbike and visit old churches, or stroll in rustic market towns. In London they would go to the pictures, or to warm museums where Ned would take John on fabulous journeys back in time.

One afternoon, Ned took him to tea at Fortnum & Mason, to meet Mrs.

George Bernard Shaw and to celebrate his acceptance into the army, the Tank Corps.

John was so nervous and so in awe of the remarkable woman that he hardly spoke but sat adoring her in silence. She was full of energy, brimming with ideas for Ned's future, pleased for his sake that the bigwigs were allowing him to join the army, the Tank Corps, but John thought that was a lie, that she didn't want him in the army at all. Then the subject changed, and she was full of praise for the book Ned was writing.

"Has she read it?" John asked Ned afterwards.

They'd walk along the Embankment, sharing a bag of roast chestnuts and, if the tide was low, throwing pennies to the mudlarks. In the evening they'd go to a music hall and then to a pub. Even though Ned didn't drink, John often thought he was tipsy, so febrile was his need to experience all the city had to offer. Ned had little interest in women, but he was always amused by their flirting with John.

"What's it like?" he asked one night. "To shag a woman."

As a young ram with a prison record, John had found girls who were fascinated by his granite surliness and were ready to let him explore them, up against a wall in a dark alley. He had fantasies of feather beds and blond women with big breasts, but he imagined the reality of his eventual wife, whoever she might be, was more mundane. In any case, a hole was a hole, or even a hand, and it didn't bother him to go for long periods of time without any release.

"Everyone makes such a song and dance about it," he replied, "but it's all over and done with in a couple of minutes."

He looked at Ned. "Haven't you ever done it?"

Ned shrugged and winked. "My balls have never dropped," he giggled.

After the pubs were shut, they haunted Piccadilly. Ned loved to chat with the homeless and the runaways and the boys who made their living on the streets or in some patron's bed. He thought it was funny when those boys called John a mystery. A mystery was someone of their own kind who had arrived among them but who would not reveal anything of himself or why he was there. John thought the boot was on the other foot; he wasn't the mystery, Ned was.

There were many things that John didn't understand. He didn't understand what pleasure a gentleman of learning and intelligence, one who had been a colonel, could get from working-class men like himself—other than the obvious. He guessed that he was not the only person who had ever beaten Ned, but he was equally sure that there were some specific reasons behind Ned's need for the floggings. It had something to do with a place called Deraa and someone who had died. Most of all, John didn't understand why the man who was Lawrence of Arabia could bear to be simple Ned.

"You're the one who's a mystery," John would say to Ned. "A bloody mystery to me."

But his eyes would be shining when he said it, because in Ned's company he never felt alone. Out of the blue, and because he didn't want to be lonely again, he offered to join the Tank Corps with Ned.

Ned was delighted. "Would you do that?"

John shrugged, not quite believing that he had made the offer. "It wouldn't help. We'd be in different units, different camps."

"I don't think that's a problem," Ned said, and grinned. "I still have friends in the right places; they could fix it in a trice."

Within weeks, John Bruce was in the army, in the same camp, the same unit and the same hut as his friend Ned, and sergeants were screaming abuse at them.

The army was no real surprise to John. He resented the bullshit, all the spit and polish, and the sergeants who roared like trumpeting elephants, but at least he didn't have to worry about his next meal. He got on all right with the other blokes after he'd established his physical ascendancy over a couple of them. They all came to recognize his guardianship of Ned, and for the most part they left Ned alone.

Ned hated the army. Almost from the beginning he wanted to get out and get back into the RAF. It wasn't the discipline or the drill—Ned was good at that—it was the other men. John knew their kind from prison and the slums of Aberdeen. They were mostly the dregs of Britain, rough, loutish, brutish men, who didn't know how to talk without constant aggression. They were there because it was steady employment and they couldn't get a job anywhere else. They were poor and disregarded, they were young and ill-educated, they were strong, working-class men chock full of furious energy, and they could be trained to absolute obedience of orders even if those orders were to kill or to march to a futile death. They were cannon fodder.

"What do you think of it?" Ned asked him one night. They were in the canteen. John had just finished a huge plate of bangers and mash, swimming in a lumpy gravy, with mushy peas.

"What the fuck are we doing here," John said. It wasn't a question.

Ned stared at him steadily, and then something of the old spark came back to him, for just a moment, and he made an odd little movement of his head, that was both entreating and very slightly feminine. "You're my bodyguard," Ned said.

Somewhat to John's surprise, Ned survived the basic training, and then he found Clouds Hill and the ramshackle cottage made the army bearable.

He bought a couple of sleeping bags, *Meum* and *Tuum* he called them, "mine" and "yours," and they slept at Clouds Hill, on the floor, two feet apart, and Ned would whisper stories of the desert, or that old city that he loved so much where he had lived before the war, and a few times he talked about a friend, an Arab lad called Dahoum. Talking about the boy always made him sad and silent, and then John would stretch out his hand, and Ned would take it gratefully, silently, and would drift to sleep, safe at last in the strong Scotsman's grasp.

Christmas was always a jolly celebration, just a few of them, men who didn't have leave or didn't have families to visit. Poppy came once, and Jock from the air force, and they were good company. But John began to hate Christmas because after December came January, and in January, the bleakest month, Ned would write letters begging to be reinstated in the air force and would be turned down, and then the Old Man would make his unwelcome presence felt.

"What's so special about the RAF?" John asked him again.

Ned was silent for a moment, and then more honest than before.

"I need to feel I have some value, that I'm earning my keep."

The third Christmas at Clouds Hill, in 1925, was the worst. Ned was depressed about his book, which was soon to be published.

"The book is a lie, a monumental dishonesty," Ned said, "and now the world will know."

They were just the two of them that Christmas. Ned wasn't in a mood to invite anyone else, and because of his shrouding bleakness, no one invited themselves. All of John's senses were alert.

Ned would sit staring at the wall for hours, oblivious of the finished gramophone record scratching away, or he would have fits of energy and write stacks of letters. John would sit, close but not too near, watching him.

"My life's a ruin," Ned said once. "I don't know what to do."

John began to worry that there was a gun at Clouds Hill, or some other weapon. One night when Ned was upstairs, John looked through the cupboards and found a loaded revolver. He took the bullets out and put them in his pocket.

Nothing happened until two nights later, after Ned had got the letter he had been expecting, denying him the RAF yet again.

It was late, John was curled up in his sleeping bag but wide awake. There was silence from upstairs, and then John heard movement. He closed his eyes and pretended to sleep. He heard Ned come downstairs, heard him go to the cupboard and open the door. He heard Ned go outside.

John got up and went to his jacket, hanging on the back of a chair. The bullets were still there. He took them out and went to the door, praying that Ned had not checked the gun.

Ned was standing in the overgrown garden, staring at the moon. He had the revolver in his hand.

He got down on his knees and put the gun to his head. After what seemed an eternity to John he heard a click as Ned pulled the trigger.

John experienced a number of conflicting emotions of which the greatest was relief and not the least a sudden desire to laugh at the look of astonishment on Ned's face. Ned pointed the gun away from him and pulled the trigger again. Another click, and Ned inspected the cylinder.

"Looking for these?" John asked him, holding out the bullets.

What happened next stunned him. John had seen tears in Ned's eyes, once or twice, in odd circumstances, but he had never seen him weep. Now the man let out an animal howl, and enormous, shuddering sobs wracked his body, as if his grief was being dragged from the very core of him.

John ran to him, put his arms around him and held him and whispered useless words of consolation. And Ned clung to him, as a drowning man clinging to a raft, and cried for love.

It got better after that. The next morning, Ned was calm and apologized for the previous night and said it wouldn't happen again, and while in the coming weeks he was still withdrawn, he was coping.

The spring of 1926 brought sunshine. One day, Ned came bursting in to find John and waved a letter at him. "I'm going back," he shouted. "They're taking me back!"

John knew exactly what he meant and couldn't help but be pleased, Ned's joy was so infectious. He let his friend have his head and listened to happy speeches of what his new life would be like. Later, when Ned had calmed down, he asked the question that nagged him, the question he had always known he would ask if this day came.

"What's going to happen to me?"

Ned turned to look at him, puzzled at first, and then his eyes filled with what might have been compassion.

"You'll be all right," he said.

John would always be all right. Employment was scarce in the outside world, but he was safe in the army. Even outside the army he wouldn't starve. A sturdy young man who would turn his hand to anything and was handy with his fists could always find a square meal, even if the supplying kitchen was one of His Majesty's prisons.

But now he would be lonely again.

Ned went off to the RAF again, and then Ned's book was published. John couldn't afford to buy a copy, but he read the praise of it in the newspapers with beaming pride. Soon afterwards, he was surprised to get a letter from Ned, saying that the Old Man was furious about the book and some of the revelations in it. Ned was being posted to India but had to have a "treatment" before he went.

John went to London, and in the attic room in Westminster where Ned was staying and where they had first obeyed the Old Man's wishes, he con-summated their love again in the only way the other would allow.

Ned went to India, and John was discharged from the army.

"Why?" he asked Poppy.

Poppy looked uncomfortable. "I dunno," he said. "Doesn't make sense to me. You're a good soldier." He tapped a paper on the desk for John to sign. "It's honorable," he said.

John went back to Aberdeen, found a job and a young woman who didn't mind his silence. On winter nights he thrilled to read Ned's letters, which were filled with the exotic sun of India. Then, in 1929, there was another almighty row in the papers and Ned came home, in disgrace with the Old Man again. John went down to London to do what the Old Man demanded, and afterwards they spent a few days together, and John wasn't lonely any-more.

They stayed faithful to each other through letters, and occasionally John would be summoned to London to do the Old Man's bidding, or he would go to Clouds Hill for a few days, or they would holiday together in the Lake District. By then John had married and had a bonny daughter. Ned was thrilled by the child and made a small settlement of money on her. Always, these days, he was surprisingly calm, as if the India business had lanced a raging boil, and the relief after the dispelling of the poison could be mistaken for contentment.

Occasionally John read small items in the paper about his old friend. Ned was said to be working on fast boats at Cattewater and involved in some speed trials. It was all secret work, important for the country's defense, but mostly the press had lost interest in him. Then in early 1935 a letter came saying that Ned was leaving the RAF and didn't know what would become of him. It was a familiar bleakness, and even though Ned didn't mention the Old Man, John packed his bag and took the train south and went to Clouds Hill, and there, for a few days of a mild winter, they relived old times.

They went for walks in the soft rain or rode on another, newer Boanerges, Ned driving, wrapped in John's embrace. They shopped in minster markets, and at night they ate baked beans and bread and jam and listened to lovely music.

John didn't speak much because he never spoke much, and there was no need to speak with Ned, who thought that silence was a precious gift. Ned talked a little about leaving the RAF, obviously rattled about it, but he seemed to accept it as the unalterable fact it was.

On John's last night, a Sunday evening, Ned took him to a little church in a village not far from Clouds Hill. John was surprised. Ned claimed he didn't believe in God, and although they often went to look at churches, they had never been to a service.

"Evensong," Ned said. "The priceless gift of Thomas Cranmer to the English people."

John didn't understand—one service was much the same as any other to him—but it was beautiful and simple, and Ned seemed happy.

Afterwards, they stood outside enjoying the evening, breaths frosty in the chilly air. The choirboys clattered home, half a dozen half-formed youths, who, minutes before, had seemed angelic and now were only noisy boys, exuberant with youth and the burgeoning discovery of life.

The lamplighter rode along the street, stopping his bike by each street lamp and turning up the gas to light the coming night. In a large house near the common, the doctor's wife was playing Mozart on a piano that needed to be tuned. Across the green, coming from an open upstairs window of a small, thatched cottage, a scratchy gramophone recording of a popular song drifted out to meet the Mozart, but the sounds ebbed and faded before collision, as if declining battle on such a peaceful evening.

They could hear laughter from inside the pub, and in the doctor's house a telephone rang. The pianist stopped, and a few minutes later the doctor came out of the house carrying his black bag, got into his car and drove away.

"Someone is dying," Ned said. "Or a child is being born." He giggled. "Or perhaps it is only appendicitis."

John smiled. Ned always had a way with words.

"The world is turning as it should," Ned said. "It doesn't need us."

Suddenly, Ned wanted to be away. He walked quickly to the bike, climbed on and started it. John got on the pillion, put his arms around his friend and they drove away from the peaceful village.

The roar of the bike sang in John's ears, engulfing him, cocooning him, marooning him with Ned on a speeding island of noise. The throbbing of the machine between his legs caused John to get hard. He pressed himself against Ned and felt no instinctive withdrawal. Instead, Ned pushed himself against John's hardness.

Ned stopped the bike on the crest of a small hill. They couldn't see much—it was too dark—but it didn't matter because the land was there, and the smell of it, the early springtime smell. Stars had appeared. They both sat astride the bike saying nothing, and the magic happened. The reflective, reflecting moon received the full energy of the unseen sun and flooded the land with softest light.

"Let's go home," Ned said.

At the station the next day, when John was leaving, when they said good-bye for the last time, John asked what Ned was going to do when he left the RAF.

Ned looked away from him, and John thought he looked older than his years, and tired. But then he found some energy. He straightened his shoulders and looked at John, and he was chipper.

"Oh, I don't know," he said. "Something will turn up."

John got onto the train, put his suitcase up and leaned out of the window to say good-bye to Ned. The guard blew his whistle, the two men shook hands, and the train shunted into life. John stayed leaning out of the window, looking back at Ned.

Ned waved a couple of times, then turned away, walked away, and the train rattled round a bend, and John couldn't see him anymore.

40

He lies beside me, sleeping now, two feet away, exhausted, spent. It's chilly—it's February—but the sleeping bags are warm as toast, I in Meum *and he in* Tuum, *and I can't sleep.*

I stare at John and wonder why I cannot love him more. He is much more than I expected, much, much more than I deserve. He is loyal and undemanding. He is always there when I need him, always happy in my company. He accepts the very stringent limits I have put upon my heart and is content with that small place I grant him. Without him and his mighty arm, I might not have survived.

He gave me a good one tonight! Twenty, thirty strokes, I lost count, and so did he; and the agony was so exquisite I almost forgot myself, almost cried out, and if I had cried out it would have been his name. I know he loves me, I have the proof of it, because he has never deserted me (only I him), and tonight I heard him say the words that he has never said before, the words that have never been said to me before.

But I could not say the same.

I have never said those words to anyone, I did not even say them to Dahoum.

But I should have! If only once, when he was dying.

I should have said them after Deraa, that cursed place, where my fear of pain was greater than my fear of violation, where my body and my mind and heart were not strong enough to keep my vow of faithfulness to him, and I did not stop a vile, invading Turk conquering and claiming as his own that part of my body that was sacred to Dahoum, my chastity.

After Deraa, when I am filled with hatred of myself, a message comes to me. Dahoum is sick, the message says, and wants to see me. My bodyguards take me to him, he isn't far away, in a village near Damascus.

He is near death, but when he sees me his dull eyes shine. I cry out to God to prove to me that He exists and let my beloved live. Are there not enough souls already in heaven, is He so greedy for one more?

But God is deaf, or blind, or cruel, or isn't there. I hold Dahoum in my arms, I don't care who's watching, who might guess how very much I love him. I hug him to me, beg him to stay with me; I am nothing without him. I tell him he should not have made the journey from Carchemish, but he stops my mouth.

"Oh, Ned," he says. "I had to see you, one last time. Do not be angry with me. Do not beat me or send me away to live among the women."

I tell him I will never be angry with him, or beat him, or send him away from me.

Somewhere a dog is barking.

"Listen," he says. "The dog sees the angel first."

It is an old proverb of his people, and it frightens me because he believes it to be true. I stare into his eyes, that he will see only me, but he smiles and breaks my heart and goes to meet the angel.

It cannot be, not yet! I have not told him that I love him! Yet what is the point of it? He always knew and cannot hear me now.

Afterwards, I try to write the words, a book, that all the world shall know that I was loved, shall know my lover's name, and that he shall have a glorious epitaph, but I fail, even at that. I write the words but am too scared by what I write (WHY?), for fear the world will damn me (WHY?). What can it possibly matter, I am damned already, by myself.

I write the words, and lose them, by accident on purpose, let them scatter to the wind, that only the wind shall know. I write them all again, but in vanity, seeking my redemption, not his monument. Just hints of him, I do not even write his name. I, who was a Prince of Mecca and might have been a King of Carchemish, do not even have the courage to write his name. And what I write is a lie. It was all a lie, there was no Arab Cause, there was no Lawrence of Arabia, there was no victory, there was only ever a gift I sought for my beloved, and my own vanity.

Yet the world offers great acclaim to me for what I did not do, and I am condemned to live with my unworthiness.

John Bruce has made my hell endurable, and I do not, have not, thanked him for it. Even though I do not love John as I loved Dahoum, I do love him in the only way that is possible for me. But I cannot say the words. I am too weak, too cowardly. I learned that at Deraa.

Is John the instrument of my salvation? No, I am not salvageable. He is the instrument of my survival, but what, I wonder, is the point of it all? Since I have nothing left to live for except a lie of a life, why does life have any meaning for me? Am I too fearful of the alternative? Do I believe in my heart—because

Mother beat God's grace out of me—that there is nothing afterwards and that Dahoum will not be there? Or that I, a sinner, am condemned to hell, while he dwells with angels? Am I too frightened to find out?

So I go on with life, and I think, these last few years at least, that I have earned my keep. I have been somewhat useful. I have done some small service for my country and would do more but don't know what. Next week I am to be kicked out of my sanctuary because I am too old. Nancy says that Winnie will find me a job, but no one listens to Winnie anymore. Others say there is a place for me, in government or out, a King's Man or a Fascist, they all want a part of me. But it isn't me they want, it is that other man they think I was, and if they knew the truth they would destroy me.

But what can the world do to me that the world has not already done? What can the world do to a broken-down A/C 2 who isn't needed anymore? What can the world do to an aging writer when he doesn't have anything to write about anymore, because he only ever wrote about himself? Who cares about a useless legend that was never anything more than a lie?

Who cares about anything?

There's only now, this moment. The days are much too long to seize, or I'm too old, and the night is fast escaping.

I reach out my hand to him, to John, to touch him gently, to grab a moment, and whisper words I know he does not hear.

(And, oh, the relief of it!)

Or does he hear? His breathing is still heavy, but he turns, and his hand falls toward me. Does he dream of me, I wonder, because even as he sleeps his hand finds mine and holds me firm in his strong grasp. He opens his eyes for just a moment, and he smiles, and I know he has heard what I have whispered.

And, oh, the relief of it!

I lie back, lit by a wayward beam of moonlight peeping in through the window, an oppressive, suffocating weight lifted from me. I am become air, and I drift on the softest breeze, light as thistledown, to the most distant stars. There's Venus, that trashy moll—the Plough and Orion, and the great, glittering path that is the Milky Way. I dance there, carefree, because I have found at last what has so long been lost. I have the answer to the question I never needed to ask.

My mother was wrong. I have the proof of it. I have found it in John's grasp. I saw it in his eyes in that brief moment when he looked at me, and I saw his eyes were shining.

I am not a sinner, merely mortal man, and only by divine comparison a failure.

41

"YOU KNEW HIM ONCE, didn't you?" Betty asked her husband. She was frying his eggs and bacon, and he was shaving at the kitchen sink.

Slaney didn't bother to reply. He didn't know who she was talking about, and Betty would fill in the gaps of his silence. She always did.

"Lawrence of Arabia," Betty said, ladling the greasy eggs onto a plate and setting it on the table. "He's dead."

It was a bolt from the blue.

"Good as, anyway, they say he won't pull through." She was looking at the newspaper that was propped up against the teapot, ready for Slaney to read over breakfast. He could see her in his shaving mirror and stared at her reflection.

"Never," Slaney said.

"It's in the paper," Betty said again and went to wake their baby daughter, Jenny, for her feed.

Slaney put down his razor, washed and dried his face and hands and went to the table. He saw the headline and was surprised that he hadn't noticed it before. He always glanced at the headline when he came into the kitchen. This morning he had been grumpy and hadn't bothered. Jenny had been crying half the night.

Ned was in a coma, in the hospital, and not expected to live. He'd been in an accident on his motorbike. No one else was hurt. Slaney sat down and read the follow-up articles, of which there were many, most of them praising the man who had been Lawrence of Arabia and calling his misfortune a tragic loss for the country.

Slaney finished his breakfast and had a final sip of tea.

"Serves the bastard right," he said to the empty room.

Slaney's feelings about Ned had not changed over the years, but they had mellowed with time. He wasn't angry anymore, and a small part of him remembered the affection he had once had for Ned. Still, his less-generous emotions dominated.

303

He got up and finished dressing. He cuddled Jenny, kissed Betty good-bye and went to work.

He'd been lucky, he thought, when he was sitting on the bus. Betty was a good wife. He wished she was less demanding sometimes, less nagging, less determined that he should better himself, but Slaney wished that about himself too. He had left the RAF at the end of his time, three years ago, and gone for a holiday to Bournemouth. He liked the seaside city and found a job there as a hospital porter. He was aware that his considerable skills as an engineer were wasted, but jobs were scarce, and he thought himself lucky to be working at all. He had found good digs with a couple of sisters, one a widow and one a spinster, and they looked after him well. He applied for jobs with various fledgling civil aviation companies, but with no success, and then a local garage took him on as a mechanic.

The country was still recovering from the Depression, and he was lucky, he told himself. Still, he felt incomplete. The following summer he met a cheerful young woman called Betty who was on holiday in Bournemouth from her home in Leeds. Both Slaney and Betty were worried they were being left on the shelf, and before Betty went home at the end of the week, Slaney had proposed and she had accepted. They married the next April and found cheap furnished rooms to rent. Jenny was born the following Christmas, and Slaney adored his baby daughter.

He did not adore Betty. He wasn't even sure that he loved her. He had thought her cheerful, and she proved to be overbearing. He had thought she was as patient as himself, and as realistic as he believed himself to be, but once Betty had found her man and had the security of her marriage lines, all her ambitions for the husband of her dreams collided with the reality of the husband that she had. There was never enough money, she complained; their rooms weren't good enough, he wasn't using his skills enough, he was wasting his opportunities.

Slaney didn't know what opportunities he had, and Betty could never tell him, but he began to understand that she was disappointed in him, and the more he understood that, the more he became a disappointment to her, and to himself.

Because he didn't want to admit that he had made a mistake in his choice of a wife, he gave himself frequent lectures about how lucky he was. Betty kept a good house, Jenny was well looked after and his dinner was always on the table when he got home. The bedroom was less satisfactory. Slaney was an undemanding husband, and Betty seldom denied him what he wanted, but he knew that he did not satisfy her as a lover. He simply didn't know what to do to make it better, because no one had ever taught him and Betty refused to discuss intimacy or what more she wanted from him.

For the most part, Slaney had put Ned out of his mind. He'd been pleased with the newspaper scandals that he believed he had created after the business in Afghanistan, and vindicated by Ned's summary removal from India. He was disappointed that Ned was allowed to stay in the RAF, and occasionally, when he read snippets in the press about Ned's involvement in the development of fast motorboats, he was cynical and wondered how an A/C 2 could have been of much use.

He supposed that Ned, as usual, was either being given more credit than was his due or was worming his way into prominence. Other than that, Ned had ceased to exist for him, because he didn't like to think about the past. The past was too great a contrast with the present.

Reading of Ned's accident reawakened in him things that were part of the happiest time of his life, memories of India—and of Doreen. Each evening he listened to the news reports on the wireless, and every morning he read the newspapers, and when Ned died a few days later, never having recovered consciousness, Slaney didn't understand why he felt so sad.

He said a small, ungracious prayer for the dead man and poured himself a rare beer. Suddenly, nostalgia flooded through him. Slaney had allowed himself to believe that he hated Ned, but he realized now that wasn't true. He hated what had happened between them, he hated what he thought Ned was, but he didn't hate Ned. If anything, now that he was dead, he felt a curious compassion. He remembered standing with Ned in a barracks in Karachi, singing a pretty song, and smiled to himself, because they must have looked ridiculous. He remembered Miranshah and how happy they had been. And he realized that if it hadn't been for Ned, he would never have met Doreen.

After his first night in Delhi with Doreen, he couldn't get her out of his mind. He and Bats flew back to Peshawar, and Slaney wrote to Doreen and sent her little gifts. He was not surprised that she never replied, even to thank him, and forgave her because he had no false illusions about her or her profession. Some weeks later, Bats was injured in a rough landing, and Slaney found himself with time on his hands. He applied for a week's leave, took a large amount from his savings and went to Delhi.

He spent every night with Doreen, even though it cost him every penny he had with him. He bought her flowers and presents. He pretended that she was not what she was, that Mrs. Windsor was a kindly aunt or other relative and that the house was some kind of hostel where Doreen was staying.

Doreen, in turn, gave him his money's worth, and for one glorious week Slaney thought himself a king. It was why he was so puzzled that he disappointed Betty in bed, because Doreen had always told him that he was a wonderful lover, strong and energetic, who made her feel as no man had ever made her feel before. Surely it couldn't all have been lies?

At the end of the week, Slaney didn't want to leave and decided he would stay an extra day. He sent a telegram to Peshawar saying that his transport had engine trouble and was delayed. He bought the biggest bunch of roses he could afford and went to see Doreen.

Mrs. Windsor sat with Slaney in the garden and gave him the sad news. Doreen wasn't available; she had other admirers. She was with one now. If Slaney would like to wait, Doreen might become available in a couple of hours, or there were several other girls just as pretty as Doreen, just as expert in bed. Doreen, she hinted, was not her most expert employee.

Slaney's world did not come tumbling down, but he was bitterly disappointed. He knew Doreen for what she was and knew the past week had been a fantasy for which he paid a hefty price, but he had set high hopes on this, their last, unexpected night together. Then he felt disgust. He thought of her being in bed with another man—in his mind some greasy, fat, slobbering old man—doing the things that she had done with him, saying the things that she had said to him. *Were* they all lies? He was suddenly sick to his stomach.

"No, it's all right," he said to Mrs. Windsor. "I just wanted to see her, to say good-bye . . ."

"If you'd let us know before . . ." Mrs. Windsor was a very practical woman and could be tough, but she didn't like to disappoint a customer and saw the hurt in the young man's eyes. "We could have made the arrangements."

"My fault," Slaney said. "I wanted it to be a surprise."

He looked at the roses. "I got these for you," he lied, and gave them to Mrs. Windsor.

She was very gracious and tried to pressure him into going with another of her girls, but Slaney wanted to be away. He took a rickshaw to the barracks and got blind drunk that night. He never completely trusted a woman again, and thus did not entirely trust Betty.

Thinking of Doreen had aroused him. He went to the bedroom. Betty was already in bed, her hair in curlers, reading a magazine.

"Have you been drinking?" she said. It sounded like an accusation.

"What if I have?" Slaney demanded.

"Not so loud, you'll wake Jenny," Betty said, nodding at the cot where Jenny slept.

Slaney saw an unromantic lifetime stretching before him; he wanted to be away, out of here, out of England, back to India, to Peshawar, to Miranshah, to anywhere other than boring Bournemouth, shackled to this woman. He wanted to go back to Delhi and Doreen. To Bombay or Suez, or to Cairo to sit in the shadow of the pyramids. To Kenya or Mozambique or Bermuda or Brazil or even the deserts of Arabia. To be anywhere other than here. To be clinging for dear life to a gun ring while Bats made a hairy landing. To be dodging bullets in a revolution in Kabul. To be outside a Bedouin tent under a foreign moon, clapping and dancing with Lawrence of Arabia. To be alive again.

He made up his mind that he would start applying for jobs with airlines again the very next day.

But he was here now, and Betty was his immediate future. He undressed, put on his pajamas and got into bed.

He put his arm around Betty.

"Not tonight," she said. "It's my time."

She'd had her period two weeks ago, but he wasn't in a mood to argue.

"Do it to me, then," he ordered.

Betty sighed and turned out the light. Slaney pushed down the sheet and blanket, opened his pajamas and lay back. Betty put her hand on him and started to work. Slaney tried to think of anything that would make this a pleasant experience, but Betty, after all this time, still didn't understand the rhythm that he needed and regarded the function as distasteful.

"It's all right," he said. "I'll finish it."

He was sure he heard Betty sigh in relief. She lay back, and he put one hand on her breasts and the other to himself and let his mind fly to Mrs. Windsor's tranquil garden.

307

Now his fantasies came. Now he saw the things that he desired. He lay in a lumpy double bed in boring Bournemouth, beside a wife he didn't love, bringing himself to pleasure and dreaming of his dusky Doreen.

But at the moment of his climax he saw in his mind's eye, if only for a moment, Ned.

42

CHARLOTTE'S SOLICITOR ARRANGED the interview. John Bruce's address in Aberdeen was in one of Ned's notes, asking Charlotte to be kind to John if anything ever happened to him. Charlotte paid for his train fare and a couple of nights at a hotel.

As John came into the office, Charlotte could see he was very nervous. She wondered if he might have been more relaxed in a less formal situation, but this was business, and she might need legal advice. She was kind as she could be; she asked about his family and told him how sorry she was about Ned's death.

"Yes, m'm," he said.

She faltered for a moment, not sure how to go on, but it had to be done, so she plunged in. "I know that you and Ned were such good friends," she said, "that you were very fond of him . . ."

She stopped because he looked at her, full in the eye for the first time, and she saw a puritan determination.

"I loved him."

He said it just as it was, without embellishment, without shame or pride, just the fact of it, and Charlotte was quite moved.

She glanced at her solicitor and wondered aloud if they might have tea. Blessedly, he took the hint and left them together.

"We all loved Ned," Charlotte said. "But not everyone is as understanding as you are, or as sympathetic. The public, the politicians, certain sections of the press . . ."

John was looking at the floor, at his newly shined shoes, and said nothing.

"It would be a very great shame if certain things about Ned ever came to light," she continued. "Things that are open to misinterpretation. If letters of his fell into the wrong hands. If more about him became known than either of us want."

Charlotte wondered if he understood her, or if not, how blunt she would have to be.

"I have made arrangements that none of his letters to me will be published during my lifetime," she said. "Several of his friends feel the same way."

He said nothing.

"Of course, we can't stop speculation, and he was a man whom people loved to talk about. But we don't want to feed those rumors."

He stared at her again, and this time she saw accusing anger.

"You think I would?" he asked her. "You think I'd blab about stuff we did—what we felt . . ." He stopped and looked down at the floor again. "It was private between us," he muttered.

"I'm very glad to hear that," Charlotte said. There was another silence. This might be the most difficult part.

"Are you all right for money?" she asked him.

"I've got a job," he said. "We do all right."

"Yes, of course, but Ned was very fond of you, and I am grateful for the companionship you gave him. If ever you could use a little more . . ."

Thankfully, he took the hint. "We're simple folk, we don't need much," he said. "But I can't say a few quid wouldn't go astray, now and then."

That was all; the business was done. They talked of Ned for a while, and Charlotte felt genuine gratitude that Ned had found this granite man. She hoped they had been, however briefly and in whatever curious manner, happy.

They had nothing more to say to each other because each was too full of the memory of someone else. John left, and Charlotte arranged with her solicitor that a small check would go to him. It wasn't a great deal of money, because Charlotte knew that she would hear from John again, in a year or two, when a few more quid wouldn't go astray.

She left the office and dismissed her driver; she wanted to walk. He followed her, at a discreet distance. He had instructions that Charlotte should never be on her own; she was old and getting frail.

She didn't know where she wanted to go but found herself headed in the direction of Adelphi Terrace, where she and GBS used to live. They had moved from there some years ago to new rooms in Westminster, pleasant enough, but devoid of the ghosts of her past. And anyway home, their real home, was in the country.

The building where they used to live was gone, pulled down for some modern monstrosity. The London School of Economics, which used to occupy the first two floors, now had its own smart building in Bloomsbury. She knew it was foolish to be sentimental, but she missed the past.

And she missed Ned.

It was here that she had first met him, a slightly shabby, bright-eyed young man who once had been a legend and who was scratching a living together while he wrote his wonderful book. She had known, at their first meeting, that she was in the presence of someone remarkable.

Or had she? Was memory playing tricks with her? Had she simply met a very lonely man who didn't know where to look for love, or what to do with it when he found it?

She thought she was going to cry, but even though she was often sad that Ned was gone from her, the bitter tears of grief all had been shed when GBS first told her of his death.

Instead, she laughed out loud, and several people passing by looked at her as if she were mad.

"He was such an infernal liar!" she said happily to a passing delivery boy, who grinned and doffed his cap and went on his way with scarcely a second thought for the dotty old lady standing outside an office block talking to herself.

Charlotte nodded to the driver she knew was waiting for her. She got into the car and was taken home.

Was he such a liar, or just a fabulous storyteller who told tall tales that he might hide his real self in the thicket of them? Why had he not told the truth about Dahoum? Was it simply that the name of this love dared not be spoken? Oscar Wilde was a real human being to Charlotte, a man she'd known, and Roger Casement. Would Ned have shared their fate? Was his fate any better?

And all that business at Deraa, it couldn't possibly have happened the way Ned had written it, because it didn't make any sense. *Something* had happened at Deraa, because Ned had talked to her about it, and she had seen the scars but not the masochist's fantasy that he had described. On the surface it bared Ned's soul to the world, so was that the reason for it? Was Ned's apparent nakedness his very best disguise?

Surely he was a bitterly unhappy man—she had seen too much of his pain to think otherwise—but often he invited his own degradation and his own

notoriety. He must have known that serving in the ranks would arouse speculation and indignation, so surely it defeated its own purpose. Or was he
obsessed by the limelight, as some believed, and had found his own eccentric
way of hogging it?

It didn't matter now. Ned had always said that people would rattle his
bones for years after his death, and that he had laid perverse clues about himself. Charlotte had done her best to help. She had no idea of the precise nature
of Ned's relationship with John Bruce, nor did she care. If it was what she
thought, then she had bought John's silence in the face of an unforgiving
world. If it was not, then she had simply been charitable to a dear friend of
Ned's who needed some financial help.

She thought about Ned again just before she went to sleep, and prayed her
customary prayer. She prayed that at the end he had been happy. She prayed
that he, who was so scared of pain but needed it, had not felt too much agony.
And she prayed that he, who had always regarded death as some kind of
defeat, had, in his last moments, embraced it as his ultimate and most forgiving friend.

43

Damn!

I didn't see those two boys on bikes ahead of me. They were hidden by the crest of the hill. Now I'm almost on them, I'll have to swerve to avoid them.

Easy. The road is slick from the shower, but I'm not going fast, and Boanerges (this latest model, anyway) is sturdy and safe.

Why is a dog barking? There aren't any dogs round here. The road is clear, apart from the boys. I've only seen one car, a black one, some distance back.

Here we go. Swing the handlebars, easy to the right. That damn dog.

Ooops! The road is wetter than I thought, and I'm in a skid. Don't panic, stay calm, swing into the skid—

Or shall I?

Boanerges is heavy, and the trees at the side of the road look so pretty. Bluebells are out, and hawthorn flecks the bushes like snow. I'm very tired, I'd like to go and lie down there for a while and think of the nothing I have to do for the rest of my life. It would be so peaceful if it wasn't for that barking dog.

Double ooops! I can't pull out of this one! (Do I want to?) Boanerges is slipping from under me, slithering toward the gravel, and suddenly—hey, this is marvelous! I'm flying!

I'm back in the Raf with a vengeance, free of gravity, whizzing through the air, lighter than any thistle! Oh, this is the life, I'm flying!

Still, I have to be very practical about this. I'm not free of gravity, and every flying machine will run out of fuel eventually.

That's what I've done. I've run out of gas. I'm coming down to earth.

If I'm unlucky, I'll crash into that hawthorn bush and break a leg or two and get some nasty bruises. I'll pick myself up if I can, or yell for help, and an ambulance will come and take me away and they'll patch me up and I'll have a few more scars on top of all the others and the rest of my life to look forward to—and that's a depressing prospect.

But if I'm really lucky, I'll land headfirst. In a millionth of a second I'll land headfirst on the ground and knock myself out. (I'm very tired, I could use a decent night's sleep, or even a lifetime's slumber.)

I feel lucky today. In a billionth of a second, my head will hit the ground and my skull will crack open and my brains, what's left of them, will spill out and that'll be the end of me.

It's so peaceful, flying, coming in for a final landing. If it wasn't for that damn dog barking, everything would be perfect.

No. I'm wrong. Bless that dog! Because now I see more clearly than I have ever seen anything before! I see horizons that were only misty and I see a river, and there he is, waiting for me on the other shore. Or is it the angel? Is that why the dog is barking?

In a zillionth of a second, my skull will crack open on the mossy ground, my brains will spill across sweet England's earth and I will go to sleep, but only for a moment, just long enough to find the strength for the last little section of the journey. And when I open my eyes, the ferryman will be waiting for me (I have already paid the fare), and Dahoum will be there on the other shore.

I can see him already, waiting for me to come and join him. His eyes are shining, even though I have failed and do not bring him the long-promised freedom. (He found that years ago without my help.) He will be angry with me that I have kept him waiting for so long and will shout his grievances at me. But he can never be angry with me for very long. I will tell him that I am very sorry to have kept him waiting, and he will smile and break my heart again, and he will see that I am crying, and, because he cannot bear to hurt me, he will hold me in his strong arms and forgive me (oh, why have I waited so long?) and we will be happy.

And we shall lie together beside the waters of Babylon and walk forever in the wilderness of Zin.

He's reaching out his hand to me and waving. I'm almost there!

Hang on a tick—there's something happening . . .

Can it be, at last, after all these years? It had to happen eventually; I've thought it had happened before, but I've always been wrong. Not this time, please . . .

No. This time I'm not wrong! Oh, thank you Janus, Juno and Jupiter!

My balls have dropped.

At last.

Afterword

THIS BOOK IS my patrimony, an inheritance from my father.

My father was one of those odd Englishmen who adored his country but could not bear to live there. As a young man in the Royal Air Force, he was posted to Baghdad and fell in love with the Middle East. He spent most of his working life, as an airline engineer, in foreign countries.

So I was born, raised and partly educated in the Middle East and Africa. I was an only son and was often the only British boy of my age in the various countries that I visited or in which we lived.

My father believed that travel broadened the mind, and he wanted to share with me his love of the East. From about the time that I was ten, during school holidays, he would send me to wherever a plane was going—Cairo, or Aden, or Nairobi. He would telegraph the airline office at my destination asking them to arrange accommodation for me, but otherwise I was on my own.

It was a fabulous childhood. A boy is no threat to anyone, and so I saw, and did, things that have only been seen, or done, by a very few foreigners. Some of those adventures appear, however disguised, in this book. But I was often lonely and dependent for my welfare, safety and friendships on the kindness of brown or black strangers.

At school in Jordan, one of those friendships ripened into something more. In my very early teens, my classmate Yahyah, born as I was in Palestine but a year older than myself, became my lover. It was a relationship of mutual consent, known and accepted by all our other school friends, and, I suspect, by many of their parents. It lasted for almost three years, until my parents and I were forced to leave Jordan during King Hussein's housecleaning of the British.

Yahyah's family was well educated and prosperous, and he was very far from being a donkey boy, but from him I learned what love can be. Thus, my portrayal of Ned's relationship with Dahoum is based heavily on my relationship with Yahyah.

From the moment that Yahyah first touched me (or did I touch him?), I understood that what we did together could not be given a name. My father, a self-professed racist who was astonishingly kind to people of other races, was also rabidly antihomosexual.

I used to borrow books from the British Council library in Amman. My father encouraged this, but once, when I brought home *The Thousand and One Nights* by Sir Richard Burton, my father asked me not to read the book. I accepted this without question and returned the book to the library, unread.

Yet already, in my mind, there was a paradox. Someone had lent us some paperbacks, and one of them was *A Rage to Live* by John O'Hara. I started reading it, and my father saw me. He warned me that the book contained some "adult" material but did not stop me reading it. I could not imagine that there was anything in the Burton book more explicit than some of O'Hara's passages, and wondered why my father had requested censorship.

It happened again when I brought home *The Mint* by T. E. Shaw. My father said it was not fit to be read by decent men. I asked him why, but he simply said that Shaw was a boaster and a braggart, and I would understand when I was older.

This time, I disobeyed my father and read the book; and I could not understand his reasoning. I found nothing particularly sexual or obscene in the book, I thought it was beautifully written, and it gave me an insight into a world I did not then know.

So I shook hands with Shaw for the first time but did not meet him again for several years.

Fairly obviously, with my background, David Lean's film *Lawrence of Arabia,* partly filmed in Jordan, made a huge impression on me. I thought it was the finest film I had ever seen, yet even so, there was something missing, something that didn't make sense. I thought I had seen a remarkable portrait of a legend, but I did not think I had met the man.

My father would not even see the movie. He would not pay good money to see anything that showed that "charlatan" in a decent light. I tried to defend the film, but my father got angry and shouted that I did not know the man— but that he did.

This was a small revelation. How had my father known Lawrence? And what had Lawrence done to earn my father's enmity? I tried to find out, but my father refused to discuss it.

Many years later, I made a film called *The Clinic*. It was simply a day in the life of a VD clinic, a comedy, and it discussed, but did not show, just about every sexual variant that exists.

My father was appalled, and in one of our last conversations before his death he asked me why I would make such a thing. I tried to defend my film, but my father simply shrugged, said he didn't understand and changed the subject.

"It's like that damn Lawrence," he said. "Why would anyone make a film about him?"

I waited, and slowly the answer came. My father had served in barracks with Lawrence—Shaw—in the RAF, in Karachi. Now the story tumbled out, and it was a portrait of Shaw—as seen by Slaney.

But my father and Shaw never became friends. Instead, my father believed all that was later written about Shaw in Afghanistan, that he was fomenting revolution against British interests. Yet even this didn't explain my father's detestation of the man.

After my father died, the tale stayed with me, and I began to read about Lawrence. It became very obvious to me, very quickly, what had aroused my father's fury. Everything that had been a puzzle started to make sense to me. I did not for one moment consider Lawrence to be "gay," because that implies a lifestyle, accepted or otherwise. What I found was a man trying to assuage a consuming loneliness, and the key to that was not Dahoum, but John Bruce.

People, men especially, seem to find in Lawrence what they want to discover, and perhaps I am guilty of the same. Perhaps I am reliving, in Ned's relationship with Dahoum, my youthful love with Yahyah. Yet surely no one would want to relive the agony of Ned's later years and imagine that much pain as his own?

Assessments of Lawrence fall into two basic groups. The first, the majority opinion, seems to be that because he was a great man, he couldn't possibly have been "queer." The second, minority, opinion, led by Aldington, seems to suggest that because he was "queer," he couldn't possibly have been a great man.

But what, I wondered, if Lawrence was both?

In *The Mint*, Lawrence writes with unsparing honesty. So to me, the dedication to "S. A." in *The Seven Pillars of Wisdom* should be read for what it is.

Equally, Lawrence's relationship with John Bruce only makes sense if it is seen for what it was, without absurd apology, or silly protestations that this does not make Lawrence "queer."

This is a novel, a work of fiction, of my imagining. Because it deals with people who existed, I have followed Gore Vidal's rule: everyone is where they should be, most of the time. Beyond that, this book does not pretend to be what was, simply what might have been.

I have invented two major characters, Slaney and Bats, and several minor ones. I have simplified the various expeditions to Carchemish.

Do not look for my father in these pages, you will not find him, even though "Slaney" is a family name.

And do not look for me. I am someone else.

All I have done is try to imagine Lawrence of Arabia as a man, not as a legend, and have tried to give their rightful place in history to those who brought him comfort.

David Stevens
Newburyport, Massachusetts, 1999